Such a union as Jane an… entered her own imagi… wanted to see on the a… that she had not yet b… tried to put herself in his … … … …more than glance at her, and she had not dared to approach him, as she might, and say: 'I am Claudine Forestier. Once you came to my grandmother's café and gave me a dream of a different life' . . . No, her aim must be to make him notice her stunning red hair, her green eyes, and the rest. She had thought there was time enough. She might now have to act more quickly. If necessary, she would put herself between them. She had not trod such a long and lonely path only to have it crumble away beneath her feet. And Jane could not offer such love for Johnny as she had ready in her heart.

ABOUT THE AUTHOR

Intending to write from the age of sixteen, Anne Griffiths spent a good many years at a number of other occupations including modelling, hotelkeeping and teaching before starting her writing career. She was educated in Bournemouth, has a degree in English and French and, apart from a period near Paris, has always lived in either the south of England or the south of France. Her first novel, *Liscombe Hall* (1991) was published by Piatkus and Penguin.

ANNE GRIFFITHS

Distant Dreams

A SIGNET BOOK

SIGNET

Published by the Penguin Group
Penguin Books Ltd, 27 Wrights Lane, London w8 5tz, England
Penguin Books USA Inc., 375 Hudson Street, New York, New York 10014, USA
Penguin Books Australia Ltd, Ringwood, Victoria, Australia
Penguin Books Canada Ltd, 10 Alcorn Avenue, Toronto, Ontario, Canada m4v 3b2
Penguin Books (NZ) Ltd, 182–190 Wairau Road, Auckland 10, New Zealand

Penguin Books Ltd, Registered Offices: Harmondsworth, Middlesex, England

First published by Judy Piatkus Ltd 1993
Published in Signet 1994
1 3 5 7 9 10 8 6 4 2

Set in 10/12 Monotype Plantin
Typeset by Datix International Ltd, Bungay, Suffolk
Printed in England by Clays Ltd, St Ives plc

For my Mother

PROLOGUE
Winter 1917

Claudine Forestier, in her room over the Café Flamand, listened for the burst of singing that would mean the English soldiers were past their first bottles of wine and her grandmother would be too busy serving them to notice her. There it was, the sad tune and something with the word 'home' in it and all the English sounds she could not say. 'Ho – *home*,' she breathed, huffing the H the way Johnny Tranter had taught her. She added a muddle of English Ss, giggling to herself and venturing one cold foot from the bedclothes to make the forbidden journey down the stairs in her nightgown.

'My little Claudine!' There he was, her special soldier, Johnny, standing out from the others because he was taller and more handsome with everything about him shining, from blue English eyes to the flash of his teeth and spurt of dark hair that would not lie flat. In the smoky room, he held out his arms to lift her over the heads of the other, ordinary young men who would soon be going into battle, as he would. This Claudine knew. Sometimes, there were weeks when the countryside around the village lay quiet, and then there would be a big battle and distant thudding of the guns going on and on. No one would come to the café but the local miners who cursed the soldiers when they were there and when they were not.

Her father had been a soldier. This Claudine knew too from the daily reminders of her grandmother whose beloved son he had been. Her father had died, and her mother, because of the war, and she supposed she and her grandmother would eventually die from it too because that was the way things were.

But this evening, Johnny Tranter placed her on a stool and pulled up a strand of her hair to admire its redness that her grandmother hated because it was brazen and like her mother's. He told her she was pretty, with his few French words, and that her eyes were beautifully green. The other soldiers admired her and teased; Claudine forgot the lonely day and basked in their attention. She leaned into the crook of Johnny's arm to keep her small self from her grandmother's sight and drew his gift from her sleeve where she kept it. It was a picture postcard of a long building with a tower and rows of windows, that seemed to lie sleeping under a breath of sky. There were specks of birds floating up into space and an avenue of trees showing the way to a welcoming door. She had never before seen such trees, nor any place or sky like that.

'Home, yes.' Johnny nodded and laughed down at her. 'My home. You come, one day.' He pointed to the name written in script underneath the picture. 'Liscombe Hall, Dorsetshire' it said, and he repeated it slowly, for her to copy. Then he laughed so much her grandmother heard. There was her frowning face over the counter, the tight angry bun of hair and the hissed words, 'Up those stairs.'

'Seventeen years,' Johnny whispered, holding up fingers to show how many; they had established she was four years old. And he added, 'I will wait,' for those were the words of a French song and easy for him to remember.

Claudine, bathed still in the warmth of him, replaced the postcard picture and let herself be lifted back to the stairway where Johnny's last smile in the gloom was enough to keep her comforted until the next evening. She would see him again then, so long as the big battle did not begin. All would be sudden silence in the café until the guns took up their thudding and perhaps he would never come back to ease her unhappiness with the dream-image of his home: Liscombe Hall, Dorsetshire.

PART ONE

CHAPTER I

1931

'One more push, Lady Liscombe!' The midwife was jovially brisk. Kate saw through a mist of sweat the watch swing and glint on the woman's navy blue chest and turned her head painfully towards the window where the sweet Liscombe sky must give her strength.

'Oh, it should never have been, not at your age, our Kate.' Susan Tranter, mother to Lady Kate Liscombe, rocked on swollen feet beside her daughter's bed.

Kate flung out her arms for something to tear at. A shout, her own shout, rang round the room. 'Oh, it is done,' she heard herself gasp.

'Thanks be to the Lord.' Her mother bathed her face. 'And there musn't be no more,' she muttered.

'A fine healthy girl.' The doctor was already rolling down shirtsleeves.

Kate said, 'Tell David, Ma,' and lay still in the damp bedlinen.

'I'll tell him there's to be no more.' Susan waddled, exhausted, to the door. 'It's a girl and healthy and no thanks to you,' she shouted furiously at her son-in-law waiting long hours in the corridor.

Lord David Liscombe took the hand of his stout and elderly mother-in-law and swung her along the main corridor of Liscombe Hall, dancing her past the dark painted faces of ancestral portraits and along to the top of the staircase where he shouted, 'It's a girl, and healthy!'

Behind him, the long patterned window framed his

head, which still seemed dark but which was almost grey now, and the wide aristocratic shoulders which his breeding made him hold as straight as always. Down past the bronze pillars, grouped about the last step, were the elderly butler Treeves and Mrs Baker, lifelong servant to the Hall and still its housekeeper. The kitchen staff, odd boy, maids and gardeners stood behind them, in their place, for this extraordinary event at Liscombe Hall, the birth of a daughter to Lord Liscombe and his wife, once a kitchen maid and now its owner in her own right, after a love affair they had waited twenty years to fulfil. They all beamed up at this man they had once feared but had grown to love in the last year or so, when his happiness with his new wife had reached them.

'Champagne for you all, Treeves,' he shouted. 'I'll be down with you once I have seen her ladyship.'

Waiting, and content to wait, he strolled dreamily to and fro near the door hiding his beloved Kate. He longed to see the glow her dark blue eyes would have at this baby safely born, the symbol of the love that had endured so long. Twenty years or more before, in their past which was like yesterday to him, for he had spent it in waiting, their other child had died. Now it was to be different. They were together with Sarah Elizabeth Liscombe, to be named after their two dead sisters, Beth Tranter and Lady Sarah Liscombe.

Lord David, humming, said the name to himself and rejoiced in the sound of it. The child would grow to be like her mother and their sisters; she would have Kate's eyes and her dark hair and healthy peasant skin, Beth's gentleness, Sarah's thought for others. She would not, he felt in his joy, carry in her any Liscombe weakness nor suffer from any Liscombe stain.

*

Beyond Liscombe Hill, down in the village of Long Trenthide, at the residence of the new vicar recently established at the Rectory, the last of the sun warmed the attic where lay his niece, Jane Beale. She too was in damp bedlinen and felt the mound of her belly weigh her into the iron bedstead. Her uncle had banished her there, to a servant's room, because of her shame, which was the weight she bore. She felt her heart beating against the burden she seemed to have been carrying for most of her eighteen years. Her heart itself must burst soon in the small space it had left. She could not breathe. Something must happen soon. Probably, she thought, she would die, and though she did not understand how, it was her own fault. Shuffling footsteps sounded on the landing outside. 'Mother?' Jane turned a heavy head towards the door. She wanted to say 'I think the baby is coming' but knew she must not, for her mother would not admit that one day there would be a baby. The fact of it had never been mentioned and Jane knew that somehow she had to bear it herself and in silence. She heard a chink of china but her mother did not open the door. There would be no tea then, and she was suddenly very thirsty. The shuffle of footsteps retreated.

She forced herself to lever her body from the bed and stumble towards the wash jug on the stand and the dusty water warmed by the hot day. And there, in the looking-glass, was her own face. She did not often look at it. Since she had been told to rest in this room, since this extra burden had begun to grow within her, she permitted herself one glance each day. She had to see that she was still Jane Beale, that there was, in her world, something of her own life, her own face. There were the blue eyes – hyacinth blue, her father had laughingly told her, in the old days before his death.

They seemed black now against her pale skin, and the mouth her mother always said was too big, was open like that of a dog. But I am panting, she thought, so that is quite natural. She was panting. She grasped her brush. If she tied back her hair into its pale, neat bun, everything would be ordinary again.

The water had a taste of dust and iron. Everything in this room where she knew she was going to die was like dust, shifting and floating in the gloom. Now there was the sound of horse's hooves on the gravel drive three storeys below, and a shout, 'Parker!' Her uncle. Jane felt herself take in more panting breaths. Soon he would be there, in the room, with his dark sweating body and her supper on a tray. To save, he said, her mother's legs. It was the only kind act he offered her mother, apart, of course, from taking them both in, out of charity. That was how it had begun. Already the birds were there, waiting, scrabbling about outside with their wings flapping. They knew it was suppertime. Mutton stew and cinnamon tart, rice pudding and steak pie . . . sickening odorous stuff that she would throw out on to the roof tiles, for the birds.

Jane leaned across the washstand as far as her burden would allow and swallowed the bile that so often came to her throat. She must get away from the window where the nightmare noise of birds' wings was all mixed up with the creak of his boots on the stair. She must somehow get herself back to the bed and let herself die there before he came, with her supper.

It was dark when she realized she had not died. Her mother was there, and a man her mother addressed as 'Doctor'. She was lying in her bed with her legs pushed up. She could see the shape of them against the lamplight from the washstand. There seemed to be more things in her room; a little table had appeared with a set of jugs steaming on it. The doctor moved away from her, his shadow fluttering and looming against the far wall.

'You say you have no idea who the father is?' His voice was low but Jane heard it. She opened her mouth; she would simply say the truth and admit that she was shameless, since she was to die anyway. Her mother would soon be able to forget that her daughter had been a hussy and a whore that Bible stories told about. Her uncle, the Reverend Stevens, liked his sermons to speak of whores. He would stand in the pulpit with his white surplice flung up over an outstretched arm and thunder about sins of the flesh.

'You would think she might have been better supervised on this holiday you so kindly offered her in Harrogate,' the doctor was saying. 'It is most unusual, in a family such as yours . . .'

Jane lifted her head; she wanted to say that her few days at Harrogate had been filled with pure happiness, but then the pain came as he said it would.

Afterwards, she could remember very little about it until she was sitting up in the bed amongst clean bedlinen. There was a very red baby in her arms and the doctor was showing her how to guide its mouth to her breast. She looked down at the man's blue-veined old hands on her skin; there was no part of her nakedness that had not been revealed to the world now. He was saying, 'It is our duty as Christians to try and sustain life where we can. Your uncle, good man that he is . . . you're a lucky girl . . .'

The alien thing, flesh of her flesh, seemed to squint up at her, waving a minuscule arm. Jane gazed back at it with fear.

★

Some two hundred miles away in a Flanders village which still bore the stains of battle, the soft September night had fallen before Claudine Forestier was able to push her baby into life. Eighteen hours it had taken her and now her grandmother had laid it in a drawer from the bedroom chest on the floor; she could hear its tiny snuffling noise.

'It's a boy, thanks be,' her grandmother announced, busy with newspaper and water and breathless from bending. 'A boy, and not another brazen hussy in this world.'

'Will you pass the baby to me, Grandmother? He must need me. I do not know . . .?' She felt she had hardly the strength to speak, barely enough to breathe. 'And will you bring me water to wash?' She was conscious of the mess of soiled sheets around her and the strange feel of her belly with the burden gone.

'You'll wait. The mite needs seeing to first, now it's entered this earth, God forgive you.' Claudine saw the woman straighten sharply from the bowls and cloths and pass a hand over her thin chest.

All her childhood she had seen her grandmother make that sign of the cross which was so much at variance with her unloving and spiteful self. She felt her first tears come in the shadowy room where her grandmother would make her wait for water, to punish her for her sins. But it had not seemed like the sins this woman had always taken so much pleasure in dwelling upon. It had seemed like love. Armand Beranger had seemed to love her; he had had a little of her childhood hero about him, very blue eyes like Johnny Tranter and the same debonair charm. She had given her heart and her body to him, just as she had placed all her child's need for love in the remembered image of Johnny.

Now she must pay. Her grandmother had at least been right about that. She must pay by accepting the burden of the baby on the floor beside her. The little snuffling sound he made seemed to call to her; she felt a strange swelling need to hold him to her breast.

'Water. Wash yourself.' The dark shape of her grandmother laid a bowl beside her.

'Help me,' Claudine said. Tears and sweat were mingled on her skin. She tried to ease herself to her elbows. 'Never mind if I deserve it. Please, Grandmother. And must I not begin to feed the baby?'

'You deserve no one's help, and I've done enough, taking you in with your shame for all the village to see.'

'I'm grateful, Grandmother. Just ... please.' She lay back; she was not strong enough to wash herself, much less lean down to the baby, without the help of this woman. It was perhaps a sin to have walked so proudly and happily away from her three years before to find her own future and a different, better life with dreams in it. She had been almost there! A post as chambermaid at a hotel in Paris, her English almost perfect with only a charming hint of accent left. Armand had said that. He had coached her in English, because he had been valet to English gentlemen. He had taught her other things besides ...

'Tomorrow you go away and there'll be no need for you to feed the mite.' Her grandmother was stripping away the sheets from damp and heavy limbs and would not let her move. Claudine felt the rough cloth of the washing glove stifle her urge to speak. *Savon de Marseille*. It was the soap of her childhood. She was going to cry and would not be able to stop. The woman was lifting her arms, dragging off the nightdress, the way she had when Claudine had soiled the sheets. Her clothes and her skin gave out café smells, men's tobacco smoke and pastis. It was all as it had been. She would never escape again. The weight of her childhood misery seemed to well up all over again in a surge of weeping.

Jane Beale lost count of the days she lay with her baby in the attic room. Her mother came and went with shawls and binding cloths. She had shown Jane how to wash the child with a little oil but there had been no talk between them except of such practical matters. She watched, vaguely, her mother's thin form which now so often seemed to be trembling; her mouth worked of itself as if she were old and toothless though Jane knew her to be around forty-five. There had been, in happier times, birthdays and special cakes and candles and handkerchiefs that Jane had embroidered herself.

She would like to ask the date of the baby's birth for she should know it, she thought, so that there could be some kind of certificate, with her name and place of birth like other ordinary babies. She would somehow have to arrange this herself for she wanted the baby to know that she had had a mother, however unworthy and defiled, and imagined that in some future time, she would take her away before the child could be looked upon by *him*. He had not come, since the night it happened, and she grew sometimes breathless, holding the baby, thinking that she heard the sound of his boots on the stairs.

One night, when the weather had changed and the wind swept the leaves up against the window pane, her mother said, turning her back to Jane at the doorway, 'The baby is to go tomorrow.'

Jane saw the woman who had long ago ceased to

care for her, hesitate, thin fingers tight on the door latch. She found enough voice to say, 'Go, Mother?'

'Your uncle fetches the baby tomorrow.'

'But is she not my baby, Mother?'

'She is your shame, your shame!' She released the latch and seemed to hug her arms about herself.

'Mother! Oh, Mother, please help me!' Jane felt herself urged from the bed; she threw out legs which yesterday had been too weak to hold her. 'Mother?' She held out a hand, to comfort this woman, to beg comfort from her, but the door was wrenched shut and Jane heard a final cry: 'Your uncle takes it away tomorrow.'

Horror and terror filled her; the man was to touch this creature whose impulse to cling to her had warmed a little corner of her heart. But she knew what she must do. She must somehow take the baby away, at once, this evening, and find some kind of establishment which took in the needy. She was needy, and so was her baby. She would search for a workhouse in the nearest town and put herself at the mercy of the kind souls who ran it, and they would see they were both safe, she and the living thing in her arms whose warmth and need had filled her with strength enough to walk the county if need be.

But fear and weakness, and the evening gloom, made her take a wrong turning and she found herself climbing a hill which had no end to it. The baby was wailing by the time she had crawled to its summit where, in clear moonlight, she could see a signpost and a stretch of hills and nothing else but navy blue sky. Fighting the impulse to sink to the ground, she forced herself to sit sensibly up against the post and struggle with shawl and her clothing so that the baby could feed at her breast. This natural act, which seemed so unnatural to her, was part of what she had to do, though it was so painful to offer up her nakedness, even to her own flesh.

She thought they had both drifted into sleep when a voice startled her. 'Here,' it said, 'you'd better come along with me.' Clutching at the shawl, Jane looked up and saw a woman standing before her, dressed in a dark collection of clothing. On her head was a man's cap and her face was dark in the moonlight, with two bright button eyes regarding Jane with gleeful interest.

'You'd better come along,' she repeated, reaching down to the baby's shawl with a hand as brown and dirty as a farm worker's. Jane looked up at a man's jacket over a long skirt of another age and men's big boots. She felt no fear, for here was a woman; she was suddenly lightened, her burden gone. 'I am to go into Dorchester,' she said, 'if you would be so kind as to direct me?' She tried to push herself on to her knees.

'You'll not be getting to no Dorchester,' the woman said, hooking the baby with ease into one arm and taking out a surprising pipe. 'Come along of me,' she said again, putting the pipe into her mouth and holding out her free arm. Jane obediently laced her hands around the woman's thick wrist. She smelt of the earth and must be safe, Jane thought, or perhaps this was a dream. It did not matter, for her strength was gone. She herself could barely lift the bundle of clothes which must go with them as her nameless baby's only inheritance.

Claudine stood in the bar of her grandmother's café, fighting nausea. The sickening drift of pastis and the smoke from the men's cigarettes brought back the memory of other evenings spent thus, prey to the men's jokes.

She passed old Jacques his usual bottle of red and the three glasses for his evening game of cards with his cronies. She knew that he had muttered something about her recovery from the little illness that so often brought village girls home again. Throwing his poor coins into the cash box with something of her past youthful contempt, she did not glance at him. She did not need to see the leer that gave a sparkle to his grin, and she would not hear the others shouting.

'Eh, eh, Jacquot, our proud Claudine needed a holiday, that's all.' But she was not proud, she had never been proud: she only wanted more than this mean life, cheap alcohol, careful counting of *sous* and no further boundary than the church and the priest's house at the end of the village street.

Fingers trembling, she re-wiped the glasses on the counter. How many evenings did her grandmother intend to make her spend here, for the show of it, so that no one could say there had ever been a baby? It was as if the last nightmare weeks had never been, as if the three previous years of her freedom had not been lived, for here she was with the smell of pastis and the smoke and the men's voices ... Only her weakness was different, the need to hold on to the counter to steady herself and the great wound in some unknown part of her body that had been meant to care for a baby.

And then it was finally over; her grandmother informed her it had been the last evening, and a short discussion took place between them.

'Here is the money,' the woman said, facing her across the table in the room behind the bar. 'Count it as your inheritance, if you wish, for there will be no more. It's enough to get you away from here, even to your precious England that you've always wanted with your fancy ways. Foreign ways. You take after your mother.'

'My mother?' Claudine repeated. It was years since she had thought of her mother, to imagine that she was a beautiful princess who was not really dead but would come back to claim her. She watched her grandmother's thin fingers working endlessly round the leather pouch, feeling the coins, perhaps already regretting their loss. '*Please* tell me about her.'

'She is dead, and she was no mother to you, believe me.' She lifted her nightcap glass of cognac to her mouth, the dark hook of her nose a sudden ugliness in the lamplight.

'And I am to be no mother to my son,' Claudine said faintly, 'because you have taken him away.'

Her grandmother placed the bag with a thud between them. 'It is best,' she said. 'It is best, for you and for him.' She sniffed. 'You had no milk. You have no place in the world nor ever will if you saddle yourself with an infant. Believe me.' With her first sign of agitation, she poured herself another glass; she never took two, being too careful to take up the ways of her customers. 'Believe me,' she repeated, 'I am doing my best for you and the boy. He is with a wet nurse now. In due course he will be sent to people who can give him a proper upbringing with no taint of scandal.' She swallowed the second glass and stood up. 'The wine carrier will take you to the station.'

Claudine stared at the leather pouch by her own glass. She had sold her baby. That was the truth of it. She had agreed to leave him for a sum of money which would enable her to begin her life again. She too rose to her feet. There was no more to be said, and it was, of course, for the best. Very well then. Tomorrow she would dress in the black suit Armand had bought her in Paris. She would fix her chic little hat with its green feather on to her hair, once more in its glossy red plaits in the latest style. The wine man's cart would take her along the village street for the last time and she would not look back. She would look forward, to the solitary life which was so obviously meant for her; it would have space in it, elegance and charm. It would have something that she had glimpsed once in a picture postcard and ever after held in her mind. Armand, the baby . . . they were not meant to be. This would be the life she should have. And there would be no hurt in it.

At the top of Liscombe Hill, inside the building beyond the avenue of trees, Kate Liscombe sat up in the windowseat of her bedroom, giving her baby its afternoon feed. Beside her sat her husband, Lord David, his arm firmly around them both, as it was whenever she would allow it. They could hear the tiny sucking noises Sarah made against the howl of the Dorset wind sweeping across the Downs outside.

'How safe it feels,' he said, 'to be inside Liscombe with both of you, my darling.'

'The wind seems rather haunting today.' Kate leaned her head against his. 'As if something were going to happen that is not . . .'

'No more of those times, darling, remember?' He watched her ease the baby's mouth from one breast to the other. 'You'd think we'd had half a dozen of these, to see you.'

'If we had, how different our lives would have been. None of those years of work in London . . .'

'You left me, remember.' He put a hand around the heavy damp breast just abandoned and bent his head to kiss it.

'How we worked, Aunt Bessie and Gideon and me.' She leaned her cheek against the cool windowpane and gazed down upon the avenue of oaks with their great swaying branches.

'Every moment together counts now,' he said, lifting his head to look into her face, which seemed to him to grow more beautiful as the months of their marriage passed.

'Do you think we have paid enough with all our pain in the past to have earned what we have now, David?'

'It is all forgotten, the pain. I sometimes think ... Ah, the door. Someone wants to take you away from me again, darling.'

Kate watched the intense joy in his face fade as a second knock sounded. 'It will not be for long,' she said. 'I hope it is Aunt Bessie.'

'Your brother Johnny and your nephew Joe,' Lord David announced, flinging open the door, 'forced up by your mother, no doubt.' He laughed. 'And here the lady is, gentlemen, in glory of motherhood.'

Kate laughed too to see her brother Johnny standing in the doorway beside their nephew Joe, an orphan they had raised between them; each had the same air of male embarrassment, and each brought with him the feel of the outdoor life he led, in the main concerned with horses. 'Come and see the first baby in the family since you, Joe, sixteen years ago!'

'I say, Auntie, I'm not much for babies!' Joe edged his riding boots across a foot of carpet, followed by his uncle who emitted one of his general grunts meant to suffice as answer. If there was difference between the two, it was in age only, for each was tall, with dark healthy skin and the stubborn Tranter hair which would not lie flat though it was so often covered by a riding cap. Each held his cap before him now, as if entering a church, and their riding outfits bore the marks of much wear. If their boots were polished, it was because Susan Tranter insisted upon it as the mark of gentlemen and they had become gentlemen by virtue of Johnny's and Kate's hard work.

She regarded them now with amusement. 'Anyone would think you hadn't seen a few hundred foals nursing,' she said.

Johnny Tranter shifted uncomfortably on the little patch of carpet he had chosen. 'That reminds me, Sis,' he said, dark blue eyes so much like her own frowning past her and her child and out to the view of his beloved Downs beyond. 'We got to get that mare in, she's near her time.' Satisfied that he had made some gesture towards her present condition, he nudged Joe's arm. 'That's right, Auntie,' Joe said with relief. 'The mare.' He turned and followed his uncle with the same urgent stride and the same slight bowing of the back, from so much time spent on a horse.

'Ought to be your time soon, old chap,' David called to Johnny's departing form.

'No damn fear!' Johnny skirted past his Aunt Bessie arriving in the doorway. 'Not me!' he grunted.

'Nor me!' echoed Joe, avoiding his great-aunt's playful push.

'If either of them two go so far as to get married, it'll be a baby horse comes out, I swear.' Aunt Bessie, a brisker, more energetic version of her sister, Susan Tranter, gave another push to Lord David's arm and ordered him away. 'Get that nurse in,' she said, 'to give Kate a rest, ain't you got no thought? We're having tea and we wants some peace to have it in.'

Glad to give herself up to her Aunt Bessie, as she so often had in the years when they worked at business together in London, Kate was soon comfortably installed with her in the adjoining sitting-room, a table with tea laid out between them.

'Blasted wind howling,' Aunt Bessie said, taking charge of the pot. 'Gets on my nerves, turning round in this great empty place with nothing to do.'

'You're not supposed to have anything to do, Auntie.' Kate laughed, accepting a teacup. 'You're seventy, and we worked all those years with never any time free, just so that we could one day have a life up here on a hill in the sun.'

'Ain't no sun,' Aunt Bessie grumbled, picking up a tiny lemon tart and biting into it. 'And not enough to do.'

Kate took a comfortable mouthful of vanilla sponge. 'No, no,' she said.

'What's wrong, dear girl?' Aunt Bessie looked up sharply. 'Don't you listen to me fretting, that's just me . . .'

Kate felt her giving her the old hard look which was the privilege of their years together. She noted with affection the newly-hennaed hair of her aunt in its outmoded Alexandra fringe and the rouged sagging cheeks. 'I cannot bear it if you are not happy, Aunt, please . . .' She took another mouthful of sponge that she did not want. 'You at least,' she said.

Aunt Bessie chose an almond biscuit and sniffed it. 'I don't want no happiness and I don't expect it,' she said. 'If you hadn't needed me after Gideon died, *I'd* have died out there in that sanatorium in Switzerland.'

'After Gideon was murdered,' Kate said faintly. 'By my son, Auntie.' She put down her shortbread. 'I can't forget. I can't be happy. I can't just live like other people, with David and Sarah and you and everyone, how can I? Every time I see David's face, so full of joy . . .' She put up a hand to her eyes to stop the tears falling. 'You and me and Gideon, working so hard together all those years . . . we were happy then, though perhaps we didn't have the time to know it.'

Aunt Bessie placed her plate carefully on the arm of her chair. 'Gideon wouldn't want us to go on suffering,' she said. 'It'd have broken his heart to know we couldn't be happy because of his death. He was the one who got you Peter when your own baby died, and he didn't ever stop blaming himself for the boy's bad ways, no more than I did for letting him bring that baby home, I should have had more sense. I couldn't bear to hear you weeping for the poor sick mite you didn't know was dead . . .' She wiped away her sudden tears with the back of a hand. 'And I can't bear to see you now sometimes, sitting by that window and living it all over again.' She made an effort and picked up her plate. 'So if it's work you want, it won't be me who's against it. And ain't hotel-keeping what we know about? Then we got to think of the future for Sarah, if things go on as they are, she'll need to be doing something to keep the place up.'

'Yes, that's it, that must be why the idea has come to me. When Sarah was born I thought of half the roof needing repair, and all our investments and stocks falling day by day with this dreadful slump. But David can't agree, can't bear to think of me working again.' Kate bit into the shortbread with a sudden burst of energy. 'Oh, I knew you wouldn't be against it entirely, Auntie. We'd never notice the wind howling against the windows again, would we? Though of course I do love it, too . . . And it's perfect for a hotel.'

'You ain't got to pretend with me,' Aunt Bessie said, inspecting the base of a miniature eclair. 'I don't know as I can wait to get started.'

'You're supposed to be past seventy,' Kate said again.

'And you're supposed to be a lady now,' Aunt Bessie replied with a hoot of laughter. 'You're supposed to sit about with a piece of *petit point*, sighing over modern ways and the *nouveau riche* what will go about making vulgar money. They sit there with dry rot and the roof leaking and no one to leave the place to.' She brushed crumbs from the crepe silk stretched over her plump body.

'We'll really shake people up, going into trade again and showing them what modern women can do.' Kate rang the bell for fresh tea. 'All the aristocrats mouldering in their stately piles . . .'

'I was born too early,' murmured Aunt Bessie, wiping her chin. 'Now, what sort of hotel you got in mind? Not Dorset inn-style, I presume, with what we got here?'

Kate laughed. Her heart lifted to hear Aunt Bessie talk business. 'We keep it as it is,' she said, 'only better, putting it back how it was – Liscombe Hall in the golden Edwardian age, with improved plumbing and sanitation and so on. We could have bridge and billiards and church on Sunday, riding and the hunt and the shoot back. Johnny and Joe will have to see to that. Johnny's even prepared to put in 10 per cent.' She paused and leaned back to take breath.

Aunt Bessie, seeing the fatigue in the face of the woman who had been more to her than any true daughter could be, did not waste time in urging her to rest. 'It'll need proper planning,' she said instead. 'We'd better start getting some figures worked out for setting the place up, new carpeting on them corridors for one thing and God knows what linen if we're to offer a daily bed-change. If Johnny's putting in a 10 per cent share, I'll put in twenty say, but it won't matter, you'll be getting it back in my will. Perhaps we can break Joe's Trust and put in something for his future . . . A share in a prosperous business shouldn't be sneezed at.'

'Liscombe Hall Hotel,' Kate said dreamily. 'How's that for a name, Auntie? And won't we be busy?'

One damp morning some months later, Jane Beale paused in her work of carrot-lifting in the top field over Liscombe Hills. Wiping earth from her fingers, she adjusted baby Mary in the shawl at her back. She was listening for the sound of hooves. Lord and Lady Liscombe were late for their ride with Mr Tranter and the boy Joe, she thought.

She and Pugs always allowed themselves this moment of respite whenever they were labouring in fields near enough to the Hall to watch the movements of those who lived within it. Now was the hour of the daily ride.

'Them's late,' Pugs, beside her, confirmed. In the time since Pugs Burrow had discovered Jane under the signpost and taken charge of her and the baby, they often had the same thoughts, linked as they were in poverty and otherwise without friend or family. The Rectory was closed – mysteriously so, Pugs had established from village rumour – but otherwise there was so little outside event in their days as farm outworkers on the Liscombe estate that nothing remained unnoted and roundly discussed.

Pugs heard the thud of the hooves before Jane. She straightened and eased a hand to her back, boots square into the earth that had given her a living since she was twelve years old. Her teeth were clamped about a smouldering pipe and everything about her was dark from its smoke and from the soil: her man's cap, all the skin on her face, and the clothing which like herself seemed to come from a past age. 'There they do go,' she said.

'There they go,' repeated Jane, straightening stiffly from the months of labour she was not accustomed to, and from the weight of Mary, named after Pugs. It was Pugs's given name but everyone called her after the place where she had her home.

And there the quartet were, on their glorious mounts, thudding along the lane below them. Leading was Johnny Tranter, as sleek and darkly handsome and exotic as his fearsome black horse. The man had thrown Jane a terrible hard blue gaze when she had been helping with the harvest, but otherwise seemed to pay no one much attention. Wherever Mr Tranter was, Joe was too, following along behind, but there was nothing of the exotic about Joe. He had once given Jane a sweet shy smile over the wheatsheaves, his face as hot and dusty as any farm worker's though he was so closely linked to the Liscombes.

Joe now offered up his cap to them with a shout of pleasure, and closely behind him was Lady Liscombe herself, a vision to Jane in black jacket and trousers, daringly astride a horse the colour of her chestnut hair. She too looked up and raised her crop, guiding her mount round past the churchyard.

Last, on a stately ageing hunter, was his lordship, dressed in fine cloth and leather, his handsome dark head raised up. 'Good morning to you, ladies,' he shouted and thundered on.

Jane breathed out a sigh as the sound of their going faded, feeling the little turbulence of air around her face their passage always seemed to create. They disturbed her air and her thoughts each morning.

'Time fer tea,' Pugs announced, lumbering off to the gateway where their tea bottle was packed in a basket with bread and whatever else she had found for their dinner. It might be a piece of cold rabbit from her poaching or perhaps cheese bought at eightpence a pound from the village shop. Today it must be cheese, for three ginger tails were also weaving their way through the carrot tops towards the basket; Pugs's cats always knew when there was cheese.

Pugs would never starve nor let her starve nor the cats, Jane thought, trudging along behind her, lifting heavy earth-covered boots Pugs had begged for her at one of the big houses. She had been clothed by Pugs, and Mary by the good grace of Lady Liscombe in clothes of the Honourable Sarah Liscombe, a baby of the same age. Jane felt she only minded charity that moment each morning when the magic party flashed by, all gleaming. She and Mary breathed dust and earth, and a film of dirt covered them when they returned to the refuge Pugs had offered. They slept in the attic of the cottage given to her by Lord Liscombe in the days, Pugs said, when he had been wrong in the head, before he had found his true love, the present Lady Liscombe. There was a straw mattress dusted with Keating's powder to ward off bugs, and the comfort and warmth of a cat or two. With the goat who sometimes joined them in the downstairs room that was kitchen, bedroom for Pugs and communal room too, animals and humans shared what there was.

Jane sat beside Pugs on the broken tree trunk that would serve as bench and eased Mary round to lie in her lap. They were lucky this morning; she slept still and they would have a little peace. Three ginger heads and three pairs of amber eyes turned in unison towards the basket as Pugs began work with knife and the

27

precious cheese. Accepting her portion, Jane gazed down over the misty field to the majestic splendour of Liscombe Hall, its line of golden stone a symbol to her of something magical, like the people who lived in it. Sometimes, looking across to the Hall where happy, open, blessed lives were lived, without dread in them like hers when she had heard the sound of her uncle's boots on the stairs to her room, she allowed herself to dream that one day there might be such a life for her and Mary.

She took her jamjar of tea and said, 'Can they really be going to make the Hall into a hotel, Pugs? A sort of inn?' She did not want there to be any truth in the gossip Pugs had heard from the other farm workers, for then the Hall would surely lose its perfection.

Pugs hesitated, puffing on her pipe. 'They do say so.' Smoke wreathed about her face and up past thick brows. 'Selling beer and cider and that.'

'It doesn't look right for it, Pugs, not with the men . . . singing and so on.' She had a memory, from their previous village, of men leaving the inn, of her uncle rampaging against the sins of drink.

'More like a palace, that place is,' Pugs agreed, puffing.

'I want it to stay so, Pugs,' Jane said, for the few moments each day when she could gaze upon it helped to lift her out of the life of trudging behind Pugs with the weight and worry of Mary on her back.

Claudine climbed the eight sets of back stairs of the hotel in Paris where she had found another post. Here was the cupboard of a room they had given her, here she read and wrote her letters of application, sitting on the bed with the coverlet about her and the smell of generations of chamberpots. Today, there was a letter with a London postmark and elegant script across the back: 'Imperial Palace Hotel'. The best in the world. Claudine took a deep breath. Let this be the one. She could aspire no higher for her next step towards a different, better life than this great hotel which held in its mere name all the glamour of English high-society.

She gazed unseeing over Paris rooftops beyond the window. Its glamour was not yet, could not yet be, for her. Here she had the same lowly work, the same long arduous day, with no one to notice her special, higher abilities. Someone at the Imperial Palace Hotel would see them, she had no doubt of that, if she could only be given the chance.

Tearing suddenly at the envelope, she could not wait to . . . And there it was! She forced herself to read it slowly:

Dear Mademoiselle Forestier,
    We are pleased to offer you work as chambermaid on the understanding that you undertake a period of training to ensure you fulfil our exacting standards . . .

Exacting standards. Claudine read the words again. Something to reach for, that was what she needed.

And even if the Imperial Palace Hotel did not look like Liscombe Hall, even if it were crushed into the centre of a city instead of lying open to the sky, it must none the less have something of the special magic she yearned for.

CHAPTER 2

The Hall was ready for its opening day. The old warm golden stone lay bathed in sunlight, all its glittery windows polished. Sun shone on the scrubbed urns on the terrace, on the glow of brass at its door, on the new tower of the East Wing, lighter than the other for it had not had its share of weathering.

Kate stood beneath the last oak by the gravel before the terrace and watched the movement in the dark space that was the open doorway. There were the new waiters, the oddboy, the butler Treeves, and Tilley the new head porter no one liked. Not much time remained now, but there would always be a last-minute rush in catering, for nothing must look spoiled.

She touched the wood of the new noticeboard which stated in bold green lettering:

LISCOMBE HALL HOTEL
OPEN FOR LONG OR SHORT STAYS
RESTAURANT OPEN TO NON-RESIDENTS

It had the Liscombe Hall insignia too, an L and an H entwined around an oak leaf.

Ice, she thought suddenly. Had anyone thought they would need more, on such a hot day? The ice buckets would be holding water before the drinks were served. But she must not go running off to the kitchens; of course Cook would have remembered ice. This moment was for herself, to absorb the splendid sight of Liscombe recreated, scrubbed and polished, glowing, and to ponder on the folly of such an enterprise in a time of depression.

'Perfect, darling, it's all perfect.' David was suddenly beside her. 'The Ford 'bus has left to pick up the local guests and those from the railway station, and I think that's all on my list.' There was a smudge of oil on the cuff of his grey silk jacket, and on his chin where the blue shadow of beard grew. Kate's heart turned over with tenderness. In converting his inherited home into a place of trade, he had baulked at no task as too lowly for an aristocrat with generations of breeding behind him.

'No regrets, dear David, now it has begun and we cannot turn back?'

'None, Kate, because it has been what you wanted. Only, perhaps, a little because you have been so much occupied with matters outside my ken.' He tore off an oak leaf from the branch above their heads and absent-mindedly rubbed it into the oil stain. 'But that's an old grumble. You were a successful hotel-keeper all those years living without me and you know more about business than I do. Remember, I let Liscombe moulder from plain mismanagement and weariness once before.'

'Go at once to Treeves,' Kate commanded, 'and ask for the right thing to take oil from silk, if it exists. If it does not, your jacket is ruined.' She turned her gaze back to the group about the terrace. 'Look at him up there, the perfect butler, a showpiece himself. Just one glance at that waiter is enough to cow him.'

'You'll have to let him retire soon, Kate, though I know he's keen enough to keep going. He's served the Hall for forty years.' David tried the oak leaf on his chin.

'But where shall I find a replacement who understands service without servility like the old servants did? And I do want the hotel to be exactly like a country house. Only Hawker seems to have the right touch.'

'You were lucky to get Hawker,' David agreed, 'but I still say you should have looked farther afield for your waiters. That Tubbs now, he's going to drop a tray some time during the course of our opening party and it may even be very shortly . . .' Even from their distance, they could see poor red-faced Isaac Tubbs stumbling under the cold eye of Treeves.

'He'll get used to trays soon. What can we expect? He's been used to carrying a pitchfork all his life.'

David shook with laughter. 'Tubbs was a failed sheet music salesman and before that a boy trumpeter, darling, so he's one you cannot claim as saved from redundancy on the land.'

'Well, he was unemployed, and Cyril was a farm worker,' Kate said, stepping on to the gravel. 'And he's doing quite well.'

'My Kate, everyone's doing well, you especially, and I shall never again say one word of reproach about your trying to help local workers. Honestly, it was a noble idea.' He caught up with her, laughing and contrite, but Kate, unusually, did not laugh with him. She was glad of the sunshine. It had been cool, under the oaks.

Her head ached and her heart had taken up that rapid beat that had woken her before dawn that morning. 'I just don't want to disappoint anyone,' she said. 'This wild scheme of ours – mine – to start a hotel to improve our income when there's still no real end to the depression . . . What if we've nothing left to pay the wages with after the six weeks' cash in hand we have?'

'Darling, don't let anything but practical matters about today spoil your pleasure in the party . . .' David began, but his wife was gone. He watched her walk up the steps to Treeves whose bony face with its thin papery old skin had never betrayed his disapproval of their offering Liscombe Hall up to the general common public, as indeed it had not, five years before, when she, once a kitchen maid there, had bought it with her own earned fortune.

Watching her move to speak quietly to Cyril Govier and then to the poor Isaac, he thought that he would be content to follow her about thus for the rest of their lives, for her skill with staff was a source of pleasure to him, like all her actions. But she had disappeared into the darkness of the hallway and he knew he must let her go.

'The awful moment approaches, Treeves,' he said, running up the steps too, but Treeves had also left him, occupied with a mental list of checks to be carried out. The oil spot on his sleeve would have to wait.

'Whatever's the time?' Aunt Bessie asked in breathless irritation, arriving suddenly on the steps behind him. With a menu card, she fanned her plump face and chest where a jet necklace lay in an upsurge of breasts.

'Nearly time for the guests to start arriving.' He grinned at her, noting with affection the blue eyes that must once have been like Kate's, the colour of bluebells exactly, with the same flash of spirit though they had faded with the years and the flesh around them drooped with age and past bad tempers. She was often out of temper now, but he was used to her and no longer found her fearsome as the new staff did. 'What about slipping some of those booking forms into the brochures we give out today?' he said. 'And when people want to book, they won't have to bother to write a letter.'

'My, you're suddenly gone businesslike.' Aunt Bessie gave him a sharp glance from the shadowed splendour of the hallway where the bronze pillars caught a glance of the sun and the old wooden floor had absorbed the morning's warmth. 'Tell Treeves or that nasty porter to see to it. Where's Kate?'

'Gone to put on her new lace dress, I think, but I wish she'd hurry. If they start coming, I'll have to give the first welcome, and they won't want *me*.'

Aunt Bessie wiped her forehead with a wisp of Swiss handkerchief and fluffed out her Alexandra fringe. She thought: they'll be torn, the whole bloody lot of them, between wanting to shake hands with a real lord and seeing the woman who was a kitchen maid and is now lady of the manor in her own right, with a murderer as a son in the past and other things besides. At that moment, with months of work and excitement behind them, Aunt Bessie wished she had not let it happen. She was too old to face the world again with Kate and push herself to exhaustion. Kate was too. They could have still kept busy, and held on to their investments until the Depression was over.

She watched the back of David's head, jaunty in the sunlight. He did not understand hotel-keeping; he was swinging on his heels as if there was not a donkey's work to be done. 'Hawker!' she shouted.

Hawker, newly appointed *maître-d'hôtel*, arrived silently by her side from the shadows. 'Don't let them bring up the soufflés too early,' she said, 'they'll fair melt this weather. Wait till the guests start getting fidgety, have the messy stuff cleared away, then bring the desserts on.'

Hawker bowed with soldierly courtesy, his long thin

face without expression. 'Yes, Madam,' he said. A former clerk, unemployed for a year before Kate found him at the dole office, he had a gammy leg from a war wound and a drink problem, but he understood service. He had taken to restaurant training like a duck to water. Aunt Bessie regarded with satisfaction the high gloss of his shoes, the knife crease of his black evening trousers, wishing that Kate had not felt obliged to gather a crew of yokels for the man to work with. 'If any children dare turn up, send 'em round to the laundry area to play. Get one of the maids to watch, or I'll see that Nanny about it.'

She moved on past the hearth beyond the first bronze pillar where, though it was summer, a fire burned, because that was the way of things past. Near it, carelessly thrown by the fire irons, was a little hamper of the kind gentlemen had taken on their fishing and shooting trips. In the alcove beyond that, some fishing rods were lodged, and an old gun propped up. The alcove also held a number of dusty overcoats, two scarves and a cap.

Aunt Bessie glanced about her, at the perfection created by herself and her niece. All was designed to look as if the gentleman himself and his cronies were about to walk in demanding hot toddies. It was as if the past thirty years had disappeared and it was 1901, the golden era, all over again. She wondered suddenly whether it did not lack the presence of a hunting dog or two but decided at the same moment she would air the idea to no one. Dogs were messy, smelly and a thorough-going nuisance and they needed no more of those.

She began to climb the curved oak staircase where generations had trodden, generations of servants and society people. It had lain almost unused in David's time; it had taken Kate to bring it to life, and there was Kate now, calling to her from the top: 'Auntie I think the time has come. Is it twelve?'

'It's nearly time, dear heart.' Aunt Bessie puffed up two more steps. 'You ready? You look it in that lace. Won't be none to mistake you for anyone but Lady Liscombe.'

Kate gave a turn in her cream lace, cut low on a bias from her hips to her calves. Her dark hair was swept up in combs and around the slender column of her neck she wore David's pink pearls, his wedding gift. 'I sometimes think I am prouder to be a hotel-keeper again. Isn't it shameful and ungrateful of me? But I do look all right for either, Auntie?' She skipped another turn on light feet in cream-coloured shoes.

'It ain't shameful!' Aunt Bessie protested, holding out a plump arm clothed in a russet shade of glâcé silk. 'Work's what you make of things yourself. The other . . . ent the same!'

Comfortable together, as they had been for over twenty years, since Kate had been sixteen and her aunt had supported her in training for an independent life in business, the two women inspected the corridor. Everything was in order, from the pink glass chandeliers to the row of framed sketches of Liscombe and the dark oak doors with their names or humbler numbers in gold paint. Pausing by the open door of the Blue Room, each glanced with a professional eye upon the glory of colour within: the blue Aubusson, the four-poster bed draped in damask that was very nearly bluebell, the cornflowers in a Chinese vase, the inlaid lapis lazuli on the walnut cabinet and screens. There was a white marble fireplace with wood laid ready and a number of water-colours showing blue-tinted Downs like those glimpsed from the window.

'It's all perfect, that's what it is, Kate, why don't we admit it? We done a good job.' Aunt Bessie gazed about her as if for the first time. 'It's come together all of a sudden, ain't it? And you were right to get this place *used*, like you always were before.'

'You always supported me in London, all those years, though we did argue, darling, do you remember?'

'And our Gideon did the umpiring and always sorted us out and we did what *he* thought was best in the end.' Aunt Bessie lifted a hand to her mouth. 'It sometimes seems like he should be here sorting us out now.'

'We do need to be busy, Aunt Bessie. Being ladies of leisure just leaves us far too much time for thinking.'

Each looked at the other for a wordless moment when past shared sorrows were allowed to surface.

'We don't think of them things no more, girl, remember?' Aunt Bessie took Kate's arm.

'I think I remember too much and wonder if I am ever to have the right to be happy. David would not understand if I said so much as one word . . .'

'That's because he ain't shared it with you.'

'And if I tried to share it with him, even now, he would be heartbroken to think he cannot make me happy.'

'Yes.' Aunt Bessie held on tighter to her arm. 'Maybe we done the best then, keeping busy, eh?'

'Yes. Let's get on down, shall we, darling?'

'Well, I ain't seen that nanny yet about keeping any children out of the way, nor the maids to check they're not plastered with American tan and Hollywood red.'

'Never mind.' Kate took a deep breath. 'Let's hope we can go on keeping them employed at least.' They set off to the top of the stairs, each absorbing the sight of the hallway below, so warm, so cunningly furnished to suggest that the gentleman of the house would stride in at any moment. 'What better welcome could a hotel guest hope for, Auntie?' Kate murmured.

'Let's hope we find enough of 'em to afford our palace.' Aunt Bessie released her arm and set off down the stairs. 'And if this lot coming now for a free party don't send us some, I shall want to know why.'

They reached the terrace just in time to see the porters and Treeves stepping forward on to the gravel ready to open vehicle doors, for in one rattling sweep, the local mayor and his wife and an entire coachload of members of the Dorchester Chamber of Commerce arrived. Then the 'bus hooted its way under the oaks bringing a party of travel booking clerks from London; there was a Daimler carrying some dignitaries from Sherborne and a Rover with higher civil servants from the area.

Each one seemed to step from their vehicles tired and dishevelled. They lifted up their faces to the sweet Liscombe breeze and looked appreciatively about, at the long sweep of the terrace, the old stone, the tables laid out with glass and silver.

Kate held her husband's arm with one hand, her aunt's with the other; they walked together down the steps to meet these Liscombe Hall Hotel guests who were the first of many more to come. 'If these were carriages,' David said, 'and the ladies were in long gowns, we would be back in the days before the war.'

'People want them times,' puffed Aunt Bessie, holding up her head to disguise the folds of her plump neck, 'or the dream of 'em, and that's what we're going to give.'

*

On evening duty at the Imperial Palace Hotel, Claudine Forestier looked along the rail of the hanging cupboard and found the honey-coloured glâcé silk evening gown she was required to lay ready. Slipping it out, she gave a smile of pleasure at the rustle of the skirt and at the tracing of honeysuckle flowers in beads on the bodice. Cool, it felt, to her fingers in the warm, scented room, and silky enough to give a shiver to her skin.

Moving soundlessly along the carpet, admiring the airiness of the cloth on her arm, she laid it across the chair as she had been shown, straps along the back, bodice and skirt in the seat, and a drape of silk pulled out as if on display in a modiste's window. Of this task, Claudine did not tire or silently scoff; this was work worthy of her special talents.

From the cupboard, she chose a pair of gold sandals and a light fox cape together with a gold pochette purse. These she arranged with care about the dress, and stood back to study the effect. A peachy light from the electric lamp gave the whole a splendid glow. Claudine was pleased with herself, although this lady was of the English aristocracy and therefore unlikely to leave a generous tip. The Americans came no more to the Imperial Palace since the Depression; she knew they had once filled it with loud and open-handed ways. Times were hard here as they were in France, but she had set herself a programme of learning from everything about her: the fall of glâcé silk, its special rustle, the choosing of fine fox fur, and even, she thought, the right cigarette holder. She had seen an amber-coloured one amongst the dressing-table scatterings.

The valet, on his side of the room, had finished his duties and was giving a final brush to the gentleman's dinner jacket for the show of it. Claudine moved quickly to look around the scent bottles and the combs; if this lady were to say a good word about her to one of the housekeepers, it would be worth more than a tip.

'Black *lace-up* shoes?' The voice of the fourth-floor housekeeper behind her startled Claudine. 'Those French shoes that you have on your feet may well do for an afternoon off, Forestier, but not for service at the Palace.'

'Yes, Miss.' Claudine bobbed before the exalted Miss Banfield as she was required to do. 'Shall I return to my room to change at once?' She was not prepared to let anything spoil her start at the Palace, not their petty regulations nor the stare the woman was giving her.

Miss Banfield looked carefully at Claudine Forestier's olive-skinned face with its green eyes cast down and dark-red hair blatant beneath her cap. Was that tone of hers insolent? Miss Banfield could not decide. 'At once,' she said, for her position demanded it, and then, for her own sake, 'I shall be back to inspect Room 302 in ten minutes.' The girl, she thought, would surely one day make a mistake and she would be able to have her dismissed.

'Yes, Miss.' Claudine held herself in check and walked sedately, proudly, down the scented corridor of the Imperial Palace, through the service room door and on to the chilly back stairs where she broke into a run, clattering her French shoes on the wooden steps. No matter how much Miss Banfield tried to find fault, she, Claudine Forestier, was employed at the best hotel in Europe and nothing would prise her away: not insular mistrust of foreigners nor the pettiness of a small-time woman with a little authority. One day, she herself would be at the very least a floor housekeeper and possibly in charge of Miss Banfield herself.

In her room, Claudine allowed herself a moment's treat and took from under her pillow a copy of *Country Life*, one of the many magazines left behind by guests. It had not appeared to be a rule that maids were not fit to take these things for their own pleasure, and whilst the maids who shared her room giggled over tittle-tattle about the page boys, the valets, or worse still the awkward boys they took tea with in Joe Lyons Teashops, she read society reports and tales of balls and weddings. She stared at the photographs of plump English misses in unseductive lumpy waistless dresses with unnecessary trains and fussy tulle adornments. They looked no better than the plaster mannequins in the windows of Oxford Street, but nonetheless she learned much from them.

Sniffing distastefully past the girl Maisie's frowsty bed, Claudine stood by the light from the window and opened the pages to the Classified Advertisements section. There it was, Liscombe Hall Hotel, in a small box of type:

> *Taste the beauty and tranquillity of the Dorsetshire*
> *countryside and country living as it used to be*
> *Riding, Shooting, Fishing, Bridge*
> *Charm and Peace in Troubled times*
> *Liscombe Hall Hotel. Telephone: Long Trenthide 02*
> *Write for brochure and tariff*
> *Special rates for extended stays*

And she had seen it quite by chance. Claudine replaced the magazine in its secret place, took off her Parisian shoes, inspected sole and heel, and pushed in the stays. She knew how to take care of her things, her grandmother had at least taught her that. She also knew, sitting quietly on her bed, that one day she would walk up the drive of Liscombe Hall whose name and image had been like a talisman in her dreams. The fact that it was now a hotel was further proof, if any were needed, that her life would be linked to it.

CHAPTER 3

Jane Beale held her screaming daughter Mary about the waist and leaned down to stir the fire. A smoulder of damp smoke rose in her face. She placed the child carefully on the earth floor of Pugs's room. On the bed in the corner, Pugs lay groaning. 'Don't cry, Mary dear,' she said, not angry for she was never angry with Mary, only overwhelmed by the task of motherhood. 'You'll waken Pugs. And you cannot have milk until I have milked the goat.'

The tantrum over, Mary regarded her coldly, as she often did, and followed her outside.

From its tether behind the cottage, the goat watched them with a silent human stare. Jane held the bucket she had washed with rain water, but that was a mockery too, for none of the milk would reach it and if it did, the goat would aim a careful kick and the warm precious stuff would soak into the grass. There would be nothing but watery broth to make Pugs better and nothing at all to soothe Mary. 'Here, girl, there's a fine girl.' She held out a useless pacifying hand towards the animal; its pale eyes brightened with malevolence. Reaching out, she grabbed at the rope, putting the bucket under a dripping udder. There was dread in her heart. Sometimes the animal would let her get this far.

'Pull her head back, Mummy,' Mary shrieked. 'Goat wicked.' She had learned more from Pugs than Jane had since they had lived in the cottage.

Jane gripped the rope and pulled. The goat turned in a flash and there she was, prone on cold earth. From the rooftop a trio of rooks rocked and cackled. Nausea filled her for she feared birds more than she feared Mary who was kneeling on the grass beside her.

'Get up, Mummy, Mary want milk.' She rattled the bucket and ran towards the goat's rope, pulling at it with fierce childish strength. A black bird clawed and flapped its way down the thatch.

Jane struggled to her own feet, for goat and bird threatened Mary and she was after all her mother.

'My dear.' A low gentle voice came from behind and there was the lovely face of Lady Liscombe, smiling. With ease, she tethered the goat against the wall. 'I have heard poor Pugs was taken ill last week,' she said. 'Jane, is it? And this is Mary who is the same age exactly as my Sarah? What a clever good girl you are to help Mother.'

Mary, dressed in smock and stockings passed on from her ladyship's Sarah, sucked earth from a thumb and regarded her with interest. 'Mummy can't get milk,' she announced.

Jane stared at the vision of Lady Liscombe, so tall and stately, so finely dressed in cloth the colour of heather. 'Don't think,' she was saying, 'that I'm afraid to dirty my hands. I've milked many a goat in my time, believe me.'

Mary obediently clutched at her hat whilst Lady Liscombe knelt and pressed her mass of chestnut hair into the side of the goat. The animal itself now lost interest in matters and rubbed its head against the wall. The rooks flew off.

Jane recognized the establishing of order, and the capability of Lady Liscombe who could subdue and milk a goat. She felt her shoulders droop. Here was further proof of her own inability to be as others were. She must stir herself and somehow cease her reliance on Pugs who now lay very sick in a tumble of sacking in the corner of the cottage. And there was no half-crown to pay for the doctor. Before she could protest, Lady Liscombe strode into the gloom where the fire still smoked, dishes were unwashed and Pugs's three cats had discarded a disembowelled bird by the door. Jane had not yet gathered herself together enough to brush the horror outside and bury it.

She stood dreaming and speechless by the doorway as Mary dipped a cup into the milk in the bucket and three cat shapes joined her. Lady Liscombe knelt by Pugs and peered into the bedding. 'I rather think, my dear,' she said to Jane, 'that Pugs has had a stroke. She does not appear to be quite conscious.'

In her blank dream, the voice of Lady Liscombe seemed to be saying what Jane did not want to hear, what she had not wanted to hear. 'I shall call the doctor and you must not worry about his fee. There will be nothing to pay. Jane?'

The vision of Lady Liscombe in the squalor of the cottage served to take away what little power of speech she had.

And here was the time she had most dreaded. Jane peered into the dark space that would eat at Pugs's flesh until she was no more. Around the charity grave, other people were gathered, from kindness. There was Lady Liscombe and the housekeeper from the Hall, Mrs Baker, with the old cook. There was Ned Perkins who had urged them to work harder at the carrot-lifting. Perhaps he was sorry now, with his red drinker's nose blue with cold, for it would be his turn soon. Or perhaps her own, Jane thought, because another terrible space awaited her at the cottage, with the fire smouldering, the goat defiant and nothing at all to eat but three potatoes and a rabbit with its throat torn that the cats had left as offering. And she must somehow leave Pugs here to be stifled by earth and climb the hill that had no end to it, towards her own despair.

That was where Lady Liscombe, returning home by car, found her – stumbling upwards in the ditch under the hedges. Jane turned her head stiffly round to Lady Liscombe's beautiful face that she had so often seen from the fields, had so often watched for with Pugs, and clenched her teeth together so that she would not burst out weeping and taint her with the wretched sorry story. She had not cried since Pugs found her under the signpost with Mary, only days old – could that period be well over a year away? Her uncle had been going to send Mary to an orphanage and somehow she knew even then, though she had been just eighteen years old, that she must not let it happen. Pugs had saved her and Mary too without question or condemnation, and her face had had in it the same sweet kindness she saw now in Lady Liscombe's. All she had to do was give herself up to it.

That evening, dressed in a blue satin gown for evening service, Kate stood with Aunt Bessie by the door of Liscombe's small dining-room. Aunt Bessie gave a critical glance across the tables set for four and six as if for a country house supper party. The great dining-hall beside it remained unused, and had done so since their opening day, for the small amount of business they had managed to attract had not warranted it. 'That Isaac Tubbs have put the fish knives before the meat again,' she muttered. 'He just can't learn.'

Kate too gave a critical glance around the room, and

found only the old problem at fault: marks on the blue silk wallpaper where the tables had been put too close to it. 'We might as well have had fewer tables,' she said, 'and saved the silk.'

'Might as well,' agreed Aunt Bessie, 'for all the business we're doing.'

'All this for five dinner guests, Auntie. Where have we gone wrong?'

'Starting up in a slump, that's where,' muttered Aunt Bessie. 'We wants our heads examined.' She jumped as Tubbs thudded his way into the room and, not seeing them, passed nervous eyes over the tables. Picking up a spoon, he puffed on it and rubbed it on his sleeve. An adjustment of the glasses then seemed to be necessary and he leaned on a table, kicking a leg and unsettling the candelabra. They could hear his breathing. Aunt Bessie shouted: 'And still you won't see the blasted fish knives, boy. Go away and leave it to Hawker!' The brilliantined Tubbs pounded off. The two women resumed their inspection and the weary consideration of their future prospects.

Kate, tired of this nightly exercise, changed the subject. 'The girl in the nursery, Jane Beale – I think we shall have to do something about her. We can't just send her back to that damp cottage. She can't seem to manage the child or herself.'

'We don't need no more girls,' Aunt Bessie began crossly, 'we can't pay the ones we've got and we can't afford no more charity.' She fanned her overheated face with a wisp of Swiss cotton.

'Charity, Auntie . . .' Kate hesitated. 'But she's up there quite unable to get herself together, I think. Nanny put the child to bed next to Sarah and Jane is slumped in a chair with an air of hopelessness.'

'We can't take the world in,' Aunt Bessie began again.

'No, but this Jane reminds me so much of myself. What would I have done without you and Gideon to care for me and my baby? I was so young, as she is.'

Aunt Bessie paused, giving her niece one of the few looks they permitted each other when their past came back to be remembered. 'Temporary then,' she said, 'you just see to her temporary till she gets herself together. No harm in another maid, I suppose.'

'We don't pay them much,' Kate said quickly so that her aunt should not change her mind. She kissed her, for their past remembered, and went unseeing out into the hall where golden lights glowed on old bronze pillars. Once she had thought the place would be crowded with the coming and going of guests. The little lift of pleasure she had known to think Jane could be looked after without argument from her aunt, disappeared. All this beautiful, unused place, with barely a guest to pass through it!

'Ah, Lady Liscombe, I was so hoping to see you this evening.' The plump form of Miss Snowe, their only long-stay resident, emerged from the shadows.

'Good evening, Miss Snowe.' The woman had nothing else to do but ruminate on complaint; discontent was written in the puffed lines of her face and the droop of her body.

'You know I don't want to complain, Lady Liscombe, but I do feel that the temperature in my room is a little low for the time of year. My chest, you know.' She pressed a fat manicured hand against her sensible cardigan.

'I'll send up a porter, Miss Snowe. He'll bring more coal and check the air flow.' Kate turned away. How many women, she wondered, were living like this one on private incomes, in spite of the catastrophic drop in stocks and shares dividends? And how could she attract more of them? Because she hesitated, thinking she might go so far as to ask Miss Snowe what had made her choose Liscombe for her stay, the woman launched into a further attack.

'It may be a more serious matter, of chimney cleaning.' Miss Snowe placed herself firmly in front of Kate, seeing her chance. 'And I must report that the maid last night spilled water around the cover of my hot water bottle and my bed was quite damp. I do think . . .'

Kate rejected the idea of giving Miss Snowe such fuel for rumination and gossip, stepping quickly to the rear of the hallway and the green baize door which would give her back her freedom. She did not want more Miss Snowes. She wanted people of sophistication and charm; she wanted the kind of cosmopolitan glamour they had had at their London hotel years before. Miss Snowe would now lie in wait for David, as she always did, and he would let her chatter for half an hour, never showing a glimpse of impatience. He had more skill with people than he realized and it was natural to him; hers had been learned.

Standing alone on the chill back stairs, she had a sudden flash of memory: of herself on a removal cart coming to Liscombe, and David, gleaming in worsted cloth on the back of a hunter. She sat upon feather mattresses and had dust around the rim of her hat with everything to learn. She wanted to go up and say to the girl upstairs that she herself had once been as poor and helpless as Jane was today. She could not, however, make a friend of the girl if she were intending to employ her, and employ she must. If she did not, it would be as if *she* were friendless all over again. And this little action might do something to retrieve the gloom of another week of poor business.

★

Two days later, Jane rose before dawn and dressed Mary who was to spend her days in the Hall nursery with the Honourable Sarah Liscombe as friend and playmate. She herself was to take up work as chambermaid, quite like any other girl.

She felt full of strength, ladling out rain water to heat for washing, sharing out the goat's milk. Her ladyship had been thoughtful to the point of sending Ned Perkins up to milk it. There was enough for the cats that Pugs had loved so much and who had followed Jane about since Pugs had died, in case she too should disappear. Today, she did not feel the burden of their care upon her shoulders. The five of them, and the goat, would somehow live together without Pugs and she would earn their daily food by going to work at the magic place that had seemed to hold happiness within it.

There, she would become like everyone else, unpuzzled, unwearied by life.

She was barely afraid at the prospect of walking across to the basement door and knocking on it, explaining her presence, flinching at the pairs of eyes that would rest upon her and the child who was born outside of wedlock.

Some of her fear had left her because Lady Liscombe, who could milk a goat and supervise the running of a palace like Liscombe Hall, had passed on a little of her own courage.

Claudine, on her afternoon off, strolled slowly along the Embankment. Carriages clattered by, and motors too, giving out their share of the fumes that made the London air so dirty. She had breathed much soot and fog in London, but it was worth it, to be touching her dream.

She turned to make her way across to Oxford Street where she had promised herself a few moments in front of the windows of the modistes and the jewellers. She never tired of gazing, judging, picking out always what was best even if none of it should ever be hers; she considered her taste to be unerring and had saved for months for the coat she now wore, though the weather was a little warm for it. It was made of fine black worsted cloth, neither winter nor summer weight, with a detachable Astrakhan collar which she had taken off today and replaced with a light jade and silver scarf. This coat, she knew, would take her through several years. Armand had taught her so much about clothes.

Branching off at the end of Regent Street, she could not help a little lift of the heart. She had made a rendezvous for tea at the Joe Lyons Corner House with her almost-beau, Pierre-André Lecomte. Hotel tittle-tattle named him such and she did nothing to deny it; it was easy so. But she could not let him become another Armand. This she knew, whilst accepting the lift to her spirits which his friendship offered her. There had been such a long lonely time since her last ride down the village street of her childhood. She had allowed no other fellow worker to glimpse her past nor her determination to move upwards and away without looking back to anything but the dream-image of the picture postcard. And had she not been right! What odd chance had led her to pick up that particular magazine, with that particular advertisement hidden in its pages?

Pierre also had ambitions; they were, she suspected, two of a kind, and he would not remain a lowly pantry chef with blood stains on his uniform for the rest of his working life, albeit at the Imperial Palace.

He was waving to her from the pavement, debonair in the sunshine with a smart trilby over his dark curly hair and the Ronald Coleman moustache that seemed stuck to his skin, olive like her own. He grinned jauntily, catching sight of her little black hat and its green feather over the crowd, kissing her hand with mock Mediterranean charm. Today he was excited, she could see. He led her to a table, ordering the set tea, holding on to a copy of the *Caterer and Hotelkeeper*.

'Look at this,' he said, speaking English, for she was helping him improve the niceties of his pronunciation; fluent English could be important to both of them. 'I can see the way for me to move on.' He smoothed out the magazine on the table and pointed to the advertisement he had circled in ink.

> *Chef wanted to specialize in the Dr Hay diet.*
> *Liscombe Hall Hotel . . .*

Claudine felt her heart quicken. This then, this place, it was more than coincidence. It was meant to be, her fate. She looked up into Pierre's face and dark eyes looking warmly, with expectation, into hers. He wanted her to be pleased. She was pleased.

She put down the magazine and took a deep breath. She had to decide at once, during the next few minutes, whether she could blatantly ask him to take her with him.

'You know this Dr Hay diet? It is one of their strange regimes, like the slimming?'

'It is one of them, yes,' he said, winking.

'And you know about it? You will get the job?'

'I am going to know more about it, and I already know something from when I worked on the Riviera.' He grinned and she noticed the charming lift it gave to his mouth. '*Voilà.*' He slid a book from his pocket and threw it on the table.

Claudine read: '"*A New Health Era* by William Howard Hay." Ah,' she said, 'you are going to know all about it.'

'And per-*haps*,' he said, forcing out his English H with a splutter of amusement, 'not many other men do. And meanwhile you are going to write a letter for me in that beautiful handwriting of yours to say you are the proprietor of a restaurant in Cannes, now retired and staying at the Palace on a shopping trip, who employed me to prepare this diet for the society ladies of the French Riviera.'

'Ah,' said Claudine, eating a fish paste sandwich without grimace. 'And if I tell such a lie, you will . . .?'

'I shall find some suitable return.' Pierre leaned across the table. 'We are the same kind of people, you and me, Claudine,' he said, 'and, look, what is there for me here, even at the Palace? Two have gone in the kitchens this week. With this sloomp still . . .'

'Ah! Sl-uh-mp,' said Claudine, 'not sloomp.'

'Sl-uh-mp,' repeated Pierre. 'If this country house place has some special ideas for getting people to stay there, it means they have enterprise and they will suit me very well.'

Claudine choked on the disgusting stodginess of a rock cake, hesitating over her question. 'I think it is a place that might suit me too,' she began, looking across at him. But Pierre was not listening. He was gazing past her at the window into the crowded street. 'My fiancée will not want us to wait any longer,' he was saying, 'a job like this . . . perhaps I will be able to get her work there too. I shall have my own department at least. It's a dream, Claudine, and I shall be able to get married. Marie wants to be married.'

Claudine stared at the mess of rock cake on her plate. Why had it not occurred to her that Pierre might be engaged? Until five minutes before, it would not have mattered. Now it very much did. She collected the crumbs into a pile. Pierre was saying something.

'Let's go out and celebrate tonight, Claudine. We are good friends and I feel today . . . oh, ready for a moment that is not work. We are slaves in the kitchens, you know, and I always take someone else's shift if I can, for the extra experience, to show how earnest I am! For a year I have only had an occasional stroll with you, my only friend in London . . . shall we go dancing tonight?'

Claudine considered him, her heart beating. This man had taken her almost to the very edge of her dream and only a girl called Marie had prevented it. She imagined some plain little creature going to Mass each morning and praying for her fiancé to send for her. Was her own dream not worth more than Marie's?

Pierre had taken her hand, was lifting her to her feet. 'I imagine you dancing very well, my slender and lovely Claudine,' he said, his face charmingly lifted and glowing with pleasure.

'I learned to dance in Paris,' Claudine heard herself say.

Afterwards, when Pierre had finally left her room to creep back to his own in the male staff quarters, amid much whisperings and protestations that their coming together was, after all, meant to be, Claudine lay in the darkness reflecting sadly upon her actions. For they had been hers. She had allowed them both to be overtaken by the power of their bodies. And how good it had felt – his arms about her, his mouth at the most secret parts of her body. She was trembling still from her own response.

She struggled to sit up and threw back the sheets. All the things that Armand had taught her, her body had remembered as if of itself.

But it must not happen again. Armand made love without love. She had made love with Pierre as if she loved him, when she did not. Double her shame then, she thought, double, for she had deliberately set out to tie Pierre to her, and moreover had no doubt that Marie would shortly be receiving a letter from him. She imagined this plain woman, no longer in her first youth, going stolidly to Mass to ask for Pierre's forgiveness. She would no doubt soon find herself another steady husband, whereas she, Claudine, was destined to live with no security, only the strength of her dream. Did she not deserve this one chance to reach out for it, now that it had come so close?

She thought, I shall send Pierre back to his Marie as soon as I can. Everything will be all right. This comforting decision soothed her enough to let her sleep, and edged away that other memory which sometimes threatened to come to her at night, of the day she had agreed to exchange a baby's future for her own.

CHAPTER 4

Claudine had time to accustom herself to her sense of shame for some weeks before she received a letter from Lady Liscombe asking if she would like to apply for the post of lady's maid at Liscombe Hall Hotel. Their chef had recommended her particular skills, she said, and they needed the services of a maid with fine sewing and knowledge of quality clothes for a regular clientele of lady guests following the Dr Hay diet.

Her heart thumping at the mere sight of the letterhead, 'Liscombe Hall Hotel', Claudine acted quickly. During the afternoon lull at the Palace, she simply packed a bag and slipped quietly down to the basement, smiling with such charm at the doorman that he failed to notice she had the bag with her. That she could pass through the door so easily, when there might have been crested Imperial Palace towels or sheets in it, seemed to her to be another tiny sign that her way to Liscombe was ordained.

Thinking that one of her first acts at Liscombe must be to repay her debt to Marie by freeing Pierre's affections, she gave no backward glance to the place that had not known how to recognize her competence. She might have given up her dream of Liscombe if they had. A post as Head Housekeeper there, with her own suite of rooms, floor service meals, a secretary and the obeisance of the male department heads, would have suited her very well. As it was, Liscombe would have the benefit of her and they would need no letters of recommendation.

The river water was dull today, and murky from the gloomy day which was not gloomy for her. Claudine took in her last sight of the Thames and walked thoughtfully, lightly, across Westminster Bridge, clutching at her dream of the handsome Johnny Tranter, whose image had drawn her this far. He would not yet be forty, and handsomer than ever, no doubt. Young men had never had any appeal for her. She had often admitted to herself that he might no longer be at Liscombe, that he might be married with a batch of children. But she knew she could accept that, for the image of Liscombe itself had danced as strongly in her mind as his. And today she was going to Liscombe; this was the last stage of her journey of years.

At Dorchester she stayed the night at the station hotel, wanting only that the time should pass, and took the 'bus the next day that would drop her on the main Dorchester road. There would be a good mile to walk after that, she was told, up the steepest hill for miles around, for Liscombe stood on one of the highest points in the county.

She felt only a little stab of fear and loneliness, standing in the silent lane when the 'bus had rumbled off. What if her dream had been false and all these long years of her life had been based on nothing? But Pierre's letter spoke of grandeur and of the gentry . . . She put back her shoulders in the perfect black coat and began to climb.

The effort she had to make seemed somehow linked to the years she had planned this moment, when she finally stood at the top of the hill and looked across to the postcard view of Liscombe Hall. There it lay, with an avenue of oaks leading up to it, almost as it had seemed in that faded sepia photograph of her childhood when Johnny Tranter had given her a glimpse of something noble. In life, it was more glorious, more noble. She held her face up to the Dorset breeze that was scented with flowers and gazed down past the oaks to the perfect line of golden stone stretched out before her, bathed in sunlight and warmth, windows gleaming, waiting for her.

Claudine took a deep breath. She was not disappointed. Here, even the birds seemed to glide and float up into the endless sky with extra joy.

Lifting her bag, she began to take the last few steps of her journey of years.

She smiled to herself, admiring the moving patterns of sunlight through the oak leaves over her head, and the flutter of the breeze in the branches. They would think she was foreign and different to walk down the avenue when she should have known her place was the rear entrance. She *was* different, to have had such a dream. And how beautiful and light its reality was, so far removed from the grey smallness of the life she had been born to.

Here, under the great swaying trees and the wide sky where the birds floated, there could be no smallness for anyone. Even the staff must share what there was.

She walked therefore down the centre of the avenue, a small figure dressed in black because black would take her anywhere. Only her hair showed a blatant glimpse of red.

And walking towards Liscombe, she felt herself opening up to the house, as it stood open to her.

Vera Cox, assistant housekeeper at the Hall, adjusted the damask curtains in the Rose Suite against the glare of the noon sun. 'Here, Beale,' she inquired of the chambermaid at work on the carpet behind her, 'there's no new arrivals today?'

'No, Miss Cox.' Jane, busy with the brush under the bed, added, 'This room's taken tomorrow.'

'I know it's taken tomorrow,' Vera said impatiently, 'they're all taken tomorrow.' She leaned into the swivel glass over the dressing-table and patted her blonde Mary Pickford curls that nightly cost so much time. 'Not that a guest would come up on foot, I suppose. What am I thinking?' She caught sight of a stray hair under a plucked brow and pulled at it. 'Nor with only one bag. I wonder . . . I tell you, Beale, if that old Mrs Baker has taken on a new maid without no reference to me, there'll be trouble. Either I'm assistant or I'm not.' She strode from the room, her tall clumsy body in cheap serge unsuitably crowned with the Hollywood hair.

Jane threw down her brush and rushed to the window. A small figure in black *was* walking down the centre of the avenue. Soon all of Liscombe would know who she was.

Meanwhile, she could allow herself a moment of pleasure, looking down upon the splendour of Liscombe Hall steps and the moving oak trees that today were giving their special high swishing sound that was sometimes like music. All this was part of her world now, and everything about the dream place was as she had imagined it, but she had rather there were fewer birds . . . a clutch of starlings was squabbling in the first oak and one of those birds – a crow or rook, she could never remember which and did not care for each was as horrible . . . She shut the window with a slam and bent back to her tasks. There were birds here, and then the ever-present food to disturb her. Soon it would be luncheon and she would have Cook to face or perhaps Gladys arguing about her new diet.

She brushed on, crawling under the bed. She was

fortunate that Dr Adlington had taken her on as a patient, giving her very nearly the same attention as the guests had. He met her in his room every other day, for weighing, to see if her daily regime needed adjustment. He had even suggested that they meet in the cottage where she went to tidy the place and feed the cats, for Pugs's sake, though she now had a staff room and Mary slept in the nursery.

There was that time he had met her by the doorway once when he was passing on his walk ... Jane wriggled away from the skirting, brushing as she went. There was exercise, too, to take off gross unhealthy flesh. She sprang up to permit herself a glimpse of her plump face in the looking-glass. One day, the doctor promised, she would be as thin as Lady Brockhampton who had left the week before, so beautifully slender you could see the blue veins under the fine skin of her face. Jane pinched one of her own cheeks until it hurt and shut her mind to the faint drift of cooking smells coming from the kitchen. With a feather duster she then began the routine insisted upon by her ladyship's aunt, a tartar to all the staff, with the habit of swooping in on them whilst they worked.

She herself had not yet been reprimanded, however, for she never forgot a crevice. First the picture frames and the picture rails, next all top surfaces beginning by the bedside. She ran the duster over the bedside books in their little carved wooden case and, carefully, behind the chest on which they stood and under the biscuit barrel; on round to the table at the foot of the bed where she had to inspect the blotter and check that ink had not been spilled on the perfect polish of the walnut surface. Here she paused, for a candle had been used; even such a small point should not be allowed to mar the perfection of a Liscombe Hall bedroom where everything had to be as it had been in the days before the war.

Changing to a hogshair brush that could reach to clean the nooks and crannies of the marble fireplace, Jane gave a little shiver of fear at the thought of Mrs Baker's praise of her careful work and her knowledge of the history and furnishings for each room. She was, it appeared, being considered for the post of assistant beside Vera now that the Hall was so busy and most rooms occupied continuously. But they were taking her too far ahead!

'Guess what, Beale!' Jane looked up at Lucy, a fellow maid who appeared in the doorway.

'What?' she asked, pausing by the bullrushes in the fireplace and smiling at Lucy who was so knowing of the world that she sometimes took the 'bus with Vera and cavorted in the *Palais de Danse* of distant modern Bournemouth.

'Did you hear the bell ringing? It was that new maid Lady Liscombe wanted – to be lady's maid, you know. Saucy, I call it, coming up to the front door like as if she was a guest. And all dressed in black like some fancy widow!' Lucy skipped across to the glass and peered at her shiny black bob of hair and the perfection of red gloss on her lips. 'But what can you expect, she's French.' She laughed and swished one leg backwards to check upon a forbidden stocking seam under her print maid's dress. 'Cox is having kittens. I bet she's telling everybody already that she can't bring her foreign ways here.' Lucy giggled, showing tiny white teeth. 'Watch out for fireworks, Beale, but we'll have a good laugh, eh?' Giving a turn about the room in a practice dance step, she winked at Jane, pushed the cap further on to her gleam of hair and slammed the door behind her.

Jane, warmed by the feeling of ordinary friendship

that Lucy seemed to offer, as she were not different, a mother of shame, as if she were not grossly fat, lingered over the dusting of the carved wooden legs of the *chaise-longue* by the window. Below her on the gravelled drive was the shy young Joe Tranter, earnestly bowing to Miss Ramsden, a guest of large proportions whom he had led along the lanes of Liscombe and was now helping to dismount from the back of Bobbin, a horse so placid that gunshot did not unnerve him. She peered down on to the beast's wide-flanked form, broad enough to accommodate Miss Ramsden, wondering if perhaps, after she and Lucy had laughed over the French maid and Vera, they could go on to giggle in a kind way about the poor Miss Ramsden that Dr Adlington himself could not help. Leaning down, she imagined the conversation they would have and how she would add that Miss Ramsden would far rather be taken for a riding lesson by Mr Johnny Tranter, head of the stables, as who indeed would not?

With the lady guest safely in the house, there he was, clattering across the gravel to Joe on his great black hunter. Jane, allowing herself to ponder on such a thing, thought how well she understood the preference of lady guests for Mr Johnny. His handsome face had a dark drawn look, with eyes as startlingly blue as Lady Liscombe's and dark untidy hair that no wind could flatten. Once, down by the basement steps as he was thundering past, she had caught his glance. It had made her shiver with a strange excitement, and afterwards she had dreamed of the way he held the reins of the horse.

She watched the top of his head, for he scorned a hat, as befitted his wild nature, and gave herself a moment's rest.

★

'Keep Bobbin out for the doctor,' Johnny called, walking his horse round towards his nephew who had finished bowing to Miss Ramsden and was inspecting his ride's front forelock to recover from the indignity of such labour.

'Not the doctor,' groaned Joe, rising and pushing back his hat. 'I'm not sure even Bobbs can stand him.'

Johnny took up the reins of the stoical Bobbin and threw them across to Joe. 'Well, he don't weigh much so it can't do him any harm. Make it a quick one, leave out Liscombe Hill, just go round to Flush and back.'

'What time?' grumbled Joe, leaping in one swift graceful movement on to the saddle of his favourite, Starlight, who had a character as young and serious as his own.

'Ah, and here he is.' Johnny's formal tone told Joe his pupil was walking down the steps behind him. He slid in the same easy movement from Starlight's back and bowed to Dr Adlington. The man was small and thin, dressed in dusty black with fine pointed boots and a hard riding hat. He put one foot up for Joe to lift him on to Bobbin. Johnny grinned as Joe's young strength almost shot the doctor over to the other side and on to the gravel. The man made his flesh creep though he could not say why, and he wished his sister had not found it necessary to employ a doctor for her guests, though the Hay Diet was bringing them in fast enough. They were suddenly prosperous, both the hotel and the stables because of it, but if there had to be a doctor, he would have wished for a simple country one with no nonsense about him, one who did not believe in fads. He would swear Adlington was a fake and knew no more of diets than he did himself.

He grunted as the man sat his scrawny body stiffly on Bobbin and swung his own hunter on down to take the side path past the Hall. He was due for a visit to his mother in the valley. By the basement steps and the grass patch where the servants hung linen, he heard his sister's voice. 'And this is where you will put out anything that needs to dry in the air,' she was saying. 'Of course, you will use the warm room for clothes that need to be dried quickly, say if a guest wishes to leave that day or wear a garment the same evening. We aim to give as quick a service as possible.' He saw his sister and beside her a girl, probably a maid. He paused. He wanted to ask her if she wished to go on offering free lessons to the so-called doctor for he was damned if he thought it necessary. The man would be glad of a job, any job, in his opinion.

'Ah, Johnny.' Kate called across to him. 'Don't go. I want to speak to you, please, about the stable bills to us. Can you wait?' Blinking through sunlight, Kate indicated the girl by her, in a smart foreign outfit, he now noticed. 'This is the new lady's maid, Johnny, she is to attend to our guests' personal needs, and Claudine, this is my brother, Mr Tranter, who has our riding school and stables.'

Johnny nodded to the girl. He saw she was very slim with a smooth matt skin and red hair drawn up into plaits around her ears under a smart little hat. When she looked up at him, he saw green eyes and parted painted lips. He thought: she could be trouble. She had on her feet unmaid-like shoes with high heels, and surely silk stockings underneath the skirt. 'I'll be coming back in half an hour,' he said, and pulled Jet's head round towards the path. He noticed the girl was looking up at him still and had time to take in her slender neck and firm rise of breast. He thought: I should quite like some trouble with her, but knew he would never dally so near to home. Setting the horse to a gallop down to the stream, he instantly forgot her.

Claudine held her breath to still her heart; there he had been before her, Johnny Tranter who had lifted her in his arms when she had been four years old. He was almost as she remembered, only handsomely aged with a slight touch of grey at the temples. He had the same thick dark hair standing up, the same dark blue eyes, looking so directly, and very white teeth showing when he smiled. He had smiled, at his sister. He had looked coldly, politely, at her. He had not recognized her, of course, nor had the name seemed to mean anything. A little girl, a child called Claudine, had fallen in love with him. He had given her a postcard of this place, his home, and the dream of them both had lifted her from the life she had been born to. Here she stood in the light English sunshine under a sweet wide sky beside the sister of the man she had followed, who owned this place. She could not have known that was so but it was, and this aristocratic lady was speaking to her in a kindly natural way that must be exclusive to the English gentry.

She turned to Lady Liscombe, Johnny Tranter's sister, dropping her eyes to the ground. 'I shall be able to start work at once, your ladyship,' she said.

'You understand I have no references for you? You came so suddenly! I think we'll have a trial period instead.' Kate was smiling at her, her voice light and unhurried, quite unlike the mean pinched tones of Miss Banfield. Claudine felt disarmed, almost as if she could tell the story to this lady, standing in the sunlight on a patch of grass. She judged her to be past forty but still beautiful as only a lady who had not had to work could be.

'I was so eager to come, Lady Liscombe,' she said. 'My friend, Monsieur Lecomte has told me what a beautiful place it is and how kind you are to the staff.

In London, people are not kind to staff, your ladyship.' She lowered her eyes and forbore to speak of her own history. She must not be so weak as to give anything of herself away; that would be for Johnny, later.

'Times have been hard,' Lady Liscombe said. 'We ourselves have found it very difficult to keep our business going, but with the Dr Hay diet, our sunshine rooms and our natural sunshine, we seem to have found a little niche.' She laughed as she turned away and walked back to the basement steps. 'Come along, my dear, I'll see you are taken up to the staff floor. We shall, I think, refer to you as Mademoiselle,' she added, going down the steps and into the passage leading to the kitchens. 'Mademoiselle Claudine is on hand to attend to your personal needs . . . It would look rather well in the brochure.' She waved a hand towards an open kitchen door where Claudine had a glimpse of Pierre in apparent dispute with a plump elderly woman. 'Your friend works in there but of course I shall not expect to find you there too.'

'Of course not, your ladyship,' said Claudine, following her down the stone passageway where she could smell the soap and steam of laundry work. She had hardly bothered to glance in at Pierre, feeling no pleasure to think of him so near to her. She would also very soon be able to clear her conscience and send him back to his Marie who had waited so long for him meekly at home, saving for their future. She allowed herself a little smile, thinking of the picture she had fabricated for herself of this woman. Forgive me, Marie, she said to herself, but I have my dream now, and you may have yours back.

CHAPTER 5

In the staff room that had once been the servants' hall, Simon Smith the oddboy bent his sore head to the wireless set on the sideboard and turned down the sound. Sid Tilley, his tormentor, had boxed his ears for not wanting to miss his favourite programme, *Saturday Night Variety*. Since their new prosperity, when Tilley had been taken back on the staff, Simon lived in dread of him, but tonight he dared pull up a chair and lean two bony elbows on the sideboard the better to hear, no matter if there were to be a party.

'Turn that off and take these two trays up.' Prissy the kitchen-maid, heavy-footed and flushed, changed already into her finest Sunday wear for this special evening when she would say goodbye to the woman she had worked beside for thirty-five years, pulled Simon's ear from habit and indicated trays bearing bowls of trifle. She did not bother to look at him but marched out, in shiny stockings, Simon noticed without interest, and fancy shoes like ladies' which did not make Prissy look like a lady. He turned the sound higher and began to laugh as his favourite comedian made a joke which must be funny, for the audience was laughing. He grinned rapturously, imagining himself in that hot heady place with a light directed upon the man with a red nose and shoes a foot long. All comedians looked like that for Simon and if there were magic in the world, one day he would have a ticket for the train to London to see for himself.

'The wireless? When there is a party?' The foreign cook who said he must be called 'Maître' now he was in charge of Liscombe kitchens, shouted at him from the doorway. 'Come and do your work if you hope to attend it yourself!'

Simon muttered that he did not wish to go to any parties, which must surely be times of dread with all servants gathered together to tease him, as they did at Christmas. He considered whether he should disobey this man who did not understand English ways but nevertheless knew that Simon was the butt of everyone below stairs. He stood there in his funny hat that looked as if it might topple over, sweat running down the dark skin of his face and a fearsome knife in one hand. Simon got slowly to his feet, eyes daringly challenging. He was going to say: 'I'm listening to the wireless, if you don't mind', but something in the man's face made him change his mind.

He lumbered across the room past Prissy's trays which he would not now take up, for the foreigner wanted him, and sullenly set to clearing the kitchen table, one ear cocked for the laughter from *Saturday Night* and his heart burning with resentment. His aching back bent over the task, he gave way to the little fear that had been lurking. With all the old staff to go, Cook and Mrs Baker and Treeves, who kept things the way they always had been, who treated him with near-respect, below stairs might hold anarchy. His difficult job could only get harder. He let a tear fall into the fish kettle from self-pity and the loss of *Saturday Night*.

In the staff room, swaying to the music of Henry Hall's band, Vera Cox took the man's part in the fox trot, swirling her backless silver dress, turning Lucy Pike who fancied herself as the apache girl in last week's film in Dorchester and had darkened her eye-brows and drawn back her hair. She flew with Vera around the table and the forgotten trifles, out of the room and down the corridor, their shoes tapping dramatically on the stone floor which this evening was theirs for their pleasure.

Even Gladys, little birdlike faithful maid to the Hall since Lady Liscombe's young days, poked her head out from the laundry room where she had gone in search of a lace collar discarded there in a pile of unclaimed laundry. Humble in the brown woollen dress she had bought from Marks & Spencer on a day trip to Weston-super-Mare, Gladys gave a little skip to the sound of the music and might have felt happy, this party night, if such an unknown future did not face her. Her heart had trembled at the news of the retirement of all three people who had played such an important part in her life since she was fifteen, forty years before. What would become of her now? Who would appreciate her worth, the care she put into the cleaning of her rooms, of all the Liscombe rooms? Even when Lord Liscombe had grown sad, between his first and second wives, she and Mrs Baker had kept the rooms as they should be kept. Lady Liscombe and her aunt hardly had time now for daily inspections, so there was Vera Cox, who knew nothing, and a vacant place as joint assistant. Jane would not be able to accept it for she was too afraid. Gladys knew that Jane felt as lowly as she did, and also that she was capable of much more than she herself would ever aspire to.

Scuttling on thin legs that never seemed to tire, Gladys carried the lace to enliven the dullness of Jane's dark blue dress which had come to her from some source, probably Mrs Baker or Lady Liscombe herself who had risen so far in the world since Gladys had first known her and giggled with her over the antics of her brother Johnny, lamp boy then.

Jane was sitting before the chest-of-drawers by the window of her room, holding a looking-glass in her hand. 'Gladys,' she said, 'I think I am a little too tired for the party tonight.' She was breathless, giving out little puffs as she often did in the past weeks; only Gladys had noticed this new habit.

'You been taking that stuff from the doctor again?' she said, studying the girl's bluish skin from the light of the window. Gladys did not believe in doctors, having never had need of one herself, but she especially did not believe in Dr Adlington whose creeping silent ways made her scurry away. 'It ent never done you no good, and what's more it ent natural.'

'I was too fat, Gladys. Fat and clumsy, that was me.' Jane put down the glass. 'And greedy, Gladys.'

'And now you eats nothing.' Gladys bustled about the room in a mechanical tidy. 'As if it were natural.'

'I eat too much.' Jane gave a breathless laugh. 'Dr Adlington says I shall soon be as slim and lovely as Lady Liscombe herself.' She stood up and put the collar to the neck of the plain woollen dress. 'Like this?'

Gladys pinched up loose folds of cloth around Jane's shoulders. 'If this fitted,' she said. 'It surely did fit two years ago when we went to Bournemouth for the day because there was no one in, not one guest, and Lady Liscombe were so unhappy she thought we'd have to close down, so she gave us a day out and . . .'

'The collar's lovely,' Jane said. 'Will you just pin it in?'

Shooing Gladys finally from the door, Jane sat down on her bed. She felt faint. It was probably, she thought, because of the work they had to do now, with so little respite from it. Every maid had a full set of rooms under her care. Then there was Vera Cox, always at her back, waiting for her to make a mistake, so that the rumour Jane was to be promoted to work alongside her would never become a fact.

She reached under the bed where she kept the bag with Pugs's cap and pipe and sacking apron. There too was the precious bottle of brandy that Dr Adlington said was the best treatment for sleeplessness. He would sometimes come into her room at night to administer it himself from a second bottle he kept just for her. She was often so drowsy from the little she had allowed herself that she hardly saw him there. She needed more of it now, before she could leave the room, for she had found it had a second function; making her brave enough to face the world. Swaying slightly, she managed to walk down the corridor of the servants' wing and on to the nursery in the East Tower where her daughter was sleeping beside Sarah Liscombe. It was easier to kiss her goodnight when she was asleep and could not turn cold eyes towards the mother who had left her to be raised amongst strangers as a kind of poor companion.

Claudine, emerging from her own room, watched Jane stumble past and allowed herself a moment's pity for the girl who was so obviously weak and such easy prey for a man like Dr Adlington. The wonder of it was, she thought, that Lady Liscombe had caught no drift of happenings in the staff quarters and in that strange cottage where Jane went daily under pretext of feeding cats! How could her ladyship not see that the man was dubious? She, Claudine, would not take off her clothes to be weighed by that papery evil creature. Only English women could be so foolish as to be swept up in the slimming craze.

Claudine felt the slim perfection of her own waist beneath the black crêpe-de-Chine dress she had bought second-hand from a London market-stall. Stepping daintily along the corridor in her Parisian shoes, she considered the problem of Jane Beale who was in line for promotion, and was moreover the pet of Lady Liscombe, with her daughter kept in style as companion to the Honourable Sarah. She herself was more capable of doing the work, though whether she could bear to stand as equal to the common Vera was another matter. But given that Lady Liscombe had not been able to promote either into the post of head house-keeper on the departure of Mrs Baker, there was also that position to be viewed as a possible personal object-ive. It would be unusual to be appointed directly to it, she knew, but surely not impossible.

She tripped down two flights of stairs, her thoughts thus occupied, and reached the baize door leading to the bigger dining-room. A band was already playing American music. Her heart lifted. Perhaps Lady Lis-combe had persuaded her brother to attend the party and there would be a chance that he would dance with her. As part of the strange reality that was the actual Liscombe, she had long since learned that neither Johnny nor his sister were the aristocrats she had supposed them to be, but the children of Mr and Mrs Tranter from the cottage in the valley, he still working with a herd of cows because that had been his life. This fact had not changed her feelings towards the place or the man. It had rather seemed to add to them. That people of peasant stock should aspire to other things, that their energy and competence should reward them with this place, merely made Johnny a more accessible dream.

She stood quietly in the doorway, a small black

figure gazing upon the glory of the Liscombe dining-room laid with a feast as if for the grandest company. In her mind, a conversation took shape between herself, as Head Housekeeper, a clutch of keys about her waist, and Lady Liscombe, to whom she described a new colour scheme of eau-de-Nil and gold for this room which was past its best.

Johnny, drinking a courtesy glass with Treeves and Mrs Baker, whom he had known since his fifteenth year, caught sight of the small figure standing with no trace of gaucheness in the door of the great room, as if she were accustomed to it. She puzzled him. She seemed to appear whenever he set foot in the Hall. It was almost unnerving, and there was something so familiar about her that he dared not search his memory too deeply. There had been girls enough in his life, used and discarded away from Liscombe, but this was surely not one of them. He would have remembered a French girl. He turned back to Treeves whose routine of years was failing him now, who did not always wait at Liscombe steps to welcome Lord David back from his ride because he had forgotten he had gone out. The hotel had been too much for him for maybe six months, Johnny estimated, seeing the vagueness in his eyes as he stood with his untouched glass, oddly a guest in the room where he so often served.

'And what are your plans for retirement, Mrs Baker?' he asked valiantly, hoping for his sister's or David's entrance so that he could avoid the girl in black and escape to his flat above the stables where his life was comfortably without questions apart from those concerned with horse management.

Kate Liscombe, at the doorway behind Claudine, took the plump arm of Hannah Fellowes, once queen of Liscombe kitchens, now to retire at the age of seventy. 'David, take her other arm, we shall have to drag her into the party,' she ordered, laughing, to her husband.

David caught up Cook's right arm and held it tight against him. 'You shall have this moment of glory, Cook,' he said, 'no matter how much you hate it. You deserve a good send-off and you're going to have it.'

Hannah, bursting from her violet silk, caught sight of the comfort of Mrs Baker and Treeves in the glorious room which was set for her too and let herself be taken towards them and Johnny Tranter. He always teased her and made her feel a woman, the wife and mother she had never been though she bore the cook's courtesy title of 'Mrs'.

Kate left the group they formed, standing quite rightly in the centre of the room, and moved amongst her staff with their unaccustomed champagne. Now they were on the other side of the dividing line between guest and servant. Only Simon and Pierre were left in the kitchens, for the guests, joining in with the spirit of the event, had dined early and could if they wished attend the party after the speeches. She noted with amusement how the staff were still bunched in their separate groups, maid with maid, porter with valet, outside staff and kitchen staff. They were still ill-at-ease, in their Sunday best, gazing at the general magnificence of their own efforts, the arrangements of flowers and the fruits and the heaped plates which they would each hesitate to be the first to touch.

She stood alone amongst the murmuring groups and took in the sight of it – hers, brought into being by her own efforts and held together by all of them, Aunt Bessie and David especially. They had come through because Aunt Bessie had remembered the Hay Diet and the fashion for slimming which was such a perversity in a time of depression. She was going to congratulate everyone this evening, not just the three who had supported her past their own retirement time.

'You are in a reverie, my darling.' Her husband appeared beside her. 'I think Hawker is waiting for your signal that the food may be dug into, and Vera and Lucy's eyes are boring into your back. I gather they want the dancing to start.' He took her arm. 'You were thinking how everyone had bravely come through and brought us to this, weren't you? You are right, my dearest, and now I think, with the younger staff coming in, you can rest on your laurels a bit. What about the south of France for us and Sarah? I want to show you where I spent all those years roaming about pining for you.'

Kate said, as she had before, 'When I've chosen another assistant housekeeper, or a head one if I can, darling. I don't want to leave Aunt Bessie to see to everything on that side.'

'Well, it had better not be that girl Beale,' he said. 'She really doesn't look strong enough. If we hadn't taken that daughter of hers into the nursery with Sarah, I can imagine they'd have ended in some institutional care by now. Don't you think so, Bess?'

Aunt Bessie joined them, holding her first glass of champagne. 'It's the daughter I can't take to,' she said. 'Who's going to start the damn' speeches?'

'You are,' they chorused, but Hawker seemed to take charge of the matter. At a nod of agreement from David, he had the music stopped and stood by the top table, a perfect specimen of old-age courtliness. He called for silence and introduced his lordship to take the floor.

There was polite applause for Lord David, still ruggedly handsome with his hair almost grey and lines of past sorrows in his face, but seeming nonetheless a natural member of the aristocracy to all of the staff. They always deferred to him, though it was his wife who managed matters as they well knew. None thought the less of him for it, certainly not those he stood to honour who had known him since his young manhood. He held the hand of blushing Hannah Fellowes, clutched awkwardly at the elbow of the stiff Mrs Baker who had learned her formality from his own mother, as Treeves had, standing beside her with only a suggestion of a tremble to his chin. Lord David spoke with charm and humour of their years of service, of the time when he had been alone before Lady Liscombe had returned to him and the Hall had been reborn.

Kate herself was barely able to offer public thanks; it had come to her in a flash of terror that these three, whom she had first known when she was a kitchen maid at the Hall, who had so ably helped to make the Hall a successful hotel, were actually leaving it and her. She simply kissed them. Aunt Bessie led the cheering and then took centre floor to tell a comical story about the cooks and housekeepers they had had at their London hotel and the night a disgruntled maid had put a dead mouse in the bed of one of them. There was relief, the moment of emotion finished, and the three stars of the evening were able to say a few words before everyone moved towards the food.

When it had been demolished, the dancing began. Jane was led on to the floor by Hawker, Claudine by Pierre. Jed Swaffield took on Gladys for they had danced together at Liscombe parties for forty years and if Jed's mother had not lived so long with her weak heart, they might have married. Vera Cox giggled at them between throwing out her chest in the arms of the valet Armstrong, this movement designed to show off the gleam of her back in the silvery gown sewn by Gladys from a pattern offered to *Woman* readers. Vera revealed a sturdy calf in the style of Ginger Rogers with the confidence of one shortly to be head housekeeper at the Liscombe Hall Hotel and have her own downstairs sitting-room. She would have to give up the pleasure of the *Palais de Danse* in Bournemouth and indulge in tea at Fullers instead. It would, Vera considered, leaning over the tables, be worth it. She might join the Women's League of Health and Beauty too. There were some very genteel members, quite unlike the coarse people at the *Palais*. She had outgrown it.

Claudine regarded the dancing of Vera Cox with scorn and allowed herself a moment of pleasure being held in the arms of Pierre without succumbing to the pressure of his body. She had tried to show him, by her busyness, by her coolness, that there would be no more times of intimacy like those in London, but he had not seemed able to understand.

It was she who first saw Jane fall at the feet of Hawker and the pale papery hand of Dr Adlington reach out to feel the pulse at her neck. There was something in the way the man leaned over Jane that tempted Claudine to turn to Lady Liscombe. She wanted to tell her about the doctor's interest in the girl, about poor Jane's weakness and the spell the man seemed to have cast on her. She hesitated, easing away Pierre's arm, and the moment was gone, for the doctor led off a procession of men carrying Jane, followed by Lady Liscombe herself.

Without the music and the dancing, the room all at once seemed hot and frowsty, full of smoke and body heat. Everyone looked pale with fatigue in the stillness, a poor end to their night of celebration, Treeves, his eyes paler and blanker than ever, led off unbending Mrs Baker who had not yet cried for the moment when she must leave Liscombe for ever. Behind them trotted Hannah Fellowes, her tears mixed with giggles because of the champagne. Mr and Mrs William Tranter, Lady Liscombe's parents, followed her, on their best behaviour for their daughter's sake, and glad to leave this grand place which had never had much to do with them. Aunt Bessie kept up a cross conversation with the waiter who had served Jane with two double brandies, and at a nod from Lord Liscombe, the band threw itself into the playing of *God Save the King*.

Claudine cursed herself for her hesitation, for with hindsight she could see that if she had made one move towards Lady Liscombe that evening and discussed with her, as two women of the world, the evil effect of the doctor on Jane, it would have gone some way towards her becoming her ladyship's confidante and therefore natural successor to Mrs Baker. As it was, she was too late and Johnny Tranter became involved, so that the parts of all three of them, herself and Johnny and Jane, were set for years to come.

It had already occurred to her that the person most concerned in Jane's illness was the doctor. When she went to her room, she found Gladys fussing around the door and reporting that the doctor was inside with Lady Liscombe herself. Digesting this information, she was still there when her ladyship appeared.

'Ah,' she said, 'Claudine, just the person ... Will you be able to spare a minute later? I want you to help Jane dress and pack a few of her things. Dr Adlington says she is suffering from neurasthenia, a severe case he says, and must have absolute rest.' She spoke in the whisper appropriate to news of illness. 'I suggested we send her away for a while to a nursing home, but he won't hear of it and proposed we send her across to the cottage. She can have complete peace there, and the doctor will spend an hour or two with her each day. She'll have the very best attention.'

Claudine sensed that Gladys stood beside her, as open-mouthed as she was herself. 'Now, Gladys . . .' Lady Liscombe did not seem to notice their surprise. 'I shall need you too. Run down and tell Miss Cox to rearrange the work on the East Wing so that you can be spared to go across to the cottage and prepare it for Jane. You'll need a strong broom and a long feather duster for the cobwebs. I hope you're not squeamish about bits of rabbit skin. Those cats!'

She was already walking away though Claudine felt herself put out a hand to stop her. She wanted to say something about the doctor but the presence of Gladys, the faith in him of Lady Liscombe who was so astute in other matters, carried the moment from her. 'Gladys,' Claudine began, 'do you think . . .'

'What, Miss?' Gladys whispered too, a hand held to her mouth in the same attitude of surprise.

'That doctor, Gladys . . .'

'I don't know nothing, Miss,' Gladys burst out, and scuttled off down the corridor.

'Don't forget to take enough sheets, blankets and pillows,' Claudine called after her, and set off herself for her morning tasks. She did not think she cared to go into Jane's room until she was sure the doctor had left it.

It was almost luncheon before Gladys reported that the cottage was ready for habitation with the fire lit, though a little smoky, and a kettle already on the boil.

Helping Jane dress, Claudine was struck by the pitiful thinness of her limbs, by her weak trembling movements, as if she did indeed suffer from some illness. She did not seem to want to speak, only murmured her thanks and some tremulous apologies which tempered Claudine's pity with irritation. 'You cannot help being ill,' she said, and was brisk, setting her mind to work on her own plans. If she could not immediately discuss Jane and the doctor with her ladyship, she would outclass Vera Cox none the less by taking charge of Jane as Mrs Baker would have done. She would organize her meals, a round of sitters by the bed, her laundry, the fire. She would also give Jane solid advice, help her overcome her problems and her weaknesses. The girl needed a friend. Claudine would let her pour it all out and there would be real ammunition then to have her put out of mind as an assistant, and in addition to have the doctor dismissed. It would not be just a question of her suspicions and what she had thought to hear through the door of Jane's bedroom one night when on her way to the lavatory.

The next day, on her third or fourth personal visit to Jane, she saw Johnny's horse before she had skirted the field beyond the churchyard. She did not take much note; Johnny was often about the paths with his hunter, but approaching the cottage door, she saw that the beast was actually standing near the corner of the cottage itself. In the doorway, a ginger cat was also gazing at the horse in some surprise. Then Johnny himself appeared, stepping over the cat, grabbing at reins, sending a sort of polite salute to her, and thundering off.

Behind him, in the silence he had left, Claudine walked on and bent to stroke the cat's marmalade head, murmuring to it to give herself time to absorb the extraordinary fact of this man's presence in this cottage.

She did not have to spend long at Jane's bedside to learn unwelcome news. All unknowing, in the way so typical of the weak and helpless she later thought, Jane had changed everything, for she said between sobs: 'I have told him. He made me.'

Johnny spurred his horse past the corner of Liscombe churchyard, round the last oaks in the avenue, stopping with a clatter on the gravel. He shouted for the head porter, pausing no longer than to throw him the reins. He ran up the steps to the door and on across the wooden floor he had first trodden as lamp boy at the age of fourteen. He did not stop to admire the bronze pillars nor the sweep of staircase where sunlight played from the great windows; he had no taste for such things and anyway did not see them. Anger had flooded his body with heat; it propelled him to the second floor where afternoon quiet made the thud of his boots the only sound. He threw open the door of number 51 without pausing to knock. The man sat there, correctly dressed all in black, writing at a desk. Prim little knees swivelled round at Johnny's entrance, the papery bloodless face pinched with surprise.

'Out!' Johnny said, his breath suddenly gone. 'Pack your bags. I'll be back in an hour. Someone will take you to the station.'

'Whatever . . .?' The man rose from his chair. 'You have no right. I shall see Lady Liscombe . . . his lordship . . .'

'No need,' Johnny said, staring with distaste at the bony hand put up to the man's hollow chest. 'Lady Liscombe and his lordship will be too busy to see you. They'll be taking statements from the other maids, no doubt, to see what other rooms have been opened in the dead of night, what other innocence has been tainted.' He allowed himself a moment of triumph as the man seemed to crumple. The bony hand moved to the desk for support. A stuttering sound came from him, a word or two that may have been something about a maid's story against a doctor's. Johnny did not stay to hear them.

His anger was gone. When it came to him it was as fierce as fire but did not last long. Neither, however, was the cause of them ever forgotten. He still remembered the red haze of his boyhood that had made him attack a teacher who had unjustly taken his penknife.

He found his sister at the bottom of the second floor staircase, sent there by some member of staff aware of the unusual nature of his presence inside the hotel. He did not begin his explanation until they were seated in her office in the basement; there was no silly questioning from his sister, as he'd known there would not be. She waited sensibly for him to begin.

'I was taking Jet nice and slow round towards Pugs Burrow,' he said, 'when I saw smoke from that old cottage of Pugs's, so naturally I went in to investigate. Thought it was tramps.'

'You would, dear. I'm sorry I never thought to tell you . . .'

'The Beale girl was lying there in the bed, the fire going, kettle on, all homely. I half expected her to get up and invite me for a cup of tea. But she was crying her head off.'

Kate tutted in sympathy. 'And you couldn't very well just leave her.'

'No. I wanted to get out sharpish and send for you, but she said, "Please don't tell Lady Liscombe" and I thought she meant because she was there but she meant because she was crying. I more or less stayed until that was sorted out and then she couldn't seem to stop.' Johnny eased his tall frame in the chair. 'Couldn't stop sobbing something about that doctor. He's ... he's been going into her room at night, as far as I can make out. Can you believe it, Sis?'

'Johnny, you don't mean ... sexual things?' Kate's face turned pale with horror. 'Here at Liscombe? And that poor girl!'

'Some sort of ... something, I don't know, it's a woman's job that, to talk to her, but there was drinking too. He's been feeding her brandy day and night – so he could creep in I suppose and start ... Ugh! Did you know she drank?'

'I suspected it,' Kate said faintly. 'I thought that was why she sometimes seemed less in charge of herself and why I postponed giving her a post of responsibility.'

'I imagine she was glad to drink to forget the other things that filthy doctor – if he is a doctor ... I told you, Sis!'

'Yes, you did, Johnny, you sensed something, but I had no idea. He's been so charming with the lady guests.'

'Been conning them too!'

Kate seemed to gather her strength. 'I must go and see him, I suppose. He has seemed creepy. David laughed at him but he always took the diet so seriously, treating it as a kind of science.' She got up.

'You're not going.' Johnny leaped to his feet. 'Send David if you must but I don't want you or any female anywhere near him. He must have some power over women or something. How else to explain it? A girl like that ...'

'She already had problems, Johnny. The child ...'

'She must have been forced then, you can see she's the innocent sort, and that doctor sniffed it out. You go over and see her, she needs your help.' He took her arm to lead her from the room. 'But here, that cottage – you know he's even been pawing her over there from what I could make out and that's been the last straw for the poor girl, lying there helpless.'

'It was his idea, the cottage,' Kate said weakly. 'I blame myself in part. I had no idea . . .'

'You just go and see if you can help her now,' Johnny ordered. 'None of it's your fault. You're as gullible as any other woman when it comes down to it. You should have listened to me!'

'Yes,' Kate said. She was too shocked to argue with her brother.

'David and I will see he's off these premises and never comes back. Leave it to us. You go and see that poor girl.'

With the doctor gone in shameful haste, Kate went across to the cottage. Jane was lying quiet; her eyes were puffed with weeping, Kate saw, and the pillow about her head damp with tears. She lit the lamp by the hearth. Someone had thought to fill it, she noted with pleasure, probably Claudine, and the kettle was full too. There was tea and milk and cocoa and sandwiches under a cover.

With the three cats about her feet, Kate prepared to make tea, pouring milk into a bowl by the hearth as a first priority. 'I'll tell everyone to make sure they bring enough scraps and milk over for these sweet things,' she said. 'I know how much you worry about them and how much Pugs loved them.'

Jane did not answer, regarding her silently from the bed, able it seemed only to nod.

'But I wonder if it might not be better for you to go away for a while? Someone will come every day for the cats.' She did not look at Jane but busied herself with tea and stroking the creatures who seemed to be asking for something else.

'If there is cheese in the sandwiches, they would like some of that,' Jane said suddenly. 'They always liked cheese. Pugs used to buy it when we had eightpence to spare. They would come up to where we were, they always knew, and the time too. They'd just appear and she'd give them a piece each.'

'I think I saw them once or twice, going across to the fields.' Kate poured tea into two Liscombe cups and took one over to the bed. 'And I've seen you come over here each day, never forgetting. I think Pugs can rest easy if she's watching over you, and I'm sure she is, my dear.' She was talking, she knew, to calm the girl's sense of awkwardness at lying there, at being the cause of trouble. But Jane's face crumpled, she could see it in the glow from the lamp.

'I didn't come for the cats,' she burst out. 'Or only at first. That's what's so terrible. Everyone thinks me good but I'm not. I came for other things, too, and I cannot forget, I cannot! You see, if you knew what I was, you could not even bear to be in the same room with me.' She began to weep, letting the tears fall into her hair.

Kate sat on the foot of the bed and said gently: 'Is there anyone I can send for . . . your family?'

'I have no one.'

'Was Pugs a relative?'

'No, she just saved Mary and me. Before that I had only my mother, my father died when I was eight and . . . a man . . . my uncle took us in, but they have gone away now, my mother and him, and the Rectory is shut up.'

'The Rectory over at Frampton? You had something to do with the vicar who disappeared years ago as suddenly as he had come?'

'I do not want to speak of it!' Jane could barely form the words for her weeping made her sit up and choke into her hands.

Kate tried again. 'Would you like to see another doctor?' she suggested. 'A proper one that you can talk . . .?'

'Oh, not a doctor! Please, not a doctor!' Jane lay back as if exhausted, muttering again. 'Not a doctor, please, your ladyship.'

'Of course not. Whatever you want, you shall have, my dear. You know everyone at Liscombe is part of the family, and I do feel responsible. That wretched Adlington! I engaged him myself, you know. He took me in and everyone else too.'

Jane covered her face with her hands.

'You must not feel to blame in any way,' Kate said. 'Come now, drink this tea and then have a nice healing sleep.'

She waited until the girl had fallen into some kind of doze and Gladys appeared, all anxious flutter, sent by Claudine to sit by the sick bed for the afternoon.

Walking reflectively back to the Hall, she made up her mind to promote Claudine to the post of assistant housekeeper at once; it was clear Jane would never be capable of assuming such responsibility, or not for a long time. She had hesitated to promote Claudine before because she had been engaged as a lady's maid and had no experience of Liscombe bedrooms except where she had offered herself to cover for sick maids in the past busy months. But there was no doubt in her mind that Claudine could do the work far more competently than Vera, whose coarse ways might not

86

fit very well with Claudine's professional and ambitious attitude. There would be trouble between them, especially when the French girl showed herself capable of the position of head housekeeper, as Kate had no doubt she would. The situation would have to be watched. And as for Jane herself, she knew that David would agree she and the child should continue to be in their care. She could never let down Jane for she reminded her of her own self when she too had had an illegitimate child to raise. She wondered who had been the father of Mary? Had there been someone vile like Adlington preying on her, or had she been the result of an illicit love affair? Deciding that she had no need to know, Kate walked on to the Hall which still held the air of excitement caused by the departure of Dr Adlington; even the guests appeared to have learned the scandalous cause of it.

Claudine had little time to savour her promotion. She moved with haste into the larger room beside Vera's with a view over the Downs. It had carpet instead of linoleum, a proper chest of drawers and wardrobe befitting her new position. It was gratifying to know that Lady Liscombe had recognized her ability; she had made an important step upwards. But there was much work to do – a full house and two maids less, for Gladys spent most of the time with Jane. She had to divide their sections between the other maids, all slow workers; it was Gladys and Jane who had worked with speed and skill.

In order to finish her duties by two o'clock, Claudine had to make up some beds herself. She did not mind. That was the least of the day's problems, where she had also to fit in her duties as lady's maid. The principal one was that of Jane and Johnny. She had twice seen him fly on the hunter past the churchyard and evidently stop by the cottage. And when Gladys had rushed back for food on one occasion, she had been, she said, sent by Mr Johnny who would sit with Jane whilst she had her own meal.

'And he told me not to hurry back,' Gladys informed her breathlessly, 'but to get some nourishing food for her and have it properly prepared. Oh, you'd think he was Lord David himself, to hear him.' Gladys fluttered her hands in admiration. Claudine paused beside her in the basement corridor, hoping for more information. Gladys obligingly gave it. 'I think he's sweet on her, I do, though I never thought it before. Whatever else can he want to sit there for with her crying fit to die?' Gladys scurried off, no doubt for further gossiping.

Claudine thought: I cannot bear it. And then: but Gladys must be wrong. Johnny could not be sweet on Jane. Such a handsome masculine figure could not care for featureless Jane, whose only charm lay in her apparent helplessness. But it was, she thought with sudden insight, there that Jane succeeded, for everyone felt stronger, better, for supporting the weak. And she was pretty, with big round frightened eyes like a kitten's.

Such a union as Jane and Johnny, however, had never entered her own imaginings. The only girl she had wanted to see on the arm of Johnny was herself and that she had not yet been able to achieve. She had her first promotion. Johnny had been more elusive, though she had tried to put herself in his way. He had done little more than glance at her, and she had not dared to approach him, as she might, and say: 'I am Claudine Forestier. Once you came to my grand-mother's café and gave me a dream of a different life.' She *could not* dare for if then he was appalled by her extraordinary single-minded effort, all for him, and well he might be, she would have nothing left. No, her aim must be to make him notice her stunning red hair, her green eyes, and the rest. She had thought there was time enough. She might now have to act more quickly. If necessary, she would put herself between them. She had not trod such a long and lonely path only to have it crumble away beneath her feet. And Jane could not offer such love for Johnny as she had ready in her heart.

Johnny, sitting on Pugs's milking stool by the head of Jane's bed, was transfixed by the cloudy blue of her eyes in a face where he could see the veins on her forehead. She had suddenly begun to talk about her child. 'When I saw my baby,' she said, 'she seemed to have the same hair as me so I thought I would be able to have someone to love, but Mary does not love me.'

'Of course she does.' Johnny shifted on the stool from embarrassment. 'All young love their mothers, you can see it in the animal world, it's natural . . .'

'She knows I'm not worthy to be a mother, and Dr Adlington, he knew it too, and he saw me come here every day and so he came in too like he used to come into my bedroom.'

Johnny felt a flood of heat spread across his back and up to his face. He had not done enough to the man. He wanted the girl to stop but did not know how to interrupt the little bursts of words that kept coming. He was, he felt, getting into deep water but could not speak nor move from the stool. He had come only to see how she was.

'He talked to me and said he could make me slim and pretty like the ladies at the Hall. He gave me brandy to help me sleep and things to take to keep me slim. It did not matter. I drank it all, for he knew how I was, how I had been, and seemed to see into my shame.' She began to rock slightly against the pillows, a thin pale hand clutched to her neck, as if she felt the need to vomit.

Johnny stood up. He felt he might otherwise lean across to stroke her and hold her, as if she were one of his sick horses. 'Is there anything anyone can do for you?' he said instead. 'The maid will be back soon and . . . oh, here she is.' At the sound of a footstep from the doorway, Johnny turned gratefully.

'You were expecting me?' Claudine, a vision in jade-coloured crêpe with her red hair dressed up into combs, stood framed in sunlight with a basket on her arm and an air of healthy robustness about her.

'Er, no, the other one,' Johnny muttered. 'Gladys or someone that her ladyship sent over yesterday. Anyway, you'll do.' He moved briskly to the door. 'Er, I think she's about to sleep for a bit. I just came . . . her ladyship asked me . . . Good day to you.'

He was gone. Without his male presence, the room seemed bare and chill. Claudine saw that indeed Jane was lying back with her eyes closed. She thought: She has touched his heart, and the realization was as unwelcome as Gladys's story. What *could* such as Jane be to Johnny?

It took her several days of watching his movements, of going across with regularity herself to question Jane in the most casual way as to his calling on her and their conversations. Jane would only say in her sweet immature way that Mr Johnny was being *so* kind to her, so generous of his time, and to a humble maid! Repressing a desire to shake her, Claudine was forced to admit no kind of duty could be involved; Johnny went to see Jane because he wanted to.

She made up her mind that Jane must not be allowed to come between the rightful couple: herself and Johnny.

On the day she decided to act, she was not off duty until nine, but that suited her. She wanted it to be dark and near the time when Johnny left the club in Dorchester where he dined every Tuesday. She bathed in Floris bath essence which a guest had left behind and dressed in the set of black silk camiknickers and camisole. Was it wicked to use Armand's gift for Johnny? Then there was the rust crêpe dress, her only one of colour beside the jade. This, she noted with renewed appreciation, brought out the rust tints of her hair. There were jet clips for her ears and a jet comb to fix the swathe of hair from the new low bun she had adopted for day duty to a knot at the crown of her head. With its centre parting and roll at each side, there was no mistaking the gleam of richness that her hair had, so unlike Jane's that she never bothered to style.

She admired the swirl of skirt from the bias cut of her dress, pulled on the silk stockings from Paris and her Parisian shoes that Miss Banfield at the Imperial Palace had ordered her to remove. If Miss Banfield could see her now, mere fourth-floor housekeeper that she would remain!

There *she* was, a perfect image of chic, gazing back at herself from the looking-glass on the washstand, a glow on her matt skin, her lips parted in anticipation of the evening to come, and a tear at the corner of her eye. She was lonely, and tired! She had so wanted Johnny to have come to her. It should not have been *this* way!

But she was not prepared to let simpering Jane walk

away with him. Putting back her shoulders, lifting her breasts showing at the low neck of her dress, she strode from the room, without her bag for that was part of the plan. Pierre saw her leave by the basement door but she called out that she was going to see Jane safely asleep, and did indeed take the path towards the church, turning back on herself to go along the rear of the Hall where no one would see her or guess at her objective.

She glanced down into the valley to the cottage where Johnny and his sister had been children and where their parents still lived. It was such a humble cottage, yet no one amongst the staff ever thought to comment on it, so much was it accepted that Lady Liscombe had risen from such beginnings. Her personality was so strong that she had overcome her start in life, feeling, it seemed, neither pride nor shame in it, nor in the terrible fact that the child she raised as her own had been a murderer. Claudine felt renewed admiration and renewed pleasure that they had had the same lowly start in life; there would be no great differences between them as she had once feared.

She had no doubts now about her present action and did not notice the chill of the air. At her estimation, Johnny should still be in Dorchester, perhaps at that very moment walking across to his Bentley. She must hurry. She wanted him to find her on the Dorchester Road or at the point where the lane turned into Liscombe Hill. She would be the poor foreigner who had lost her bag and missed her last 'bus home.

Johnny, confused by his evening drinking, and by this last glass of whisky that she had somehow poured him, regarded the girl who sat upon his sofa beside him. He could smell a faint flowery scent. Her bare arm, next to his, reflected the glow from the lamp he must have lit himself. He had seen her walking alone out on the Dorchester Road in the dark, with her purse and her 'bus gone. He had been obliged to offer her a lift, of course, and there she was, turning her face towards him with parted lips and eyes a haze of green.

'Here,' he said now, 'I'd better be taking you back.' And he leaned forward to place his glass on the table near her. Her arm touched his where he had rolled back his sleeves from the heat of the room and the whisky she had given him. He could not tell whether it was by accident or design but she appeared to have fallen a little behind him and then her lips were on his neck and that smooth warm flesh of hers made something explode within him – all the senses that the other girl had awoken in him, spending hours with her, giving way to tenderness though he could not touch her. It all exploded within him until he was spent and he had to say that he was sorry, sorry. But the perfect form of her body matched his exactly!

Jane, rising shakily the next day, bathed her limbs in heated rain water, the way she had before Pugs died. She dressed in the clean cotton dress Gladys had washed and ironed for her and tied back her hair with a blue ribbon. This she could do for herself now though it might take an hour.

'There, my lovely,' she said to Tom, the head cat. 'Perhaps Gladys with our breakfast next, or Mr Johnny out early?' Her heart thudded from weakness, and the thought that Mr Johnny would surely come that morning some time for he always did. She was overwhelmed with spoiling since the night when it had all begun when she had suddenly felt too weak to dance at the party. She had fallen before, in her own room and had once lain all night. No one knew the true shame of it, but Mr Johnny had heard about Dr Adlington and still came to see her as if she were an ordinary girl and had some ordinary illness to be asked after.

'The milk's coming,' she said, for she and the cat had heard a movement at the doorway but there had been no horse thudding up the path. She was glad it was not yet here for the early mornings were when the strange weakness very nearly overcame her, though she forced herself to rise.

'Here we are.' It was Lady Liscombe's voice. 'Milk and breakfast. Even Simon's busy this morning, my dear.'

'Oh.' Jane tried to get up. 'Please don't, your lady-ship, I must stir myself and get back to work.'

'Nonsense, what an idea!' Kate brought a rush of fresh air with her, placing a basket by the hearth and making tea from the kettle all in one movement. 'You are not well enough yet.' She regarded Jane from behind the teapot. 'And as a matter of fact, I have had a very sensible suggestion put to me this morning. About the sea air. It's already decided, Bournemouth it's to be for you, and no arguing.' She laughed, unpacking bread from a napkin and a delicate piece of bacon Pierre cooked 'specially for Jane each morning. 'I'm sending Gladys with you, since you can't go alone. She's given the Hall forty years of faithful service and deserves more than a couple of day trips to Weston-super-Mare. I haven't told her yet, but I've booked it by telephone. She'll be so excited, and so will you be once you get over the shock. It's a sort of spa place, on the cliff top.'

Jane thought: I cannot go. I cannot move from this chair. She thought: I shall not see Mr Johnny.

*

94

Johnny's stableboy took him the news of Jane's departure, having been ordered to drive her and Gladys to the station. Johnny started the boy's work himself, leaning a negligent arm from a stable door as the car swept off across the gravel. He had a glimpse of her pale face and those eyes staring across at him and thought that it was just as well. She was such a delicate girl, with such a painful experience behind her. The other one, the girl from last night, was far more his type, though he would have to disentangle himself from her clutches very shortly. Kate would not like him to be involved with a member of the staff. For the moment, if she were willing, he was too, and he was tired of professional women. She would not be likely to be indiscreet. He must make a visit to the chemist. He must also try and remember her name. She had a charming accent, and what a neat little body!

Johnny leaned on. A sense of well-being made him reluctant to saddle up the two horses booked for afternoon lessons. Well, he grinned to himself, French women certainly had a reputation for such things. There had been one or two in the war . . .

Claudine heard the car because the stableboy spent so long cranking it. There was Gladys, all of a flurry, sending little squeals up through the open window of the Blue Room where Claudine was checking the maid's work. She saw only the top of a hat beside Gladys and a glimpse of Jane's blue dress and coat. She saw Gladys kiss Mary goodbye with more love than Jane ever seemed to put into an embrace with her child and she felt again Johnny's arms around her from the night before. There was still on her skin, the feel of his roughness where he had kissed her. Her mouth burned, and her throat and her breasts as she stared blankly from the window. At last, she had lain with Johnny Tranter.

But treacherous tears were creeping down her cheeks. If only Johnny had come to her of his own accord, if only she had not had to force their meeting! How lonely she had been, with the knowledge of her plotting. And then he had apologized for his passion.

It must not matter. She wiped away the tears. This was only the beginning for her and Johnny, and the tableau being played out below would be the last of her making. Johnny would very soon realize that he loved her as much as she loved him and there need be no more. By the time she returned, Jane would be forgotten.

Johnny did not forget Jane at once however, and a few days later, Claudine found she was breathing in curative sea air for herself. Johnny had told her to meet him on the Dorchester Road. There was a furious ride with the wind roaring round his open Bentley roadster and this most unusual remark from his lips. 'Beautiful place, Bournemouth,' he said.

Claudine hardened her heart afresh against Jane and muttered her agreement. They had screeched to a halt on the cliff top; before them was a stretch, acres, Claudine thought, of blue sea with a ribbon of sand around it and this pile of unnaturally green and white cliffs. 'It is like a painting,' she said. 'Or a postcard.'

A postcard had helped to bring her to this point. Beside her Johnny had set his cap at a jaunty angle, his blue eyes squinting into the sun. 'Spiffing spot,' he said jovially. His arms looked very strong and tanned beneath the yellow sports shirt he wore. There were fashionable grey flannels and golf shoes to complete his ensemble and he looked not at all like the Johnny she knew at Liscombe, always so lean and hard in his jodhpurs and riding coat with a masculine air of horse work and stables about him.

Claudine tried to smile into the sunshine that must have burned her nose already. She wanted to be with Johnny at Liscombe, not here, in this gaudy place with the sunlight on the water that made her eyes smart and the sign written in big letters: HIGHCLIFFE HOTEL. That was where Jane was, and he had brought her here to see Jane.

'Let's get on down.' He levered himself out of the car and ran round to open her door, bowing with mock gallantry over her white gloves that had dust on them from the drive. There was grit down her white dress and must be on the skin of her face too in spite of the veil.

'We'll have tea,' he said, shading his eyes from the sun and peering down the cliff where there was a path from the sea and a lift. A strange high sound of people and children shouting floated up.

They had tea in the hotel and Claudine thought he had gone to ask for Jane because he disappeared while the tea was ordered and then could barely sit still long enough to drink it. She sat gazing at the picture view, waiting. If it were true, that he had come for Jane, what was she to do?

Tea dispensed with, he seemed to want to run down the path ahead of her, and it was more than a path, winding round and down so steeply that a blister formed on her toe. He even doffed his cap to the people climbing up and Johnny was known at Liscombe for his taciturn ways. Perhaps, she thought, stumbling down with her feet burning, Liscombe is not really his love at all, nor horses, and what he yearns for is an enervating place like this one where there was no shade from the sun. Suddenly he reached the bottom, for he called back to her, and there they were, standing on a hot sandy concrete promenade amongst a mass of children, all shrieking excitement. There was a strip of beach dark with people in deck chairs, looking out to the glittering water. She heard Johnny shout: 'They're up this way somewhere,' and said, wearily: 'Who?' but he did not hear. She knew he had meant Jane and Gladys. She followed behind through the crowd, keeping her eyes fixed on his yellow shirt. He stopped at a noticeboard which proclaimed:

WOMEN'S LEAGUE OF HEALTH AND BEAUTY
Classes daily here 2.30 to 3.30 pm

On a section of the sand that was roped off there were rows of women and girls in blouses and, she saw with distaste, shorts. Only the English could be so vulgar. They were leaping about to the orders of someone on the promenade and she did not look for Jane because she knew she was there.

Johnny pulled his cap down to shade his eyes from the blistery sun. What a terrible place, he thought, what heat, what noise, what gaudiness. But he had already seen Jane, because Gladys had been drawing the eyes of the watching crowd. She was giving out little squeals, her tiny birdlike legs making wild movements. Jane was beside her, the last on the farthest row by the sea's edge.

As the lady in charge bellowed, 'And up, up, up!' everyone leaped into the air with their arms outstretched. Gladys fell over and Jane stopped to help her. He had known she would be kind. She was not laughing at Gladys but repeated the movement for her. Johnny could see her fine white skin, her frail neck, her slender limbs in the blouse and shorts. They suited her. He imagined the blue of her eyes that he could not see for she was squinting up at the woman in charge and youthfully, earnestly, leaping up and up.

'Now out and . . . out . . . and rest. Let yourself go down and down.' Jane leaned forward with everyone else, head swinging dangerously to the sand. That seemed to be the end. There was some movement and the women began to separate. Jane led Gladys towards the sea. He could just see the two of them approaching the water like the novices they were, one toe at a time. He felt himself let out a breath of relief. She was all right. He had only wanted to know that.

'We'll walk along to the pier at the other end,' he said to Claudine whom he felt rather than saw at his elbow. 'If you like. Then if there's a film you want to see . . .' He set off, turning once. Jane was lost in the mass of other paddlers. It did not matter. He had only wanted to see that she was all right. The girl beside him was much more suitable. And her body matched his exactly.

CHAPTER 6

Heat lay in the valley and on Liscombe Hill. Even the oaks did not stir. All Liscombe windows lay open to the stillness. The staff moved fretfully about their tasks in the near-full house which had, since the departure of Dr Adlington, added other guests to its slimming ladies. The chef included French cuisine on the menu and they had earned a solid reputation for upper-middle-class comfort. With the Depression more or less over, people felt inclined to spoil themselves without looking over their shoulder at the mass of unemployed, though there were nearly as many.

Today, inside the staff attic rooms, the air was thick with heat and rumour of the kind that overwork was likely to bring. A quarrel had simmered for days between Claudine and Vera Cox, uneasily linked as assistants under Lady Liscombe, over a matter so small as the correct way to clean a mother-of-pearl firescreen with a film of cigar smoke on it.

Gladys leaned from her attic window and breathed the thick air, hearing behind her in the corridor running feet, the slamming of a door. She tutted for the days of Mrs Baker when quarrels were quickly suppressed. There would, she muttered to herself, have to be a reckoning and she did not wish to be any part of it, though anyone could see Miss Forestier was the better of the two. She could easily take the part of Mrs Baker, although she was foreign. Perhaps *because* she was foreign, thought Gladys, without prejudice.

Liscombe Hall required class; Mrs Baker had had it and Miss Forestier too in spite of her spending some time alone with Mr Johnny in his flat of an evening.

She allowed herself a moment to watch Mr Johnny thunder down the hill to his mother's cottage on the horse he rode for pleasure and waited to see her friend Jane emerge from the basement steps, on cue for her afternoon trip to the cottage for the cats. There was the basket on her arm, carrying the milk and any scraps left from luncheon service. Gladys felt her heart constrict: let there not be any drink in it! She could not always trail her, not all day through work and meal times and the long night when Jane could not sleep.

She jumped from the window seat and scrabbled in a drawer for the sampler she must complete, for the great day itself, 6 May 1935, was already well past. There was Queen Mary's head only half finished, the King's not begun. She must get down to it at once.

In the cottage that had been Pugs's, that had seen the climax of her terrible illness, Jane knelt on the floor by the old range and put out three dishes of milk with three slivers of roast beef. Throwing a rat's tail from the window – she was lucky, there were no horrible dead bird's feet to dispose of today – she proceeded to the next part of the afternoon's ritual. While the cats washed, she rinsed their bowls in water from the rain butt, swept the hearth, and then it was time. She took the bottle from its hiding place in the chimney breast with the others, some empty but three happily full. Sitting in the chair that had been Pugs's, she drank slowly from the ration she would allow herself.

The cats came one by one from their toilette, turning their bright knowing eyes upon her without condemnation. It was too hot for her lap but they grouped themselves about her on the cool stone before the grate and slept while she dreamed, feeling herself, just for that moment, comfortable and unjudged. The images of shame and weakness went round and round in her head, growing dimmer until she could forget them and even forget she had once had a hope that someone could know of them and still find it in his heart to love her.

At the other end of the Hall, in the East Tower, Kate Liscombe sat by the open window of the nursery, watching the afternoon lesson of her daughter Sarah, and Mary her companion. Both were breathing heavily over a copy of *Josephine and her Dolls* at the nursery table, supervised by Nanny and the little tabby cat, Suki. The competition between the two girls involved being the first to decipher difficult words like 'quacky'. Kate leaned against the warm wall; even the nursery curtain seemed damp with the heat, like her own silk dress which she must go and change.

And there it was, the quarrel. 'Qu . . . ack.' It had fallen to Sarah to read the particular sentence where Josephine spoke to her toy duck.

'Quacky, dear,' prompted Kate, and knowing the story by heart, added, 'Quacky, dear. Just think for a minute.'

'I knew it, didn't I, Nanny? I knew "quacky" and Sarah didn't.' Mary's high thin voice broke the nursery peace. Kate saw her elbow poke into Sarah's plump arm. The cat took a delicate paw away from the page and leaned with sympathy upon the hand of her beloved small mistress. Sarah went stubbornly on, but Kate said: 'Nanny, I think that is enough reading for today. Perhaps you should walk the girls to the stream for some air. It might be cooler down there. They can play by the water and go and have a glass of milk with my mother.'

'Granny!' Sarah clapped her hands from pleasure, ran to her mother and put tender arms about her knees. 'Can we go to see the horses and go along to Grandpa and the cows after?' The child had big dark blue eyes, like her own and her sister's had been, and dark curls which today were damp around her forehead and neck.

'May, not can, my darling,' said Kate, kissing a hot damp cheek. 'You may do all that this afternoon because it is hot, too hot for work.'

'I am better at reading, I am, aren't I, Nanny?' Mary, holding back from the kiss that she too would have had, clutched the reading book and gave her friend a look of triumph.

'Little girls don't boast,' Nanny said sharply, regarding her second charge with distaste, Kate noted and not for the first time. It was unfortunate that Mary simply was not an attractive child. 'Of course, your ladyship, *Miss* Beale often calls to see her daughter at this time of day, and if we are down with Mrs Tranter ...' She folded her hands over her plump belly, pursed her mouth and blinked in a manner which told Kate she did not approve of Miss Beale's single status nor of children being taken down to play by streams and drink milk in humble cottages. The woman's pretensions had never pleased Kate, but she knew them to be a peculiarity of nannies in general. It was most important that Sarah loved her, and she did, she thought, stroking back her daughter's hair. But then Sarah loved every living thing, from her haughty little cat to the frogs in the stream.

'Oh,' she said absently, 'if Miss Beale does call in, she'll guess you have gone for a walk. And if I see her ...'

'Go and put on your pinafores, girls,' Nanny bustled off, no doubt to fetch her own hat and coat, Kate thought with amusement, for whatever the weather, nannies dressed. 'Of course, if the storm should break whilst we are out,' she heard her mutter, 'I won't answer for the consequences.'

Kate walked back down the stairs to the first floor of the rebuilt East Tower which held their bedrooms and Aunt Bessie's. She leaned negligent arms on the bedroom windowsill, looking out into the still air and the silent oaks. She was just in time to watch Jane slip down into the field which had Pugs's old cottage in it. Her cat visit, she reflected, was more important than a word with her own daughter. Jane was recovering well, though, and was capable of any task if only she would let herself believe it.

Kate stirred in the heat. She did not want to think of staff problems on such a hot day. How strange the Downs seemed, rolling out to the horizon. They seemed to stand as clear as a drawing against the day. All of Liscombe was quiet and sleeping. There would be a few screams, a little hysteria, if the storm were to break. Summer storms on the top of their hill tended to be noisy and dramatic. Kate smiled to herself. She would welcome it as another Liscombe spectacle to show off.

Now, it was too hot. She was filled with lassitude; she wanted to think of nothing.

She was almost dozing in the heat, when the sound of Johnny's horse on the gravel outside startled her into wakefulness. Rousing herself, she peered down to see him gesturing towards her. 'Come on down!' his frantic arm said, with that fearful black horse of his rearing up. Mother! she thought, her heart giving a painful leap. She was down the two flights of stairs and out on to the steps before the sleepy porter had crossed the hall to see what the commotion was.

'Sis!' Johnny was hissing, as if they were back in the days of their youth. 'Go down home. Father's got bad news.'

'Mother, Johnny?' Kate felt the blood pound to her head in a rush of fear. She might have gone down that morning, but did not, from distraction, from laziness.

'No, no, not Mother. The cow, you know . . . he was afraid . . . get on down, do.'

'Not the worst, Johnny, not the very worst that he feared? I'd forgotten.' Kate stuffed a hand into her mouth, standing helpless on the steps and looking out beyond her brother at the Downs and the oaks which would never be as they were any more.

'It's sure.' Johnny tried to still his horse. 'The vet's down there now. You'll have to close this place up, he says. I've got to go and tell all the men.'

Kate walked blindly round to the basement. Foot-and-mouth disease. Her father's precious cows to be slaughtered. Everything that moved to be slaughtered. Burning, burning in the ditches. Death and isolation on Liscombe Hill and in Liscombe valley. She stumbled down the hill where her father waited with the very worst news that could afflict them.

The officials were already there: the veterinary officers, the man from the Ministry of Agriculture, the police, all sent for the closing of Liscombe and the area around it. There was a cluster of people by the door of the stables and two or three vans parked by the dairy.

'Is it certain?' Kate said to a man in rubber boots to his thighs, standing by her parents' cottage door with his pencil held ready to mark her reason for standing there as if she were not Lady Liscombe, owner of all the eye could see. She might as well own it no more, Kate thought; these men could behave as if they owned Liscombe for they would have total power over it.

'It's sure, madam,' he said with the necessary grimness, narrowing his eyes. 'I've got a lorry due with all the disinfectant in Dorchester, and no one's to leave, no one, especially not those children running about up there and liable to go spreading it elsewhere.'

Kate turned. Behind her, tumbling down the hill, was Sarah, always ahead, bonnet hanging by its string around her neck. Nanny's high voice shrieking 'You'll fall', did not stop her arriving with a shout of joy at her mother's side.

'What are all the mens, Mummy? Where's Granny?'

Kate put a hand on the child's head. 'No Granny or Gramps today, darling. The men have come because . . . the animals are ill and they must be taken away.'

'The horses and the sheep and the cows are poorly?'

Kate watched her eyes widen with distress. 'Not the horses, Sarah, but all the others. The horses can stay, they must stay so as not to go spreading the sickness anywhere else, but the sheep, the pigs and the cows must be taken away.'

'To hospital?' Sarah asked, her hot hand taking her mother's.

'To hospital, yes,' Kate said. If it could be true! To Nanny, arriving breathless with Mary in tow, she said: 'You had better take the children back to the Hall. There's some trouble here with the animals.'

'No one must leave the area, is that clear?' the man shouted from the cottage doorway. 'And no one must stay around either. It won't be a pretty sight.'

Kate signalled an urgent silent message to Nanny and she took both girls' hands to march off with them up the hill. She watched Sarah's frantic little face pleading with her from under the replaced bonnet. She thought: there will be many more tears before this dreadful time is over. She would not even be allowed to send the children away so they might not know the full horror of it. Turning her head painfully back to the man with the notebook, she said: 'I believe my father and the veterinary man wish to see me?'

The man, hesitating with the realization that she was Lady Liscombe, had the grace to change his tone. 'I believe Mr Tranter has returned to the dairy with the vet, your ladyship.' He bowed.

Kate crossed the little bridge over her own stream and walked slowly up to the cottage. A heavy sunless light seemed to have darkened the colour of her mother's sweet peas. The fragile blossoms drooped as if they had been parched of moisture and all along the stone floor beneath her feet the shadows seemed to weigh heavy too.

'Mother?' she said.

Mrs Tranter, a plumper, more tired version of her sister Bessie, sat watching two kettles bubble on the range. 'I'm making them men tea,' she said. 'The mites didn't see me? Sarah mustn't know about the beasts going off like they must.'

Steam lay in a still layer in the hot air. Kate saw a bright patch of colour in her mother's cheeks and her sudden burst of tears. 'And how will Father take it? His cows ent never had no real sickness, not so as they all go off to die.' She stuffed a corner of pinafore into her mouth.

'Let's make this tea, Mother,' Kate said, moving blindly across the room and grasping a kettle holder. 'How many spoonfuls of tea, do you think?'

Her mother did not answer. Kate ladled four spoonfuls into the two brown pots put to warm on the range top. Nothing could make her mother forget to warm the pots but everything today would be mechanical, Kate knew, and none of it would matter. For the moment, it had only just begun. She laid out the cups and saucers from her mother's dresser, the set of Blue Willow and the new Crown Derby china she had given her that was never used, for fear of breakage. 'Twelve cups, Mother,' she said. 'I'll let you pour out. I'll go and tell the men to call in as I pass. I must go and see the vet and Father, and then find David. He doesn't know yet.'

Down by Home Farm stables along the stream men were rolling barrels of disinfectant and tossing hay into heaps. Her own people, sweating in their shirt-sleeves, doffed their caps at her offer of tea, eyes squinting in the strange hot light, saying all that could not be said in words. The silent sympathy seemed to loosen something in her. She felt her own tears threaten, but blinked and nodded back. They and the strangers in their rubber boots would be duly disin-fected from head to toe and go back to their normal lives; Liscombe would be still and silent and empty. The livestock would be burned, somehow. Kate jerked her head up towards Rookery Hill and the sullen sky where the dark shape of a policeman was outlined. Where would they be burned?

She began to run, her silk dress damp around her legs, wet to her back, the dry dusty earth puffing around her chamois leather shoes. They would burn them there, in the valley, and all the smoke and the smell of their poor flesh . . . 'Pa!' she called. 'Don't let them!'

There was a movement around the dairy, strange unaccustomed stirring for it was not yet milking time. It would never be milking time again, not there, not for many weeks. The beasts who sensed change, who leaned hot heads on each other's flanks, gazed at her. At a glance, she could see no blistered skin, no salivating jaws, but then those affected would no doubt be dead already. These would die in case they carried the disease.

The veterinary man, whom she knew slightly, was standing by the dairy door, he too in high rubber boots, with his face red and sweating under his cap. His hand was up, he seemed to be gesturing her away.

'It's all right,' she said, panting. The air seemed pressed down on to her chest; her voice came from somewhere high in her throat. 'It's all right – I shall throw my shoes away. I mean, burn them, of course, it does not matter. Where is my father?'

'Don't come in, your ladyship,' the man said. He had caught her arm, but Kate brushed it away. 'I want to see my father,' she said, and there he was, lying on the stone floor, his head with its few poor hairs lodged against a milking stool and his hand stretched out to the cleaning channels where water ran. It was clutching a piece of paper.

'Heart attack,' a voice behind her said.

'His heart, yes. Is that the paper telling him all his cows must die?'

'I'm sorry, I had to give it to someone, it's the regulations.'

'Then regulations helped to break his heart,' Kate said. She put a hand up to the slow heavy beat of her own heart. 'He could not have borne to see them die, not all at once, massacred and burned.'

'No. I've sent for the doctor. They'll have to let him past.'

'I shall ask my men to take him home. My mother would not want him to lie here all alone.'

'Of course, your ladyship. And his lordship?'

'My husband and aunt have a few more moments of ordinary happiness. They know nothing yet.' Kate bent and touched the leathery skin of her father's face.

'I'm afraid someone will have to come up to the Hall to inform your guests. I was thinking that perhaps his lordship . . .'

'Don't worry,' Kate interrupted, 'I am well aware of matters which must be dealt with. The guests and staff kept within boundaries, everything to be disinfected – shoes, boots, wheels – and only people such as yourselves to be allowed in and out.'

She walked to the door of the dairy where her father had spent much of his days for the last twenty-eight or so years, since they had come to Liscombe. 'But of course I am sure my husband will soon be home to help you deal with matters you consider to be the male province.' She did not wait to hear his apology but trod with slow heavy steps back along the path towards her mother's misery. She thought: how lucky we are to have our own churchyard.

She did not know how much time had passed before she heard about David and Aunt Bessie. She sent Johnny down to be with their mother. Her father's body was laid out on the bed he had slept in for all his married life. Comfortably cradled in feather down, he had the air of sleep. A doctor had been allowed in to certify his death and was being disinfected. No undertaker was to be permitted; they must order his coffin by telephone. She was saying to Hawker, in the strange high voice that seemed to have become part of her: 'How fortunate it is, Hawker, that we have our own churchyard,' when the telephone rang and he, already in charge in his own smooth way, answered it. She had a premonition, standing beside him, that something else had happened, for his pale thin skin seemed to blanch. She heard him, as if in a dream, say: 'I am afraid there has been an accident, your ladyship. Lord David, Mrs Villiers . . .' She could not move. Hawker poured her a glass of brandy and some time must have passed.

She knew afterwards there had been a dispute as to the return of their bodies to the Hall. No one had known what to do. The newly-disinfected doctor made the decision to have them taken to the hospital mortuary, and of course she never saw them again.

It was her fault, for if she had not sent the man down to find them on the Dorchester Road, David would not have set the little Vauxhall to its top speed and would not have crashed it turning up their hill, the place where they had first met. Apparently, Aunt Bessie had lived a little longer than he had.

She felt that she would sit in her office chair with the glass of brandy in her hand until she could go down the hill to meet their coffins, coming home, and with the burst of thunder that was the storm rolling across the Downs, she heard herself give a little cry, looking at her hand holding the glass, at her own flesh turned to stone. In some distant part of her mind she thought she heard the thud-thud of guns shooting the cows and sheep but it might have been the sound of her own heart.

When the Liscombe church bell tolled out its one funeral note, there was smoke drifting round the tower from the pyres built to burn the dead animals on the Liscombe estate. There had been four hundred and thirty-two shot. Dozens of men had had to be brought in to dig the ditches, one beyond Home Farm stables, the other past Pugs Burrow. On the day of the other, human, funeral, their smoke seemed to meet around the Hall and the church, blackening the windows, creeping along the terrace and amongst the procession of mourners who were mostly staff, for no one outside of Liscombe was able to attend unless they were in a position to stay on there for a number of weeks. Of the guests who had not yet had permission to leave, a few chose to join the staff but most stayed behind their closed windows. Liscombe telephone lines still hummed to the sound of their angry voices demanding to be released, protesting the urgency of their business.

The smoke caught at the throat of the exposed mourners. There were stifled coughs, little splutters to add to the sound of their shoes crunching across the gravel. The smell of burned meat was already in their hair and their clothes.

Behind the church, the smoke seemed to be caught amongst the family gravestones. There was the tomb of David's great-grandfather, the memorial stone of his grandfather, lost in battle at Trafalgar, the head-stone of his father, the fourth Viscount Edward David Cecil, killed on his horse when David was ten. There, too, the grave of Harry Liscombe, David's son, killed in the Great War, first buried in Flanders itself by Johnny and finally brought home in 1919.

Kate had not yet ordered any headstones, but had been able to decide the three of them should all lie in a row by the little stone wall which would give shelter from the Downs. Gideon, her own and Aunt Bessie's working partner, was there already, and her son, Peter. She would just be able to catch a glimpse of them if she looked from her bedroom window in the tower, where, she supposed, she would spend most of her remaining life, for she would never again have force and energy enough to leave it, not once the whirling of her mind had ceased enough to give her rest. She would rest then, as David and Aunt Bessie and her father were resting, until the time came when she could leave Sarah and join them.

The vicar said something about eternal rest but she had not listened to him because of the dreadful moment now when she must face the three gaping holes by the wall. She held her mother and her brother's arm. Mrs Tranter stood in dignified silence as first her husband then her sister were lowered into their graves, seeming to crumple only as they disappeared from her sight.

Kate was not able to turn her head to watch them take up David's coffin. In there, his body. They would not let her see him. His neck, they said, had been broken. She stifled the sickness that rose from some-where near her heart and clutched at the memory of the feel of him, holding her. That was real, not this choking air and the smell of animal flesh, not Aunt Bessie and her father both gone forever, and this man, the only one she had ever loved since her sixteenth year when they had first been together. There was the dark oak wood and the darkness of the space that would be his. She could see the brass plate and the clod of earth someone had thrown in. It must have been herself. Her mother was bending now and then Gladys came from behind her to do what she had begged to do, throw in three flowers, one for each of the servants who had known and loved David Lis-combe for so long: Treeves, Mrs Baker and Cook. Kate leaned forward. One clod of earth, three flowers for David. She must give him something to comfort him in his long wait for her. At her neck, his pink pearls. She would wear them no more. She pulled them off and threw them on to the flowers. Now she must leave him. Goodbye, David. Goodbye, Aunt Bessie. Goodbye, Pa.

The group of people behind her parted. She took her mother through them and on to the path that was a few short steps from the gateway leading back to the Liscombe terrace.

'Not far now, Mother,' she said, and saw on her mother's face beneath the half-veil a smudgy trail of tears she had contained and now let free, mixed with the smoke. If they could have taken the animals away to burn! Kate felt a spasm of nausea beneath her heart.

'I ent going nowhere, Kate, so it don't matter.' Her mother let herself be led into the line of birches by the kitchens and watched dumbly as Kate was very sick, holding back her veil, retching against the smell of the smoke and the urge of the sobs she had thought were spent.

Mrs Tranter made an effort, gazing hopelessly at her daughter's white face with its dusting of smoke. 'It don't matter,' she said. 'We ent got nothing to do now.'

Johnny Tranter stood beside his nephew Joe as the vicar finished the business around the three gaping holes. Now, he thought, he and Joe were the only surviving male members of the Tranter and Liscombe families; Joe himself the only one left of their mingled blood, with little Sarah in the nursery. Of all their interlinked history then, it had come down to this: counting who was left.

'Soon be over, old chap,' he murmured to Joe, standing hard by his elbow. It was the only comfort he could give. He was not good at offering comfort but it was all left to him, with David Liscombe gone. He would miss him. Well, he had avoided family responsibility until now. You could, if you managed to escape the trap of marriage. He coughed. Blasted smoke. Riding out the mares that morning, he had seen the poor legs sticking up from the ditches. It had been a pitiful sight, and the terrible smell would haunt them all. He would never eat meat again and thanked God there would be no funeral feast. With no family to attend, David's daughters, their husbands, all the local gentry, too, forbidden to come, it would have been a mockery to hold a funeral feast for the staff.

He stepped forward and shook hands with the vicar. 'You'll come back to the Hall?' he said. Someone would have produced a drinks tray, he supposed, or opened the bar. He needed a drink; his throat needed a drink.

He walked behind the vicar, nodding from courtesy at the rows of sobbing staff, all wrapped about in the smoke, who parted to let him go. Jane did not look up at him. She had on a touching little veil. They were dressed in black, as neat and formal as they could make themselves, but it was a poor end, he thought, for a viscount, not that David would have cared. Aunt Bessie would have wanted a better show. He smiled, thinking of Aunt Bessie. He would miss her. He turned and grasped Joe's arm. 'Come on, old chap,' he said. 'You and me must go and do our duty at the Hall. The only men left, eh?'

At the gateway there was movement. Claudine had placed herself in front of the group of staff. She seemed about to hold out a hand, as if to take his other arm. He thought, she believes her place is by my side. That is my fault. I must make this a chance to end it.

PART TWO

CHAPTER 7

Claudine shivered, pacing about on the cold stiff earth under the beeches. Eddies of bitter wind spat water from the morning's rain into her face. She pulled at the collar of the riding jacket, tried the hat again upon her head, removed it, resumed pacing. The clump of beeches at the east side of Liscombe Hill was not the place for a serious consideration of her future but she wanted to see the very moment when Joe brought the steadiest old horse from the stables to the paddock for Jane's riding lesson. She had to see if Johnny was going to be present, strolling up to the gate as if by chance, as he often did. Sometimes, since the funerals, it was the only moment she caught sight of him all through an empty week. She had gone up to an unused staff bedroom in the West Tower many times, to watch him, with Jane and the horse. She did not know how she could have let matters between them go to such a point, when once she had shared his bed, and love.

She paused, peering down the hill through dull misty air. When this dreadful Sunday was over, it would be decided. If he felt nothing for her, if there was today to be no glimmer of feeling, no look that said he had not forgotten, that one day they would be together again, then her second plan, as yet hardly formed, would be put into operation. It too depended on the actions of others. For the moment, she was waiting, shivering, mud spattered already on the fine riding boots that had been glossily black when she had taken them from the store kept in the past for lady guests who had a whim to go riding. The jodhpurs seemed to billow out around her hips, but the jacket fitted to perfection. Claudine paced anew, dreaming. When Johnny saw her dressed for his horses, he would see how much they could have to share. And she would like horses, once she had learned to mount; she would do that better than pallid Jane, playing at the helpless little girl! It would be thrilling, riding beside him, thundering across to Rookery Hill where he kept his old war horses that had the shrapnel scars still showing. She would care for them, take them carrots, become a country woman, for Johnny.

There was movement below her suddenly. Claudine took in a deep breath. There was Joe, in charge, heaving Jane on to the back of the great Dobbin. Soon Johnny would be there. He would be striding across through the bitterness of the air, all energy, his handsome dark face lighting up with the pleasure and surprise of seeing her on one of his beloved beasts.

She left the beeches and strolled along the rear of the Hall and down to the paddock. Joe saw her first. He blushed crimson to the rim of his hat as he stuttered out: 'I say, Mademoiselle Forestier has come.'

'I have, Joe,' she said, forcing out the words through stiff cold lips. 'I have come to learn to ride too. If I may. May I, Joe?' She leaned casually on the paddock gate.

'I say!' He rushed across to meet her, flinging the reins across Dobbin's back.

Jane sat carefully waiting, too fearful to pick them up in case the horse took any movement as a signal to go forward. Over the width of its shoulders, she saw, without rancour, that Joe had taken Claudine's slender gloved hand to shake it formally. She guessed at the look of admiration on his boyish face. She felt no resentment at his obsession for Claudine or the fact that they spent so much of their time together talking about her. She put a tentative hand on the ripple of horse muscle beyond the saddle that was supposed to be of leather but must be iron. 'Don't move yet, old boy,' she implored. She would be patient until they remembered her presence. Joe was opening the gate, guiding through a laughing Claudine. She was, Jane saw, a woman of beauty under the hat, with firm olive skin, her face a perfect oval outlined in black, a glimpse of dark red hair about her neck, its bun secured by a riding net. Claudine always managed to dress for whatever part she played, Jane thought, and recognized her own moment of insight: Claudine sometimes played a part.

'Jane!' Her clear, barely-accented voice reached across the field. 'Master Joe has agreed to teach me to ride too. Look at what I have been able to borrow from the stores. Look at my jodpores!' This was the girls together part, Jane thought, but with no bitterness. She wished that she herself could play a part. Perhaps everyone did and that was why they all found life so easy.

The touching hesitation over the word 'jodhpurs' seemed to send Joe into rapture. 'Jod*fers!*' he corrected, taking her arm and leading her along the grass that earlier rain had begun to muddy. Dobbin moved forward to greet him, shaking his beautiful dark head, massive body lurching. Jane's heart lurched with it. She gave a little scream, clutching at slippery leather and sliding sideways.

'Grip with your knees, lean back,' ordered Joe, but lifting her down with a showy masculine movement for Claudine's benefit. 'You go and have a rest by the gate,' he said, and turned away to help Claudine towards the beast. Her head barely reached his mane but she gave a high laugh, Jane heard, trudging away, knowing that neither would pay her any more attention. She thought: Claudine never laughs like that. She trudged, her legs weak from the effort of sitting on Dobbin. Claudine could not care for Joe, not when there had already been Mr Johnny, and she could not care for riding, particularly on a cold winter morning. What therefore could be the aim? She reached the gate and fiddled with the latch.

'Here, let me do that,' a voice said, and it was his strong brown fingers managing the gate.

Jane's heart thumped. She had forgotten to hope that he would come, because of Claudine. 'Good morning, Mr Johnny. Thank you.'

'Johnny to you, Jane. Surely we are friends by now?'

'Yes!' She scraped round the gate, avoiding his arm.

'What's she doing on that horse?' The words startled her. 'Miss Forestier, I mean. Not the sort, is she?' Jane was obliged to turn around to answer, and found herself gazing up into the face that so often appeared in her day-dreams. There was the startlingly blue gaze upon her, crossness in it now, and the coarse dark hair that always stuck up at the crown like Joe's; a shadow of a beard, a thin mouth that did not smile, the hard drawn face that people said still showed his suffering in the Great War. He had once, Gladys said, been a wild charmer, hooting his way through life, a breaker of girls' hearts down in Dorchester. She gazed, forgetting to answer. 'What can she be up to?'

Jane found some words. 'I think Claudine may like country things now,' she said.

'Humph!' He turned his handsome hard profile to stare across at Claudine perched on Dobbin's back. Jane took her eyes from Johnny and saw with satisfaction that Claudine appeared to be gripping the saddle with some force. She said: 'Riding is not as easy as it seems.' There was an unexpected shout of laughter. Johnny turned to her with a grin that lit his eyes and softened the lines of his face. The grin broadened as there was a shriek from the field. Dobbin was lumbering towards the gate and his true master with a look of sparky determination.

'Dobbin!' Joe called.

Jane did not stop to see the rest of the scene but walked quietly away, turbulence around her heart from the moment with Johnny.

Claudine saw the dark sweating hide beneath her seem to heave. She felt a wave of nausea. She was falling. The wretched boy was shrieking at her to grip with her knees but her knees barely reached the animal's sides and anyway had no strength. 'It is not trained to stop,' she shouted, without daring to take her eyes from the great beast's back though she was aware that Johnny had jumped the gate. The creature seemed to wind its awful head around him. 'Oh!' She managed a giggle of relief. 'How strong your horse is!'

'It's me here, not Joe.' Johnny looked up with a cold frowning stare. 'No need for that girlish nonsense. Get off Dobbin at once. You're upsetting him.'

'Help me down, Johnny.' It was the nearest she had been to him all the long months since the funerals. There was his dear lined face that had once looked at her in the act of love. She felt all the silliness of the last half-hour, and gazed silently into the blue of his eyes, willing him to show her some mark of what had been between them. They both ignored the boy's voice in the background. Only Johnny and she and the horse stood there, locked in a tableau of her making.

'Get down yourself – you got up there. Slide down, Joe'll catch you.' Before the hard stare, Claudine flinched. He had seen through her, had guessed the game had been for him. And he did not want her. It was as clear to her now as the throb of blood at his firm dark neck. 'I cannot,' she said after an age when each seemed to read a wordless message.

'The boy'll help you,' Johnny said, 'just this once.' To Joe, he said: 'Help Miss Forestier down.' His gaze did not leave her. Claudine forced her right leg to scrape across the horse's back. If he had not gazed, so icily, contemptuously, if she had not held on to the saddle with her left hand, she would not have wrenched it, half falling off into Joe's arms, he so overcome by her nearness that he did not hold her.

'I have twisted my wrist, I think,' she said. There was indeed a spasm of pain. She let Joe bend over it so that she did not have to look into the cold face of Johnny. He took his time, walking around the beast but watching her. She clenched her teeth to stop herself from trembling. It was final then. If there had been a ghost of feeling there, he would have reached out to look at her arm. But he did not want her near him or even near one of his precious horses.

'I say, Uncle, shall I give Miss Forestier lessons with Jane?' Eager Joe had not understood.

'Certainly not. She's not at all suited to it, you should see that yourself.'

'Perhaps it is because I am a French woman.' She forced her stiff mouth into a smile, offering a sparkling glance up at him, and one to Joe, to thank them. Once Johnny had liked her Frenchness, had been enchanted by her accent, as Joe was. And more words slipped from her, as if of themselves, though she knew it was a lost cause. 'But may I try again, Johnny dear?' An air of disbelief took the coldness from his face and a gust of wind whipped a final fierce blow into her face.

'Certainly not.' He made no attempt, for Joe's sake, for her sake, to cover the matter with good manners. 'Certainly not,' he repeated, and stood there, waiting for her to leave.

Somehow getting away from the field, Claudine strode back along the path towards the basement entrance and the beech trees where she had waited in hope and had been foolish enough to suppose a different end. She wrenched off the silly hat that made her head throb and threw it into the bushes. Very well then. *So much the worse for Johnny*. It would be his loss. He could only love horses. Horses! And she had dreamed so of him. All those years since her childhood, she had dreamed of Johnny and Liscombe, and now he rejected her on pretence of decency. It was months since the deaths had made Liscombe fold in upon itself.

Walking down the basement steps, on along the corridor, past the empty laundry rooms which could soon be full of heat and steam again, she thought: there is still Liscombe. I can awaken Liscombe and then I shall have work, more satisfying, more enduring, than love. Somehow, she would have to put her second plan into operation.

She reached the kitchens and called out: 'Pierre!' because she still had him too. 'Oh, Pierre, I have hurt my wrist, look. Have you any ice, please?' She thought she looked as piteous as she felt; a layer of cold had settled around her chest. Mud was spattered up to her knees.

Pierre looked up from his task at the table. 'Let me

see,' he commanded, wiping his hands and taking her wrist in warm broad fingers. 'Take off your jacket. Whose jacket is it, *mon Dieu*?'

Claudine allowed herself a trace of a smile and let him remove the garment with the familiarity of past intimacies. 'The hurt is bad,' she said and let fall a genuine tear from weakness, from the efforts of the failed morning, and the sudden comfort of Pierre's fingers.

He looked thoughtfully into her face. 'You have been doing Englishwomen's things and that is no good,' he said. '*Des folles*, they are, madwomen.'

'*Oui*.' She leaned a little against him. There was still Pierre as well as Liscombe.

The nasty winter rain had set itself to drum down on the valley in earnest by the time Kate Liscombe sat down for Sunday lunch in her mother's cottage. She felt a glimmer of her old past self as the last of her family, the Tranters, sat around the scrubbed deal table with the old range black-leaded to a gleam of jet throbbing under the saucepan of apple suet pudding. A drift of clove escaped from its muslin cover, as it always had through the nearly thirty years of Sunday dinners since they had come to Liscombe and their new life had begun. She and Johnny had sat around the table on her afternoons off kitchen-maid duties at the Hall, with their brother Billy, later killed in the Flanders mud, with their sister Beth, dead in the Great War too after giving birth to Joe, the child of her love with Harry Liscombe, David's son, who was shot by a sniper's bullet out in No Man's Land.

She sat watching Joe's glowing dark skin and dark hair, so like Beth's, and his grey eyes the replica of Harry's and David's. He would have been called

Liscombe, Viscount Liscombe now, if things had been different. He was pushing roast rabbit into his mouth with fine Liscombe fingers calloused by stable work. Those hands were a symbol of the Tranter and Liscombe mixture, she thought, brooding, with her fork raised to her mouth. Aristocrat and peasant; Joe had the blood of both and had no inkling that she had asked her solicitors to set about making a claim to the title on his behalf though he was illegitimate, so that David's title should not be lost forever.

'Kate!' Her mother's voice. 'I didn't get them rabbits brought down for you to sit over.'

Kate took an obedient mouthful as if it was a time long past when they sat as undepleted family waiting for the sound of their father's boots scraping on the doorstep.

'I'll have another leg, Ma.' Johnny played his part and reached out for the dish of roast potatoes. He had not cared for rabbit since his young days when he had taken pleasure in the poaching of them. They were a dry meat when roasted but there was no beef or lamb on the table now, since the funerals.

Mrs Tranter pushed over the gravy boat and served her son and grandson with more Brussels sprouts. 'Not like Father's, these,' she muttered. 'He'd hardly had time to plant his out.'

Kate looked round the table at the four Blue Willow plates heaped with food. Heat and steam made the room seem an oasis of comfort from the rain and the wind that sped along the valley outside, sending up scurries of water and whipping at the neglected Easter-planted potatoes in the garden. But it was not cosy. She gazed with horror upon the drying stain of gravy around the meat on her plate. Every day there was this, food to be eaten, custom to be followed, and all the time the cold hollow in her chest, the layer of something almost tangible that followed her and sat where she sat. It was, she knew, loss and grief and the knowledge no one could ever come back, could ever again be touched with love or the everyday routine of life. They had all been there over roast or stew, apple pudding or thick creamy rice, Beth and Billy, her father, Aunt Bessie, David, and long, long ago her son Peter who was dead too.

She put down the piece of rabbit she had been going to put into her mouth and tried a forkful of potato. She felt faint with dizziness. Sometimes, when she *knew* they were all gone, there was such a feeling of horror within her. She forced out some words, looking across to sweet Joe who dared not speak for fear of offending her or the grandmother who had raised him and who now sat, in a heap of gloom, her hair shockingly white, the droop of her body past changing. 'I saw you this morning teaching Jane to ride down in the paddock. How is she doing?'

Mrs Tranter spoke for her grandson, ignoring the stain of red that crept across his full healthy cheeks and the fact that he was almost twenty-one years old. 'She's doing as well as you can expect, at a lady's occupation, a maid what you employs and whose got some kind of past we're not allowed to mention though the proof of it's squabbling up there in the nursery this very minute.'

Joe picked up a rabbit leg and protested. 'I say, Gran . . .'

'No, Ma.' Johnny pushed aside his empty plate. 'The girl can learn if there's a horse free, I've told Joe.'

'But I say he's to keep away from that French woman up there.' Mrs Tranter swallowed an unwanted

Brussels sprout. 'With *her* fancy ways. A little maid what makes up to you and makes you feel strong and manly is one thing, I suppose, but the other one . . .'

'Gran!'

It seemed to Kate that the blush that spread across Johnny's face was as dark as that on Joe's. She heard Johnny splutter something and felt a touch of warmth against the cold band around her heart. There was to be a family argument. She was glad of it. If her mother could find her old fretful interfering self and Joe and Johnny could seem like little boys at the table again, perhaps there would be something in their lives that might become ordinary.

In the Liscombe Hall kitchen where only staff and family meals had been prepared since the previous summer and the closure of the hotel, Pierre and Claudine sat at the table together. The staff beef hotpot was still bubbling in the oven and Pierre was preparing the upstairs food that would not be eaten.

Claudine, from habit, had changed into her housekeeper's black and wore around her waist the badge of her office: Head Housekeeper. In her hand she held a copy of the *Caterer* whose pages had recently stimulated her thoughts. 'It does say here that the Americans will be coming to England for the Coronation this year. Look, I told you.' She turned with urgent fingers to the page where an article carried a big headline: RESURGENCE OF HOTEL TRADE.

'They won't come to Dorset.' He smoothed his moustache with the back of his hand. 'And I've told you, my dear Claudine, do not confuse the old slump with our very personal one.'

'No one can come while we're still closed.' The satisfying clank of keys about her waist as she leaned across towards him had lost its charm. What use to have been given the post in an empty shell? And somehow she must start upon her second plan or she would not be able to retrieve the day, this gloomy Sunday, that she had set as decider of her fate.

'No one will want to come whilst it rains. Has it rained since Christmas? It feels like it. Listen to it on the windows.' With his usual calmness when at his kitchen tasks he continued pressing beef into a mincer, his fingers sticky with blood.

'Pierre, please listen. I cannot do this on my own.' She looked restlessly round the room, at the copper pans hung unused in their rows, at the new electric stoves without burden, at the empty space of table where maid and boy should have been. 'Surely you don't want this all to disappear, all your work, the reputation you built up?' She dug a thumbnail into the worn white wood and pushed away the bowl of raw meat that Pierre was now forcing through a sieve. There were splashes of blood on the enamel. 'You know she won't care for that beef pudding and nor will the nursery.'

'Her ladyship must eat and the child too. They need good honest blood to build them up.' He put a mouthful of meat into his mouth and chewed. 'The beef I bought from the other side of Sherborne is *superbe*.'

'We were doing so well. Can't you see, we can again? All it needs is for something to help her ladyship into making a decision about reopening. She's already got her most important staff, me and you and Hawker, and if there's a possibility of getting some good solid trade in . . .'

'I tell you, her ladyship will not open again.' Pierre got up and began wrapping the sieved beef in muslin. 'You,' he said, turning his amber eyes upon her, with the little touch of sadness that was so often there, 'because you have no heart, cannot understand that hers is broken. Anyone but you, dear Claudine, could see that her ladyship is heavy with grief. She has lost her beloved husband, her aunt, her father . . .'

'I think you are in love with her. Heavy with grief!' Claudine felt a sudden rush of envy for the protective emotion that Lady Liscombe aroused in everyone. 'I think that is why you stay here.' She too rose from her chair. The atmosphere was suddenly changed. They faced each other, and the comfort he had offered her only an hour before was gone. And she must have Pierre and his comfort when she needed it.

'I do love her,' he said coolly, 'but I shall not stay here, in spite of that. What true man could not love such a woman? She has grace, beauty and *true* feeling.' He put a hand against his heart in an exaggeration of Gallic charm, and his eyes were as cold as Johnny's.

Claudine cried out, her glance evading his eyes, slipping down to his dark chin where the beard grew so quickly, to the thick handsome neck and his broad strong hand on the white jacket. Every part of him was familiar to her. 'You cannot go! You did not tell me! I thought we were friends.'

'We were friends.' Pierre bowed across the table at her. 'Some time ago in London we were friends. And one night, in London, I thought we were more than friends. I thought perhaps you and me, Claudine, one day, a little restaurant of our own. That is what I thought. But I was foolish.' He laughed without warmth, showing the touching gap between his front teeth. 'I did not know you were the kind of girl to use her body. No, I did not know that.' He tied the muslin with impatient skill and threw it back into a basin.

Claudine held her breath. So there was going to be

truth between her and Pierre too. Well, she did not want it. She could not face it, not today. 'Of course I did not. What a strange thing, to bring all that up again. I explained to you before. I thought . . . you persuaded me that night . . . I did not want it . . . Men are always the same.' There were rare tears in her eyes, threatening a weakness she could not allow, not when she knew Johnny was finally lost. 'I was lonely that night, I did not mean it to happen. I was ashamed afterwards.' Even to herself, the words sounded false. And they were not false, she had been ashamed!

'Do you suffer from shame, *ma chérie*? I do not force women, as you know. I accept you as you are, you see, or I have been willing to, until now. I gave up my Marie. I was waiting until you would realize Mr Johnny was not the man for you. An Englishman who will never understand you as I have. Are they not ashamed of love, ashamed of the senses? Don't they all prefer their horses and their shooting and their fishing by the cold river? No, Claudine?'

She gave a little gasp, staring back at the face of the man who was so familiar to her and who now so suddenly faced her with ugly truth. 'I am sorry,' she began, because she was. Pierre had been waiting. She had half known it. She had not cared but now did for she must be left with something. 'I am sorry,' she repeated and did not know how to go on. What if there were no more dreams, if her second plan crumbled away too because other people would not play the part she assigned them in her mind?

'Johnny . . . it was just one of those things that happen.' She heard her own voice rise in panic. 'He seduced me. I did not dare speak out about it. He's Lady Liscombe's brother, an important man, part-owner of the Hall.' She walked round to Pierre, to take his arm. Was it not true, that first night by the fireside when there was whisky? She did not want to remember. 'Johnny uses women,' she said, 'and then casts them aside. He is not a decent man like you. I thought he was serious about me.' She lowered her eyes because he did not look at her and tried to lean her face against his shoulder. 'Pierre!'

He took his arm carefully from her hold. 'Do not shame yourself by play-acting,' he said, and turned away to stack bowls and mincer. 'Simon!' he shouted through the doorway. 'Clear this table.'

Claudine pushed past bony Simon lumbering in, leaving her keys and the awful scene behind her. She did not care if the boy who was not a boy but a man of thirty had heard, for he would understand nothing. Her legs weak she walked along the corridor past all the rooms she had had charge of since the foot-and-mouth disease and which now suddenly seemed full of worthless things. What matter if she looked after the silver and the Minton and the silk brocades when Liscombe was a shell, when the fabric of the past two years lay bare, exposed by Johnny and Pierre? Why had it happened today when it rained so and when she had woken with such a spirit of determination to set her own fate in motion once more?

Pausing by the door of her own special room with 'Head Housekeeper' and her name written on it she faced herself: she *had* seduced Johnny, she *had* used Pierre to come to Liscombe. Her punishment had not been long in coming. But none of it mattered. Her second plan had not yet begun. It would work, this one, because she would make it work. She would then be paid for the pain of today, of the past months. Its secondary objective had come from the last hour; it would make Pierre stay at Liscombe and not leave her.

'Claudine!' She was startled by Jane's voice, sudden in the gloom and silence of the basement corridor.

'What is it?' she too whispered. There had been much whispering in Liscombe corridors during the past months.

'I want you to come and have a look at Sarah.' Jane's thin pale face with the big eyes appeared at the bottom of the nursery stairs. 'She doesn't seem well. I want you to come and look at her.'

'I know nothing about children,' Claudine said, 'and why isn't that nanny back?' She found herself almost pleased to stand by Jane, her only friend now at Liscombe, in England itself, in the world, she thought, with pity for herself. And she had not been allowed to learn about children.

'You know she's still at her mother's looking after her, I don't suppose she'll ever be back and there's no one else. I'm frightened, Claudine, Lady Liscombe thinks Sarah is suffering from grief still but I think it's more than that. You're so sensible, Claudine . . .'

'Oh heavens, Jane,' she began with her usual impatience, glad to find it in her, to find something of herself that had not changed in the last dreadful hours. 'Oh, I'll come. Go on, I'll follow you up.' And she was glad to have a moment when she need not think of herself, and all the hurts of her past.

In the nursery, both children glanced up at her from their drawing books. There was Mary, tight little face and small eyes quite unlike her mother's, showing no welcome, and beside her the Honourable Sarah, dark blue eyes the same as Lady Liscombe's and hair almost as black as her father's had been. On her face there was a smile but moving closer Claudine saw that the girl's cheeks had not their usual rosy glow and there were shadows in her face that no child should have.

She was leaning her head on her hand as if too tired to keep it up and the hand that held a blue pencil lay still on an untouched page. Claudine made an effort. She sat down beside Sarah. 'Chef's cooking you a nice lunch,' she said, 'with rice pudding to make you feel better.'

'I not want no lunch, Claudie, thank you. I tired.' Her head drooped so far that the dark hair fell upon the page. The little tabby cat Suki that was her shadow stirred from her spot around the jug of dried flowers and went to settle amongst her curls.

'Nanny says we must eat lunch,' Mary chanted. 'Nanny says she'll cut Suki's tail off if she sits on the table. Nanny says Sarah mustn't talk baby talk and she does.' She clutched a red pencil and drew a cottage in hard red strokes. No one answered her.

Claudine felt a strange surge of tenderness seeing the line of eyelashes on Sarah's face that she now thought had a yellow tinge to the skin and an unhealthy flush of fever in a stain across her cheeks. She got up with a scrape of a chairleg and gestured Jane from the room. Outside the door, she said: 'One of us, or someone, must try and tell Lady Liscombe that something is wrong. I don't know how.' But as she said those words, she realized she did know. It would be perfectly simple and moreover could be made part of her second plan. She did not want the day to end with only failure to review when she lay sleepless that night. She wanted no thoughts of sick children to haunt her.

Jane was stuttering on, staring back at her in the corridor, not realizing Claudine had decided. 'There is only you and me here,' she was saying with a note of panic in her voice. 'There's Hawker, she might listen to him, there's her mother, but she's in a worse state than Lady Liscombe and anyway can't walk up here now, she feels too poorly. How awful everything is since the funerals, Claudine . . .'

'We've got to make it better, there's got to be an end somehow.' She found a note of energy in her voice because a tableau was forming in her mind of herself up here on the nursery floor again. 'Look, give me some time to work things out. Say I bring up the nursery supper tray tonight, quite casually, saying I'm giving you the evening off, then I'll start some sort of conversation with her ladyship. It will be perfectly natural to speak of Sarah.'

'You'll have to be careful, daring to suggest something to her ladyship like that.'

'Leave it to me, Jane.' And she moved away with her old rapid stride, running down the stairs to retrieve the keys that were a symbol of her rise in power. 'When was I ever tactless?'

Oh, often, Claudine, Jane thought, peering down into the gloom at the disappearing glow of red hair. Now she had the afternoon to wait in fear in case there should be argument to come, added to the usual misery of Liscombe since the funerals. And this would be her fault.

After lunch, the rain began again, hard enough to make the oaks in the avenue droop their great branches, swish and creak in enervating rhythm. Simon Smith forced his bicycle on down the hill for the afternoon with his mother, Hawker rode behind him for the reluctant duty visit to his wife. Only Gladys was left in the dark twilight warmth of the staff hall with the wireless and Richard Tauber singing 'You are My Heart's Delight'. Unable to bear recent turbulence in royal circles any more than those of Liscombe, Gladys had unpicked the head in silk of the golden Prince of Wales and was now engaged on a new sampler of his ordinary brother George who had been obliged to take his place as King. Beginning the G for George VI in blue thread, she shut her mind to Jane's whisperings as the tea tray was being prepared and was only vaguely aware there was added tension in the air.

The sudden apparition of Johnny Tranter in the nursery gloom startled everyone present. Mary was listless over a reading book, Sarah lay on her mother's lap with her head nestled into her. Kate Liscombe had her arms about her daughter and gazed at Suki lapping cream from a saucer amid the disarray of the tea tray on the table. They all looked up as the dark male presence strode into their world where little happened but the slow progression of the days and meals that no one wanted.

'I say, Sis.' Johnny scraped back a chair and sat down noisily opposite his sister. Suki stared, a fringe of cream about her chin, until he was settled. The flutter and rustle of his arrival amongst the sitters at the table subsided. Sarah's eyes drooped over the sucking of her thumb. 'You'll have to do something about the servants.'

'Staff, Johnny,' Kate corrected. 'And what must I do?'

'Sort them out. They're running wild downstairs, doing what they like.' His hard blue eyes moved about the room and across to the window where the cleared sky showed a pink tinge foretelling frost. 'And why is the lamp not lit nor the curtains drawn? Or this mess cleared away?' He took up a salmon sandwich and pushed it into his mouth. 'You'll have to make a stand.'

'Nanny says you mustn't talk with your mouth full.' Mary shot him a look of spite, which he returned.

'I will, Johnny, one of these days, when I get matters sorted out.' Kate sent her brother a silent message of sorrow which he did not see.

'Nice sandwiches,' he said. 'I bet they scoff them downstairs most days.'

'Even staff need to eat, dear, it doesn't really have any importance.'

'Well, like Ma said, they don't need to be coming down to our pastures and sending Joe silly.'

'Gladys says he's mooning over Claudine.' Kate gave the ghost of a smile.

'*She's* had the cheek to appear all dressed up and demanding lessons!' Johnny took an angry bite at a couple of sponge fingers. 'Joe could hardly function afterwards and there was that new mare to ride out.'

'Joe has to go through the older woman stage. Remember you and that fancy Mrs Strangeways you had a taste for, the Captain's wife over at West Frampton?' Kate gave one of her old giggles. Mary and the cat looked across at her in astonishment. 'Ma was all of a flutter in case the husband came over to give you a whipping and you . . .'

'All right, Sis.' Johnny did not want to remember the embarrassment of Lucy Strangeways. 'I'm just saying it's not good letting the servants get out of hand and not know their place anymore. When or if you eventually reopen the hotel there'll be no end of trouble and you'll have to deal with it. Jane's all right,' he said, pausing over shortbread, 'she and Joe are like a couple of old schoolfriends together, or brother and sister almost, but the French girl . . .' He decided against the shortbread and brushed crumbs from the sleeve of his jacket.

'Johnny,' Kate said softly, 'don't be nasty about her, you know it was different once.'

'Yes!' Johnny said. 'And that just proves what I'm saying. She's got above herself and thinks she's someone. I know I shouldn't have started it, I regretted it straight away, but I tell you, she's . . .'

'Sssh!' Kate said. 'Not here, Johnny. I thought you respected women. I hate to hear you speak like that.'

'Well, never mind.' He strode across to the door and pulled the bell. 'I'll get the maid to clear up this mess and I'll light the lamp myself. God, what has this place come to?' All the pairs of eyes in the room watched him fiddle and curse over lamp wicks.

Kate realized he did not want to leave yet and waited for him to say what else he had come to say. She saw him go to the window and drag across the curtains, shutting out the clear dark sky, the chill of the coming night. He chose next to go to the fireplace and rattle the coals, sending up sparks and a puff of smoke. And then it came. 'What about opening the place up, old girl?' He threw on more coal from the scuttle. Suki padded over to watch operations which would give warmth for her nap. 'Only you can't . . .'

'Sit about here doing nothing, fretting?' Kate finished for him.

'Right,' he said and turned to look at her. The few precious seconds of her brother's sympathy were harder to bear than all the anxious day-long flutterings of everyone else. Kate's throat tightened; she could not speak and anyway had nothing to say. She gazed at the new fire making a frame of light around her brother's long legs in their brown boots, around the slight stoop of his shoulders from too much time spent on a horse. 'Bess'd have wanted it and David. Anyway, think about it, old girl, do.'

Kate watched him finally leave with regret. She would have liked a proper talk with her brother, about David and Aunt Bessie and Pa and all the problems of Liscombe, but had somehow not the strength nor the will. She hugged sleeping Sarah to her and lifted her over to the other side.

Claudine did not allow herself to flinch from the pain in her wrist, carrying the heavy tray up two flights of stairs. There was power in her own resolution: to seal her fate that very afternoon.

She found Lady Liscombe seated in the nursery with Sarah on one side, Mary on the other and a model farm laid out with stables, barns and manor house. Mary had two fistfuls of lead animals clutched to her and little Sarah was weeping. 'I don't want no sheep nor any cows on my farm.'

'It can't be a farm without cows or sheep in it, Auntie, and Nanny says Sarah mustn't talk baby talk.'

Claudine saw her chance. 'If everyone drinks their milk,' she said, placing the tray on a sideboard, 'I think I might find a better French game up my sleeve.'

'Oh, Claudine, would you? Isn't it a dreary day.' Lady Liscombe leaned wearily back in her chair. Claudine whisked away the board holding the farm, levered Mary's fingers from the lead animals and with one movement had crossed the room to put the whole without ceremony into a cupboard. Within minutes she had organized a game of Simon Says which involved undressing for bed at the same time. As she called out the names of the parts of the body and of clothing in French, there were squeals of rivalry and delight. But as she cried, 'Lift *le genou*' for the third time, Sarah, mistakenly thinking she must lift her knee, fell. Mary began a jig of triumph.

Claudine realized the child could not get up again. She had rolled herself into a ball of weariness and her own task was simplified.

'Mary, go down to your mother in the kitchen, please.' Mary stopped dancing and looked at her in astonishment. 'Because I say so,' Claudine added, forestalling the question 'Why?' already formed on the child's cross face. They flashed each other a look of dislike but Mary obeyed.

'What is it, Claudine?' Lady Liscombe, slowly, was leaving the table. 'Sarah?'

Claudine lifted the child. Her head lolled back. She had fallen as quickly and deeply asleep as a sick animal. 'Sarah?' Lady Liscombe said again in the hesitant manner she had taken on after the funerals when all her old force had been dragged from her. 'Can she be ill, Claudine?'

'I think she may be very ill, Lady Liscombe.' There. It was done. Later would be the moment for her own objective. She went on, for Jane, for the child, for Lady Liscombe herself, because Sarah was ill. 'Jane and I have noticed,' she said, holding the girl against her breasts in an automatic maternal gesture. 'She is so hot and yet so pale and we both thought, well, she has not been quite herself.'

Kate Liscombe knelt beside her and put out a hand to feel the child's face. 'Hot, yes, poor darling. She has not been well, you see, Claudine, since . . .'

'Yes, Lady Liscombe.' She used a louder, more urgent voice to startle her from her blankness. 'But perhaps it is more than grief. She is more poorly now than she was those dreadful days, you may not remember, when she shut herself in the old gypsy's cottage where Jane lived, with Pugs and those three ginger cats and Suki. She shrieked and shrieked then for fear the men would shoot them, she was hysterical, but she's different now.'

'Yes,' Lady Liscombe said, her face a sudden tight mask. 'I think I'll put her to bed and sit by her. Will you keep Mary downstairs? She's not a restful child.'

'May I sit with you a little while, your ladyship?' Claudine took a deep breath, ignoring the startled look turned back at her. 'I have something to ask you.'

'Very well. Of course, Claudine, what a good idea. We'll have a chat. It has been such a dreary day, hasn't it? How's the riding? I *did* see you out there in the paddock?'

They put Sarah to bed beside Suki. She was still deep in soundless sleep, her little body seeming lifeless, sunk into the mattress. They each sat watching her in the nursery gloom until Claudine spoke the question she had been rehearsing since she had first formed her two plans. 'I am thinking, your ladyship, that it may be time to open the hotel again.' She waited for Lady Liscombe's quiet set face to turn towards her.

The nursery clock ticked, the only sound between them, its Mickey Mouse nodding.

'It is strange you should say that today, Mr Johnny has just suggested it.' Kate leaned over Sarah, smoothing back damp curls, and moved to touch the little cat who stretched and breathed out a purr. Claudine sat still, waiting, the pain in her wrist a sudden throb. 'But I don't think . . .' Her words trailed off.

Claudine offered her first trump card. 'I do understand you don't feel well enough yet but you see, Lady Liscombe, I know that Pierre is thinking of leaving and if he does, Liscombe's cuisine . . .'

'Pierre, leave?' Her ladyship seemed shocked into attention. 'Oh, without Pierre . . . Where is he to go?'

'Please, your ladyship, do not ever tell him I told

you. Pierre likes to keep personal matters close to himself. He has told me, of course, because I am his friend. I think he feels unused here after building up such a reputation and a chef cannot afford to waste his early years.' Lady Liscombe was again making tender movements over her daughter's pillow but Claudine knew she was listening. 'I thought,' she went on, 'that is if you felt you could agree, we would do all the work for you, the three of us, Hawker and Pierre and me, and it would stop Pierre leaving.'

'Much depends on one's chef and a good one is hard to find.'

'Yes, your ladyship.' In the silence, the wind sent a little cloud of smoke into the room from the chimney. Claudine thought she should get up to attend to the fire but dared not disturb the train of thought she had set in motion. 'A good hotel is not easy to find either,' she said.

'Especially not a good one outside London, and this was. Liscombe Hall Hotel. I dreamed I could make a marvellous hotel here and look what happened.'

'You could again . . .' Claudine broke in. 'We could again. It is still a dream place.' She paused, watching Lady Liscombe's bent head. She could almost tell this woman the whole of her own story and release the burden of the dream of Liscombe that she had had and never told to anyone.

But Lady Liscombe's attention was gone again. She was smoothing her daughter's head and said: 'Her hair is not so glossy, is it?'

'No, Lady Liscombe,' Claudine said clearly. 'I think you should send for a doctor at once and I think you should let your heads of department do their job of reopening this hotel.' She let out a breath and went boldly on with her last trump card. 'There is some

143

movement in hotel trade,' she said, 'in case you are wondering what sort of start we could make, without the Dr Hay diet and so on.'

'There is, Claudine?' Kate looked vaguely across the cot at her with a hint of a smile.

'Americans,' Claudine said and then, quickly, to stop the raise of her eyebrows, 'they're coming back to England. The world slump is over and the Americans are coming back, especially for the Coronation this year, and there are two new liners coming out – one's in operation already, offering real luxury across the Atlantic. Royalty and luxury, that's what the Americans like, and we can offer them both!' She realized that her voice had risen but did not care. Sarah had not woken although Suki watched her through the slit of one eye and sighed.

'The Americans don't come here to Dorset, Claudine dear, though I don't say they won't start coming back to England.'

'We make them come, we attract them.'

'Really?'

Was she imagining it or did Lady Liscombe look at her with something of her old sharpness?

'With the right advertising.' She had much more to say. She could tell Lady Liscombe how she herself had seen the old Liscombe Hall advertisements and remembered every one, how she *saw* how the Americans could be attracted by the aura of Liscombe as she had been.

'Without the right advertising, we would certainly have no chance.'

Lady Liscombe rose to her feet. That was enough to make Claudine realize her own instinct had been right. Her ladyship wanted to hear no more for the moment. Claudine was satisfied however that the seed was sown.

It had been Lady Liscombe's old sharp look, or the glimmer of it, that had told her. She too rose. 'Shall we talk about it again one day, your ladyship?' This she knew was boldness itself for her ladyship had silently signalled her to leave.

'Yes, Claudine.' And, as she reached the doorway, Kate added: 'You remind me of myself, when I was your age.'

Claudine stood with her hand on the doorknob. Lady Liscombe had moved to the hearth and the interview was truly over but Claudine recognized the sudden warmth around her own heart and it was not solely triumph.

She could not assure the rest of the staff that the time of their long wait might soon be over, but she and Jane none the less tried to make the evening a celebratory one. At least it had been said, that Sarah ought to see a doctor, and Lady Liscombe had listened, seeming to waken from the dream she had been in. It was, they agreed, a beginning. Pierre set himself to concoct a special supper, Hawker suggested they might allow themselves the rare privilege of a bottle or two from the cellar. Her ladyship would be the last to complain about that and they had permitted themselves nothing at Christmas. With a new feeling of comradeship and hope, they laid the staff table with a lace cloth, setting out linen napkins and upstairs silver and glass. But they had all become so unaccustomed to jollity they could hardly do justice to the meal. Even the Châteauneuf had not begun to warm them, for the weight of the last months lay so heavy, and what if Lady Liscombe were to slip away from reality again? Hawker went for a third bottle before anyone wanted to try the lemon ice-cream Pierre had been working on.

Claudine was watching Jane hesitate over her glass of water when Hawker discreetly passed her by and refilled Gladys's glass. It was unspoken between all of them that Jane should never be allowed near the scent of alcohol and only Hawker and Pierre had access to the cellars. Afterwards, she could not remember what had prompted her to say what she did, blaming her own weakness in taking too much wine herself so that she was unwary. She said, hearing her own voice very loud against the irritating jingle from the gramophone: 'Go on, Jane, have a glass, just one, it won't hurt.' She took up the bottle herself before Hawker or Gladys could stop her, for they both shouted 'No!' at the same moment. Her eyes met Jane's over the table. There was fear in them, and panic, and need. She pushed the glass forward, the deep red of the liquid prettily outlined in cream lace. 'It's such a good wine, isn't it, Hawker, that it can do you no harm and if it hadn't been for you, Jane, suggesting I speak to Lady Liscombe . . .'

Hawker turned on her his pale, hooded eyes that so seldom revealed thought or feeling. Now there was anger, she knew, and was it warning? She could not tell, but it did not matter for she herself *must* be linchpin at Liscombe and Hawker *must* keep his place. Beside Jane, Gladys's little bird-like eyes blinked frantically. Her hand with its knuckles swollen from work and rheumatism reached the glass at the same moment as Jane's. There was a struggle with fingers around the stem of the glass. Claudine watched, breathless. She had time to shout: 'No, Jane, I was only teasing,' but Jane had won and the glass was at her mouth. A dribble of red dripped on to the cloth and she held it out, empty. 'I should like another, Claudine, if you don't mind. After all, it was my idea to speak to Lady

Liscombe.' She hiccoughed, her cheeks a sudden crimson.

'Only because you were afraid to do it yourself,' Claudine said sharply. But there was a wave of nausea around her heart at the sight of the sickening relief in Jane's eyes. What had she done, starting Jane on that old fearful path? Pierre's dark face was looking down the table at her in disgust. That was the second time today, her dear faithful Pierre. She had not known he was dear to her. From today, of course, it did not matter; it did not matter because Lady Liscombe would very soon come to her for a little of her strength to get the place begun again. She saw that Hawker had risen from his seat in silence and taken up the bottle. Pierre stood too and Gladys jumped up, pulling at Jane's arm. They were grouped together, against her, staring at her, but it did not matter. It was better so. She did not need their support. She would do far better without the obligations of friendship. Friendship only meant weakness.

From a corner of the room, the singing voice madly relaunched itself: 'Happy days are here again, the skies above are blue again . . .'

Simon Smith appeared in the doorway, rain dripping down his waterproof cape. 'Who's been messing about with my records?' He sneezed.

'You are just in time for the washing up, boy,' Hawker said. 'And here, take this wine. Why not? At least you're as simple as your name and will do no harm by it.'

For the first time in her life, Claudine took a glass of brandy to bed with her, to ease herself into sleep without reviewing the turbulence of the day. Before sleep came, however, she had time to realize that she had lost love, and perhaps friendship too, although the misunderstanding with Pierre might be healed. But Liscombe and her dream of it was going to be reborn. And she had no reason to flinch from her self-imposed and single-minded purpose, because it was all that she had.

CHAPTER 8

'Why did she get up at four o'clock this morning and sit over that typewriting machine in the office tapping away like a madwoman then?' Gladys asked Jane over the table in the staff hall where they were first to breakfast the next day.

'I don't know, Gladys, why do you think she did?' Jane forced a spoonful of porridge into her mouth.

'Put some more syrup on it, it'll go down easier.' Gladys, making an effort not to notice Jane's nervous forcing of food, none the less could not prevent an aura of concern pervading the room. She pressed on with the subject of Claudine Forestier. 'Because she's meaning to take your place close to Lady Liscombe, that's why,' she said, chewing on a doorstop of cold toast. 'She's not content with forcing her ladyship to open the place again, she wants to become one of them secretary women as well as Head Housekeeper and before you can look round, you won't have no say in nothing.'

'I don't want a say in anything, Glad.' Jane put her spoon on the grey mess in the bottom of her bowl and took up her teacup with relief.

'I cut you this nice thin piece of bread and put honey on it.' Gladys pushed over the plate Jane had known was destined for her. 'Mr Hawker told Chef she's a spiteful piece that needs to be taken down a peg or two and they was whispering.'

'Chef! That reminds me, Gladys, I'd better warn

Chef the doctor said last night Sarah might be needing to eat liver, for her blood sickness. He may have to send out for it.' Jane took a rapid mouthful of bread and honey, for Gladys's sake, and got up. 'And I must take her ladyship's tray, Glad. Thanks for the bread, it was lovely.'

Gladys's round eyes, as bright as a robin's, gazed into hers. Jane gave silent acknowledgement of the entreaty in them and said: 'It's all right, don't worry, I haven't.' She knocked into the door post as she ran from the room on unsteady legs. The morning's weakness was bad, since the brief lapse at supper, and was one of the many things to remind her of the past. There must be no more lapses, *she must not let herself down*, as her ladyship had once so sensibly suggested. But this very minute, if a glass appeared by magic in her hand, she would drink it.

Warmth would flood through her and relief and strength enough to make her legs work, to make her throw back her breakfast with an easy laugh.

'Careful!' Claudine appeared in the basement gloom. 'Shall I take her ladyship's tray up for you?' Jane hesitated. She did not like taking up the heavy tray when she did not feel strong, when the china was likely to rattle as she set it on the table and Lady Liscombe give her a look of concern. It was however best not to hesitate with Claudine. She had given her a flash of those green eyes, swung on her heel and was in the kitchen before Jane could recover herself. 'I had it ready,' she said sweetly, carrying the tray which also had on it, Jane saw, some office-type papers. She had no time to ask what these might be for Claudine had passed her with an effortless stride on legs that were not long but as sturdy as a pony's. Jane realized she did not want Claudine to take over the tray, not even for one morning. If she were not Lady Liscombe's special attendant and confidante, what would she be?

'Hurry with the cleaning, Gladys,' Claudine said, sitting at her desk two days later. 'And tear these pages into small pieces, please.' Passing her rejected sheets from Sarah's drawing pad, Claudine frowned over the final version of her advertisement.

'Yes, Miss.' Gladys obediently tore the sheets into strips – not without, Claudine noted, muttering over them. She wanted Gladys to glimpse the drawings and the scripted words in their little squares before she made the presentation to Lady Liscombe. There need, she thought, be no mistake about who had been the instigator of Liscombe's renaissance. From devilry, she turned around and said: 'What do you think of this sentence, Gladys? "Find again the savour of the past"?'

Gladys's swollen fingers paused over the wastepaper basket. 'I don't know nothing about history, Miss, I didn't have no schooling.'

'What about "Taste the pursuit of Kings and Queens"?' Claudine persisted, because she wanted them all to wonder about her activities, because they were all against her. She saw Gladys's birdlike features twist into diligent thought. 'Will it make people want to come here, do you think?'

'I always said to Jane that guests lived like royalty at Liscombe, Miss,' Gladys said eagerly, 'but there's no guests now.'

'There will be, there will be, Gladys.' Claudine rose from the desk with a thrill of pleasure. This moment, when she had something prepared to show to her ladyship, was very much like the one when she had stood at the top of Liscombe Hill for the first time and it had all been spread out before her, waiting. She picked up the papers and put them into an old menu folder. 'Don't touch the magazines, Gladys,' she said, indicating a pile of society journals on the desk. 'I may need to make a further study of them. And leave Miss Sarah's drawing pad and pencils.'

She left the office with the satisfaction of knowing that puzzlement had settled into Gladys's mind and would have been voiced in the staff hall. They would all wonder but need know nothing yet. Each one of them would benefit from her actions and she was glad of it; she wanted in fact to retrieve a little of the warmth of the friendship she had felt.

She found Lady Liscombe waiting for her in the nursery with the odious Mary working at sums beside her. 'How is Miss Sarah, your ladyship?' she asked, sitting now with the ease of familiarity, folder, notebook and pencil in businesslike fashion before her.

'A little tired, Claudine, and still in bed. The doctor will be coming again this evening. I can't think how I let things go on. Well, I've got you to thank . . .' Her voice trailed off.

'I'm sure it's just that, what is it called, anaemia, your ladyship.'

'Yes, it's to be hoped.'

'I've brought the drawings and plan I promised.' Claudine pushed forward a sheet where her final work was displayed with a neat square drawn around it as it would appear in the advertising pages of magazines.

'That's *my* drawing paper,' Mary began.

'It's Sarah's,' Claudine said sharply. 'Miss Sarah gave me a whole new pad yesterday, your ladyship, she's so sweet, isn't she?'

Lady Liscombe took the page in her thin hand. 'I didn't know you could draw, too, Claudine,' she said, with a suggestion of a smile on her hollowed face that had once, Claudine thought, with a pinch of sympathy, been so vibrant.

'It's not a very good crown,' she said, 'nor a very good Liscombe, but I drew the two towers and the line of windows quite easily though I've never had a drawing lesson.' She almost added: But I know the shape of it by heart. Its image has lived with me since I had a postcard of it from your brother. If there would ever be anyone she recounted the tale to, it would be this woman who had herself fought for so much. She too must have had a dream in the beginning or how else would she have become what she was?

Lady Liscombe said, 'I like this, Claudine. How enterprising you are.' She began to read aloud. '"Find again the savour of the past." Perhaps flavour would be better there?'

Claudine held her breath; she had not shown even the mildest surprise at being presented with a sample advertisement already fully drawn by her Head House-keeper.

'"Taste the pursuits of Kings and Queens." I like that, they *did* go about the country houses once, still do I suppose, for the hunt and the shoot. "Country Living as it used to be." Yes, we used to offer that. "Hunting, Riding, Shooting, Fishing, Accompanied Tours, Royal Table Kept." And this little crown at the top – it's to give a suggestion of royalty, is it?'

'Yes, it's to link it all together, your ladyship, as I told you yesterday. You see, royalty has been so much in the news lately, with the old King dying, Edward VIII abdicating, this new Coronation, I thought we might use the general atmosphere of the country. And with the Americans starting to cross the Atlantic on the new liners . . .'

'Yes, my dear, but as I think I've said, I've never seen an American in Dorset.'

'They're coming to London and . . .'

'But to get them to come here? We'd have to have advertising set up, say in the London hotels, and by then they would have made arrangements for their stay with passages booked home . . .' There was, Claudine saw, a droop to her shoulders again, her moment of interest gone. But all the energy was going to come from herself, so it did not matter. She began, very quickly, so that she got everything in at once: 'We advertise in American magazines, starting at once like Honywood Hotels have done – they had their own agent in America too. It was all in the *Caterer*, the great success they had in the twenties, and there's absolutely no reason why we should not do the same, I've worked out the whole scheme.' She paused for breath, knowing that a flush had spread from her neck to her cheeks. This moment was perhaps vital but before she could go on, forcing words into Lady Liscombe's vagueness, her ladyship had seemed to make an effort. 'Honywood?' she said. 'Yes, I seem to remember, it was very successful.'

'Because they had a good idea and pursued it.' Claudine leaned across the table, ready to say more.

'Yes.' The great blue eyes that had once been the colour of bluebells looked back at her. 'Yes. Well, all right, let's say I'm in favour at first glance. Why not, after all? Will you write me out a letter to Honywood's head office? They might be helpful.' She rose and pushed the drawing back to Claudine. 'That I do like. It might well work though I'm not sure about too much royalty. We might have to stick to suggestions of the old aristocracy. Anyway, come up and see me tomorrow. And will you send Chef up now? We have to do something about the liver that Sarah's supposed to eat. She really can't get it down, the poor lamb.'

Claudine collected her papers, her heart thumping. She dropped her pencil. Mary ran round to pick it up, passing it to her with an unchildish look of interest. 'Thank you, Mary dear,' she said, fooling no one. She felt suddenly weak with exhausted effort.

'You *do* remind me of myself when I was your age, Claudine.' Lady Liscombe smiled at her from the nursery bedroom doorway.

She was conscious of another flush, of pleasure; everything was going to be all right.

'Gladys! The doctor says Sarah might die. Oh, Gladys!' Jane, bursting into the staff hall, put two hands to her white face. Gladys stood up, dropping her teacup with a thud upon the table. 'Die!' she echoed and could not move, her hand poised, her mouth open as if to scream.

'Die? That little mite?' Hawker, carrying a tray of glasses past the doorway, stopped, all the drinker's colour leaving his face. 'Chef! You heard this?'

Pierre called Claudine from the laundry room and with unspoken accord everyone gathered together to sit around Chef's table, Gladys leading Jane so that she could recount the story properly. No one objected when Simon took it upon himself to join them. Jane gazed from face to face, reading horror in each, and dread.

'Lady Liscombe won't believe it,' she began, 'but I heard. The doctor says Sarah doesn't have a blood disease after all. She's got some kind of creeping paralysis and there may be no cure. He went on and on. He asked me to be there. He thought Lady Liscombe would faint but of course she didn't because she didn't believe him.' Jane gasped for breath. 'She sort of smiled at him and said, "I shall get the best doctors, I shall go to London. I shall take Sarah at once to Switzerland. Thank you so much, Doctor." She was as calm as could be. She said I was to come down and tell you they would be leaving. She says she wants to see you all before she goes. She says she knows she's leaving Liscombe in good hands.' Gladys broke in with a cry of assent. 'And she'll soon be home again with Sarah. That's what she said. So you're all to be around and she'll come down. And I'm to telephone the stables to ask Mr Johnny to borrow the Ramsays' Rolls. Sarah won't stand his Bentley coupé nor the train, she says.'

'If you ask me, the mite won't be able to stand any travelling.' Gladys could not sit still. 'She'll want us for the packing, Jane?'

'We'd better go up,' she agreed, not moving. 'There's so much to think of. It'll no doubt be summer before they come back, they may need light clothes.' No one answered her.

Into the silence, Simon spoke. 'That little girl won't never come back,' he said, with a note of hysteria in his high boy's voice. 'Nor won't her ladyship. She'll sell this place, she won't have no heart for it after, and we'll all be out of a job.'

'Shut up, boy,' Hawker said mechanically. Everyone stood with him and went to their separate areas of work, as if it were a normal day, although nothing had been normal since the funerals.

Claudine said no word to anyone, finding herself suddenly alone in her sitting room. She could not remember having walked there. She had, she knew, to think very quickly. Sitting at her desk, opening a file she reread the wasted lists:

Advertising plan for the reopening of Liscombe
Schedule of magazine placements
Reopening staff requirements

There was even one of former staff she knew still to be in the area. Everything would have been simply a matter of time and her own progression. What use now if the child were to die? Claudine gazed unseeing at her work. She had a sudden flash of memory, of Sarah's face at the window, the time before the funerals, horror and determination in it, because the men with the guns might come and shoot the cats. She who so rarely allowed herself tears had wept at the sight, shouting up to Sarah that they would not shoot cats. Hawker had wept, and Pierre and Jane and the wretched boy Simon. She had woken at dawn the next morning, weeping all afresh. There had been a dream, a nightmare – why had the memory come so vividly now? A boy, a little boy with red hair . . . and Sarah's face had been at some other window, not screaming, dumbly sorrowful with a deserted child's despair. Her pillow was wet. She had been crying for a long time.

A tear fell now and spread on to the file. She rose from the chair. There must still be hope. Sarah was suffering from grief and shock and must not die. She needed to get away from the place that had shown her a blissful view of life for her first five years and then had broken her heart. The doctor, a fool of a man, a charlatan, would not understand that. How could a blood sickness become paralysis?

She picked up the folder. She must not give in now.

All of Liscombe lay silent in the damp wintry air. Kate could not take her last glimpse of the Downs beyond the oaks where she and David had used to ride.

They were in mist and a little mist seemed to sit along the wall sheltering the three graves. She would like to be able to say to her husband, her aunt and her father: look, see how my heart is near to dead from loss of you. How can I bear more?

She had found the black funeral hat to go with the black suit that would take her into the office of the doctor who would save Sarah. Its feather touched her cheek as she closed the door of the bedroom that she and David had shared for such short happy years. Walking blindly along the corridor, down the great staircase, past the stretch of mullioned window that today let in no light, she forced herself to remember nothing, to fear nothing, to hope for nothing.

They were all on the steps to see her leave, the core of staff she had kept on to maintain the rooms, keep the garden in order, for the future, for Sarah's inheritance. The stableboys, the gardener and his boy, stood with caps clutched, beside Gladys who was sobbing, and the handsome chef. There was Claudine and Jane. Johnny and their mother stood by the door of the borrowed Rolls where Joe rubbed at the headlights with a duster, to hide his love and embarrassment.

Kate paused in the doorway where she had stood many times to admire the sweep of the avenue and the great rustling oaks. She held out a hand to each of them, all wordless as she was. Even Claudine was quiet, a little apart, free of the folder which was now safely inside her own day bag. She wanted to say to her: 'Take Pierre, you and he match', but of course could not, and anyway it was perhaps too late. She had tasted too much of the thrill of achievement to become a mere wife. 'Keep those plans going,' she said to her instead, and was regarded with a smile of complicity from sharp green eyes.

Jane gave a gasp, taking her hand, face pale with sympathy.

'I'll be home, everyone, just as soon as Sarah is well.' She forced herself to walk down the steps. 'Look after Liscombe.'

'We will.' It was a chorus.

She turned away, her shoes crunching on the gravel, the only sound a hiccough from Gladys. The mist was thickening to drizzle, cold against her skin. She watched as Hawker carried out Sarah in her blankets and put her in the back seat of the Rolls where a bed had been made up. Her mother watched too, dry-eyed, as she was herself. They were both beyond tears. 'Look after Joe and Johnny, Mother,' she said. In her arms, her mother's plump flesh seemed to have shrunk. She leaned up to kiss the cheek of her nephew which had both boy's flush and the prickle of a man's beard on it.

Good. It was all finished now.

Her last sight of the place she had bought as the pinnacle of her life's work, where she had lived in late joy with the only man she had ever loved, was of a thin line of staff, each one with hand raised to bid her goodbye.

Johnny pushed the car into second gear and they sped off under the oaks. Kate closed her eyes, arms encircling the makeshift bed where weightless Sarah lay.

CHAPTER 9

Spring was near, blossom was turning to leaf in the Liscombe gardens. The oaks were all in bud and Sarah had not died. Still undergoing treatment in a London clinic for a rare complaint none of them had ever heard of, Sarah needed her mother with her but Lady Liscombe had been able to find time to send orders to Liscombe for its reopening. The new notice-boards were already up, one at the bottom of the hill just past the Post Office, the other by the last tree of the gravel drive.

'Liscombe Hall Hotel,' it said, under the Liscombe emblem. 'A Royal Welcome: Hunting, Shooting, Fishing, Kings' Table Kept.'

Johnny Tranter, obliged to act as overseer in his sister's absence, sat stifling in the basement office, trapped by the telephone, tugging at the collar around his neck. It was worse, he thought, to be stuck there, when the air was light outside and the horses were friskier, scenting spring. 'OK, Sis,' he was saying. 'Right. Thank God, I say. You know I'm no good at this sort of thing. When's this manager coming then, for Chrissake? Noon Monday. And he's ... Percival, Percival! ... Pemberton. Right, well, sounds ... No, I'm not laughing, Sis, I don't care what he's called as long as he gets here and I can get on with my own work. Yes, the river's filling up nicely. I've taken on that Duffall chap to help with the pheasant stocks. If we're going to offer a proper shoot ...' He gazed up on to the half-window. There was a glimpse of foliage in an urn on the terrace, and beyond the swaying canopy of oak branches almost in bud. 'Of course, the stables are as before, no problem there but I shall take on a couple more boys. Yes, you'll telephone tomorrow. How's Sarah going with that new exercise treatment? I'll bring Mother up to help next week if that chap settles straight off.'

He slammed down the receiver with an impatient sigh. Like all women, he thought, his sister, once launched, never stopped talking. But if that were a sign things were improving, he was glad of it. He pulled again at his tie and avoided the sight of the piles of paper on the desk that had, without his noticing almost, become his. Thank God that was all to be over, with this Pemberton coming. Percival! Johnny got up and threw a few sheets into the wastepaper basket, shuffling the others into loose piles. This was no longer his work. Only the servants to see now, for the daily few words that had somehow become routine.

There they all were, around the teacups in the servants' hall, with Hawker at the head, like the old butlers, next to Claudine whom he avoided looking at, Chef at the end near the door in case there should be need to run to some over-boiling pan.

Johnny made an effort, standing in the doorway: 'Morning,' he said. All eyes turned his way. Hawker rose to offer him a chair. 'No, I won't sit down, thanks. Only one thing today, I think, and that's good news. The new manager's coming, noon on Monday. His name's Pemberton and he'll no doubt soon have everything shipshape for the opening. I think we'd better all be about to welcome him. His rooms should be got ready, that doctor's old rooms, Lady Liscombe says, and ... well, I know her ladyship can rely on you.'

He smiled at Gladys, avoiding Claudine's face; it was enough to feel her willing him to look at her. Jane had her sweet head bowed over her cup as she always did so there was no need to stay any longer. 'Good day to you,' he said, and strode thankfully back towards the basement door and his freedom.

The staff stood grouped about the terrace steps at noon on Monday, very much as they had to see Lady Liscombe leave. Only Jed decided he was not needed and would dedicate the day to the first mowing of the lawns. He had shod the donkey in its leather shoes and was leading it up and down the rich green stretch by the churchyard so that he could none the less be witness to the event, a strange one. There had never been non-family management at Liscombe.

Pierre was grumbling that he was not a servant to wait upon new arrivals as if they were all back in the old days. Simon muttered about his aching knees until Hawker silenced him. No one seemed to look forward to welcoming the man who was to help carve out their future. They frowned into the sunlight; the sky was still cool, the sun low. Perhaps after all spring was not so near as they'd thought.

It was Gladys's sharp ears that heard the sound of a motor car, and then a little bullnose Morris came into view. They watched it make a hesitant circle around the gravel and pause, engine running. A head with a tweed cap poked from the window. There was a pale featureless face and the gleam of a monocle. 'Liscombe Hall?' a high clipped voice asked. Simon, standing well out of the way, started to giggle, for where else could it be, with the noticeboards out, and anyway who would come up Liscombe Hill if they were not destined for the Hall?

Hawker stepped forward, both butler and maître d', and said, 'It is, sir.' He opened the car door and the man stepped out, long thin legs first in checked plus-fours, long thin chest clothed in tweed. He threw some keys to Hawker, his glance sweeping across them and along the line of golden stone that had become theirs, with the myriad windows that were their life's work, the steps they had scrubbed, the great brass door knob that shone because of them, the glow of oak flooring behind that they had polished. All this they had cared for, watched over, and this pale young man who was too tall and too thin merely glanced around. He said nothing about its perfection, only: 'Take my bags in, will you?'

Hawker threw the keys and the task at Simon and stood back to watch the man walk up their steps.

Claudine saw a monocle hanging on a grubby ribbon around his neck and, surprisingly in one so lean, rather full lips. She heard him ask, 'Where are my quarters?' to no one in particular and step limply into the splendour of the hallway where the bronze pillars glowed and the little telling items that had been left out, the gumboots, the butterfly net, the fishing rods, indicated it had once been the residence of gentlemen.

She watched him breathe in air that was warm from the fire at the hearth and scented from the bowls of pot-pourri. It was all as Lady Liscombe had laid down years before. She herself had seen that it was so and this man, this interloper, for at once she knew that he was that, merely glanced about him with a sniff of disparagement. 'Bit old hat, what?'

She stared at him and could not reply. Hawker, beside her, said briefly: 'You'll find your room at the top of the second stairway, Number 51', and threw him a key. Claudine saw that Hawker, impeccably the showman on every occasion, even before the most crass war-profiteer guest, threw the key at this man who did not know how to appreciate Liscombe. Neither she nor Hawker moved to show him up, although they had agreed they should both do it, as equal heads of department. Neither moved, but when the man went forward as if to mount the fine oak stairs, family and guest stairs, Hawker was all bustle.

'We usually go up by the rear stairs, sir,' he said, ushering the man through the door behind the reception area.

The rest of the staff, still gathered by the front steps, had watched this tableau. No one spoke, but Claudine knew that the man's position amongst them had been decided. She felt all at once an immense weariness. How could Lady Liscombe have thought him suitable for the Hall? How could she not see they did not need him?

Six weeks later the man had done nothing to alter her feelings. There was no pleasure for her now to know that she had helped re-awaken Liscombe; there was no pleasure in her daily work at all, although some kind of routine had become established because they were near to opening.

That fine May morning, Claudine was occupied in setting up the office for the daily staff meeting. She was careless; everything she did held no interest for her and had lost its purpose. Liscombe was not going to blossom ever again. She threw notepads and pencils on to the table. 'Don't bother to dust, Mrs Bassett,' she said to the daily woman she had engaged. 'It's only the staff meeting. Go and see Miss Cox about washing down the dining-room paintwork.' The piles of paper on his desk were more disordered than in Johnny's day. How could the man have any clear idea of matters in hand when staff rotas lay mixed with advance bookings and wine orders?

'I say.' Pemberton stood in the doorway. 'Your Miss Cox was very nearly rude to me this morning, Mademoiselle, and I won't have it.'

'She is not *my* Miss Cox,' Claudine said sharply. 'It was you who suggested we take back the old staff, because it was easier. I told you she was rather coarse in her manner. Sir.'

'Why is this room so untidy? Can't you get it cleaned up?' He let his monocle fall and stared crossly round the room, not at her, never at her, Claudine thought, though his eyes were so pale it was hard to know where they settled. She saw with distaste the limp lock of hair, his petulant mouth. There was ash from his cigarettes on the black manager's jacket, on his black tie and down the striped trousers.

'I cannot spare a maid or a daily, and anyway you would only say they disturbed things.' She waited for him to give his usual fretful answer but he did not bother.

Hawker slipped in to sit beside her, in his shirt-sleeves as always, which was his signal of contempt for this man, and Pierre followed. Each chose to murmur a word to Claudine, for the show of it, because the three of them were locked together in disapproval of Pemberton.

'I say, you three, I'm waiting to start. If you've got time to waste, I haven't. And that 'bus company's name you gave me's no good. They won't play.'

'What do you mean?' Claudine asked.

'They won't do the tours, I said, they won't play.'

Pemberton slumped into his chair and put a long leg across the desk. 'I said to them, you'll be sorry, it'll be an important coup for you to transport Liscombe guests around Dorset – and you should have heard them. Rustic rudeness!'

'But they were anxious to do business with us when I telephoned them last month for you,' Claudine protested. 'They said so much per day, driver included, never mind how many guests, up to the maximum the 'bus could take.'

'Ah!' Pemberton lit a Craven A. 'And I said we'd pay so much per guest – we might only have one or two to start with. Can't afford to throw money away.' He blew smoke into Pierre's impassive face. 'So finito the tours.'

'We have no tours at all? But there are two American parties coming the first week and wanting, expecting,' Claudine said, '*expecting* two or three trips around to see the great houses and the countryside.'

'We'll have to make some excuse. Anyway, next on the agenda this morning is the dining-room. I want a fountain in it, Hawker.'

Here, Hawker woke up. 'A fountain?' he asked quietly. 'Actual water, in the dining-room?'

'Right first time, old chap. Got an estimate here. £504 19s 6d. Of course some of the panelling . . .'

'Water tiddling away while people are eating?' Hawker stood and pulled at his shirt collar. 'And five hundred quid? Do you know how many meals we shall have to serve to get that back? And if you go refusing to give guests what you've promised, we'll fail before the end of the summer.' There were purple patches on his cheeks. Claudine wanted to put out a hand to calm him but hesitated; let Hawker say what had to be said. 'I tell you, sir . . .' His voice was shaking with a sudden fury, he who so seldom showed any feeling. She and Pierre seemed both to hold their breath as Hawker struggled to control himself. 'I tell you, sir, you will very shortly find yourself without a restaurant manager unless you leave dining-room matters as they are.'

They all watched him march to the door, ramrod straight, the drinker's tremor of his hands stilled by his anger. Then Pierre stood. 'I think, sir,' he said, his accent all at once assuming its old thickness, 'that I must show my support for my colleague. I too give notice that Liscombe can no longer count on my services.'

Claudine watched him too leave her alone with the man who was going to ruin Liscombe. Far better that it had lain in limbo than this, for there could be no rebirth after Pemberton. But he sat there, a little paler, she thought, shrugging his shoulders.

'Temperamental, aren't they?' he said, reaching for another Craven A. 'They'll come round. Jobs aren't that easy to find. Now, about the hallway. Have you got your notebook?' He could not look up at her. 'I want all that old stuff cleared out, the old boots and coats and so on. I want it modernized. I'm thinking along the lines of glass, say, and chromium. I'm going to get one of those designers in.'

Claudine got up, forcing herself to speak calmly. 'That old stuff,' she said, 'is what we have to offer.' She walked to the door. She would not bother to follow the conventions of the staff meeting any longer. Soon there would be no staff to meet together. 'Excuse me, I have to see to one of the cleaners.'

He did not bother to try and stop her. Even he, she thought, must now realize things were going badly wrong.

Walking slowly back to her own office, she knew she must act again for Liscombe, to save it from Pemberton. She longed for the presence of Lady Liscombe, so that all could be explained. How quickly she would see the follies of the man! But no one had access to her ladyship but Johnny, and Johnny . . .

It did not matter; she must put personal matters aside, for Liscombe. She would go and see him, on business, and not let herself weaken. Putting up her chin, she reminded herself how far she had travelled by keeping a firm and steady purpose hidden within her.

'Johnny, I have to talk to you, please. About the hotel.' Claudine stood in the gloom of the stables, and breathed in horse smell. She could have grown to love it, as Johnny did, if he had let her love him. Instead, she had thought she had Liscombe, but Liscombe was crumbling away under Pemberton. Johnny was somewhere around the back of a horse and would peer out soon to answer her. She waited. She had not bothered to change. Such cheap wiles were finished. She had grown beyond them. And anyway, she had lost Johnny.

'I've got the vet to see.' The voice, low and gruff, impatient, still dear to her, emerged from the dimness. 'What is it?' His most lined, darkest face appeared from the rump of a brown creature, his eyes still the bluest of blue, as Lady Liscombe's had once been before her world had stopped.

'It is the new manager, Johnny. He is not quite as a manager should be, we think, Hawker and Chef and I, and perhaps Lady Liscombe should know about it. They are both threatening to leave and then we'll have nothing.'

'He'll need time to settle in.' He grasped the horse about its head and stroked its muzzle. The horse put its nose into Johnny's hand. Each leaned with love against the other. Claudine felt her heart give a little twist, from pain, from regret. She and Johnny could have been like that together and she would give it all up now, her keys and her power and her present burden of worry, if he reached out his hand like that, towards her.

'He's had time,' she said, 'and he understands nothing about Liscombe as we do, he wants nothing to be as Lady Liscombe wanted it, he spends too much time on foolish plans when what we need is people here first, as her ladyship used to say. Do you remember – bodies in beds? That's what we need before we can afford to spend anything, and then we must please them first, not fail to offer what we've advertised. *And* he wants to stop our advertising – the contact in New York, all the London things Lady Liscombe organized. She'll tell you, we'll have no business if we don't advertise.' She heard her voice rise.

Johnny, the horse's head happily nuzzled into his neck, watched the passion that transformed Claudine's face. 'I can see there's plenty wrong with him.' Her face was beautiful when she forgot herself. If she had not wanted too much of him! He felt a rush of desire for her, for the body that had so exactly matched his. 'I'll be going to see my sister before she leaves for the south of France. Sarah's latest treatment, you know . . . I'll give her your report on him and we'll see what she thinks.' He moved away to safety behind Tess. 'I think she took him on in a hurry, planning to go away somewhere warmer, for the child.'

'Yes. Thank you, Johnny. I do not think she can have known how he would be, destroying all that she's built up!' Johnny saw her framed in sunlight, her sturdy little body perfectly dressed in some new style that became her, a working outfit that was in accord with her position. She knew how to behave when it came to work matters. There was a flush still on her face. He dared to shoot a glance at it. He had seen some pertness before, but there was none there now, he thought, but genuine feeling. He watched her move towards the stable door. 'I say,' he said. He wanted to offer something more. 'Her ladyship has a very high opinion of your capabilities and does appreciate how much you have done to hold the place together, you and Hawker and Chef.'

'Yes?'

'Yes,' he said. He hesitated. It might not be a good idea to let her think too much of herself. But he would like one more moment. He had missed her in fact. He had been tempted, on more than one evening, to stroll across to the staff hall and put himself in her way. But it would not have been fair, he knew, to begin again on a relationship which could have no future for her. She would have to find herself a husband before it was too late.

He said, so that she would turn back and he could see the slender firmness of her neck and the pretty sweep of that red hair, 'She has often spoken of you.' He was about to go on, searching for something to say, when the boy Joe appeared at the stable door and the moment was over. There he was, all legs and arms and blushes. Johnny had grinned himself about the obvious pash the boy had on her but now heard himself burst out, as sour as an old man: 'See the lad about that end stable. There's oats dropped all over the floor, he's not fixing the bag on properly. I've told you both about it before.'

He watched Joe slope off followed by the girl, managing to make her walk provocative under the working skirt, and turned back to his task with a curse.

'Claudine!' Well away from his uncle, doubling back behind the bushes, Joe contrived to re-appear in Claudine's path. 'I say.' He had a bright patch of red on each healthy cheek. His attempt to grow a moustache had produced a bush with a chestnut glint in it, like his mop of hair that had the same tufty growth as his uncle's. He too, from his tallness, had a slight stoop about the shoulders from years spent on the back of horses but there, Claudine reflected, the resemblance ended.

'Yes, Joe?' she said lightly, for she felt light-hearted, in spite of Pemberton, because of Johnny.

'I say, Claudine,' he said again, 'what about a run out tonight? There's a new roadhouse down Wareham way, with a new band . . .'

Claudine's glance went down to his polished boots that reflected back a glimmer of her own image, all black and white. Joe stood his ground. She heard him take a deep breath and answered him, from pity, as kindly as she knew how: 'That would be so nice, dear Joe, but I don't think I can, not tonight.' And yesterday, she would have said yes at once, to comfort herself. An evening bathed in Joe's adoration was pleasant enough but now, suddenly, she did not want it. She had never cared for boys and with the image of Johnny still with her, she could not bother with Joe. 'Ask Jane,' she said, smiling at him in warm friendship. Joe was a sweet and nice boy; he would match very well with sweet nice Jane. 'I do think Jane needs a change, Joe dear, she's been working so hard getting the hotel ready and she's still worried about Sarah.'

'Jane doesn't much care for dancing.' His face had lost its blush, his eyes their excited glow.

'That's because she's too inhibited, Joe. Try and take her out of herself a bit, will you? For my sake? I like to see my staff happy, you know, and when we're open, there will be little time.'

'Very well,' he said stiffly, 'to please you, Claudine.'

'Thank you. Dear Joe. I'll lend her my nicest dress and you must teach her the new swing step.'

Knowing that his gaze followed her as she went slowly back across the stable courtyard, she resolved to help the friendship between the two shy young people. It would be the least she could do and she really did not need Joe's admiration any longer. Turning the corner she saw that all the swaying oaks were almost in leaf. She had not noticed that only half an hour before. Soon Liscombe would be in flower and with Johnny's help, she was going to see that Pemberton did not spoil her plans. There would be cars crunching across the gravel, guests spilling out all summer long. She was here, at Liscombe. Johnny had looked at her. He had smiled, in a friendly way. He did not, today, seem to hate her. She must not let herself consider there might be more, but she was filled with joy because the hatred was gone.

'Forestier!' Pemberton was shouting from the top of the steps. How foolish he looked, so long and thin and somehow unsavoury, ash about his tie.

'Yes?' She would not call him 'sir'. Let him run down the steps towards her. He *was* coming down. Claudine almost laughed. Very shortly Lady Liscombe would hear from her brother some of the horrors he was trying to introduce and something would happen that would not be to his advantage. Elation took her on past him and his mumbling about the clutter in the hallway. Everything would remain exactly as it had been.

She had only a few hours to wait. She could hardly believe that Johnny had gone so far. But he had driven up to London almost at once, it seemed, to speak to Lady Liscombe himself. And there, just as she was preparing herself for supper, was his voice on the telephone in her sitting-room.

'My sister says to keep your own department and the others going as they always have been for the moment. She's taking Sarah across to the sanatorium in the south of France and hopes to be able to get back for a trip home shortly. Until then, discreetly, you in particular are to keep an eye on things.' Claudine held her breath. Johnny had lost any suggestion of the formal business tone he usually adopted for hotel matters. 'My sister,' he had said. 'Of course, it's got to be done as cleverly as possible, she doesn't want the man's authority with the rest of the staff to be affected in any way, it would not be fair to him.'

'Of course, Johnny.' Claudine gripped the receiver.

'If you can, get a look at as many of the letters and orders he sends out as possible. Who's doing his typing?'

'We had a girl coming up from the village every morning but she left last week because he was always shouting at her and was never satisfied with anything she did, although he would never give her exact orders as to what he wanted.'

'Right, well, try and get someone else in. Do you know anyone who can type?'

'Well, I can a bit, Johnny, and Jane. We taught ourselves over the winter, for something to do . . .'

'OK, see that Jane perhaps . . . not yourself, of

course, you're too valuable elsewhere. I'll talk to you again in a day or two. I'm staying in town.'

'Very well, Johnny.' Claudine was breathless from the intimacy of his voice. 'I . . . we'll be waiting to see you then. I'm sure we can manage matters between us.'

'Of course we can. Goodbye.'

'Goodbye, Johnny.' Claudine held on to the receiver that had given her such sweet contact. She was not alone, fighting the world, fighting Pemberton. There was Johnny with her, and Jane to help, and Liscombe would rise like a phoenix from its very near destruction. Pemberton would have destroyed it, if she had not set *his* destruction in motion.

'I don't know how to be a secretary, Claudine.' Jane slumped over the nursery tea table, her eyes rounder and bigger than ever.

'You've only got to type and answer the telephone.' Claudine poured tea with energy. 'Anyone can do that. Where's Mary?'

'Down in the farm stables, watching the horses. And I can't, Claudine, I can't!'

'Once you thought you couldn't be maid even, but you could, you were the best. I'd like to have you as assistant now, you're better than Vera because you care about things. If you were not needed in the nursery sometimes, you'd have the job. I think we'll put that girl Monica to looking after Mary when she's not at school and . . .'

'Mary doesn't go to school yet, Claudine.'

'Well, she ought to, at least whilst Sarah's away. Don't you think so?'

'I hadn't thought . . .'

'Quite,' Claudine said wryly, crunching on a ginger

biscuit. 'We do a lot of your thinking for you, me and Lady Liscombe.' She looked with impatience upon the drooping form of Jane and wished she could put some of her own force into her.

'Does Lady Liscombe think Mary ought to go to school?' Jane copied her gesture over a ginger biscuit she did not want.

'I think so,' Claudine said vaguely, and went on before Jane could realize this was no answer. She thought: her ladyship would, if I could put the prospect to her. She said: 'I'll ask Joe to run you down to the school tomorrow to see the headmistress, then I'll put it to Pemberton that he needs a secretary, a proper one, on the premises, in such a way that he will think it's his idea – and there you are. Now, come on, you'll be late. Here.' She picked up two garments from the back of a chair. 'I've brought up my jade and one of my blacks for you to try and a comb for that hair of yours.'

'But what will I have to *do*, Claudine?' Jane rose mechanically, for she was used to following Claudine, and put a hand towards the black dress which had a glow of jet around its neckline. 'You know I can't wear black.'

'You can guess more about being a secretary than he has about being a manager,' Claudine said briskly, handing her the black dress. 'You just answer the telephone, listen to what he says, type out his letters – especially the ones about booking rooms because they'll be the most vital. Don't send the worst ones, the ones you think might cause trouble or unnecessary expenses for Liscombe, until I've seen them.' She walked with firm stride towards the nursery bedroom where Jane now slept with Mary.

'We can't go that far!' Jane gasped. 'And did Mr Johnny think I should work in the office?'

Claudine held the door and hesitated. She did not want there to be any lingering hope for Jane over Johnny, even if all was lost to herself. 'I suggested it to him and he agreed at once,' she said, permitting herself the small lie.

'Then I suppose I must do my best,' Jane whispered, trotting after her.

'You always do, Jane, that's the whole point. You've got to start believing in yourself the way I believe in you. Try on the jade first, it might just make your eyes a bit darker.'

As Jane stumbled into jade crêpe, Claudine gazed past her to the window where the sky over the Downs had that special evening light, cold with a touch of dusky pink. Liscombe sky in the spring. 'It really is most urgent, Jane,' she said, 'there's only a few weeks to opening. We can't waste time. You must get Mary to school and start in the office.'

'Perhaps then he will improve.' Jane, fiddling the fastening at the back of the dress, had let herself be convinced already. 'If we report to Lady Liscombe . . .'

Claudine thought: I don't want him to *improve*. I want him to leave. They, she, could manage very well without him. She was not at all frightened by the prospect. As Jane fluttered over her appearance in stark black before the nursery looking-glass, a little picture formed in her mind, of herself walking down the front steps by the side of Johnny who was saying, to a vague group of guests, 'And this is our Head Housekeeper, Mademoiselle Forestier, who very capably runs Liscombe.'

CHAPTER 10

Kate Liscombe turned the hired Wolseley in to the lane that was Liscombe Hill. Today she was going home because her brother had asked her to, because the new manager was upsetting the staff and steering the hotel off-course. Whether this was from incompetence or an inability to see what was truly needed there, Kate had not been able to decide. Distance and time had blurred her feeling of what the Hall should be, what it had been, although she knew that at the corner, where the lane turned up, her own life at Liscombe had begun and ended. At that place, she and David had first met. She had been sixteen, a girl on a cart, covered in road dust, and he almost forty, weary of marriage, of life itself.

Carefully, Kate edged the car up in fourth gear, pushing aside the recognition that at the very same corner, David and Aunt Bessie had met their deaths. She still could not bear to bring back that memory; all she could remember was the horror of not being allowed to see their bodies so that she could realize they were gone from her.

Sunlight was bright on the bower of trees above her, on the neat little squares of ploughed fields she had let out to tenant farmers. A faint distant sound of rooks calling came through the open car windows, a scent of foliage, of the dark damp places beneath the hedgerows. And there, at the top, was the fresh shock of seeing half of Dorset exposed under a pure sky. She had forgotten the sky of Dorset.

Home was here, and not at the nursing establishment in London where she had spent fruitless months with Sarah, nor at the sunnier place in France which promised more hope for her recovery. She drove on under the avenue of oaks, letting the rustle of leaves, the moving shadows, the sudden crisp crunch of the tyres on the gravel, tell her that she was home again. The beauty of the golden stone lying there in sunlight was a surprise quite fresh too. She had been away so long and not let herself think of it. She had thought of very little but Sarah's treatment, Sarah's exercises, Sarah's stoicism.

There was movement around the terrace and front steps, a glimpse of black and white in the hallway. The staff had managed Liscombe very well without her. She decided that she must first remember to thank them, because at first glance Liscombe had kept its perfection.

Hawker, in baize apron and shirtsleeves, saw her peering crossly round as she drew to a halt. Kate noticed one or two boys run off, sent no doubt to inform everyone of her sudden arrival. She did not move, sitting quietly with the engine cut. She did not want to come home to Liscombe; it held too many memories and she perhaps had not the strength to fight for its survival any more.

Hawker opened the door. 'Good morning, your ladyship,' he said, bowing. 'Welcome home.' He would not, she knew, betray surprise or any other emotion, but she thought she saw in his pale eyes – something, perhaps relief, perhaps pleasure.

'Thank you, Hawker. I hear you have been coping very well.' 'I hope so, milady.' There was, she saw, increasing redness around his nose, across his cheeks. She hoped he would be able to keep in check the easy path to drink. 'Is Mr . . . is everyone well?' She did not want to reveal the fact she had come to Liscombe for Pemberton, although everybody would guess it. She forced her stiff legs to stand beside him.

'Oh, look, your ladyship, Miss Sarah's little cat has heard your voice.' Suki, a dark gleam of tabby fur, was streaking along the terrace wall towards them. Kate scooped her up, nestling her face into the warm body and the burst of purring. She had an excuse for a tear or two of weakness. The cat scrambled down and jumped into the car, sniffling expertly along the seats. Exchanging a look with Hawker, Kate thought she saw her own speechless sorrow reflected back to her. 'When Suki has finished looking for Miss Sarah, will you put the car away?'

Now she had to gather herself together to face more. The old staff appeared for their welcome. Johnny leapt up the steps. Everyone talked at once, asking after Sarah, after the journey. They stood in a group and vaguely watched as Suki stepped from the car and set off along the gravel. Gladys said, work-swollen hands clutched to her mouth, 'The cat'll wait there an hour or two. She does most days.'

'Then she'll get cross, from waiting, and will come home. Chef has to give her something, for consolation.' Jane made an attempt at humour. Kate noticed that she seemed a little less frail, standing in the sunlight beside a glowing Claudine, and she had on a business-like outfit of skirt and blouse.

'I hear you're being very useful in the office, Jane, and Mary goes to the village school?'

'You'll hear all the news later.' Johnny did not allow her to wait for a reply, and she wanted none. Kate felt dizzy from a sense of strangeness there in her own hallway, though the same people who had waved her goodbye had gathered to welcome her and though the air was heavy with their sympathy. 'Send some coffee up to her ladyship's room, Hawker.' Johnny led his sister up the staircase. They left behind them a faint feeling of dissatisfaction. Each member of the old staff had a story to relate to Lady Liscombe and was anxious to begin it.

Kate did not ask for their reports. She sent for Pemberton almost at once, pausing only to book the telephone call to Sarah's doctor in France, and met him in the basement office.

'And then, your ladyship, I have had these estimates made up for a fountain to be constructed in the restaurant.' Percival Pemberton sat gracelessly at the desk he had made his. 'They're here somewhere.' He had not, Kate noted, felt it necessary for her sake to have the heaps of paper cleared from his desk nor to have a ready list of matters they should discuss. Within five minutes, he had rambled through housekeeping and kitchen problems, prepared to settle none.

'I think,' she suggested mildly, 'that you should let Miss Beale set up some kind of filing system in this office.'

'No time for filing, we're opening next month.' He threw some memo sheets, a sample box of cigars and what must be one of his own ties, on to the floor.

'I don't need reminding of that fact,' Kate said sharply, her gaze travelling with distaste from the ash on his jacket to his bitten fingernails as he reached for a cigarette and lit it without asking her permission.

'I don't care for cigarette smoke,' she said. A flush spread around his pallid skin and reached down to his neck where the Adam's apple trembled. 'Ah!' He stubbed it out and handed her a sheet of paper from a building firm covered with his own tiny figures down the column where 'For the sum' stated the amount of £502 15s 4d.

'How,' asked Kate, 'would our restaurant profit be increased enough to justify the paying out of £500? Do you know how long it will take? Have you worked it out? Will anyone come to our restaurant because it has a fountain in it, a useless fountain trickling water, a most irritating sound if I may say so, especially when one is trying to enjoy conversation.'

Pemberton's red lips dropped open. One pale fishy eye, that Kate had not noticed before, blinked behind the affected monocle. A sudden physical distaste for him made her voice rise. 'And whilst we are on the subject of unnecessary expense, there is absolutely no need to replenish the cellar stocks. My husband laid down a very adequate reserve with the help of our old butler. Mr Hawker is keeping a capable watch on it and he and I know we shall not need to buy in for some years to come. Unless a very special year comes up. Hawker will inform me if that should happen and I distinctly remember telling you, Mr Pemberton, that there would be no need for you to interfere in . . .' She hesitated to use such a strong word, but repeated it, for it was meant, 'To interfere in either cellars, restaurant or kitchen. These are usually the responsibility of an assistant manager anyway, but in our case, as we have such competent heads of department, I chose not to appoint one but you as manager instead.'

She rose from her chair to escape from the glassy stare of the monocle. Mr Pemberton rose too and bowed sulkily. A sudden terrible memory, of her son Peter's sulky face, made Kate take in a gasp of breath. She knew she was being unfair; she had chosen this man from a number of others, she had interviewed him, but now she could not bear to be in the same room with him. And she had no faith at all in the capabilities of a man choosing to destroy panelling that was centuries old on a whim for a needless fountain.

'I suggest,' she said, 'that you concentrate on getting business booked into the hotel, as I asked you at your final interview in London. You told me then you had a number of promotional ideas but so far all the ideas put into operation have been those of my old staff and they seem to have been introduced in spite of, rather than because of, you.'

Kate trod wearily back along the basement corridor towards Claudine's office. At least, she thought, housekeeping matters were completely in hand and would have had no interference from him. Once she had laid down stricter guidelines as to his expenditure, she would be able to return to her daughter.

Her only worry, she reflected, in the housekeeping area, was how she could tactfully advise Claudine on the wisdom of having a happy staff, from the merest daily woman upwards. She paused outside the sitting-room which was by tradition a housekeeper's personal sanctum and privilege. Kate allowed herself a fleeting smile, remembering her own sixteen-year-old self standing in the same place and Mrs Baker finally giving her a job as kitchen maid. She had been, even then, sure she could achieve more, and she had, surpassing any girl's dream by owning this very place. She stood thinking of her old struggles, brooding upon what life would have held for her, if there would have been so many sorrows, had she never gone beyond servant life, when the sound of Claudine's voice came through to her.

'How many times do I have to tell you?' she was saying. 'If you don't check the maids' work properly, they'll get slack and we'll lose our reputation.'

'We've got no reputation, we're not even open.' It

was Vera Cox's voice Kate heard; the two had never got on and Claudine should have vetoed the renewal of Vera's employment.

'We're practising for our guests.' There was a rattle of teacups from the room, the slam of keys.

'What guests!' Vera hooted. 'And I tell you I *did* check that lavatory this morning. Someone must have used it since.'

'Vera, there was no Bronco in it. It doesn't smell of Jeyes. It has not been cleaned this morning. Anyway, who would have dared use it? You are not doing what you're paid for. Your job's to check everything under your control, and if you can't manage to do that, you will not be employed here. I took the trouble to get you taken back on, Vera.'

'You don't know what the staff get up to when they can, and all for nothing. There's no guests in, after all, you can't blame them.'

'I don't, I blame you.' To the sound of Claudine's rising voice, Kate gently tapped on the door. Inside, Vera stood by Claudine's armchair, an ugly flush of red on her big-boned face. Claudine herself sat comfortably by the window, tea for one laid out. And she seemed not to find it necessary to stop for Kate's sake. 'Just as I've been saying. Once the staff get out of hand because we've allowed it . . .'

'Oh, Lady Liscombe.' Vera turned towards her. 'It's not fair, it's not! I can't keep the staff all keyed up when there's not much to do. *And* Mr Pemberton keeps countermanding my orders. Miss Forestier does too. You do, Claudine, you do!'

'Only when it's absolutely necessary, Vera dear, and we know, don't we, Lady Liscombe, that staff need to be kept after. Mr Pemberton wanted me to bring our experienced staff back, but sometimes I wonder . . .'

Kate smiled. 'Go and have your tea, Vera, will you, and send someone to collect Miss Forestier's tray. You and I will have a proper chat before I leave.'

'Yes, your ladyship.' Vera closed the door behind her, giving out a loud sob.

Kate sat in the second armchair, where Vera should have been, and gazed reflectively upon the silver tea-tray, on Claudine herself, in her black silk stockings and well-cut black suit, at her glossy red hair, her olive skin, all so well-groomed that she had the air of having just passed from a beauty parlour. She must, thought Kate, spend much time on her appearance. 'You look very much the part,' she said, 'and I am not at all sorry I put you in charge of Liscombe Hall housekeeping.' She paused. With businesslike air, Claudine picked up pad and pencil.

'You seem to think I have some instructions for you?'

Claudine nodded. 'Each night,' she said, 'I write out a list of tasks for the next day, anything to be re-checked as not satisfactory, anything to be chased up, suppliers and so on, the upholsterer perhaps if I am not pleased with his work, the carpenter if I have fault to find, and then of course on my rounds I notice something and have to remind Miss Cox of her duties.'

Kate gazed on, at the girl's sharp green eyes, at the perfect line of her cheekbones, her crisp use of English. 'Do you sometimes find something good? I believe one of your complaints about Mr Pemberton is that he fails to notice good work.'

'Good?' Claudine asked, frowning, one fine dark brow an arch of surprise.

'Yes, good, in your staff's work.' Kate paused again, hoping that Claudine would realize her point.

'It is not my job to find good, or ever to be satisfied, your ladyship.'

'Oh, Claudine, my dear, think. Maybe it is not, with suppliers and so on, their sense of worth doesn't depend on you. But Vera and the maids ... all of them, I am sure, working away to the best of their ability most of the time. They have no place here if they don't but ...'

'Certainly they don't,' Claudine put in. 'I dismiss anyone not up to our standards, Lady Liscombe.'

'I used to find that dismissal was not often necessary, although I suppose, Claudine, when I was your age, I was rather more impetuous than I became. I learned better later, you see, and it was partly because, when I came to have maids working for me, I could remember my old self, when I was a kitchen girl and no one noticed me except to criticize. I felt worthless and resentful, full of loathing for the old farmer's wife who employed me before we moved to Liscombe. She never stopped carping at me, she could not bear me so much as to look up at the sky from her window, so naturally I did as little as I could, skimped everything and even once left a pail of water in her way so she tripped over it. I was never so pleased about anything as that woman's cut knee.'

She laughed at the memory as Claudine stared at her in astonishment. 'And then you see, when I came here, Cook, Mrs Fellowes, she noticed how much I wanted to learn, how well I was prepared to learn, by cutting the beans into perfect even strips, say, or giving the raspberries an *extra* sieving so the jelly should be the clearest ever made. She made me feel I mattered at Liscombe and, Claudine dear, I think that you might do a little more in that direction yourself. Do you think you might be able to? It really is the only ...'

Claudine stared still and stuttered. 'I . . .' she began. A dark red flush spread up from the neck of her blouse.

'Otherwise, I could not have expected such a fine successor to Mrs Baker as you have been.'

Claudine bowed her head over the notepad. 'I have not thought very clearly, have I?'

'You certainly have in most things. I feel absolutely confident that you can run your department competently – more, with as much skill and attention to detail as Mrs Baker. You're young to have worked out how best to deal with people. Some never learn it. They go on blunderbussing their way through life, upsetting people who need not be upset. I suppose it can make one feel powerful, having a number of staff in one's charge, but to get the best . . . I only speak from long experience, Claudine.'

'Yes. Oh, yes, I can see.' The flush remained on the skin of her cheekbones.

Kate got up. 'I have perhaps had to speak rather more brutally than I might, but I am leaving soon, for Sarah, and I need to feel . . . You see, I know how much you have done for me, for Liscombe, in my absence. I rely on you too heavily, I think. I don't want anything to spoil the smooth running of your department at least, and I have had one or two mutterings from your women.' She saw Claudine's mouth give a little twitch of surprise. 'Don't blame them too much. With me away, they feel uneasy. I do too. I wish sometimes we had just left the reopening for next year.'

At last Claudine forced her eyes up and looked at her. 'No. No, we have been right, your ladyship, it will all work out. I know the staff have been against me. I am bossy, is that the word? I know I am, and I am French too, a foreigner!' She seemed to relax, giving an open smile.

'A foreigner!' repeated Kate, laughing too. 'Well, I have been grateful for my foreigners, both of them, you and Pierre. I shall see you both later in the day for another chat.'

She was gone. Claudine did not waste time reflecting on her words. Each one of them was driven into her mind. She went straight to the staff room where she found Vera, still red-eyed, sitting with Gladys. Both stopped talking on her entrance and looked guiltily at the clock. 'It's all right,' Claudine said, 'don't get up. I've been thinking, Vera, that there is no need for us to go through this charade of evening duty just for practice. You're quite right. And I'm wondering if you might get me a list made up of any of the things you think are not perfect yet and we'll concentrate on those. What do you think?'

Startled, Vera sat back at the table. 'There isn't many,' she began, and stopped. 'Maybe the lavatories? They maybe don't bother if they think they haven't been used. They must check to see. Then some of the curtains need the hems turning. We'll have the time for it if we start at once.' She turned a sullen face up to Claudine but seemed to warm to the thought of a list. 'Then there's some wear on the older carpets, nobody's thought of that. We could get them turned. The women'd be willing if it was urgent and we didn't have all this useless cleaning to do.'

'You're quite right, Vera.' Claudine felt herself force out a note of lightness. 'You get the list done for me and we'll meet for coffee tomorrow to discuss some kind of new routine. We'll have it in my room, nice and quiet.' Vera's mouth had dropped open in surprise. Claudine stifled her usual remark about fly-swallowing and thought she saw in Vera's face the same dislike, the same resentment, that she herself had felt for the floor housekeeper at the Imperial Palace. It had taken Lady Liscombe's quiet words to remind her of Miss Banfield. She would try not to forget her again.

Kate Liscombe found Claudine's report on her breakfast tray the next morning. With a wry smile, glad that she had not destroyed all Claudine's confidence, she read it carefully. She spent the rest of the morning with Mr Pemberton himself, had lunch in the small dining-room with Hawker and Chef. She rode around the Liscombe estate with her brother during the afternoon, had tea with her mother, supper with the family, Johnny and Joe. All the old staff watched her coming and going, whispering in anxious groups. Gladys was found engaged on unnecessary cleaning outside Pemberton's office door but no one was able to guess the way Lady Liscombe was going to act. When the news became generally known that she planned to return to France for the following Monday, only Claudine seemed surprised at the shortness of her stay. The others seemed to think that she had done what she had returned for; Pemberton's chastened air, the correspondence that was suddenly answered, typed and posted, his giving orders to staff only through their heads of department, all this convinced everyone that he was transformed into a proper manager.

Claudine, sleepless in bed on an unseasonably hot night, only thought that they were easily fooled, and that Pemberton would find his old ways once Lady Liscombe had returned to Sarah. And she would not so easily hasten back either. Perhaps she did not care that he wanted to strip out the country house clutter of the front hall and have it painted orange and black.

Nothing had been moved yet. Nothing had been *said* yet about her own report listing all his whims and foolishness. Claudine threw off her bedding, hotter with shame at the remembered conversation with Lady Liscombe. There had only been a few gracious words of praise from her since, about the fine state of the rooms, the excellence of the refurbishments.

She left her bed and put on her dressing-gown. The gloom of the dark hot night had helped her make up her own mind. She would set into operation her emergency plan, beginning that very moment. Night was the time for such things.

Jane too was sleepless and heard the scratch at her door, hardly protesting when Claudine led her back into the room and began to whisper, 'You're to get me his keys, Jane. Don't ask me why, just get them.'

Jane's mouth moved from the silent question 'Why?' to the spoken: 'How long do you need them for?'

'A few minutes, but no one must know or ever have so much as a glimmer of suspicion about either of us.'

'Go down and wait for me in your sitting-room.' Jane seemed to take a gasp of breath as she spoke. At the door, there was a little hesitation. 'You're sure you really need them?'

'Liscombe does. Lady Liscombe does, because she hasn't really seen yet the damage he's doing to us in spite of my . . . our report, Jane.'

'She can't,' Jane said, 'because she's too worried about Sarah even to bear to stay here long enough.'

'Then you've answered your own question. What are you waiting for?'

Claudine herself was the first to know how successful those night-time activities had been. After midnight the next day, she stood at her window behind the

Liscombe terrace and heard the phut-phut of his little Morris fade away under the oaks. Pemberton was speeding secretly off into the night. How typical of him that he should leave in underhand fashion. Silence then and eerie white moonlight moving the shadows around. He would not return, she was sure of that, though he had not been guilty of one particular act. She had hidden the cash, one hundred pounds in ten shilling notes destined for staff wages, in a place she would now forget but it was as if he had stolen it and if he had left so suddenly, it was because the questioning had made him feel guilty of other things, other thefts perhaps. It did not matter to her. He did not deserve Liscombe and because of her prompt action had now left it.

She turned dreamily back to her bed and fell into a tranquil sleep, because she had saved the Hall, and with it her own and everyone else's future. She felt not the merest suspicion of shame for only Pemberton had suffered and he deserved to do so.

Well into the morning, with the sun already high over the Downs, Johnny Tranter went gloomily up the basement steps and into the light. He was very late for his ride, with hotel trouble interrupting his life yet again.

Reaching the stables, he heard Jet frisking about at the sound of his boots. He gave her a perfunctory embrace and set to with the leathers, calling the boy to saddle up gentle Pegs for his sister.

'Johnny!' There she was, making an effort not to keep him waiting after the wasted hours with the police, her footsteps running across the gravel as if she were a girl.

'Let's get on out,' he said. 'Boy! Bring the horse for her ladyship.'

'I think I have missed this, Johnny.' Kate breathed in horse smell, watching her brother's expert fingers with the leatherwork.

'You come on home as soon as Sarah's well. Your place is here, you belong here where you've always been.' Johnny led his gleaming beast out into the sunlight. A stableboy appeared leading the docile horse Pegs who always seemed to have a smile around her face where age had turned the dark hide to white.

'Oh, Johnny, all the old problems are back with Pemberton gone. I would never have thought he'd be a thief.'

'Get someone else quick as you can. See if one of your London contacts can't lend you someone, or perhaps have someone just retired who might come for the summer.' Johnny linked hands under his sister's boot, a familiar action from past years, and lifted her easily on to Peg's back. 'By then, you'll have found a proper manager.'

'For a non-business person, you sometimes have some good ideas, Johnny.' Kate held Pegs still whilst he lifted himself on to Jet in one casual movement, long legs fitting themselves into place, hands taking up the reins.

The horses crunched off across the gravel and round the splendid line of stone that had been part of their lives for thirty years. Johnny said, putting out a hand to touch the worn corner of the terrace wall as they passed: 'Or we go back to considering the sale of the place if we can't pay for roof repairs and the usual upkeep.'

'Run a hotel without proper management or give up our home. It seems rather tough either way.' Kate, with Pegs keeping well away from Jet's hindquarters, also leaned down to touch the warm stone. 'I wanted all this for us and for Sarah. I wanted Sarah to be mistress here, even if it were a hotel. I saw her becoming one of those modern businesswomen. You know, independent, serene, married only if she really wanted to be, children or not, as she wanted.'

'You maybe should let the girl grow up a little first. Maybe just let her be a wife and mother like every other woman.'

'Johnny, she may always be in callipers!' Kate pushed Pegs on across the gravel and past the terrace steps.

'Don't worry about that now.' He tried to keep Jet at the same pace though the horse bucked at the terrace urns, at the high swish of summer wind round the west corner. Kate heard him calling out words to soothe her because he did not want to be worried by her worries. 'It doesn't mean no one will want to marry her. She'll always have a healthy inheritance whatever you do about the Hall. She won't be without suitors.'

Kate watched her brother's firm body over the horse, the back of his handsome head; his maleness would prevent him from ever seeing the arrogance of the remark. 'That is absolutely what I do not want for Sarah,' she said into the wind. She did not care if her brother heard her. She spoke for herself and for her daughter. 'I will never let her marry herself off if I can help it. I will fight to my last breath to make Sarah understand that she is worth more even though her legs are crippled.'

'What, Sis?' Johnny turned his dark head against the wind as Jet set off round the basement area and down the hill to the cottage by the stream where their mother waited for her morning visit.

'Sarah will *never* need to marry herself off!' Kate shouted.

'A spinster's no good to anyone. What'll she do with herself?'

'She'll run this place as I have.' Kate set Pegs to her best speed down the path trodden each day by Johnny's horses. She could see her mother waiting in the blue doorway. She knew, now, that she would not sell Liscombe; Sarah needed Liscombe because of all the men like Johnny who would think she needed one of them, who would regard her weak legs with pity and think her blessed if she could buy herself a husband.

She reined Pegs in so that Jet's great black body could fly over the stream and land with a thud amongst their mother's marigolds. 'Come on, old girl,' she said, leading her horse across the plank bridge. 'We don't need to show off.' She must not, she knew, begin a pointless argument with her brother, who had not always shown the usual male arrogance. He was only sometimes thoughtless, and there was, after all, no reason at all why he should put his mind to the subject of women's position in society. He had chosen not to keep a wife himself because he did not want the constraints imposed by marriage. He had been honest in that. And he had helped her make up her mind today.

'I shall keep Liscombe, Johnny,' she said, easing her leg rather stiffly across Pegs's back, tying back the reins and showing her a patch of fresh grass by the old pigsty. She forced herself to put on a smile for her mother. 'What do you two think of Hawker?' she asked, stepping into the warm steamy kitchen where her mother's kettle was on the boil.

'He drinks.' Her mother shuffled over to the range and fiddled with the teapot.

'He's a drinker.' Johnny was all male strength, striding into the room, flinging back his chair, seating himself, filling up the space between window and table.

'I was thinking maybe I could make him acting manager, for the summer.' Kate too pulled out a chair and sat down in her old place. She was suddenly very tired. She wanted to have done with all of it. She waited for the explosions of protest that were not long coming and let them pass. Very well, she thought. I shall make Mademoiselle Claudine Forestier acting manageress, and I do not care what any one of you says or thinks. That is how it will be because I cannot bear any more. She would not, she decided, musing silently over her teacup, have made the decision if Johnny had not had one of his moments of traditional maleness.

She called a staff meeting almost immediately on return to the Hall; there was no point, she thought, in delaying matters further and she had no wish to change her own mind, sudden though the decision had seemed. It was not sudden; it had occurred to her months before, when it had not been necessary, that Claudine would make a creditable manager, that her adaptability, her willingness to shoulder responsibility, her ambition itself, were all that was needed. It would have saved a good deal of trouble and expense, she thought, sitting at Pemberton's heaped desk, to have had the courage to appoint her in January. It had been Claudine, she remembered, who had suggested the time for reopening had come. Had it been with fore-thought for herself? Had she herself dared to imagine such an outcome?

Kate stood up. She would not, she decided, ask Claudine. The girl might very well not be truthful. There was about her an air of reserve, allied rather strangely with an eagerness to please and a steadfast willingness to work. David had said she was a mystery. Kate put a distasteful finger into the pile of letters on Pemberton's desk. Claudine would clear this with energy and speed. She would not baulk at typing correspondence herself; she would undoubtedly work far into the night. She would not shirk real decisions by inventing the need for false ones. And although she had responded well to the advice on how to get the best from her housekeeping girls, her main problem might be attitude to the rest of the staff.

Kate left the office and went down the corridor to Claudine's sitting-room where she had asked her to wait. She felt a flicker of interest within herself, wondering how the girl would receive the news. 'Claudine?' She did not waste time on preliminaries. The girl turned towards her from the window. She could not see her face because of the light. 'Your ladyship?'

'I have decided to appoint you acting manageress for the summer.' There was a clear intake of breath from her. 'At the same salary as Pemberton, of course, although I expect some people would ask you to do the same work for less. In addition, the same allowance for clothing, fifteen guineas for the year.' Claudine was walking towards her. Kate could see now the expression of astonishment on her face. With the treacherous thought herself that this was only for the appearance of it, that Claudine's true feeling was one of triumph, she paused to chide herself. She had no reason at all to think that Claudine felt triumphant. The idea of it had come from nowhere and was an unworthy one. 'You know there will be difficulties simply because you are a woman?'

'Yes,' Claudine said. 'But they are used to you, your ladyship.'

'I do not think it is quite the same. Forgive me, but ownership . . .' She thought, from the straight look, the quick answer, that Claudine had considered the matter before. But it did not matter. Ambition was what was needed. She sighed, from fatigue, for the tasks that the day still held for herself. 'I think you can overcome prejudice as long as you remember that you must do better than any *man*!'

'I shall do better than Mr Pemberton!' Claudine stood there as straight as a rod; no girlish fluttering, no astonishment now.

'Yes, that is to be assumed,' Kate said, gazing into the girl's eyes; she could read nothing there. 'Remember too that every member of staff, even poor Simon, needs to feel they are worth something.'

'You have taught me that already. I shall not forget.' Her voice was warmer now. If she had had time, Kate thought, there might have been much they could say to each other. 'Don't let any of them have any excuse to call you shrill, or a harridan, or a witch or worse. Keep your voice low. You'll need skill to deal with any man you have to reprimand, but you will have to find your own way in that.'

'I will, your ladyship.' Her face had softened, Kate saw.

'You can telephone me whenever you wish, and in your weekly written reports set out any serious problems . . .'

'I shall be as like you as I can!' Claudine suddenly burst out.

Kate smiled. 'Until you find your own way. Now, let's get the staff meeting over with and we'll run through the budget for the summer. If we can have an average 85 per cent occupancy until October . . .'

They walked side by side along to the staff hall

where the whisperings of the collected company stopped at their entrance and became a loud excited buzz at their exit after the brief announcement of Claudine's elevation.

The first person to offer Claudine congratulations was Jane, entering the management office with some timidity although one of the desks in it was her own. She sat down putting her fingers automatically on to the typewriter keys, looking blindly down at her note-pad where the last instructions were Pemberton's. 'Telephone the 'bus company and accept their conditions for the tours.'

Claudine sat opposite her at the desk that had been Pemberton's, separating the papers into different piles.

'Congratulations, Claudine,' Jane began. 'Is it . . . is it . . .?'

'Is it what?' Claudine's face sparkled back at her. Jane saw she had changed into her new suit of black crêpe de Chine and had added a little silk ribbon at the neck of her blouse that had almost the air of a tie. She often appeared with new items of dress to fit the occasion. Her afternoons in Dorchester seldom ended without packages.

'What you . . .' Jane could not form the words. She had noticed Claudine's expenditure of clothes before but now that matter too suddenly dislodged itself from the back of her mind.

'What I wanted?' Claudine finished the question for her.

Jane however had wished to say, 'What you had planned?' The very daring of it on her part made her gasp though she had failed to form the words. 'Yes,' she whispered.

'I had not thought of it, Jane. Honestly.' They

regarded each other over the space of the two desks. Jane knew how easily Claudine could use her words.

'Honestly, Jane. I don't mean I had not thought how much better I could do the job. I thought that often. But I did not dream Lady Liscombe would appoint me. I suppose because there are no lady managers in hotels, are there?'

'No,' agreed Jane, although she only knew about Liscombe Hall Hotel and the mutterings half-an-hour before between two waiters and the new sous-chef. She wondered if she ought to suspect the word 'honestly' slipping from Claudine's mouth.

'It is not going to be easy for me.' Jane recognized the underlying request for sympathy. Everything was easy for Claudine; she did not need her sympathy, and it would not be given, not yet. 'No,' she said.

'Will you help me, Jane dear?' She did not answer. She wanted Claudine to say something about the night of the keys. Feeling the eyes upon her, she did not flinch but gazed back into the greenness and the unreadable message contained in them. 'You have helped me before, so much.'

'Yes, I have helped you, Claudine, by spying on him.' Jane took a breath. 'And that night . . .'

'Because we are friends, yes!' Claudine broke in.

'Friends,' Jane repeated. 'Claudine, *did* you take the hundred pounds or did you just go up for the keys to search amongst his papers? And was it with the very idea that he would have to be dismissed?' It was said. She watched Claudine sweep her eyes across the mess on the desk and struggle with her answer, tapping a pencil and her slim shoe in unison. In discomfort, thought Jane. 'You didn't just take the keys to get more proof with orders and things from the safe?' She would not let it go.

'Do you really need to know, Jane?' Claudine looked frankly at her and laughed. '*I* think you would rather not know, for if you don't, you cannot be burdened with it. Isn't that right? Already, you are wondering whether you should have copied his letters, as if no one had any right to see them. But they did. Especially Lady Liscombe. Aren't you?'

She laughed again. 'I do know you, you see, Jane, and I know what's best for you. If you thought I'd stolen the money with your help, you'd be having nightmares about it. Anyway, come on, we've got work to do. Let us get on. We'll start by cancelling the order for two dozen cases of Château-Latour we didn't need. I believe he meant to drink most of it himself. Have you got your notebook? Say something like this . . .'

Jane took up her pad and began to write, driven by the force of Claudine's voice.

The first letter dictated, Claudine searched amongst the mess for the second in importance: the cancellation of a number of boxes of Partaga cigars which had been destined for the smoking habit of Pemberton himself. Tearing into a scattering of pieces the promotional letters offering him special prices for all manner of things he might well have ordered for his personal use, her mind asked: *was* this what I planned? Had the theft of the cash been intended to lead to this very moment when she sat at the manager's desk and dictated letters to a secretary? She gave a little laugh, gazing blankly at the price list for cheeses, each weighing sixty-two pounds aged by a special method for thirteen months . . . She could not have dared to dream so far! She looked up at Jane; she wanted to say to her: 'I only wanted to have him dismissed, to have his dismissal immediate instead of after his ruination of

Liscombe.' She said: 'I wonder if Pierre needs any more Stilton for the summer?' to Jane's stare. Her hand shook a little as she passed Jane the letter from the cheese supplier. 'Put that aside to show him later.' And her mind whirled on. She had quite forgotten where she had hidden the hundred pounds and the theft was of no importance. As if such a small point could matter beside the fact of saving Liscombe!

And now, quite unexpectedly, she had complete power over it. Her fingers, on the papers, trembled just a little. Had she not simply supposed they would manage without him?

Jane watched Claudine work her way through Pemberton's papers with her usual command and assurance. Nothing, then, could startle her, she thought, nor cause her the slightest unease; not even the running of this great place that would soon have dozens of staff and guests in it, all requiring guidance or attention.

If Lady Liscombe could see her now, so much the opposite of Pemberton, she would have no doubts about leaving her in charge though it was not usually the work of a woman, even if Claudine might have taken the hundred pounds in order to trick herself into the post. Perhaps, she thought, it did not matter if she had plotted and stolen, if she was using stolen money to dress herself in grand ensembles, so long as the end result were to be for the good of Liscombe.

She bent her own head to the work in hand with as much determination as she could muster. She too was guilty, if Claudine was, but she must put the fear to the back of her mind where the others lurked. It would all be worthwhile if this dream place could go on. How lucky she was, finally, to be part of it.

CHAPTER II

There was no group of staff out on the steps to witness Lady Liscombe's second departure. Only Gladys, up first for her own early morning tea, heard the car on the gravel and leaned from the staff floor to watch. Mr Johnny had brought the hired motor from the garages. She could see his dark head and long legs walking round it. He wiped at the windscreen in damp air that foretold a fine day. Then there was the new manageress, Mademoiselle Claudine Forestier, crunching across the gravel beside Lady Liscombe.

Gladys dried the mist she had breathed on the windowpane with her arm and felt an unaccustomed thump behind her eyes, she who never suffered from headaches. There had been uproar in the staff quarters since the announcement of the disappearance of Mr Pemberton and this new appointment. There were some who threatened resignation, Vera for one, two of the waiters, Sid Tilley, his underporter, the sous-chef. Gladys ticked off a mental list and struggled with her own feelings on the subject. No matter how pitiful a manager Mr Pemberton had been, she felt, he was none the less a man, and no matter how competent Miss Forestier had always been, she was a woman. Her concerns should be those of housekeeping only. Tilley was right in that, Gladys decided, and there was no denying it.

Rashly leaving the scene below, she scuttled off in search of aspirin; she did not care if she had not seen the final moment when Miss F. stood there shaking the hand of Lady Liscombe as if she were someone. She did not want to see it.

'You do realize you will have to put up with a lot of resentment?' Kate stood by the driver's door. 'Some will undoubtedly threaten to leave though they may have no other work in view. They will be overhasty. Talk frankly to them if you can. Bring the matter out into the open. Ask them to give you a chance! That'll startle them so much, they'll agree.'

Claudine gave one of her frankest laughs, showing small healthy teeth. She was again immaculately dressed, Kate noticed, and she had been at work in the office an hour or more. She understood that important point as Pemberton never had: self-projection, in management was one of the first essentials, and neither staff nor guests would respect anyone of sloppy appearance or lazy work habits. 'I think you'll cope. The summer should pass easily enough if the bookings keep coming in and you can keep the staff with you. I think they all believe in Liscombe.' She put on her driving gloves and eased herself with her usual grace into the hired Wolseley.

Claudine stood back as Johnny leaned into the car to kiss his sister's cheek and mutter something. He slammed the door and they stood together, as if united by a common bond, to watch as the Wolseley nosed into the avenue under the oaks. The sound of the little motor faded away as each stood with hand raised to wave. Silence. Claudine thought she could hear her own heart beating, because Johnny was near to her, because Lady Liscombe had left her.

'Well.' Johnny spoke first, dropping his arm. 'That's that.'

'Yes, Johnny.' She dared not look at him.

'You'll be all right?' He started to move away, with a crunching of boots.

'I hope so.'

'Her ladyship has faith in you.'

Seeing that he was beginning to walk off, Claudine turned the full force of her gaze upon him and said: 'I am a little afraid, Johnny.'

He hesitated. Perhaps, he thought, Kate was wrong and Claudine's courage now failed her, facing the enormity of dozens of staff to organize and keep to the grindstone, of the soon-to-arrive hotel guests who would be like all hotel guests: troublesome and pernick-ety. He let his glance move from the dark red hair, damp from the mist, down the smooth matt skin and parted lips, her slender form perfectly dressed in black and white, jacket caught at the waist. He tried to stifle the rush of warmth that spread from his loins.

'If I need you, Johnny, may I call on you? If there is some matter a woman cannot cope with? I know I shall have problems and there may be . . .' She gazed back at him, keeping her eyes on the blue of his.

'Of course,' Johnny broke in. 'You know that.' He remembered suddenly the afternoon at the paddock months before. It was as if it had not happened, as if there had never been anything between them but this pull towards each other. He backed away, muttering, 'Any time.'

Claudine flashed a full and open smile at him, and went back up the steps in a neat easy stride and a glimpse of black silk-covered legs.

Johnny stopped to watch her disappear and cursed himself, his hot blood, the afternoon at the paddock when he had thrown away his second chance, and her devilish female ways. What he must do now, he knew, was to keep as far away from the place as possible.

And he would also keep Joe away from it, especially if the boy's threats to run away to Spain to fight for the Republican cause were as empty as he supposed them to be.

Claudine made herself walk away from Johnny though there had been something in his glance today which spoke of admiration. Perhaps this new role of hers would make him admire her, could bring them closer together. She paused beyond the oak door; she had possibly been too open in her request for help. And yet he had not backed away. She walked on, glancing automatically around the hall where Tilley's boy was clearing out the ashes of yesterday's fire. Soon the daily women would arrive and the hall would take on a cosy glow.

Claudine took a deep breath, resolving to put Johnny to the back of her mind. She would allow herself to think of him only when they were actually together. There would be some moments, she would make sure of it. She wanted to feel his eyes upon her, in admiration, and something else this morning. Warmth. She paused, considering. She must not think of such things. There was this first, this hallway, this great building, almost hers, because at last she had charge of it. She had never dreamed of reaching this far, had she? Claudine could not remember now how far she had thought she might rise, but it did not matter. Lady Liscombe had chosen her of her own free will.

'Clear out all the ashes, Freddie,' she said. 'No cheating.'

'Yes, miss.' The boy, kneeling on the hearth shovelling ashes into a bucket, looked up at her, white dust on his face and hands. 'Madam,' he amended, and returned to his task with a hearth brush to get at the corners.

Madam! Claudine allowed herself an inward smile, and stifled it. She must not indulge in pride before the staff. Suddenly sombre because Lady Liscombe's talk was engraved on her mind, she moved to adjust the angle of the cricket bats laid as if by a careless hand against the wall. It had been her idea to have summer sports things out in the hallway, the bats, tennis racquets, a croquet hook. And she had others ready, many ideas for the running of Liscombe, for the presentation of Liscombe to its first new guests. She felt almost dizzy, light-headed from the vista of the months to come when she would raise Liscombe Hall Hotel to new heights of perfection and Johnny himself would find excuses to come and catch a glimpse of her.

She knew she must curb her bossiness but it was easy to be bossy when your mind worked more quickly than everyone else's. As she walked on with light steps, forbidden pride swelled up within her. She was so often right, too, and most other people wrong in matters of hotel-keeping, in the organization of work, in matters of style. How nice it would be also to become as well-loved as Lady Liscombe herself. She paused, wondering what her ladyship's first action might be in her place, when she had resentment to face, particularly male resentment. She stopped by the reception desk and the answer came to her. Lady Liscombe would *charm* them into giving her their support. 'That is what I must do.' She had not realized she had muttered aloud until the voice of Tilley broke in.

'You speaking to me?' There was rudeness, belligerence there. She did not respond with a demand for a polite form of address but offered him her most engaging smile, for she was going to begin with Tilley. 'Mr Tilley,' she said sweetly.

*

Two months later, though it was high summer, the fire burned comfortably in the hearth of Liscombe Hall Hotel entrance. Beside it a pair of gentleman's cricket pads stood as if left there by chance by the gentleman of the house. There was an air of comfort about the scene as if at any moment he himself and some jodhpured cronies might burst in baying for sustenance.

Instead, a number of guests were leaving the dining-room after their late English breakfasts. A sweet smell of coffee and toast lingered as the guests blinked into the sunlight glancing off the bronze pillars and discussed activities for the day. A large woman stood apart from the others of her party, her voice very loud.

'I said I wanted to see the manager.'

'I am the manager, madam.' Claudine bowed slightly to the very rude American lady.

'A slip of a girl?' The woman moved heavy jowls that were not flattered by the dark red of her lipstick nor the severe hairstyle that suited the finer features of Mrs Simpson. 'I say, Art, there isn't no manager here. No wonder we get second-class meat for our supper.'

Claudine risked a slight smile. 'In England, madam, in the country, rabbit is considered to be a fine and subtle meat, most health-giving and indeed a true aid to slimming.'

'You mean you lose weight on rabbit? Art, come over here. This girl says you lose weight on rabbit.' She eased an arm under the mass of her bosom and held up a lorgnette to consider Claudine more closely.

'That so?' The woman's husband, as lean as she was plump, ambled over to peer at her too. 'You mean my wife should try and force some of that stuff down?'

'Not only is it a light meat,' Claudine went on, turning the full force of her green eyes on the man, 'but it is one that can truly be considered the food of kings. Henry VIII, you know. And Chef takes great pains to follow the old recipes. What you had last night, Mr Eckberg, was the very same dish that has been served for generations in the homes of Dorset.' She paused, allowing a moment for Mrs Eckberg to mutter to her husband. 'The very same,' she said. It was true, but she preferred not to go too far into the matter. 'And the beef on the menu this evening, well, that comes from our own land which has been in the Liscombe family for always. If you would care to honour us with a second visit later in the year, we would be delighted to arrange for Mr Eckberg to follow the local shoot, as all the English aristocracy have done over the centuries.'

'My Art can go shooting?'

'The sport of kings, madam.' Claudine swept her charm back to Mrs Eckberg.

An exhausting ten minutes later, she had taken a second booking for the Eckbergs who went off to the dining-room to order cold rabbit for their luncheon. Mrs Eckberg did not care to be deprived of a meat that was health-giving and slimming too.

Claudine was able to attend to her next task, soothing the sensibilities of the attaché from the German Embassy in London. This guest had been offended by a chance remark of the barman whose father had been killed in the Great War. Two months of dealing with the whole spectrum of staff problems at Liscombe had taught Claudine the wisdom of Lady Liscombe's attitude. She had already spent time with the barman, to listen to his side of the story. Pemberton would have stormed at him in accusation, so building a resentment which would fester and grow. She herself might once have done that, thinking that the guest should come first. Now she knew that the self-respect of the barman was the most important. It might not much matter if the guest did not return, but she would have problems in finding a good barman who recognized guests by name, who knew their preferred drink and would produce it before they asked. And the guests who thought they were special enough to be recognized by a barman, were happy ones.

Next she saw, referring to the list she wrote out each morning, was the matter of an increase in cleaning staff. With the hotel more or less full all summer, the maids and daily women had to work overtime and it was becoming too much. There would be little illnesses soon because they were worn out. She remembered Lady Liscombe had taught her that one very busy summer when she herself was still assistant and railed against their absences.

She strode into the office where Jane was at work on the typewriter. 'Jane, telephone the dole office, will you, please? Say we want another daily maid who can come up on the 'bus each morning with the others, and perhaps another daily woman. If we take on a new one to do the basement, Mrs Bassett can start concentrating on the dining-rooms and the bars. What do you think?' She almost always referred any problem to be resolved to Jane, for voicing it was helpful in itself.

'A daily woman's only eleven shillings a week.'

'Yes. But say it's for the summer only, what's left of it.'

Jane made a note on her pad, without further questions, Claudine noted with pleasure, where once she would have bombarded her with queries in a search for reassurance. Jane, she knew, had grown in confidence with her.

'If you're taking on more staff, I need another *commis*.' Hawker, coming into the office with familiarity of custom, threw himself into the chair near Jane. 'That Austrian boy can cope very well on his own, I've only given him half a section, the area by the door, but he deserves a boy. I can put him on to the others' days off if he's got a boy.' He rolled up his shirtsleeves and mopped his face. 'Dear God, you should have seen that Dutch family. Cheese for breakfast, and beer! I suppose you could say that's following an old tradition if you like.'

Claudine laughed and sat herself down at her own desk, for a moment of respite amongst her friends. 'We could offer the Eckbergs a truly royal experience, have the staff – no the servants – all in the dining-room with them, put in a great table, everyone eating with their fingers . . .'

'Throwing the bones to the dogs lying around in the straw!' Jane wrote again. 'So I ask for another *commis*. And shall I put the need for the extra staff in the weekly report to her ladyship?'

'Yes, but she won't question it,' Claudine said with the sure confidence of someone who had received a contract confirming the permanence of her post that very morning. 'Is someone bringing our coffee, Hawker?'

'Yes,' he said, yawning, 'but Chef's not joining us. He's having a fit over that mackerel. He's made up some dish for it and now can't get it.'

'He'll sort it out. Someone can go down to Poole quay if necessary. But if it can't be got, we'll put a simple note of explanation on the menus. If you tell guests straight out that a mistake has been made, they just accept it.' Claudine ran her eyes down her list of tasks remaining.

'You've learned quick, Forestier.' Hawker winked at her as she grinned across at him. 'We're proud of you. Shouldn't be surprised if her ladyship doesn't confirm your appointment before the summer's up.'

'*You're* proud of me, Hawker?' Claudine laughed. 'I did not think I would hear you say that.'

'I'll also say you need have no fear I have my eye on your job.' He leaned back in his chair and yawned again, though his eye was sharp enough, looking back at her. 'Don't think I haven't seen you being careful I keep to my restaurant . . .'

'Oh, Hawker, I haven't done any such thing!'

He gave a shout of laughter. 'My! I like you, you know. You've got spunk and you haven't faltered. Has she, Jane?'

'Claudine has been wonderful,' Jane began. 'I don't know how you can tease her, Hawker . . .'

'Well, she's done a lot for you, Jane. Haven't you put on a bit of weight, and didn't I hear you dare to speak sharply to old Tilley the other morning?'

'He was making personal remarks,' Jane said, 'about Mary.' She flushed. 'I heard him. She ran out of the 'bus and he said something about her living in style, a . . .' She hesitated. 'A bastard child,' she finished.

'And you gave it to him good and proper, quite right,' Hawker said, 'but a few months ago, you wouldn't have dared.'

'No.' Jane offered a timid smile to Claudine. 'It's because I'm too busy now to suffer from what people say about me. Claudine has made me feel more confident. I think sometimes I'm a different person since she practically forced me to work in this office.'

'I told her she could do it, Hawker, because I knew she could, and because I needed her here, but I won't have Tilley saying personal things. I'll speak to him myself.'

'No, don't, Claudine, I'll manage him.' Jane got up to answer the door to the boy's knock and took the coffee tray. Claudine and Hawker exchanged a look of friendship and Claudine felt a surge of warmth inside her. Today, everything she had learned seemed to fall into place. She thought that, though sometimes her body throbbed with fatigue from her feet to her head and she could not sleep from exhaustion, there could be no better job than this, manager of Liscombe Hall Hotel.

CHAPTER 12

'I suppose you could say we've had almost eighteen months of success before Hitler started upsetting things,' Claudine said with some bitterness. She sat in the basement office with Jane preparing the monthly report to Lady Liscombe for September 1938. 'Even last winter we had 40 to 50 per cent occupancy. Now, these summer months, it's dropped to below that.'

'Ninety-two percent during Christmas,' Jane reminded her.

'Yes, but *no* advance bookings for next month. I know the Americans won't come for a while, and we can't blame them. No one would want to cross the Atlantic if there might be a war starting in Europe any minute, but I was planning on some of those comfortable English types we had last winter.'

'I can't think that anyone will stir from home even if the Prime Minister is supposed to have sorted out Hitler and given him Czechoslovakia to keep him quiet.'

'Plenty of people think it will, Jane!'

'Yes, but why are they building air-raid shelters and digging trenches in the big cities then?'

'To keep people employed perhaps?'

'Perhaps,' said Jane quietly. 'Anyway, shall I just write the truth for Lady Liscombe? I wouldn't be surprised if she decides to come home, you know. She can't want to risk Sarah over in France if there's to be a war.'

'They'll be safer in France than here,' Claudine said, slamming shut her folder of notes. 'They've got the Maginot Line to protect the country whereas it's almost sure we're all going to be gassed to death.'

'Do you think so, Claudine, here in Dorset?' Jane's face took on its old look of tremulous fear.

Claudine stifled her urge to get up and shake her. 'You'll have your gas mask!'

The shrilling of the telephone made them both start. Claudine picked up the receiver and listened. 'Lady Liscombe,' she mouthed to Jane and gave a laugh at the extraordinary coincidences that life held. 'Just as I . . .' she whispered.

Claudine clutched the instrument as if it could bring her ladyship nearer through the clicks and whirs of the international telephone service. 'Yes, yes, your ladyship, how good to hear you. You *and* Sarah coming home? To stay? That is good news . . . and . . . yes, no, very well. Yes, so few bookings I have been hoping for your advice. Ah. Yes. Very well.' Jane watched with dismay as the pleasure on Claudine's face turned to blankness. 'Yes, I'll get your rooms ready, everything will be ready for you. Yes, of course I will. And your mother, yes. Thank you, your ladyship. Goodbye.'

Claudine put down the receiver with a clatter. She was not able to speak at once. Jane said: 'What, Claudine, what? Is it Sarah? You look dreadful.'

'No, Sarah's fairly well, she can get about with the callipers.'

'Then what, Claudine, tell me.'

'Liscombe. It's Liscombe. She doesn't think there's much point in trying to keep going. She says if there's going to be a war, we must offer the Hall for the war effort, as a nursing home for officers, something like that.'

'Oh, Claudine, what . . .'

'So that's that.' Claudine pushed away her papers and got up. 'I'm going to tell Mr Johnny, he must know, and then the staff . . .'

'Can it be sure? To say such a thing and then if it is a false alarm?' Jane left her chair and held out a hand to Claudine. 'All your work, their work . . .'

'And yours, Jane. I think I could not have gone through some of the bad patches without you here to tell it all to. You've helped me see things in perspective.'

'I just listened, Claudine. You've helped me more. I sometimes think it cannot be me here sitting talking to people on the telephone as if I were a proper Miss Smith.'

'You're more than a Miss Smith, Jane. I hope I haven't always treated you sharply.'

'No, only sometimes, and I put up with it because you've had such a load on your shoulders. And because we've been friends.'

'Friends, Jane, yes.' Claudine gave her what Jane knew to be her best look, open and frank, without guile. 'And I wish we could have gone on sharing the load together.' She held out her hand. 'Whatever happens now, thank you.' Jane watched her walk slowly to the door. 'I shall go and tell Mr Johnny. Will you walk down and see her mother? She'll like to hear the news from someone she knows. Ask her if she needs anything, a woman to clean again, anything like that. Never mind her pride, tell her.' Claudine offered Jane a full smile.

It was as if, thought Jane, there had never been anything in her that was not straightforward and for the benefit of other people. 'I'm sorry, Claudine,' she said, 'about Liscombe, but one day, it'll all happen again, after this old war. I wish they'd get on with it, really, and over with.'

'Yes.' Claudine walked down the basement corridor, mechanically out and up the basement steps, not pausing to look in on gloomy Pierre who had foretold this disaster.

Even the extraordinary fact that Johnny hardly listened to her tale but instead asked her to join him for dinner did not lift her gloom.

'And *you* think there will be a war, Johnny?' Claudine sat beside him in the old Bentley coupé. He had taken a long route to the restaurant for dinner and had stopped on a hill.

'I do, old girl, as a matter of fact. That's why I asked you for a quiet talk. Shall we get out for a look at the view?' He threw his long legs from the car and strolled round to open her door. Claudine's heart stirred at the sight of him. In spite of herself, in spite of their unspoken resolve to keep to the kind of friendship hotel business needed, her body still stirred to the slight stoop of his shoulders, the hard strong profile, the way his blue eyes could smile at her, even his calling her 'old girl'. She had always known that she would love no other man.

'Is this the famous Bulbarrow Hill?' Claudine gazed about her at sheets of fern amongst clusters of trees and at the distant roll of blue hills under a twilight sky.

'You can see Bristol, two counties away,' Johnny said vaguely, pointing to the horizon where a misty sun was slipping down.

'I have recommended this view to guests many times but I have never come here myself.'

'You've always been working, I suppose. Shall we go and sit on that log over there?' He led her past a clutch of silver birch trees and in through pines, taking off his jacket and laying it out to protect her dress. 'You've worked like a slave, you all have. My sister does realize.'

'We have worked hard, yes, and I think we have all been tired this year, though I've kept holiday rotas to try and cut out the squabbling below stairs. I have loved working, Johnny. To have been given such an opportunity! I think I have kept her trust in me.'

'You have. I appreciate it too. I'd have more to do without you taking on so much, but I do think there'll be a war, in spite of poor old Chamberlain and his "peace in our time". Silly old fool! He seems to think Hitler is some ordinary bloke who can be reasoned with, and he isn't.' He turned to look at her. Claudine saw the lines of his face soften, the touch of silver at his hairline against his dark skin adding to the handsome air that he carried with him. She took in a gasp of breath. They had not been so close since two years before, since the funerals, and here they were with the early autumn dusk falling and the only sound their breathing and the crackle of twigs underfoot.

'Bookings have dropped to nothing so Liscombe is already suffering, whatever Hitler does.' She forced herself to keep a businesslike tone to her voice.

'Yes.' He smiled, staring into her face. 'And that's going to be the least of it all. Shall you go home?'

'Home, Johnny? I think my home is Liscombe now.' She wanted them to go on sitting there and never leave the place. The sun must have quite dropped for the air had become dusky. She could only see an outline of the dear face she knew so well though she had made herself forget it. A faint scent of horse, of cologne, of Players tobacco, that she remembered, filled her senses.

'Yes,' he said again. There was a little silence.

Claudine thought she felt the air soften and become still around them; only he and she existed in the world because Johnny went on: 'I think your heart is here.' It was not she who moved forwards, afterwards she was sure of it. Johnny himself put his mouth to hers and it all began again. He kissed her around her eyes and neck, bit her swollen lips that had yearned for him. They giggled a little breathlessly, hanging her dress upon a pine branch, following it with his shirt and all the other items one by one until they stood naked together in the darkness and did not need to see. He laid her in a mass of fern, cool and damp against her skin, and each moaned and gasped for the other with only night creatures to hear.

Claudine lay finally shaking, as limp and spent as he was, her arms around the sweet stoop of his shoulders. 'Two wasted years, Johnny,' she said.

'No,' he said. 'It was worth it. Anyway, you and me . . . I thought it . . .' He eased himself up. 'It seemed not a good idea, not at Liscombe anyway. And I'm too old for you.' He put an arm under her neck and lifted her up too. 'Look at you, you're covered in twigs and God knows what.' They laughed, brushing unknown things from bare skin, each touch a caress until they had helped each other dress, both trembling from emotion and spent passion.

Claudine felt her heart would burst with every touch of his fingers, at the feel of his arm under hers. 'Johnny, Johnny,' she repeated, trying to do up the buttons of his shirt, 'Johnny,' trying to put his foot into her lap to tie the laces of his shoes. 'It has been such a long time. Why have you waited so long?'

'Didn't seem right, not with everyone knowing, my sister and all.' He cupped his hands around the breasts under her dress and around the curve of her neck, the line of her cheek.

'Was it because you fell in love with Jane?' She tried to catch the shadows of his face in the moonlight.

'It don't matter now,' he said. 'I can't remember. She's only a girl.' He fumbled about for a Players Navy Cut.

'She's nearly my age,' she said, breathing in the familiar sweet smoke.

'Well, she's no woman, not like you.' He put one strong lean hand under her dress to touch the flesh of her belly.

'You thought you liked her because she seemed so fragile and helpless.' Claudine dragged back the memory of that time.

'Well, she did seem to need help, but I wasn't the one to give it.' Johnny honestly searched his mind for the reason why he had dreamed of Jane and rejected this woman of flesh and blood. What flesh! He groaned, withdrawing his hand. 'Two bloody years wasted,' he muttered. 'Better get going, you'll be cold.' He took her hand and led her back to the Bentley and the now cool night. Distant lights showed and a faint murmur from a car travelling along a road. He leaned her across the bonnet for a last embrace. 'We'll come here again,' he said gruffly. 'I don't like . . . not with all those people we know.'

Claudine let herself be put in to the car seat and pushed aside the matter of the two wasted years. It did not matter now. All her skin burned from Johnny's touch, her blood throbbed from his thrusting into her. It did not matter, because there was this now, Johnny beside her.

He started up the car with an explosion of sound. 'I'm not much of a bloke, you know,' he said, 'don't expect too much of me. Let's just . . .' He struggled. 'I haven't much to offer a woman.'

218

'Why not, Johnny?'

'I've lived through . . . other things and now I can't seem to stand restriction somehow. Can't explain it, old girl.' The car in gear and purring off down the hill, he took her hand in his free one. 'Perhaps that's why . . . anyway, can you stand me as I am and not try to be a full-time woman type?'

'I can't be that,' Claudine laughed. 'Not with Liscombe still needing me. If it's to be a home for officers, I shall have some sorting out to do, storing the valuable things. And shall I be a . . . what? An alien, if there's a war, Johnny?'

Johnny shouted with delight as she forced out the word for the first time, though it had been on her mind. 'When you keep that little bit of accent,' he said, 'and lose your air of perfection, that's when you get to me – but you won't be an alien!'

They had reached the bottom of the hill and were turning for home. Claudine thought there was something else she must tell Johnny; it was time to recount her journey towards this exquisite moment.

'Johnny, stop,' she said, 'stop somewhere. Put the motor off and listen.' She scrabbled on the floor of the car for her bag and opened it. 'Just recently, I have had to wrap it up. It was wearing so thin, the paper.'

'What paper, my dear?' Johnny, tender and patient, still filled with love, obediently drew to a halt by the laneside.

'The postcard you gave me.' She withdrew from an envelope the faded worn card that had given her life its purpose. Johnny switched on the interior light so that he could see it. 'Look,' she said. 'A view of Liscombe.'

'A very old view,' Johnny grunted. 'The Hall's only got one tower, so that must have been taken, let's see, before my sister bought the place and had the tower rebuilt, late twenties that was, so it was before 1920-something.' He peered across her shoulder.

'I know the date of it, Johnny.' She passed the card to him. 'Careful,' she said. 'Turn it over. Read out what it says.' She gave a laugh of delight watching his dear head bent over the precious thing which had led her to him. One day, she had promised herself, she would reveal it and here was the moment come.

'What? What is this? It looks like my writing on the back.'

'Oh, it is, Johnny, it is. Read it out to me though I know it by heart. You wrote on it the day before you left our village.'

'"Dear Claudine,"' Johnny read, '"this is where I live, in the Dorsetshire countryside. It is a fine place. You must visit me one day." Me?' he asked. 'And you?' He turned his head and a blank gaze towards her. 'Me and you?' he repeated.

'Yes, Johnny, yes. You and me, since I was four.' She grasped his arm in hers and laid her head upon his shoulder.

'It isn't possible!' His usual gruff tone rose in disbelief.

Claudine laughed again. 'It is absolutely possible,' she said. 'I was a little girl about four, you used to come to my grandmother's café . . .'

'You are talking about the war?'

'Of course, my darling. You used to come every day for about two months. I think your army was getting ready for a big battle or something, and every evening a group of you would come there and drink. You used to tease me. You used to say I was pretty and you'd throw me up in your arms. These arms, Johnny!' She hugged him tighter to her. 'I always thought I was not pretty, my hair was too red, I was too naughty, but you showed me I was pretty. No one else ever had. I was such a miserable lonely little thing.'

'One day you sent me this card, this card here, Johnny, to say I must come and visit you. The schoolmaster translated it into French for me but I knew I would learn your language one day. I knew I would visit you too. I dreamed and dreamed that one day I would, and I did! And here we are!'

She stopped for breath and hugged on, not noticing that Johnny's body had stiffened, that he was staring ahead through the glass to the darkness. She did not notice that he said nothing further, that she had been able to take the card from him and replace it carefully into its wrapping envelope and back into her bag. 'This has never left me all these years,' she said, 'this card and the dream of Liscombe and you.'

'You dreamed of me for years?' Johnny said dully. 'Years. What is it? Twenty or more years, and you came to Liscombe because you plotted to all that time?' Before she could take in his words, Johnny had wrenched open the car door and pulled himself from his seat, lighting a cigarette all with the same angry movement.

'Johnny?' Claudine did not understand. She too struggled from her seat and joined him in the cold air. 'Johnny?' She tried to catch at his jacket as he began pacing around the vehicle, kicking at the tyres as he went. 'I don't understand. We were so happy. Have you not understood about the postcard?'

'I've understood all right! I've understood.' He seemed to try and calm himself, standing away from her by the front radiator, twisting a hand around the Bentley symbol. A swift-moving moon showed the shadows of his face, the deep fearful frown that had replaced his look of love. Claudine stumbled on the undergrowth, trying to reach out to him. 'Don't.' He moved around to his own side. 'Here, I'm sorry, get back in. I'm taking you home.'

'I don't understand, Johnny.' Claudine, shivering beside him, waited until he had started the engine and roared off. She opened her mouth to ask for explanation though the fast beat of her heart told her she knew there was badness to come.

'Wait,' he said, setting the motor to a high speed, turning wildly round the lanes. 'Just let me think this through.'

He would not speak or let her do so until he reached the point where Liscombe Hill turned up from the main road, then he paused, letting the engine run while he said, very clear and cold: 'Claudine, I'm sorry. I'm not the sort of man who can stand the kind of passion you describe to me. It's unbelievable. You've had a dream of me that's not real. You have followed a false image. I tell you, I can't bear it, I can't bear to think of you thinking of me all those years. I thought we were two of a kind, people of the flesh if you like, free and easy, no claims, no stifling togetherness.' He took a deep breath. 'I didn't think it wrong to make love to you. I didn't think it would do you any harm. On the contrary, I thought it was what you wanted. And if I've kept away from you, it was because you were getting too close. That's the truth you wanted. I thought you were thinking of marriage, and I'll never marry. Never, do you hear me?'

'I hear you.' Claudine tried to make herself pitifully small. 'I did not think of marriage . . .' she began.

'Worse!' Johnny shouted. 'You thought worse than that, dreaming of me all those years. God!' Furious skilful hands worked at the gears. The Bentley roared off again up the hill and under the oaks. Claudine noticed dully that a light switched on at the staff floor and the night porter turned up his lamp at the window by the front door to see what the commotion was about. She thought: We have had no dinner, and I must never be near Players Navy Cut again.

'You'd better get out,' Johnny said. 'I'm sorry, I'm sorry, that's all I can say.'

Claudine gathered up her bag and forced her stiff body to move, struggling with the door handle. 'Oh, Johnny!' It was both a cry of distress and a plea for understanding. 'I'm sorry,' he said again, and started the Bentley up, thoughtlessly loud, crunching across to the stables.

Silence. Claudine stood in disbelief, gazing blankly at the mocking façade of the Hall. Liscombe to go. Johnny gone. She could not move, but leaned her head against the unyielding wood which proclaimed Liscombe Hall Hotel open and stared at the approaching night porter who was asking her if she were well.

She passed the days until Lady Liscombe's return in a blur of routine. She slept heavy dreamless sleeps and could not waken at her usual hour. The skin of her face, her fingertips, seemed numb but she did her usual work of winding the hotel down after the summer season. There were lists to be made of the staff to be laid off, of furniture to be cleaned, or paintwork to be redone.

She did not leave the Hall, did not look from the window for a glimpse of Johnny passing on his first and second rides down to see his mother. She sensed, however, that he had not taken them or if he had, had ridden down the back way, to avoid her.

Her last task, sitting at her desk on the afternoon of

Lady Liscombe's arrival, was to write out her letter of resignation. This done, she laid it beside Johnny's letter to her. It was also brief.

Dear Claudine,
I am sorry about the Bulbarrow evening and all that
has been between us over the past years. The fault is
mine, believe me, although I cannot understand why
you have not mentioned the matter of your home
story before.
I think it better we avoid each other from now on. I
very much regret hurting your feelings but have always
known we should not have become involved.
I feel reassured to think that you will one day find a
chap worthy of a fine girl like yourself.
　Yours,
　Johnny

She folded it again and put it in her bag next to the postcard. Her own letter she placed in an envelope addressed to Lady Liscombe. She then waited quietly until she heard from the open window the sound of Lady Liscombe's voice and some squeals from Gladys.

She got up from her chair and went across to watch. A stone urn marred her view, but she could just see her ladyship in a beautiful and certainly French ensemble of an amber colour. Lady Liscombe was turning to help her daughter from the car. Sarah's legs appeared first, wrapped about in iron contraptions. The legs seemed very thin and she herself very tall, grown several inches. Claudine felt herself warm a little to the sight of the child weeping at the vista of Liscombe, her home, and the way she set off, a miniature crutch under each arm, towards the statue of tabby fur that was seated on the terrace wall feigning indifference.

Mary's nose would be put back where it belonged, Claudine thought with a glimmer of interest. She herself would not be there to see Sarah take her rightful place as princess of Liscombe, she would neither see nor know anything of Liscombe again, so she need not watch Sarah, Mary, or the little cat now circling the iron legs, or indeed Lady Liscombe herself, though they would shortly have some conversation.

With everyone else safely occupied upstairs, she left her sitting-room and went down the corridor to the kitchen where Pierre, back on duty for evening service, was making himself tea.

'They are here,' Claudine said, seating herself opposite him. There was nothing to surprise him yet for she often joined him for tea. 'Sarah's grown several inches, but her poor legs look very thin in the callipers.'

'She is very brave and will force herself on though she hurts. It is the English stiff upper lip. I think even that little Suki has it. Did she let herself welcome Sarah yet? Has she forgiven her?'

'No, she doesn't like the irons.' Claudine accepted a cup of tea. 'You do not seem very cheerful. You are not going to rush up to welcome them home?'

'And you?' Pierre did not grin at her but dipped a sponge finger into his tea. 'You are usually in attendance.'

'I shall not bother today.' Claudine sipped tea through numb lips.

'That is not at all like you.'

'No.' A scent of damp vanilla cake reached Claudine. 'Did you not have a pleasant afternoon with your Miss Frobisher?' she asked, although the question did not come from a desire to know; it was mechanical.

'My Miss Frobisher and her mother have plans to

settle us in one of those villas near South Street, in Dorchester,' Pierre answered reflectively, sucking his fingers.

'They plan to get you to the church?' Claudine tried to gather some interest in Pierre's long-standing girlfriend.

'And before I have hardly succeeded in kissing her cold little mouth,' he said sadly. 'So goodbye Miss Frobisher. Her Wednesday afternoon off from the bakery shop has been quite wasted and now she will have to set her sights on another poor *crétin*. Two years I have walked out with her and what has it brought me? A few chaste embraces in the cornfields, a caress in the back row of the cinema, and her trying out her new name, Mrs Pierre Lecomte.'

'I could see she was not right for you,' Claudine said, pouring herself more tea.

'Mmm.' Pierre too reached for the pot. 'In any case,' he muttered, 'there is to be a war and I must go home.'

'You think so?' The war was of no interest either, but Claudine made an effort.

'Yes. It is the same as last time, Germany making threats, no one wanting to believe it. It could be the third time in what – seventy years – that Germany tries to overrun our country, Claudine, and I ought to help defend the Maginot Line, to stop them if they can be stopped.'

'Yes,' Claudine said, and suddenly allowed his words to have an impact. 'You will go back?' she asked, jerking up her head and seeing his pale face unabsorbed even by the matter of tasting his sponge fingers. 'Liscombe is not home to us, is it?'

'Of course not.'

'How soon?'

'I cannot tell. What need to stay here when we have only eight bookings tonight? The boy Kurt could cook for eight.'

'If there is a war, the Austrians will have to go home. They'll be the enemy now Hitler's taken Austria.'

'Yes. I think I will return to London at once, Claudine. Why wait? In the city, there'll be real, immediate news. How do we know what is happening in this backward place?'

Claudine did not bother to remind him how much he had loved the backward place. She did not bother to remind herself. 'I'll come with you,' she said, rising from the chair and sparing only a quick glance for the astonishment on his face. 'I have already written out my resignation. I only need to see her ladyship over a few essential matters. She will be able to manage the place herself from now on, especially if it is to be for officers.' She let her voice tail off. 'We could catch the evening train, Pierre. I don't think we need wait.'

'You will need to pack.' Pierre got up. He asked no questions, and Claudine was grateful.

'I shan't take everything,' she said. 'I'll leave a box of my things for Jane, she's much the same size.'

Pierre gave a whistle. 'Now, my dear,' he said, 'I know that it must be serious.' He did not smile but simply added: 'I will ask Joe to look after my motor-bicycle. Is it all right for Joe to know?'

'Joe, yes.' Claudine reached the kitchen doorway. 'But no one else please, Pierre.'

Walking back along the corridor, she wondered vaguely if she had seen Joe drive since his return from Spain. The poor boy had come back ignominiously with an injury which could be termed a war wound only by the most generous-spirited. He had shattered his right foot after shooting himself with a rusty gun he could not handle, in training behind the front Republican lines. Claudine thought suddenly: Lady Liscombe. She could, if she wished, relegate her lady-ship to the position of Dowager Lady Liscombe. Joe was still in love with her, or so he claimed. Even his time at war in Spain had not changed that. The flash of memory that came to her, of the afternoon on his boat when he had asked her to marry him and claimed he would one day be Lord Liscombe, failed to warm her.

She walked blindly on and there was another flash. It was as if she were in a dream or a nightmare. One hundred pounds in ten shilling notes. Where had that memory come from and why? There was the spot where she had hidden it; her feet had taken her there by themselves. She had put the four fat bundles in a Pemberton kind of place but no one had found them.

The store had a pleasant smell of cigars. She felt a longing to sit down in the cool scented place and stay for a long time, resting, but there would be no point for she would only have to get up.

And now on to the room that she had once loved, to the clothes hung in their careful lines, to the shoes in their stays and the small bag she had brought to Liscombe. That was going to be all she would take with her when she left it.

With Claudine and Pierre both gone, Kate Liscombe let the hotel trade run itself down naturally. She sent the Austrian chefs and Swiss waiters home and en-gaged a plump lady cook with maid to cope with all the kitchen work, once more reduced to catering for a core of staff. She felt a little wryness, watching Miss Boyle at work on the kitchen table where once she and

Mrs Fellowes had kept the old ways. Miss Boyle did not agree with fancy foreign cooking either.

She let the turn of the year pass, celebrating only the fact that Sarah could walk, with pain and weakness, almost across the width of the nursery that must now be termed the schoolroom for she was eight years old. There would be a governess for her soon, and then boarding school so that she should grow as much like other girls as possible. It seemed a happy sign when Jane made the unexpected request for a proper tenancy on the old cottage beyond the churchyard, and she and her daughter moved in after repairs were done. But she had then to admit that the days and nights were long without the old bustle of nursery life.

A week after the estate workers, the staff and her family were fitted with their gas masks, she faced up to the inevitability of change and offered Liscombe to the War Office.

And the moment came when Liscombe once more lay quiet and waiting.

PART THREE

PROLOGUE
Christmas 1938

After some hesitation, Claudine began to write on the blank side of the Christmas card, 'Dear Jane,' and then her pen seemed to go on of itself.

'You will see Pierre's desire to go home to fight came to nothing and of course there is still no war. We have taken a short lease on a restaurant. I am the waitress! We have mostly foreigners in, refugees. Pierre would like to be in the French area of London, Soho, but could not get one there.

'I often think of you and Liscombe.'

Signing herself 'Claudine', she reflected that, for the first time, she understood the tradition which had grown from the wish to keep contact with the parts of one's past. Christmas cards were just enough.

Putting it into the postbox with Pierre's card to his mother in the south of France, she could not suppress the little rise of hope for one in reply.

She had an envelope with a Dorchester postmark by return. There it lay in the doorway with the bread-man's account, a big white envelope addressed in Jane's schoolgirl writing. She opened it casually whilst Pierre was busy in the pantry and read the letter folded inside Jane's card.

Dear Claudine,

We are so happy to have news of you. Lady Liscombe said she hoped for word this Christmas and sends her best wishes to you both. If there is really no war, she says, then Pierre will make his name in London.

Everyone is well here, those that are left, but the Hall looks horribly empty and shut up with most things in store. Lady L. is not sure what the War Office might decide to use it for yet but she is of course keeping busy with war work already, being on the Billeting and the WVS committees. It is better for her to be occupied than brooding.

Sarah is getting stronger and only needs the callipers to go out, the poor darling. She's as sweet as ever. Lady L. asked me to let Mary go back to the nursery with her for lessons and companionship and I could not refuse, especially as Mary was only too willing. You were quite right to persuade me before you left to get the cottage on a proper tenancy in case I can't stay at Liscombe. It makes me feel quite grown-up again and now Lady L. has pushed me into learning to drive, you would hardly recognize me. I have some low moments but try to remember the advice you left in the note with the beautiful clothes (I am keeping them for best).

I too am doing war work, at the Red Cross office. I *drive* into Dorchester every day and almost feel I belong with all the other women working about the place. I often hear your voice urging me on, dear Claudine, and miss you.

Joe talks about you too. You are still his elusive dream woman, Claudine. He has not yet recovered from the injury in Spain. It is painful for him to ride, I think, but he refuses to let it show.

We both send affectionate greetings to you and Pierre for the festive season.

Claudine showed the letter and card casually to Pierre

and put them both on the sideboard with those from his mother. A faint warmth had come to her with the renewed contact with Liscombe. But she supposed she would not write again.

CHAPTER 13
September 1939

The little restaurant in the Chelsea street was not yet open for lunch. Claudine stood in the doorway blinking into the late morning sky. There was Sunday silence in the street and only a few odd strollers, foreigners mostly, and refugees noticeable from the odd cut of their clothes. It would be they who came into Chez Pierre later, wanting *saucisson aux lentilles*, or sauerkraut to remind them of home. They would pass over a reluctant shilling or two when the time came to pay their bill and would sit long over the coffee, for comfort and companionship in the city where everything was alien to them.

Claudine heard herself sigh and turned back into the dark room where the tables were set as Pierre had wanted, French-style with checked cloths and carafes for wine, baskets for the piled bread. There was no 'roll and butter extra' here and the menus were still written in his hand though it was weeks since he had left London for France and the French army.

'Good morning, *chère* Mademoiselle.' The chef, Mordecai, whom Pierre had employed to take his place at the stoves during his absence at the now almost-certain war, smiled with Italian charm and melancholy both at once as he reached out his hand to bow over hers. Impeccable in his whites, Mordecai breathed admiration, sympathy and some of the fear that today she was glad to feel too. She had been numb for too long. 'There is to be some announcement, the Prime

Minister will speak,' he said. 'Shall I turn on the wireless?'

Claudine nodded. The heat of the sun had left her. She shivered and pulled up a chair to the corner table where the wireless had been installed since their arrival the year before when there had been other feared news announcements. Mordecai sat solemnly opposite her, gold-rimmed glasses at the end of his nose, black moustache a shadow of Pierre's but reminding her of him none the less. Seeing his dark-skinned hand on the table by her own, Claudine said: 'We are both foreigners here. Shall you go home?'

'This is my home, I have a daughter here, grand-children. And you, shall you follow your . . . *monsieur* back to France?'

'I think I have no home, Mordecai.' Over the sound of the anonymous music, his sympathy reached her as he said: 'You might perhaps have, shall I say . . . married your *monsieur*, then you would have a proper status.'

Claudine forbore to laugh and thought without shame or emotion of the marital bed upstairs that she and Pierre shared. Pierre had assumed they were part-ners in business and life but she herself had simply let him assume it, having no feeling or wishes on the subject. She made an effort for Mordecai. 'Perhaps we shall marry one day,' she said, forcing a stiff smile to her face that had seemed to be set in a mould for so long. At the same moment, she knew she would not marry.

'I am not made for marriage,' she heard herself go on, surprised at herself; there was so little she had been used to express recently. 'I cannot bear the thought of the restriction of it . . .' She stopped, for those were Johnny's words coming out of the past.

Mordecai lifted a finger to his mouth. The music had ceased. And there were the expected words in the old man's thin voice. 'I have to tell you now that . . . this country is at war with Germany.' It had come. Claudine stood up. There were some cries out in the street. The news was spreading. There might be relief, now that the waiting was over. She thought that she herself might feel relieved but had lost the habit of allowing herself to feel much. The wireless voice went on. 'We and France are today . . . going to the aid of Poland . . .' Mordecai got heavily to his feet beside her. 'I think I shall soon be classified as an alien,' he said, in his near-perfect English that had mostly London in it and only a little Italian. 'But first I must put on garlic and some onion to fry, for the *lentilles*.'

He moved into the kitchen beyond and Claudine set herself to her morning tasks amongst the poor furniture included in the rent and holding no interest for her. All her life here she had had no interest in it. She had worked for almost a year, mechanically, beside Pierre, as hostess, waitress, keeper of the books. Pushing straight tables and chairs, wiping ashtrays, it was only now that she recognized this period of her life was to come to an end; she had been in a limbo. Pausing to turn off the dial for the wireless voice had reached the words 'May God bless you all', there seemed to be a short gap filled only with her restless movements about the room, when a banshee wail started up from the street. The air-raid warning. Her heart gave a leap of fear. She turned to meet Mordecai coming from the kitchen with fear in his eyes too but the true male's concern for her. 'Go quick,' he said, 'down to the cellar. I will bring our gas masks.'

He took two glasses, too, his plump body stumbling down the stone steps, the gas masks over his shoulder.

There was the space they had cleared between the wine racks, with two stools, blankets, biscuits. They sat regarding each other in the gloom. Some people had said annihilation would not be long coming and here it was. Claudine hugged her arms about herself and found her voice. 'Will there be gas and bombs at once, Mordecai?' She spoke to calm herself because there was a sudden trembling in her limbs. She could not believe she had let herself ignore the possibility of her own approaching death.

Mordecai passed over a glass of wine. 'If we are to die I think we might very well take our last sip of this 1919 Châteauneuf.' She heard him take a gulp. 'I shall go up first, later,' he said, 'and see what there is to see.'

The glass was cold against her lips and smelt of garlic from Mordecai's fingers. 'I do not want to die,' she said, drinking. 'I suddenly do not want to die.' There was a throbbing in her head as if all the months of numbness had left her.

'I am glad,' he said. 'I wondered how long it would be before you threw off your ...' He searched for the word whilst he poured himself a second glass. '... your sorrow,' he finished. 'You have suffered something, a bereavement perhaps?'

Claudine considered, sipping the warm garlic-scented stuff. 'Yes, Mordecai,' she said, for if they were to die there would be no harm of speaking of Liscombe now, 'a kind of death. I lost something I had dreamed about for years and years, since I was a child.' She held out a glass for more wine. 'The dream I had might have seemed, to anyone else, too far away, too impossible, wildly impossible for the child that I was. And yet I reached it, and when I reached it, it was all gone, slipping out of my grasp. Perhaps,' she said, clarity coming to her with fear, 'you can never hold what you dream about, even if it is a place which cannot move away or die, which cannot reject you.' There was a sound over her head, interrupting her. 'Is that it? Have they come, Mordecai?'

They both stood and listened. A definite movement came from the café above, and a voice called out, 'There is someone?' It was Siegfried, a regular Sunday customer.

Claudine ran up the stairs behind Mordecai and heard him ask, 'Have there been bombs?'

Siegfried laughed. 'It was false,' he said, 'a false alarm, so people are saying in the street.'

'No gas?' Claudine joined them.

'No gas, but is there chicken soup?' Siegfried's dark serious face lifted at his own joke.

'There is soup, Siegfried,' Claudine cried, light-headed from relief. She had never permitted herself to use a customer's name before. She hardly knew she had known this young man's name but now suddenly she grasped his hand. 'I thought we were going to die, and did not want to!' She was able to joke and soon everyone was joking with the release of fear. The room was full of people and gossip: there would be sixty thousand people dead from each bomb dropped, there would be hundreds dropped, starting soon, but it would all be over by Christmas. Some said they had heard there were already dead on the other side of London but there was jollity because none of those present had died yet. And there was still time, even now, for more talk and settlements.

Through the long hot afternoon when the café was closed, Claudine checked her blackout arrangements and for the first time longed for Pierre's presence. For almost a year she had lived beside him with a cold heart. Kneeling on their bedroom floor over the kitchen, she sewed the hems of the thick black curtaining she had put up according to official instructions. She had been as indifferent to Pierre as to the coming war. She had tried to ignore all government warnings too. All of it had been part of her own strange unwanted life in London and had given an added unreal quality to it. Now she must face matters. There were sandbags to check and lighting and chinks left by this hot heavy dark stuff that was going to close her into this room where she must lie alone and wait for the aeroplanes to start coming. Her heart would lift if Pierre were to walk down the street to her now and take over the sandbags and the blackout and her loneliness.

Afterwards, she thought that her first night in blacked-out war London was the worst she had ever spent, after the night that Johnny had thrown her long years of love at her.

She did not know then that it was to be the first of many dark nights shut up alone with her thoughts and the wireless. She was driven very soon to begin writing to her only friend.

Dear Jane,

I am worried for your safety and the safety of Liscombe. The wireless says nothing has happened yet but sometimes in the war they do not tell the truth, do they? They say the evacuee children are being sent to the country and every time I hear the word country, I think of you and Liscombe. I remember the sky and the trees and the air and openness. I think the dark is the worst. And, yes, I am afraid, Jane. So there, that is an admission from me.

You cannot imagine what London is like.
Everything is black, no light *anywhere*. It is incredible
that this great city should have no lights. It is different
from the country darkness. Do you remember we used
to sit up in the nursery with the window open to the
dark sky and it was beautiful, not frightening? I hope
you are not extra fearful with this war, Jane. You
know you are braver now and there can be no danger,
not at Liscombe, it's too far away and anyway they'll
only bomb the factories and the docks.

I expect you have been able to make plenty of
friends by now, working in that office. Here I seem to
have been too busy to do anything but be dogsbody in
this place and it is too late now, everything is changing.
I wish you were nearer, we could have our old
arguments and I could bully you the way I used to. I
could get you really smartly kitted out here before the
war shortages they keep talking about get a grip on
everything. Pierre bought me a fur coat last winter.
He said a woman needs one in a time of war and, yes,
you are right, only a true Frenchman would have
thought of it. He is stuck somewhere as a weather
forecaster instead of being in charge of food
arrangements. Armies apparently never put their men
into the jobs they know. They should have women in
charge, we could do better, because we would have
more sense.

Do you know, Jane, I heard your voice, as I wrote
those words saying: 'Well, you would, Claudine!' I do
miss you, you see.

Write to me, tell me that everyone at Liscombe is
safe.

My dear Claudine,

I showed your letter to Lady Liscombe. We were both so relieved to know you're well and safe. She says you must come here to Liscombe *at once*. She will not be wanting to worry about you all alone in the city when the bombing does start, she says, so you must come for her sake. She has enough worries as it is! Isn't she sweet?

And she does mean it. I need you too, Claudine. So many girls are joining up to help the war. Lady L. made me send for an application form for the ATS but I haven't filled it in yet. I know you'd *make* me. I can hear your voice saying that of course I can do it.

You would be safe here, and your old self, because of course nothing warlike has happened here and although we are supposed to black-out at night (Gladys has had such a time of it sewing all that cloth!), it is not the same. As you say, we are used to the dark at Liscombe.

There are a lot of troops about in the camps and tanks seem to be moving about the lanes, getting in my way. I think the biggest difference here is the noise all around, the marching of boots in the streets. It's an amazing change.

The other thing is the evacuees, loads of grubby children wandering about looking lost and filling the schools, getting into serious trouble for doing non-country things like throwing stones at birds and poking sticks at cows. Lady Liscombe has cleared all the Hall except for the East Wing, in case it should be needed, but I think the billeting committee would be afraid to put such a collection into the Hall. Anyway, she thinks she will move out herself soon, if the whole of the Hall should be wanted for any serious war business. She'll take over the three cottages that the old staff used to have, do you remember, Mrs Baker and Treeves and Cook? Well, after Treeves and Cook died, Mrs Baker went to live with some relative no one knew she had. I think, to my shame, that she plans to take me and Mary with her into one and I cannot find the energy to move down myself first to save her the trouble. In a way, I know I ought to do it but I would also hurt her feelings if I did. You'd make me do it, if you were here, but then I think of the complications, Claudine. If I do join the ATS I cannot look after Mary again as well, you see.

Talking of children, there are a number of new ones here I haven't yet mentioned. It's Lord David's daughter who's to blame – she's brought her brood here, all seven of them, rather nasty plump children, spoilt every one. They've taken over the nice rooms at the rear of the East Wing. You'd be furious if you could see them writing on the wallpaper. I daren't go up there and it's not my business but you can imagine Gladys chasing behind them with cloth and pail, all of a dither, and muttering to herself. Mrs Browne – Lulu, Lady Liscombe calls her, and it doesn't suit her, she's too fat and faded – just looks on indulgently and eats chocolates. She'll be no use if there's a war but she talks of taking the whole lot of them up to Scotland to one of her sister's places. Lady Berwick, you know, she came down once or twice, tall and rather glam but somehow tired? We'll be glad to see them go. I'll drive some of them to the station myself.

Hawker's joined the Air-Raid Precautions group already. Won't he be good at being officious? And Simon's in the Local Defence, pitchfork ready . . . Come and see for yourself, Claudine, you belong here in the same strange way that I do. We both so dreamed

of it as happy and it has been, partly, for us, hasn't it?
It's not been dull, anyway.

Just wire down the time of your train.

With best regards and love from us all.

Jane.

This letter moved her more than the one from Pierre.

My dear Claudine,

We continue to receive execrable food and I
continue to struggle with weather patterns about
which I know nothing and cannot bring myself to feel
any passion. I know nothing and feel I shall learn
nothing.

I dream of you at night, my darling, and dread
news which might come of England being attacked.
Keep yourself safe first, then see to the café if you can
because it is our future.

A thousand kisses to my own dear one. Keep brave.
Some say there'll be no battle at all, just this waiting
until a final agreement is reached somehow. But I
think the Germans are getting themselves ready.

My love to you,

Pierre.

Claudine read each one several times before beginning
the automatic tasks of the day which would have its
own momentum from the established routine. She was
brooding about Liscombe over the vegetable stocks,
counting onions and tomatoes, when Mordecai came
early into the kitchen. Already hot and sweating, there
was an air about him of subdued excitement as he
wiped the rim of his hat and threw a newspaper on to
the table.

'Something has happened, Mordecai?' she asked.

'No.' His soft brown eyes, looking at her, were none the less a little sharper, she thought.

'I have not had the wireless on,' she said.

'Not the wireless. I have seen something I think is of interest to you, my dear. But perhaps I am mistaken. Sit down. Let me make a real cup of coffee, my own *espresso.*'

'Mordecai!' Claudine said. She could not sit down. 'I shall put the wireless on, I have heard nothing.'

'Not the wireless,' Mordecai said again, 'the newspaper. Look at the last page, first column where it says Personal.' He indicated his copy of the previous day's *Evening Standard.*

Claudine took up the paper with impatience but obediently began to scan it. And there it was: FORESTIER, CLAUDINE. She felt her skin prickle, and read on. 'If anyone should know of the whereabouts of Mademoiselle Claudine Forestier, formerly of St Vincent-le-Comte, Normandy, now believed to be living in England, would they please contact Messrs Wilcox, Morring and Brownless, Eastcheap, London EC1.'

She forced her eyes to take in the words again. There was no mistake. Someone, somewhere, was looking for her, and it was someone from her former life, before London, before Liscombe, that she had very nearly forgotten about, for she had only been waiting for Liscombe then.

Mordecai was humming a little tune over the making of the coffee, but his glance, she knew, was upon her. She had to say something to him. 'This seems to be me, Mordecai, but I cannot think what they want.' She had found her most brisk, careless tone, but it did not fool him.

'I shall accompany you to this office,' he said, 'for the matter might well be something to do with your dream, no? And what is more,' he went on, not wanting an answer, 'we shall go this afternoon.'

'Oh, Mordecai, I don't think I shall bother and anyway, I don't need . . .'

Mordecai placed his plump body in the chair beside her. 'My dear,' he said, 'do not hide from whatever it is. You must go, and I shall come with you as your *monsieur* is not here to do it. I am only an old widower with too much time to spare who looks upon you already as another daughter. We shall leave at exactly three o'clock. Now drink this coffee because I cannot bear to see it wasted.'

Claudine drank the dark scented stuff that had been a small pleasure in her day even during the period of limbo that she had been living in. Here was that time come to an end. She had thought the war had ended it but there was something else left unresolved. Fate, or whatever, had decided she should not be left unscarred though the war had not touched her. She thought: Grandmother is dead and has left me her café. Then: she is dying and wants to see me but I cannot go because there is the war and she will die without any remorse being voiced on either side.

During her morning tasks, she relived a variation of scenes with the woman who had beaten her for stealing five *sous* from the cash box under the counter of the café she had owned and run. She had been most prosperous during the Great War when the soldiers had gone there in great laughing groups to sing songs and drink themselves to a stupor in case that should be their last night on earth. Johnny had been one of them and the dream of faraway Liscombe had begun. Before that, there had been a mean living eked out from the miners' daily pastis.

Her grandmother had smelled of pastis. Claudine

had a sudden clear memory, as she dusted the bottles on the bar between kitchen and café, of her grandmother leaning over her bed with the strong drift of pastis – and something else. She could not remember what it was. Claudine stopped dusting. How unwelcome, this memory; how much she had had to forget. And there it was, the one put so far away: the baby lying on the floor in a drawer and her grandmother promising money for her freedom.

But freedom was as hard to grasp at as everything else in life. Her eighteen-year-old self could not have known there would be other payments to be made. Here was another demand. Polishing bottles, Claudine recognized that she would have to go to the lawyers' office and face what she was going to be told.

There was a thin old man across the desk. He was saying: 'You are the grand-daughter of one Madame Hortense Flamand, of the Café Flamand, St Vincent-le-Comte, Normandy, and the mother of a child born on the tenth of September at that place?'

Claudine opened her mouth to protest but could not form the words. Her head seemed to swell and she felt an urgent need to remove her hat.

'This child, Paul-Edmond Forestier, known as Paul-Edmond Flamand, is now in need of care, and is at present lodged with Jesuits outside the village of St Vincent. That is since the death of Madame Flamand, I understand.' The man paused and turned over a page. 'I do not know the date of the decease . . . no . . . no . . . but the fathers have written to my fellow solicitors in Normandy with the request that the boy be removed to a place of safety in view of the coming hostilities. They themselves are moving south and sending any children with relatives back to them.' He stopped and seemed to peer at her in the gloom. 'I have made the matter clear to you . . . er . . . Mademoiselle Forestier?'

'Yes.' Claudine prepared to leave her seat. It was over. The buzzing in her head would soon cease and she could leave this place and this memory for ever.

'Here are the relevant papers passed on to us. This is all we have been requested to do and I shall write and inform my colleagues that I have carried out their instructions. Good day to you, Mademoiselle.'

Claudine took some papers he handed across the desk and muttered goodbye in return, folding them into her bag.

Mordecai took her arm as she left the office and remained quiet as he led her to a taxi and they returned to the café. He poured tea as they sat together in the silent kitchen. She was at last able to take off her hat and release the formal jacket she had felt obliged to wear for probable news of a death. Mordecai's unspoken sympathy beside her was such that she felt she must repay him. 'My grandmother has died, Mordecai,' she said at last.

'Ah. I am so sorry,' he replied, and stirred sugar into her tea, passing her sweet biscuits too, for the shock.

Soon it was time to begin evening service and so nothing else had needed to be said.

Then, with Mordecai and the customers gone, she was left alone in the hot night with London black and quiet around her and another demand for payment.

But she could not be a mother now. *It was too late.*

Staring at the papers, she forced herself to try and read; her eyes were blurred, the lamplight was too low. Here was her name all the same. Mother: Claudine Marie Forestier. And then Father unknown. Born 10 September 1931. Paul-Edmond Forestier. Clipped to this birth certificate was a folded sheet, signed by her grandmother, passing the boy to the care of the Jesuits. He would, then, have become a priest. Was that not usual? She forced herself to try and remember; young boys went on to seminaries and then they became priests.

A priest with red hair! They would dress him in black and put one of those black hats upon his head, to hide it, and crush his spirit – her spirit, that he must have had – and he would become as dour and life-denying as her grandmother, his great-grandmother, making the sign of the cross, talking of sin.

She knew that she was crying. But the tears were silent and did not hinder her progress down the stairs to the cellar. It was perfectly plain to her that she could ignore this demand for payment from the past. She had not given the solicitor her address. He should have asked for it but did not. Therefore, no one concerned in this matter knew where she was and she would answer no further newspaper plea. This would be an end to the matter. Soon she would be able to forget too; there was much that she had forgotten.

She had not, however, destroyed her grandmother's letter and had gone so far as to bring it with her from Liscombe. Behind the brick, itself well-hidden in a corner of the cellar, was the letter and her other secret from Pierre, the Post Office book for the £100 she had stolen to stop Pemberton destroying Liscombe. Her fingers acted of themselves and took out the book and the letter and she held up her torch to read it. It had no date on it nor any address, but she remembered it had come to Liscombe a full six months after her own plea, and the only one she had ever made to her grandmother, for news of her son. That had been made the day after the funerals when Sarah had locked herself in the old cottage with the cats so they should not be shot. How she had cried herself that day, at the sight of the girl's face, despair on it and determination and horror all together.

She was crying now. Claudine saw that her hands were wet; the scrap of paper her grandmother had condescended to post to her was wet too. She laid her face in her arm and slipped to the ground, leaning up against cold stone. But she did not need to read the note. She knew it by heart. 'Your son is leading a good Christian life. I have seen to that. Do not concern yourself with him. He does not need you. May God bring you one day to the path of righteousness.'

Now she must get up, fold the new papers with the letter into the Post Office book and put the whole back into the secret place. She did not want Pierre ever to find them. Theft and deception were faults he might not accept. None of it would ever come to light, she thought, wiping her damp face with a sleeve. Probably all of London would be rubble once the war began in earnest, and all of them blown to pieces. Then nothing would matter.

Stumbling as far as the kitchen, Claudine held her hands under the cold water tap at the sink and bent to splash the heated skin of her face. It was too late for her to be a mother. Water ran into her neck and down into her blouse. Cleansing water. She splashed on until she was gasping with the force of it.

Finally, breathless and shivering, she saw her own staring face reflected back at her from the looking-glass, green eyes all glassy, mouth an 'O' of horror. She did not want to look at herself and she could not stay here.

Tomorrow, she would go back to Liscombe; there must be comfort at Liscombe. She should never have left it.

*

The next day she fixed a notice to the café window: CLOSED UNTIL FURTHER NOTICE, it said. And she gave in to a rising sense of panic, half-running down the street, past the closed cinemas, the shuttered shops, the government notices shouting orders about blackouts and CARRY YOUR GAS MASK ALWAYS. Her own flapped clumsily against her hip and Mordecai puffed up behind her with a suitcase. She had refused a taxi, wanting to walk once more across Westminster Bridge as she had the last time she had gone to Liscombe and there had been such hope in her heart, for her dream was so close.

'It was here, Mordecai,' she said, stopping in the centre of the bridge across the Thames, 'I stood here years ago on my way towards my dream place.'

Mordecai, about to answer, she knew, to encourage her to offer more of her secret past, paused to wipe the sweat from the band of his Panama hat and she hurried on. She did not want to tell him any more about it, or even to remember the day. It had been grey and dark then, the river had been churned up into a dark swirling mass. Today there was a shimmer of heat and the water lay gently lapping, almost blue.

She set off again, hurrying because around her everyone else was hurrying and the beauty of the day seemed more ominous. Lorries were thundering across, soldiers leaning out to whistle and cheer. The bridge and hot tarmac trembled under her feet.

At the station, there were still groups of children being sent off, with their labels pinned to chests, for the safety of the country. Each had a cardboard suitcase or tied cloth bundles. There were mothers weeping and teachers calling out names. Claudine stepped carefully past a small boy alone by the ticket barrier, evidently lost, his face a white mask of bewilderment.

He was too frightened to cry, Claudine saw and a forbidden flash came to her, of another small boy in another country.

She turned back, elbowing her way furiously through the packs of soldiers, the clanking sound of their boots the new undercurrent of all life now. She could not go to Liscombe. She could not run away.

'I have changed my mind, Mordecai,' she said to his astonished hot face. 'I have something to do before I go back . . . I have no refuge to run to anyway.'

He took her arm and asked no questions, walking back along the bridge beside her, taking off the notice from the café window and starting luncheon service very much as if nothing had happened, although it had, Claudine knew.

It was the sight of the café, door open to the sun, a tentative Siegfried already approaching along the street, that helped her. I have this, she thought. This is all I have, this and some untidy matters yet to be resolved. Then she had to run out for bread because she had cancelled their order.

Routine took her through the rest of the day. Mordecai's gentle eyes were upon her, thoughtful but undemanding, and when he was gone, there was the darkness and her loneliness. She must, she knew, flinch from neither for she had to take charge of herself again.

Shutting out the world with the black-out curtains, she turned on the wireless so as not to hear the beat of her heart in the hot stillness, though she would have to get used to that too. She let the sound of the band music fill the silence that was to be hers. The very Englishness of the rather silly comedian, Arthur Askey, should, she reflected, getting herself tea, make her feel her solitude, her separateness, even more, but it did not. She had spent after all seven years of her life, most of the adult time, with such innocence. She liked it, it was what she knew and it was part of the life she must hold on to. What was this boy, who might have been hers, used to? She put his papers, the sole thread that was between them, on the table beside the teapot and the Post Office book. Did he have to rise at dawn, in the cold, and start the prayers and the singing? Did he have to atone for his mother's sins? Was he, even there, suffering the brunt of boys' taunting? Bastard boy! He must hate the mother who abandoned him to this fate.

The Nine O'clock News and Big Ben were booming out by the time she had finished. She had written a simple note to the fathers that, in view of the expected bombing of London, she was not in a position to offer her son a home for the present time. After the war, she thought, when everything was ordinary again, when she could be the woman she had been, confident, able to feel again, then she would try and be his mother. If it were not too late.

She was able, however, she wrote, to send a money order for the sum of £100 which she hoped would pay for the boy's lodging with them during the period of the war. She left the envelope open for the money order to be included the next day and did not re-read her words. Neither did she re-read the brief will which she had next drawn up. It left to her son all her worldly goods, the contents of her bank account and a half-share of any remaining lease on the café, which she and Pierre had jointly paid for from their Liscombe salary savings.

She would take this to the solicitor in Eastcheap the next day, send off the letter and money order . . . But what if the fathers had already left, to save themselves and one little red-headed boy?

Duty was done; she could do no more. And by dawn the next day, she stumbled down the stairs with a final resolve in her mind: to get on with the business of earning a living in wartime. For that, she would use what she had – this café, a business. Drawing writing paper towards her for the making of a list of things to be done, she wondered how she could have remained passive for so long. To live, she had always needed work. Only that had ever given her any sense of contentment or fulfilment. She needed it more than ever now. And she needed it to have something to offer a strange little boy who was going to look upon her with resentment and hatred.

Mordecai was startled by her first remark on returning from her tasks the next day.

'We're going to change. This is war, Mordecai, even if the bombing hasn't started yet. We're going to serve English-type food, because that's what's going to be available once the shipping restrictions begin, as they say they will.'

'English food?' Mordecai asked sadly, grasping at the nearest *saucisson* hanging from the kitchen ceiling and breathing in its scent.

'It's what people want,' Claudine explained. 'Egg and chips, pot of tea, bread and butter, tenpence. It's all along the Tottenham Court Road. I'll cook the egg and chips if you like and can we get one of those urns for constant tea?'

'We don't have to have the thick cups and saucers and the rock cakes?' Mordecai asked, as crestfallen as a big spoilt boy. But he was glad, she could see, that there was energy in her.

'No rock cakes,' she promised. 'We're just going to adapt, and we're going to work. There's always money to be made in wartime, Mordecai, and we're going to make some.'

'Ah,' he said, looking at her over the top of his glasses, a long quizzical glance that reminded her of Pierre. She turned away and handed him one of her lists. She was not going to think of Pierre or of anyone else, including herself.

So, as the winter cold made wartime London drearier than ever though the threatened bombing had still not begun, and even the buses had almost ceased to run because of petrol restrictions, Claudine settled into a new, uneasy life where there was work. It filled her time and tired her body. When the theatres and cinemas reopened, she kept open too until the last customer had crept back out into the blackness of the London night to make their careful way along the familiar streets by feel and sixth-sense.

She tried to make the café as much like a friendly London pub as possible, for pubs had never been so popular. Far from staying at home in the darkness, Londoners seemed to need to congregate in warm crowded places, with their lights and companionship. She understood that and was grateful. She learned to produce anything that was asked for, from French onion soup, guided by Mordecai and approved of by him, to the warm beer and Scotch eggs she had to deal with herself.

There was so much pleasure to be found too in the amount of money to be banked; she only occasionally realized the irony of money deposited when the banks themselves might soon be blown into oblivion.

When shipping restrictions made food rationing necessary, she did not complain, simply filling in the forms for special stocks allowed for communal eating places. She in fact became busier, but knew that all of it was certainly temporary and could only be some kind of hiatus in her life. There would be other matters to face when it was over.

CHAPTER 14

The postal service from France, they too in limbo
waiting for the real war to begin, was erratic, but
allowed through the letters from Pierre somewhere
near the Maginot Line with his unit.

Soon this will be over, *chérie*, and we can plan our
future properly. I am not sure I can quite believe a tea
urn and the warm beer. Can you not have the beer
kept cool by putting it in the basement and having a
pumping system installed to bring it up? Tea I can
accept, since you have seen where our business lies,
but warm beer, Claudine? If it has to be warm, then
please have Chez Pierre painted out and Peter's Place
put there instead so I cannot be associated with it!
  I suffer from boredom and cold feet and a cold head
from taking weather readings at all times of the night.
And for nothing, *ma chérie*, nothing.

Claudine read the letters Jane began to send regularly
with a mixture of her old irritation and a sharp nostal-
gia for the days of their common past in the basement
of Liscombe. There was always first of all the silly
matter of the fact that Jane must keep her exact whereabouts secret, as if the censoring office would be
keeping particular watch on the letters from ATS
ambulance drivers. She supposed Jane's position to be
near the Belgian frontier with the British Expeditionary
Force. Newspapers made no secret of the fact that

they and the French armies were waiting for Hitler's next move, but meanwhile Jane had the advantage of being important and newsworthy herself. Swallowing her scorn at the thought of Jane eagerly camping out with other English girls as if in some great open-air boarding school, she could not help a touch of admiration as she read her Christmas letter recounting the terrible cold that had spread over Europe.

I have been billeted with a farmer and they have given me a feather bed in the attic. There is thick ice inside and outside the windows. I try and push myself as far down in bed as I can and pull my spare vest over my head. There is no hope of having much of a wash. It is hard enough getting ice melted for the animals and the coffee. At least there is still that here, Claudine, and the husband has cognac in his for breakfast. I can understand that too (but I don't get any, don't worry!).

Just driving is difficult enough, though of course there are not battle-wounded yet, mostly troops with frostbite that we have to take to the field hospitals. If we were a bit nearer the French side, I might see Pierre. I would give up my spare vest for a bowl of his leek and potato soup and some of that liver fricassée of his. Do you remember? There are eggs here and slices of ham from the enormous sides of pork they keep hanging near the hearth. Their horse sometimes has icicles in his mouth, poor darling. Don't tell Sarah if you go down. Why don't you have a few days' holiday, Claudine, before it all begins? Joe would like to see you! He writes to me every week, mostly complaining about not being allowed to join in though he has begged all the Services to take him.

If you could see me here in the Army like other

people, Claudine, you would be amazed. I sometimes feel totally confident, driving along the French roads, map reading. The other girls treat me like one of them really, never realizing there is a gap in my life that I can't talk about even to you. No one knows about Mary, of course, and there is no need for them to know, as you have so rightly said. I just tell them nothing and you are right – it is almost as if it has never been. When her letters come, I say they are from one of the children I was nanny to, just as you said, and it works. I would not be here without your advice.

Claudine snorted to herself but nevertheless read the letter again over her breakfast coffee. The change in Jane's life had been as great as her own, she reflected, dressing in haste in her white overall which held the odour of yesterday's cooking and was another casualty of war shortages. There was no longer freely-available soap. She could not understand where it had all gone. For the troops, they said, but the troops had surely only the same need for soap as they'd had as civilians? Squeezing out a careful amount of toothpaste as instructed in the posters, MAKE DO AND MEND, she gazed at her own firm skin that had not yet suffered from lack of cold cream and wondered why it was she minded so much about Jane taking leaps and bounds towards the outside world. Perhaps, she thought, allowing herself a mere touch of the lipstick it was rumoured would soon be impossible to find too, it was because her own life had become reduced to this mean little flat and the cooking of 'sausage and scrambled egg, fried bread, cup of tea, ninepence'.

She felt sometimes that she had no further horizon than the doorway of Chez Pierre which she had already had re-named in red paint: Peter's Diner. The cold winter light showed her a strip of street, a sandbagged chemist shop and a notice indicating the nearest Air-Raid Precautions post. Another sign showed the way to the brick shelter everyone said would never withstand the kind of bomb the Germans had stockpiled ready for them. People walked past wrapped about in a mixture of clothing against the cold and would soon come puffing steamy air to sit morosely about muttering over the cold and the restrictions and the Great Bore War that was the curse of them all.

On the chemist shop wall there was a poster. PROCEED QUIETLY WITH YOUR AFFAIRS, it said. Claudine stared at it, rage in her heart. What if I run about screaming? she asked, of the cold air and the empty room. What difference will it make? If ever she stopped to think, if the early morning brought her a letter, even if there were a statement of her growing bank account too, she felt she would not be able to bear the long hours of work that awaited her. And today, it was New Year, 1 January 1940, and nothing had really happened. Staring again at the hateful poster, Claudine thought of the bureaucrats who must be loving their tasks, multiplying regulations and admonitions on posters and placards yards high that shouted at her. She would look at no more, would listen to no more, and today, she was going to ask Mordecai to take charge of the café on his own.

She was soon marching smartly along the street in the three-quarter-line fur Pierre had bought her the winter before when war had seemed to come a little closer. He had spent money they could ill afford on it. She was, she decided, grateful, although there was almost money enough in the bank to throw away on another already. Suddenly, that did not matter.

She kept her head averted from the foot-high letters demanding that she SAVE FOR VICTORY, deciding instead she would neither save nor be quiet, she turned into Oxford Street and the department stores which already had gaps in their windows. Where had it all gone? She did not care if corsets were needed for parachutes, lace curtains for sand-fly netting, mattresses for life-jackets. She did not need any of those things. Today she was going to buy herself a smart little hat and a smart little dress and she was going to go dancing with the man from the American Embassy who sometimes, often in fact, had supper at the café, just to see her.

Teeth gritted from cold, self-induced rage and bitter helplessness, Claudine pulled the cowl of fur around her face and stopped to consider the poor displays. Whatever she bought, she would look smart. No one was as clever at looking smart as she was. It was of no help to the war effort for her to deprive herself of her smartness. She had no intention of helping the war effort. She was going to go on making a good deal of money and tonight she was going dancing. The war had not even started yet. Let Jane help the war effort with her silly earnestness and the grotesque uniform and her transporting of the frost-bitten!

Whilst Claudine cooked egg and chips, sausage and chips and pie and chips, leaving the task to Mordecai only when she went dancing with her American, Jane went on carrying the sick rather than the battle-wounded to the field hospitals. As the cold winter eased into spring, there were mostly cases of appendicitis and toothache.

One fine May morning, however, she was woken from her billet by shouts from the farmyard. Racing to the attic window, she knew at once something real had happened. Below her, an ATS private was astride a transport motorcycle. 'Get on down, Beale, we're on the move.'

'Has it started?' she shouted back but knew that it had. The farmer's wife pressed a piece of bread and cheese into her hand as she threw herself on to the pillion of the machine, only half-dressed, with hat and knapsack. She had time to think she would be under orders for failure to present herself properly, dropped the bread into the farmyard dust and did not realize how little either would matter.

Private Callow slowed the motorcycle as they approached the country crossroads and as the engine quietened, they could hear another familiar sound, of an army convoy on the move.

'Hear that Beale?' Callow asked, wiping a khaki shirtsleeve over her face.

Jane, one foot lodged in the dusty earth, scanned the turn of the road where she had so often sped on her bicycle to carefree days cleaning ambulances. 'Can it be them already?' she shouted and had time only for a shock of surprise that seemed to clutch at her heart as a vehicle appeared. It was one of their own. Behind that lorry, there were others and in each a pack of soldiers they had known and waited with during the past eight months. Grinning faces leaned out to call to them, 'Blimey, women!' still a favourite with the men and then, 'See you back in Blighty!'

'Must be expecting to see Fritz off in a day or two. Bet they don't,' gasped Callow.

Their own ambulances brought up the rear of the convoy and they were gestured to follow on. Soon they learned, as the convoy bivouacked for the night, that Holland had fallen and Belgium was invaded by the

German Army. They themselves were going on up into Belgium for a last stand.

There were two or three days on the road after that. Jane could not remember how many. She had been duly reprimanded for being without full kit, was given no replacements, but it did not matter for there were no inspections nor any place to wash nor change, and the battles were not far off – they could hear them.

Jane watched and waited, hot and grubby under a clear sunshine unmarred by cloud. Her heart leapt uneasily every time a messenger roared along the lanes past them and on to where their disorganized units were based. Some of these disappeared in the night. Lying in her bunk inside her ambulance, she listened to their going, the thud of the men's boots, the careful revving up of their lorries. She prayed only that she might now, at last, be equal to the task she was trained for, so that she might earn her place beside the rest of the world as worthy. She composed in her mind, for comfort, her weekly letter to Claudine. 'Dear Claudine, Today we are near the battle lines. Perhaps we shall have to go and fetch the wounded soon. Everything is on the move, no one knows anything for certain, not even which way we are going. I am trying not to panic. I wonder now if I can manage to do what I must. I wish you were hear to shout at me that of course I can . . .'

Then there was someone banging on the side of the vehicle. 'Get up, Beale, we're moving back.'

She could not have heard the words very clearly, for when she had scrambled in the half light into the front of the vehicle with her co-driver Corporal Jennings, she said, fatuously she saw afterwards, 'I've never been to Belgium.'

'Well, you won't be going there now, won't be no

Belgium once Hitler makes it German, and we're moving *back*, idiot! Trust you to get it wrong.'

Jane pulled on her hat and unfolded the route map. 'Which way to Blighty, then, Corporal?'

'God, Beale, fancy joking when your army's going into retreat!' Jennings pulled on her own hat and grasped the wheel with her capable hands, a solid, big-boned girl. Jane saw that Jennings would not fail now, as she might. 'Sorry, Corporal,' she said weakly.

'Look, we just follow the others and if there's any wounded, we pick them up. Even you can't make a mistake now.'

They had rattled on, without real news, in a convoy as the sun beat down and the country roads were turned to dust. There was a stop ordered and everyone was out making tea by the roadside when Jane suddenly noticed that an officer was standing in the road, looking into the sky. He began to shout, gesticulating wildly.

'Planes! Get down. Get down, everyone!' Jane shaded her eyes to look up.

'Get under cover you fool.'

Jennings's arm shot out to grab hers and she found herself face down on some tussocky grass that made her sneeze. She pressed her face closer and felt for the humble protection of her tin hat as the whining that was so familiar to them all from the newsreels back at home became a shriek. She felt a rush of air. The field around moved. Earth rose and fell. The whine became a shriek and then there was a fierce and violent rat-tat. Machine-gun fire raining down on them.

There were some dead but she herself had not died. Jane, rousing herself, feeling along her stiff limbs, saw hazily that around the field and the road where her ambulance seemed whole, there were bodies. In the grass beside her was blood. Jennings's blood. There was Jennings with a hole torn across the back of her neck. 'Goodbye, Jennings,' she said and knew that she would be the least of it. Their officer was already on her feet and calling out to her.

'Private, your ambulance seems all right, try and get it started up with Jennings whilst I get a party to load it with the wounded.'

'Jennings is dead, Major.' Jane got to her feet, earth in her mouth and scratches on her skin but with her hat on straight. The very words, the cool announcement of death, seemed to give her strength. 'But I'll start it up and be ready to move when you say.'

Afterwards, she remembered she had the engine running as smoothly as before and was about to go to the help of the first stretcherload being placed in it when the planes came back. She had no time to see what was happening behind her but she heard her Major shout: 'Try and get the vehicle to safety, Beale,' and she did. Her fingers seemed to find the skills she had known they had. She made straight for a field where there was corn in bud and beyond, thirty yards off, a clutch of trees that promised shelter. Making a snap decision, she turned the wheel and raced for it. She and the ambulance would have been saved, she thought much later, when she had time to try and remember, but a clutch of roots in the dry earth had made something crack underneath. What she knew, then, was that her head was filled with the sound of the shrieking from the fighter planes, then the ripping machine-gun fire, and then no more. When she came back to consciousness, there was silence, and dark coolness from the trees overhead. She was lodged against the window rim of the ambulance, her head stiff, a bruise upon her forehead. She listened, waiting for the sound of German troops. Her watch told her that she had been inside the vehicle like that for perhaps an hour. It was half-past four. They had stopped for tea at half-past three, because that was tea-time. Peering cautiously about her, she saw that she was alone in the cluster of trees. A faint glimmer of lightness told her that the corn field was not far off. How extraordinary, she thought, that I should remember where I am. Now I must be sensible. She was perhaps in enemy territory but would not know yet. With her uniform, they would make her a prisoner-of-war and then she would have nothing to worry about for she would be taken care of.

Putting her legs stiffly out, and carefully, easing the rest of her on to the ground, she allowed herself only a tiny start of fear at the sound of a grunt, a man's grunt, in the wood beyond.

She looked straight towards the sound and searched behind her on the seat for her hat which would make her more official. And then she saw that a man in British regimental uniform was dragging himself along the path towards her. He had on a clerical collar underneath the uniform. He was giving out the little grunts as he eased himself along. In the dusky light between the trees, she could see that there was sweat on the yellow skin of his face. She had time to register all this as she walked towards him and called out, for there was nothing to fear now; they would be prisoners-of-war together. 'Father? Wait, let me go and get help.'

The man looked up at her, easing his bulk towards a tree trunk. 'Help, my child? I may be beyond help.'

'Of course you are not!' She found herself able to run towards him, but stopped. The man was her uncle.

She saw that it was he from the skin in folds around the collar that was the symbol of a man of God. And there was the same pleading in his eyes that were a kind of glassy brown without depth, mask-like, as they would have to be so that no one could see into them. It was the same, all of it, as it had been years before when he had gone pleading and cajoling into her bedroom and reached out a hand towards her. He was reaching out to her now and there was recognition, for he said: 'Is it Jane? Can it be Jane? Thanks be to God. Run for help, child, run.'

It was the same but different. Jane circled round the body on the ground. He could not get up. His hand had moved to clutch at the root of a tree. His breath came in gasps. She circled on round him and saw that one of his legs, the right one, was a bloody mass and he could not move.

Into her heart came a leap of joy. Overhead, it seemed at the very same moment, there was a piercing shriek from the sky. The fighters were back with their guns and she was glad, for this man was surely going to die; the machine-gun fire was coming just so that he would die before her.

Round and round his body she went, watching him try to lift himself up to see her. And in the silent wood, she laughed. She heard herself laugh and he groaned.

'Jane! What a happy coincidence. Your mother will not believe it. Are there lorries still on the road, my dear? Is there any sound of our own guns fighting back?'

'What if they are?' she heard herself say and paused by his head that had rolled back into the earth. 'I think I can hear our guns, yes, but the German planes will get them as they'll get us.'

Flesh bulged over the white of his collar, flesh that had touched hers. There was dirt on it, and blood. She did not want the planes to come back too soon. She did not want him to die quickly.

In London, the newspaper headlines were clear and stark. BELGIAN ARMY SURRENDERS, they said. Reading them, Claudine thought bitterly that she was not surprised. Pushing the paper across to Mordecai at their coffee break, she said, 'The Belgians always were cowards. We French never trusted them, and we were right, you see!'

'Ah,' said Mordecai, older and wiser, 'you have suddenly found your Frenchness?' He peered over his glasses at the map on the front page which showed that the British and French armies had been reduced to holding a narrow strip of land only thirty miles long. Little swastika symbols showed where the Nazi troops had moved across the Belgian border and were pushing down into France. 'And I thought it was the British always thinking the *French* cowards,' he murmured, 'but it says here they are making a glorious rearguard action together.'

'Rearguard!' Claudine exploded, moving restlessly around the kitchen. 'Doesn't that mean they must be retreating? What about the Maginot Line, and where can Pierre be?' She thought blankly: how far south did the Jesuits go?

'And what about your friend in the ladies' army?'

'Jane!' Claudine pulled out a chair and finally sat down with her now-cold coffee. 'I can imagine her somewhere, frightened half to death. Now it isn't a game, is it? All that English jolliness, doing their bit. She'll be cowering somewhere sobbing and they'll take her prisoner or . . .' She pushed aside a sudden picture that flashed into her mind. 'What *is* a rearguard action, Mordecai?' she said, and did not wait for an answer, going on so that she could shut out the image of Jane suffering what other women had suffered in other wars. 'Surely they've already taken the women ambulance drivers to a place of safety?' Her heart turned over because another image came all unbidden, of Pierre somewhere with a limb torn off, fighting for his next breath. She got up for the memory of his warm amber eyes looking at her sadly and gently, knowing she did not love him, made her take a gasp of breath. 'Thank goodness we are busy here,' she said. 'Is this batter risen enough?' She peered into a gas stove. She had never had any reply from the Jesuits after her money order, though she had written twice more . . .

Mordecai, going to the stove with an oven cloth, took out the dish of light batter where rows of sausages lay curled in a perfection of brown crispiness. 'Maybe one day soon we shall be cooking sauerkraut again, for the occupying forces. German soldiers.' He dropped the platter and moist tears joined the sweat on his skin. 'If they are so close to the French coast, maybe it will not take them long to get their foul tanks across here.'

Claudine stared with horror at the sausages. 'If they do, Mordecai, we shall never serve them. We'll get rifles and go into the cellar and shoot out at them. But you don't think Churchill and the British Army will surrender this country?'

'Most of the British Army is out there fighting with the French. They can't be here at the same time.' Mordecai wiped his face with a kitchen cloth and shuffled heavily across to fetch his frying pans.

'Well,' Claudine said, throwing the dregs of their coffee into the sink and turning swiftly away to begin a whirlwind of mechanical activity that would last the day, 'someone will have to stop them, somehow. What have all the shortages, all the savings, all that damn making-do everyone's been so proud of – what's it all been for if it doesn't stop them coming here?'

Joe Tranter, in his bedroom in the terraced cottage that now housed him and his grandmother since their own had been given over to the War Office, turned up the volume of the wireless. His heart beating with rage and impotence, he heard the call and listened again as it was repeated.

'All owners of small craft are asked to report to their nearest naval port or to the port of Dover . . .'

'I have a small craft,' he shouted back and ran to the bathroom, all tangled up in pyjama bottoms. He almost fell and cursed his weak ankle that had done more than keep him from joining up and doing his bit. It had filled him with shame though the fault was not his.

But now he was filled with joy. Here was something he could do and would do, and no one was going to stop him. Throwing water over himself, he felt his heart swell with anticipation. His mind ticked over like clockwork: compass, rations, water bottles, Channel map. Gone were the low spirits of the past months when he had festered in the country because none of the armed services would take him; gone now, would be the furtive creeping about because all the other young men had left. Here was why he had not been taken. He had a mission to carry out.

He did not shave. There would be no time for shaving where he was going. He paused only to cut away the moustache he had grown to make himself look older, for Claudine. No need for such ruses now, and when Claudine heard of his actions, her lovely green eyes would glow – for him.

'Gran!' he called down the stairway, knowing that she lived mostly to be behind him, cajoling, supporting. 'I need early breakfast.'

'Whatever for?' Grumbling, still in her nightgown, Susan Tranter none the less put the kettle on the stove, and got out bacon and eggs from the pantry.

Running down the stairs, to show that his ankle was as strong as any other man's, Joe hesitated around the truth and finally told it. 'I'm going down to the bay where the boat is because they're asking for small craft to go across the Channel and take off as many of the troops trapped there as possible. It's the only way the British Army can be saved and be able to defend this country, Gran! You seen my sea maps? I think I had them in the sitting room.'

'What's the Navy up to then?' Susan Tranter, used to discussing war matters with her grandson for his need was so great, added, 'Ain't the Navy there, and what about that last stand?'

'It's all over, Gran, and they need chaps like me with boats.' Rucksack in hand, Joe wrought havoc about sitting room and kitchen as he collected his needs for a sea trip. He had not thought he could use the boat this year, with no petrol being allowed and with the sea planes taking up the whole of Poole bay. Disguising a grimace of pain as he fitted on his hiking boots, traced to a box under the sideboard where his grandmother had put them away for safety, he said: 'Thanks for the dubbin on these, Gran. They're nice and soft, and I don't know when I'll be taking them off next.' He laughed with joy for the adventure ahead. 'Will you do extra bacon, for sandwiches, and where are those old flasks? I'd like some tea, if you can manage it.' He kept talking, to keep her in a muddle of activity and to stop her thinking of reasons to prevent his going.

Soon he was chewing on three fat yellow egg yokes and thick slices of bacon, avoiding the faded blue of her eyes as she stood with her hands crossed over her belly, gazing at him.

Stumbling finally through the door, he dared not turn back to see her watch him leave. Nor did he glance next-door where his aunt was installed with Sarah and that nasty Mary in the cottage that had once been Mrs Baker's. All the family was now living in the three old retainers' cottages in Long Trenthide. His uncle had the other to himself but was now fortunately away at the Ramsays' where he had set up his new stables. The War Office had taken the whole of Liscombe Hall and he was glad of it now; he could get away more quickly, and was indeed very shortly on the back of Pierre's motorcycle kept in the back shed in a fine state of polish. It had all been decreed, he saw that, even to the fact that he had stowed a little forbidden petrol in the boat. It was all meant to be, he realized, revving up with the leg that only gave him the merest twitch of pain, that this gleaming machine lay ready, that he had been injured in Spain, for glory awaited him. 'Tell Uncle Johnny and Aunt Kate I *had* to go,' he shouted towards the doorway where he knew she would be, watching. She would be weeping by now but there would be more weeping women in England if no one went to get the Army out.

Joe, struggling with his little boat *Rosy* out in Dunkirk harbour, ducked back into her as he heard another round of strafing start up from the east; a high violent scream over the turmoil of the bay where there was smoke and burning oil, from the town itself ahead, from some of the craft around him. Shells fell. The Stukas screamed away again. He was covered in soot.

An arm with a rifle still clutched in it appeared out of the churning sea, and the body of a naval man with a leg gone.

He tried to ease *Rosy* round a trawler split open at her heart and burning, and followed the friendly shape of the barges he had followed all night across the Channel. Rocking in their swell, he set himself and *Rosy* to begin the task he had been ordained to do: save as many soldiers as possible from the French coast where they had been driven by raging German tanks and shells. They were ahead of him in the murky mess on the beach line, hundreds and thousands of men, stretched in queues, waiting for the little boats that had been sent for which could get well in to the shallows and then be able to carry them out to the larger boats heading for home and safety. Some of the men were wounded and lay in the sand, but he could see dozens in the water, patient, with the sea up to their necks and oily smoke billowing about, prey to the shells and the machine-gunning but with nowhere else to go. Some were fighting back, rifles held up and shooting into the sky as the next line of bombers dived for them.

Joe managed to anchor *Rosy* in amongst them. A score of sodden men grabbed at the rope he offered. Sixteen had boarded her before he realized she was listing and could take no more, though faces looked up at him from the water and held up their hands.

'I'll be back,' he shouted, and pulled up his ropes. He dared not look behind at those he was leaving and how many of them there were! He kept himself and *Rosy* steady, moving her out stern first to a pleasure boat from Brighton that would in turn take them to a destroyer about to try for home.

He breathed out a sigh of relief as *his* men waved to

him from the rail of the pleasure steamer, and set off again with fresh energy towards the massed and waiting. He took in one with a gunshot wound in his arm, one with an eye torn out and three who were weeping, their strength gone, and on with more until *Rosy* was bursting. They held on to their rifles and their helmets as if they were still going to fight and cursed for the Air Force which had not been ready, not for this. They said no word to Joe, but 'Thanks, mate.' He did not need thanks.

It was his privilege, he thought, and worked on though stiff with exhaustion and with hardly any petrol left for *Rosy*. All her boards and cabin were awash with water and oil and blood; she had taken some gunshot in her bow. They were each of them still almost whole however though every ten minutes the enemy planes swept across the beaches. Sand and sea would fly and more men would fall to roll against the others at the water's edge. All the time the sun burned down for he had worked far into the morning. The stench of hot oil and smoke and decay made him retch and he vomited once when he tried to drink the tepid water from his bottles. A bigger boat passed him two cans of petrol at one stage, and once he had just off-loaded a dozen men on to a tug when a shell hit it dead centre. Her boilers blew up in a jet of scalding water and he heard the men he had almost saved screaming as their bodies arched out, clothes torn from them. He could do nothing but haul those he could back in and let them lie moaning, skin and hair gone, until a naval boat edged in to take them off.

He had made another trip or two. He had lost count of the hours. His skin was as black from oil and smoke as that of the burned men. His eyes, he thought, were caked with it, but he could see well enough, all that he needed to see, and that was his fifty metres of churned and filthy sea and the queue of his men that never got any shorter. Then *Rosy* was hit by a shell, or so he supposed afterwards. He knew that a Stuka had just screamed its way overhead. He had not heard anything fall, however, just felt himself drawn up in a swish of hot air. Then he was lying on the sand, or what once had been sand. There was a little blue and white piece of wood with *Ros* painted on it beside him, and the rest of *Rosy* was gone. Sooty hands reached out for him and pulled him into the shade of a lorry half-buried in sand. He lay beside a man with a black mass of blood at his chest. 'Sorry,' he said, 'my boat's gone, but I'll try and get you off if I can.'

There was no answer. Joe saw that his eyes were closed and he was dead. Other wounded soldiers lay around him and said nothing to him either; there was perhaps nothing to say.

He lay back and looked up at the region of the sky. It was a pretty navy blue now. He had not realized the day was gone, but his task was not finished yet. He would rest for a moment and then get up to see what else he could do to help, before he got himself home.

Jane knew no more of her long day until she awoke. She was lying on sand and above her there was a dark navy blue sky with massive black clouds in it. She lay dreamily cocooned in near-sleep, watching the black clouds, inky black billows across the velvety sky. There must be a fire somewhere. But it all looked very pretty and her uncle was dead by now. She had watched him dying. She felt as weak as a kitten.

'Stay there, lady, we'll get you off somehow.'

She raised her head to look towards this voice and saw a pair of army boots stepping over someone else lying near. In fact, there was a great line of bodies with her in some dirty sand. There were pieces of wood embedded in it, and Army equipment, helmets, rifles, half a lorry.

'Where are we?' she said to her neighbour, too weary to keep up her head.

'Dunkirk beach,' he muttered in reply, coughing. He seemed unwilling to lift his head to speak to her either but could not resist adding, 'What's a woman doing here?'

'ATS driver.' Jane leaned her head back into the damp, dirty and comforting sand and became aware of noise around her, guns, explosives, shrieking. 'Is this the retreat?'

'It would be if there was anywhere to retreat to.' He coughed again, painfully, she could hear it.

She forced herself to sit up. 'I can give First Aid,' she said, coughing too and knowing that the black billows of cloud were smoke.

Afterwards, she remembered tearing off her shirt and underslip and making two or three tourniquets to help the men with bleeding limbs. Then someone took charge of her, a naval officer, and dozens of pairs of willing arms lifted her along the groups of men waiting to be rescued. She remembered the slight coolness of the water and realized how burning hot the air had been, from fire and smoke. She was almost dropped being passed up on to the deck of a small boat. 'Blimey, a woman!' someone said.

The second time Jane woke, it was to find herself smiling up at a nurse dressed in something startlingly white at Dover dockside. She said, 'I have let my uncle die,' and heard herself laugh.

The nurse said, 'There, there, my dear, all over now. We'll soon get you a nice cup of tea and you won't half feel better. You've been dreaming, dear.'

Jane closed her eyes against brightness. 'I would like to go home to Liscombe,' she said. 'If that isn't a dream too.'

When Joe woke, the sky had turned to black. At once he knew that it might be night-time, or it might be from the smoke. Raising his head a little, he could see that the turmoil around the sea's edge had not changed much but there was a difference. There was a kind of quiet.

'Has the bombing stopped?' He turned his head towards a body beside him. There was a bandage over the man's eyes. He could see, because firelight seemed to be flickering somewhere above and behind them. It was, he thought, like lying by some great hearth.

'Think so, hours since,' the man muttered. 'Can you see to get any water, mate?'

Suddenly, Joe felt there was grit in his throat and he could hardly answer. 'Is there any water?' He put out a call to anyone nearby.

'Water, you must be joking. The bloke wants water! Where's he been then? There might be some left in that oil and blood down there but it'll be salty!' A dozen voices hacked out a laugh. 'If you can walk, mate, go and get us all some.'

'I can walk,' Joe called eagerly. Here was something he could do before they took him home. He turned away from the shore and began to drag his body up through the sand towards the flames that must be Dunkirk burning. There would be water there somewhere. He'd have time to save a hundred men from dying of thirst. Once off the sand, he would run. He was stronger, fitter than any of the men lying here. He would show he was fit to serve.

*

Pierre thought that if he were to survive, the thing he would most remember about the retreat was the sound of boots marching along the back roads of Belgium. And after that, the sound of German soldiers shouting '*Schnell! Schnell!*' along the columns of men. He in his French unit and behind that the rows of British captured had no need to know the language. This word clearly meant 'quick!' The *caporal* beside him had estimated there were 15,000 captured French, British and Belgian men in this convoy alone. Their guards were of the worst kind. Crack troops were still seeing to the rout and these young louts were riff-raff, inglorious foot soldiers fit for nothing more than lording it over the captured, and they loved their little share of power.

The dead chicken he was hiding in his Army knapsack had stopped dribbling out its blood and he thanked God for that small mercy. He would have to carry it a day or two more before they could eat it raw, he and the *caporal* and the cook from the Brits with whom he had much in common. A cook thought of food. He and Jack Goode had already, two days before, almost wept at the sight of the German soldiery slaughtering a bull for their own consumption from a passing Belgian farm which later would not be able to breed more stock. They had left a dozen cows! But then, military pillagers would not be inclined to think of the future, and would not care.

Rape, pillage, murder, he muttered to himself, the chicken heavy and warm in the small of his back. Rape, pillage and murder for the brutes and for the conquered, a tin bath filled with a horse's head and a few bits of green stuff, with a pound or two of stolen potatoes. Food, or the lack of it, filled his thoughts, and he was glad of it. He mostly kept his head well down and kept on marching, though his boots were now almost worn down to nothing and his feet burned. He did not want to see the farmland and the little groups of Fresians for it brought back memories of Liscombe. He marched on, through his sore feet and the pain of his limbs and the suppurating sore around the wound in his neck, because survival was the issue and he intended to survive.

In his head, he composed a letter to Claudine. 'Go back to Liscombe,' it said, 'where you will be safe from all this. They will not get that far for the Brits will not let them.' This however brought his thoughts back to the wide clear sky over Liscombe which somehow must be the very same as the pure sky of this beleaguered place, where there were cows though not, he supposed for long, and where there was corn which would be left to rot like the bodies of the shelled horses.

He set his mind to rage instead, and kept his eyes skinned for the sight of another stray bird in the hedgerows whose head he could as quickly pull off before it could squeal and that would be another meal towards his survival.

CHAPTER 15

Peter's Diner
Chelsea
22 June 1940

Dear Lady Liscombe,

I am so sorry to hear about Jane and Joe. What a trail of disaster! And to think Joe took after his father – so brave! My heart goes out to poor Mrs Tranter. Her boy, whom she loved so much. Please do tell me when I shall be able to go and visit him. I shall find time somehow although of course I understand that he wants to see no one yet. I did know he had gone out to Dunkirk, he sent me a postcard from Dover. I could hardly believe it. He said he was going to try and visit my old home village so I just hope that is not what he was trying to do when the shell hit his face.

And our poor Jane. I begged her not to volunteer for overseas duty but once launched on her Army career, I think she felt she must prove herself further. I have telephoned the nursing home in Guildford where they have sent her and have arranged to go and see her tomorrow.

No, I have no direct news of Pierre although I have spent a lot of time at the French Embassy and with the Red Cross trying to find out something.

I hope in many ways that he has been taken prisoner because they are apparently keeping to the Geneva Convention at least and treating their prisoners-of-war with respect.

As for London, things are very much the same now that the fears of an immediate invasion are fading. We saw the Dunkirk men coming through in hordes. I believe some came down as far as Dorset before they could be washed and treated by doctors. 320,000 saved, amongst them Joe and Jane, but not Pierre, yet. It is perhaps not too late, I hear some are still believed to be free in France with a hope of escape later.

I do not think I can bear to know that Liscombe is in the hands of the War Office, and all the hill and the valley too. What are they doing up there? I can imagine that Mrs Tranter *is* muttering about it being MI5. It sounds like it.

I shall write again as soon as I have seen Jane.

With very best wishes and all my sympathy, for Joe. Claudine.

Peter's Diner
Chelsea
24 June 1940

Dear Lady Liscombe,

I saw Jane yesterday as promised, and you are right, she is extremely unwell. The doctors say she is undergoing some kind of breakdown and I must say I am very worried. She talks in sudden bursts about strange things, like the birds outside. Did you know she has never liked birds? I have some memory of her screaming once or twice when they flew near her head round by the cottage, but I did not take much notice then. The other thing is eating. She has never eaten much, as we all know, but now it is quite an issue. They do not want to force her here, they say there must have been some kind of trauma connected with food during the period of her escape, but I am not sure that is wise. She is thinner than ever. She also is occupied with worrying about Mary – she concealed her existence on the application form for the ATS and now feels guilty for denying her motherhood.

All I can do at the moment, I think, is go to see her often and listen if she wants to talk. The doctor I spoke to said talk can be healing, so let us hope it is. If she improves physically, I would like to offer her a home with me temporarily – what do you think? I shall feel less lonely and she might be able to help me a little in the kitchen. She will feel needed, with work to do. I have just lost my chef, Mordecai, a dear man. He is sixty, Lady Liscombe, an Italian who has been here since he was a boy apprentice of fourteen. He loves England and they have taken him away as an alien now that Italy has declared war. I never so much wanted to murder anyone in my life as that policeman who came for him! He's in the Isle of Man in some dreadful camp. I have written to the Home Office to appeal for him and am hoping for a proper answer as to what harm Mordecai could ever do against the English or the war effort.

Someone stuck a poster on my cafe door with FRENCH COWARDS written on it. I have tried not to take it personally, not being in any way responsible for the battles, lost or not, but it is very hurtful.

I shall write again, Lady Liscombe.

With kind regards

Claudine.

Peter's Diner
Chelsea
26 June 1940

Dear Mrs Tranter,

Thank you so much for your letter. I cannot tell you how distressed I have been to hear about Joe's dreadful injuries. As soon as he is able to receive visitors, I shall go and see him. I am sure there is much that can be done for him with modern medicine.

He must be very patient, and you too, dear Mrs Tranter, must be patient with him.

I am so glad he is near you, at that place outside Wareham which has such a good reputation, and I should think he will get an award for his extreme bravery. You must be so proud of him, and that he should be a hero, like his father!

I am sorry that you blame me for his going to France in such an impetuous way. Yes, I know he did have a foolish passion for me. I hope I did not do too much to encourage it.

However, I do understand your distress and send you and dear Joe my best wishes.

Yours sincerely,
Claudine Forestier

Peter's Diner
Chelsea
5 July 1940

Dear Mordecai,

I cannot bear to think of you there with all those people, cramped in dormitories as if you were a common criminal. I have written twice to the Home Office demanding your release and shall write again this week if there is no reply. Siegfried tells me (and he has had the sense to get naturalization, Mordecai, I just wish you had) that there are to be some appeals set up for the Italians and others who have been here for a long time. I am hoping for your case to be heard at once if that is so.

I need you here, my dear Mordecai, for I cannot run the café without you and the café is for the war effort. If that is what they want, I can provide it. What better good than to go on feeding people in a warm and comfortable place? I have my friend Jane here with me and she is trying hard over the toad-in-the-hole, but it does not match yours. To be honest, she is not very good in the kitchen and cannot get on with things without being told what to do, but the poor girl does not like food so cannot be expected to cook with pleasure!

I am posting you under separate cover some of your coffee which the Americans are sending over, thank heavens, and the last *saucisson* of all. I want you to have it. I only hope it is not lost in the post.

I miss you, dear Mordecai.

With my love,

Your almost-daughter,

Claudine

Peter's Diner
Chelsea
20 July 1940

Dear Lady Liscombe,

Jane is safely installed in my second bedroom and is being a great help, although getting in rather a state when service starts up. Then she manages very nicely and is liked by the customers.

I took her to the doctor again yesterday and he is pleased with her progress. She swallows the calming pills and sleeps well. Something still troubles her though and I am hoping she will be able to talk about it one day. The doctor says it is a kind of shell-shock, like the soldiers in the last war used to suffer, but she says it is not that at all. She enjoyed France and all of her war work, she says, even the rout, because it was so exciting for her. Yes, she does sound like a girl sometimes but I am not sure she will ever change. Perhaps we should not want her to, she would not be Jane!

There is news of Pierre at last. He is on the list of

captured men being taken to a Stalag in Poland. Apparently the Red Cross is to start sending parcels out soon so I think I must find a Red Cross office here in London so that I can feel I am doing something for him. No personal parcels are being sent out yet but letters are and might one day get through. So I have already written.

I hear I may be allowed to appeal for my chef's release so that is good news too. He is such a dear man, much like a father (I never had a father, you know), and a little like Pierre too so you can imagine how much he means to me.

By the way, Jane keeps saying that she feels she ought to come down and see Mary but I am sure it is from a sense of duty rather than affection, and the child shows no affection to her, so I cannot see that such a visit could help her recovery. Please let me know how you feel on this. You have always been so much closer to the child than Jane has. She admits to it and being a poor mother seems to be one of her many worries. The fact that she denied the existence of Mary in order to get into the ATS weighs very heavily in her mind, and also the fact that now her little cottage has been taken over with the Hall by the War Office, she has no home except sharing Mary's room in your new little place. I wonder if you might be able to arrange to rent another cottage in the village for her, or failing that, if I am not bombed out, perhaps she ought to consider making her home with me for the duration of the war?

I know you will give all this your usual consideration.

With kind regards.

Yours sincerely,

Claudine Forestier

Peter's Diner
Chelsea
15 September 1940

Dear Lady Liscombe,

Yes, you are quite right, we in London are now part
of the front line but for the moment the café still
stands and no bomb has dropped on our street. The
constant raids are terrible, though. We hardly sleep
and the café is busier than ever because people do not
like being alone. I have to close at ten o'clock at night
because the regulations say so but some of the
bombing is during the day. The sky over the Thames
towards the east is often a terrible blood-red. There
have been a thousand fires and all the air is filled with
the smell of smoke and soot, and plaster from the
wrecked buildings. I shall never forget the smell nor
that red sky and sometimes at night it is as if the old
lights were on again, but it is the docks burning.
Clever of the Germans, really, to start so many fires,
they can see their way as they bomb.

Jane and I go to the cellar once we are closed and
sometimes Mordecai, my chef, stays with us because I
dare not let him walk home. It does him good, I think, to
feel he is helping us just by his male presence – he is a
true gentleman, but of course if anything were to
happen, I should be devastated if he were hurt. He has
lost all his strength in the prison camp they sent him to.
If my appeal had not got him out, I wonder if he would
have survived. When I saw him walking down the street,
with his suit and his collar too big where he had almost
shrunk from the misery of it all, I could have wept. I
feel certain, however, that with work to do and us two
frail females to look after, he will one day be his old
self!

Jane's medical is coming up next week and she is

determined to apply to a different unit, one of those signal places where she intends to help with our defences! I am not sure they will take her but she seems much steadier in her mind than she was and even eats a little more. I think they intend to bomb the entire city to rubble but *I* intend to keep my business going as long as I can. You once said to me you prospered with your restaurant during the last war and I really cannot complain in spite of rationing, or because of it perhaps, because people eat out more than they ever used to with their 2 ounces of butter and 4 ounces of bacon or whatever is allowed for home use. I see the horse butcher along the street has more customers than usual too.

Jane and I often talk of Liscombe. It was such a dream place for both of us and we see it in our mind's eye as lying perfectly calm and beautiful on the hill, waiting for someone who cares to return to it. I hope MI5 or whoever it is up there is looking after it properly as we used to do. Jane is also seriously worried about their cooks feeding the ginger cats well enough. I have told her the War Office will at least get good supplies of food so they won't starve.

I write to Joe each week, as Jane does, and he dictates a short reply to us. I write to Pierre too but of course do not expect an answer. Once the Red Cross parcels begin, I shall at least be able to hope he is getting something to eat. I cannot bring myself to start knitting socks for him but Jane keeps herself busy with needles whilst we are down in the cellar during raids.

We were so happy to hear that Sarah has buried her callipers in the garden with a ceremony of goodbye. How is that delightful Suki of hers adapting to life in the village?

With very best wishes to you both and to Mrs Tranter.

Yours sincerely,
Claudine Forestier

Sometimes, spending so much time on correspondence, Claudine began another missive. 'Dear Fathers,' it said, 'I have had no confirmation that you received my letter asking you to take care of my son for the duration of the war. I am most anxious now that so much of Normandy is part of the German exclusion zone and there is no possibility of news getting in or out ...' *Why* had she not let him come the year before?

And that was the problem. There was nowhere to send this plea. There was no mail between Britain and France now and not even underground news from that place in Normandy. So she could not learn whether the Jesuits had made their escape in time, much less their present home, or the whereabouts of a slim young boy who had for her the face of the child at the station when she had been going to run to Liscombe.

It relieved her a little, however, to write the words, as she did several times, even if she afterwards had to tear up the precious wartime paper into tiny pieces.

CHAPTER 16

Claudine was in the kitchen because there had been a lull in the bombing overhead. Now the distant familiar sound began again, a rumble and a kind of whine, from the planes coming back. In the weeks since it had begun, they had learned to know where they were headed. Standing by the counter with tray and two cups of Oxo, she listened. Yes, they were coming towards them, no doubt along the river.

Jane's voice called up from the cellar, 'Hurry, Claudine, they're near.' Not hurrying, for Jane was often fearful though no bomb had yet fallen in their corner of Chelsea, Claudine moved towards the cellar door. But the door surged up, she remembered that afterwards. Her hand held wildly on, as if with the power to hold it. Beneath her feet, where suddenly there were no slippers, the brick floor was gently breaking apart. A soft plop of plaster fell nearby.

'I'm coming, Claudine, hold on.' It was Jane's voice again, but why were her own limbs trapped in some glue-like substance and how had she come to be lying at the bottom of the cellar steps?

There was something clinging to her skin, dampness and dirt and plaster. She could smell that, she could taste it. Through something that was covering her face, she saw a light that was Jane's torch and then Jane's hand reaching out to wipe her eyes. She spluttered as something fell into her mouth. 'Cough it out,' Jane was ordering her. She coughed obediently.

'More,' Jane said. Claudine coughed, then retched because she could not help it though warm saliva and bile was mixed with the mess in her mouth and where she rested her head. 'Sorry,' she said.

'Here.' Jane lifted her head and put something dry underneath it. 'Be sick again if you can. Now, where does it hurt most? The electricity's cut, I'll have to save the torch and light the lamp.'

'I don't think anything hurts.' Claudine spat out plaster, and tried to rub her eyes into the cloth that was probably Jane's dressing-gown. 'But I can hardly see,' she began, and at once knew that all her limbs hurt, that she would never be able to move again. 'Ouch!' she cried. Jane's fingers were moving all along her body. 'Oh, don't touch along my back!'

'I don't think it's broken, nor's anything else as far as I can see. Have you coughed up any blood?' The torch was shining into the mess around them. 'Don't think so. You may be just bruised. In a minute I'm going to try and help you to move along to the wine store where our beds are. You'll be better lying there.'

Too weak to protest, Claudine began to drag herself inch by inch over the rubble, Jane supporting her head and shoulders. 'I've crawled up to have a look, the whole of the top of the stairs is blocked,' she whispered, as if whispering were necessary. 'Probably the entire café itself is blown through and all we've got to do is wait here until the fire brigade dig us out. We're lucky, Claudine, both in one piece.' She set up and lit the safety hurricane lamp by the light of the torch.

It was an hour or two before Claudine could admit that they were indeed lucky. She wiped patiently at her face with a piece of cloth that Jane had dramatically torn from her nightdress, then sat propped up on the camp bed beside Jane's, listening for the sounds above.

At first, it did not seem strange that they could hear nothing. The bombers, they said, had simply passed to another site.

But then, as Jane's watch said that it was six o'clock and they supposed it was still working properly, Claudine's having been blown from her wrist in the blast, they asked each other why there were no thuds, from the digging of the fire brigade?

They finished the coffee from the flask. Jane ate some biscuits from the stock tin. She slipped away several times to make her way through the rubble at the bottom of the stairs to establish they were indeed blocked and that there was no chink of light through which she could peer. She made one attempt to start scraping away at the brick and stone until Claudine called out to her to stop. 'You'll risk bringing the whole lot upon your head, Jane. Leave it to the experts.'

But the experts did not come. It was suddenly noon, how could that be? And then it was tea-time, half-past three. They drank the last of the metallic-tasting water from the water bottle and argued about it because neither had thought recently to change the water in it.

'We got rather arrogant, thinking *we* would never be bombed.' Claudine managed to ease herself from the bed just enough to reach to the shelves for a bottle of brandy. She poured the liquid on to another piece of Jane's nightdress and wiped the cloth over her face and hands. 'It is suddenly very hot. Are you hot?'

'Stifling,' Jane agreed. 'I wish we had tea. Everyone has tea at half-past three.' She leaned back against her pillow and wiped her sleeve across her face. 'We need more air in here.'

'The English have tea at half-past three, not the whole world. Typical of you to think everyone's the same!'

Jane refused to rise to the old bait. 'I remember,' she said, 'even when my unit was making its way to the coast, when all was lost though we didn't realize it, we still stopped for tea by the roadside. Right in the middle of the French countryside with the German bombers making their way towards us. There we all were brewing tea on those little stoves, everyone going behind the bushes to, you know, and suddenly an officer stood in the road and shouted the planes were coming.' Jane sat up. 'I think I'll have some of that brandy as tea, Claudine, and a biscuit, there are some left. I'm so thirsty, and hungry too for that matter.'

'Don't eat too many.' Claudine sat up too, wincing at the pain in her back.

'There's at least half a pound here, look. Go on, you've eaten nothing since supper.' She held out the tin.

'Since supper yesterday,' Claudine said. 'You can only have a drop, you'll be tipsy.' She passed Jane a glass, took a biscuit and sank back against the pillow. 'We've been here fifteen hours, Jane, and if they haven't found us yet, haven't even started digging yet, then we may be here longer ... so just ration the biscuits, and tell me more about your big adventure in the army. You must have had a shock when you found the guns were real.'

'I did!' Jane laughed, too used to Claudine's teasing to take offence. 'My first shock was finding Jennings dead beside me. She was my co-driver and always mean to me, a real bullying type although I suppose I deserved it.' She coughed over the second biscuit. 'Oh, I wish it were not so hot down here!'

'Why did you deserve it?' Claudine asked. 'Go on. Now we've got all the time in the world, tell me why you deserved Jennings bullying you.'

'Well, I don't know . . .' Jane took a sip of brandy and then a gulp. 'I suppose I did silly things or said them.'

'You've got to stop thinking you're always in the wrong, my girl. How many times have I told you? You are no sillier than anyone else and it's only because *you* think you're a fool that everyone else does. Oh, I shall have to take off this dressing-gown.' She was panting, she thought. 'What time is it now?'

'Ten to four. They'll be coming soon.'

'Anyway, you had the last laugh over Jennings, didn't you? She died and you didn't.'

'I almost did.' Jane held out her glass for more brandy.

'No, you'll get hotter, and you don't drink any more, remember? How did you almost die?'

Claudine felt her eyes close and tried to think of Liscombe and the sweet light breeze under the oaks.

'. . . and then,' Jane was saying, 'I saw that it was my uncle lying there on the ground with a great wound in his leg. I circled round and round him, round and round, Claudine, laughing with joy because he was dying and there in the wood he was in my power, just as I had used to be in his.'

Claudine tried to make her thoughts work in the hot fuddling air. 'You mean, your own uncle . . . Mary?'

'Yes. He used to come to my room and say it was our secret, our very own secret. That my mother must never know, she'd be cross. He'd taken us in, you see, after my father died. I was about eight, I think, when he started. He would not have servants, my mother had to do all the work, and he used to bring up my supper, to save my mother's legs, he said, and I never could eat it. I used to throw it out of the window on to the attic roof, for the birds. I cannot stand birds! The sound of them, hopping frantically about.'

'They used to know the time, you see, just as I did, only they were pleased when it was supper-time and I used to stand there, waiting. I'd hear his horse on the gravel, that would be the first sound, and a little time would pass, then the smell of the supper would come up the stairs: leek soup, cinnamon tart, lamb hotpot, rice pudding with nutmeg. Horrors, horrors, Claudine! It would all run down the roof into the gutter and the awful birds would scrabble and claw for it, their wings flapping, flapping, and sometimes I would be sick.'

Claudine heard her panting with the effort to get out all the words she needed to speak to free herself. 'I knew there was something, Jane. I'm so sorry.' There were tears on her own hot skin, because she was too weak to hold them back. 'Go on. I understand all about your hating food now, I'd be the same . . .'

'You can't possibly want to hear. I'm so disgusting, Claudine. Yet surely I should still be a mother to Mary and love her the way other women do?'

'*You're* not disgusting. Don't you see!' Claudine struggled to sit up and lean across to Jane. The lamp was almost out now but she could see Jane's flushed stricken face with her mouth stretched open in a long silent sob. '*He* was disgusting. You were a little child . . .'

'I should have stopped him somehow.'

'A child? A child's physically powerless. I suppose you should have tried to tell someone . . .'

'My mother!' Jane burst out. 'I wanted her to know, she *should* have known, she was my mother, but even when . . . the baby was there, was coming, they sent me on holiday to an aunt's, my first holiday ever. I was so happy but when I got back my mother said I'd been sinful, and the doctor did too. He said I should be ashamed, my uncle was a saint to keep me. He showed me how to feed the baby . . . he had awful red fingers *handling* me. All doctors . . .'

Claudine leaned across to touch her shoulder. Jane struggled to sit up and gain control over herself, but Claudine told her to go on. 'Don't you see,' she said again, 'that you were powerless, a child? Listen, listen.' She tried to put the usual force into her words. 'Imagine Mary or Sarah in the same misery. Would you think them disgusting, would you blame them if it happened to them, God forbid?'

'No, no.' Jane wiped at her wet face with her arm.

'Just think of that.' Claudine found she was speaking in quick breaths. 'Look,' she said, 'the lamp's going down. Shall we save it and sit in the dark for a while?'

'I'd rather have the dark. I'd rather you did not see me now I've told you, Claudine.'

'You can't be blamed for anything. We'll talk about it again, later. Let's be quiet now and rest. My head's begun to hurt rather, and anyway, we must save our strength. Are you too hot to bear?'

'No. They'll be coming for us soon. We'll hear the digging.'

'Yes.'

'Claudine? Are you awake?'

'Almost. What's the time? Flash your torch.'

'Ten-past eleven.'

'Nearly twenty-four hours now.'

'Yes. Claudine?'

'What?'

'When I was a child then, I couldn't help it, could I? I couldn't help being . . . bad?'

'You were not bad, not in any way bad. A child isn't, only in little spiteful ways like your Mary sometimes. And no girl can fight against a full-grown and disgusting male of the very worst sort, now can she?'

'No. But I have been bad since then, and not just a poor mother!'

'You don't mean that horrid doctor? I've been thinking, you know, trying to work that out. I suppose you let that creature . . . touch you, because of the others. Or do you mean bad because of a proper sexual relationship? Because that's not bad in itself.'

'No, no, of course not, Claudine. No one has asked me, and I couldn't . . . hope anyone would love me.'

'Don't go on with *that* any more, you're more lovable than some.' She took a deep breath for breathing was suddenly more difficult than it had been only a few minutes before. 'More than most really. We ought to save our breath but tell me just this last thing. You can't have done anything as bad as me.'

'I bet I have.' Jane took deep breaths in between the forced tight ones. 'I let someone die.'

'In the retreat?' Claudine had time to form a strange floating picture in her mind of Jane running away from her wounded.

'Yes, I told you, in the wood, my uncle. On the ground . . . and I laughed and tortured him. He wanted water and I sprinkled some on his hand. I did leave him the bottle in the end but told no one . . .'

Jane's words were slurred, as were her own, Claudine thought.

'I let him die, a man of the cloth, because if I'd told someone . . .'

'Well, good, I'm glad.' Claudine tried to put some last energy into the words. 'Revenge is damn sweet, I say. My God, I hope he suffered first. I hope he damn well suffered agony! Did he ask forgiveness, do you think? Do you think anyone could forgive that beastliness?' She struggled for breath. 'Shall we open some wine? I think we need something. There's wine here, and *calvados*.'

She found she could not force her legs over the side of the bed to reach either, but Jane had, she said, plenty of strength left and to prove it broke the top off a bottle of wine with one swift movement. She had the strength to eat too, though Claudine could not. There seemed to be something in her throat that was sticking there. But she drank the wine gratefully and went on talking, holding the torch for a moment or two so that Jane could crawl about the tasks more easily.

'Revenge was sweet to me when I stole that money and Pemberton was blamed.'

'You did take it!' Jane gasped out, kneeling beside the bed.

'Mm.' She felt herself give a reminiscent smile. 'Worth it but bad, wasn't it, to anyone else? Not my only badness either.' Her hand was suddenly too weak to hold her glass so she forced herself to finish the wine. A momentary surge of energy filled her and enabled her to go on. 'Had an affair too, you know. I was a hussy, a blatant hussy, like my mother. I gave up my heart and my body without a ring on my finger. And I did not even feel ashamed – I suppose I should have been. But of course he left me . . . he mocked me because I believed that he loved me.'

Jane reached for the torch from under the pillow. Shining it on to her friend's face, she saw an ugly red patch across Claudine's cheeks and her lips had an odd white look, dry and powdery.

'Claudine?'

'I'm badder than you, so there . . .' The words were hardly formed. Jane could hear a strange popping sound from her lungs.

Leaving on the torch long enough to eat three biscuits, swallow more wine and crawl to the bottom of the stairs, she began to dig, moving bricks and rubble carefully aside as she made her way up. She paused once, because she could hear Claudine talking. She took the opportunity to wipe away the dust from her face, so that she could breathe more easily, she did not need to see, and she thought she heard Claudine speaking. 'And then I had a baby too, Jane, do you hear me? I had a baby, a boy it was, and I gave him up in exchange for my freedom. Listen to me, Jane, for someone must know, someone must hear me . . . I sold him, you see . . . and I sold him twice.'

Jane listened and wiped her face and went on digging.

CHAPTER 17

Claudine spent almost seven months in hospital, first in one near Portland Place, and when that was bombed, safely in Hampshire. The hairline crack in her skull mended and so did the crushed ribs but she had been so long prone by that time, she needed physical therapy to get her limbs in action again and was weakened too by the poor hospital food, so that anaemia became another problem. Lady Liscombe sent forbidden fresh eggs and butter and Dorset bacon but they did not always reach her.

Her only visitors were Mordecai with a flask of real coffee, and Jane once she had been released from hospital. Jane had suffered only shock and exhaustion, having spent twelve hours digging a careful hole large enough for her cries to reach the rescuers. She was to receive a medal for her bravery and endurance and these might also have hastened her acceptance into a new Anti-Aircraft (Mixed) Battery being set up on the Kent coast where ATS girls were to be welcomed as searchlight and tracking operators in order to free men for the guns that would bring down enemy aircraft.

The bombing of London had eased for that year and other cities were being targeted, but London was half-emptied of its citizens, those that had survived and could do so leaving for quieter areas. Accommodation was easy to find and Jane had paid a month's rent on the upper half of a house in Kensington for them both. She intended to spend only her shorter leaves in Dorset with Mary.

With two days' leave from the Ack-Ack station, newly uniformed and proud to be so, Jane took Claudine there by hired car one bright spring morning. Standing by the window of the near-empty flat, for furnishings were more difficult to find, she said, 'I don't like to leave you alone, Claudine, and where on earth are we going to find a bed, or two if I'm to spend some time here?'

'*I* shall find two this very morning,' Claudine said, adjusting the curtains. 'The lady in the next cubicle told me they can be had for 2s. 6d. second-hand and she also said that "they" would give me £9 compensation for refurnishing.' She laughed, looking down into the London street where cold sun revealed all its shabby wartime reality, sand-bagging and boarded-up shop fronts and the old posters torn. 'Good heavens, I am glad to be *out*!'

'You may be out, but you're not well. I'll put the kettle on, I did have time to get one yesterday, and there's tea and milk . . . and, oh, I remembered matches for the gas!'

Claudine heard her moving about with a new busyness and wryly refused to reflect upon the change in their relationship. Time for reflection was over, she'd had too many weeks for that, staring at ceilings. From today there was to be activity. 'Mordecai says he'll bring coffee tomorrow but remind me to call in for that form for a new ration book on my way to the station.'

'The station?' Jane stood with hand poised over a brand-new teapot. 'Where are you going your first day? The doctors said . . .'

'I don't care what they said, Jane.' Claudine went across to her new sink. 'I'll rinse out that pot and the cups. How many did you manage to buy?'

'Four. Here.' Jane passed over a box. 'Blue and white stripes, that's all there was. I think they'll allow you special clothing coupons too ... but where on earth are you going? To Liscombe at last?' Her face, that had something new in it Claudine could see in the daylight that was not the same as hospital light, allowed itself to brighten. 'Oh, that will do you so much good, Claudine.'

'Stop being so careful, Jane. I'm not sick now, and no, I'm not going to Liscombe.'

She shook water from the teapot and two of the striped cups, for there was no tea towel, Jane had forgotten that. 'I mean I'll walk to the station with you, not go to Liscombe!'

'Why ever ...' Jane watched the kettle coming to a boil.

'You know why.'

'He's not there.' She looked up at Claudine who met her gaze. The gas made a busy little fuzzy sound. Everything that was left to be said, had been said between them during the long hours Jane had spent at her bedside. She could not hide from her now, so she did not say, 'Who's not there?' because it would bring back the old false plane their friendship had been on. Water bubbled in the kettle. Jane dragged her gaze away and poured it on to two precious spoonfuls of her own tea ration. 'Johnny's off on some war work. When I went down for your old suitcase of clothes, Lady Liscombe told me.'

Claudine poured milk into the two cups. 'I still shan't go. Did you manage a little sugar?'

'I did.' Jane took a screw of paper from her handbag. 'Enough for you for a day or two.'

Adding half a spoon of sugar to each cup, Claudine said, 'Did you have time to go and see Joe?'

'No, but he won't see anyone except his grandmother and aunt. He can't bear having half a face. There's to be another operation apparently.'

They each leaned against the wall by the window in the table and chairless room.

'I feel if I insisted, if I just went into his room to be the first step over with, he'd pass some sort of hurdle. He can't mind *me* seeing him. We were like brother and sister, and both with funny childhoods.' She could say this freely now and as she did, Jane turned with a smile towards Claudine. 'I could never even think of saying that before. You know how much you did for me, just listening, don't you?'

'You did a fair amount for me,' Claudine said drily, 'like saving my life.'

'A good enough exchange because you saved something in me, and gave me a life. Here I am, taking charge of you, and part of the fighting defences. My God, I sometimes wonder if it can be the real me.'

'That's just what it is.' Claudine forced herself away from the support of the wall and walked across to the stove for more tea.

'You do think so?'

'I do and I'm glad.'

'I'm glad you found *his* name in the lists of Dunkirk wounded in that old newspaper. Knowing he'd survived, in spite of my leaving him to die . . .'

'I'm glad he didn't die too.' Claudine held out her hand for Jane's empty cup. 'Because he has the rest of his miserable life to face what he did to you. He can never hide it from himself now, do you see?'

Jane gasped. 'I hadn't thought of that.'

'I had, and I'm glad. Death would have been too quick. You see, I'm nastier than you.' Claudine laughed, passing her the full cup. 'Now, come on, you'll miss your train and I don't think you should go AWOL or whatever it is.' She wanted, suddenly, for Jane to be gone so that she could get on with the plan that had come so clearly to her as she lay in hospital and the letter had come, re-directed by Mordecai. There had been two others, grey cards stamped all over with official symbols, from Pierre in his prisoner-of-war camp, saying that he was managing well enough. That had been to cheer her, she knew, but his writing was tiny and shaky, hardly his. She dared not think of him and when the other letter had come, she had known that would be easier.

It was an odd, ambiguous note on formal military-style paper. It had puzzled and frightened her a little, for someone somewhere had known about her and she did not know them. Then when the captain came, in reply to her reply, she saw that she had purpose and would find strength enough to follow. 'Remind me to get some writing-paper on the way to the station,' she said. She was going to answer the captain's suggestion but no one, not even Jane, could be told about any of it.

Claudine returned alone to the new lodging where a Jewish family rented the ground floor, trying to live silent and careful lives in the new hell which was London under the Blitz but which must be safer than the city they had left. She did not suppose they would ever trouble her. The place seemed now as if it were empty though she could detect the slight drift of cabbage soup. She did not mind. This was to be a temporary place, perhaps, for the new life she intended now to begin. There was, after all, nothing left of the old, not even the shell of her little business. All she had was a considerable sum of money in her banking account and the core of herself that she would take forward simply because someone, somewhere had asked her to. On the grey wartime paper, standing by the stove, she wrote the letter that would open it up to her.

Dear Captain Townsend,

I have given some thought to the matter we discussed in the hospital last week after your first letter had surprised me so much. Please let me know when you have time to offer me another interview.

She thought there would be a week or two before he replied, and set about making her body work again, going on foot to buy the few pieces of furniture she would need and again along Oxford Street, searching for underclothes that were not too utility, for a tube of lipstick, a hairbrush, a toothbrush, toothpaste itself, for she had been reduced to nothing. She felt a lift to her heart, for the sunshine and her new freedom and the whole wartime world spread out before her. She had now no constraints of any kind, only her body, her weak limbs, her giddiness, to hold her back.

In fact, the reply came rather too soon. A letter labelled 'By Hand' was delivered to her two days later. It asked her to report the next afternoon to an otherwise secret address which she was to disclose to nobody.

Very shortly, there she was, sitting on a hard wooden chair at the secret address, talking to a major whose name she immediately forgot. He was very like the captain who had gone to her hospital bed to talk to her. Somehow, she was important to them. She tried to listen, though she had lost the habit of listening; she had lost the habit of dressing too and felt uncomfortable and unappealing in the skimpy wartime dress though her hat was fiercely smart because it was one of her old ones.

'And so you see,' the major was saying, 'we need ladies in particular who can speak perfect French. French nationals for preference, youngish but not too young, old enough to have acquired a bit of nerve, intelligent, without too many ties . . .'

'I have no ties,' Claudine broke in. And she had not, or only a flimsy paper link. Would her war effort for France be enough to earn a stronger one?

'To go back over.'

'I go over to France and fight?'

'Not fight in the usual sense, but just as important.'

Claudine had a vision of Jane in her uniform earnestly manning a great gun. 'Like the ATS girls?'

'Some of our girls are ATS actually, or that is their cover, but no, not fighting in the usual sense like your friend Miss Beale.' He smiled at her gasp of surprise, with his pink skin and blue eyes impeccably an English gentleman. 'No, underground work. You will have to learn things you might not think suitable for a lady. How to handle a gun, how to lay explosives, how to send and receive morse code, how to survive on the land, how to kill if necessary . . .'

Claudine eased her aching back against the chair and considered, letting him go on. The man was a spy; he knew about Jane and certainly much else. They wanted *her* to be some kind of spy. Well, why not? She would learn to be whatever they wanted, just as she had learned to be everything else she had been and would be no more.

'It's all right,' she interrupted him. 'When do you want me to begin?'

'As soon as you've got your first cover story. You're joining the FANY organization, a rather superior group of young ladies a bit like the ATS girls. That'll be your official position from now on but the rest you do not talk about.'

'Can you just tell me who you are and what this place is?' Claudine got up to shake his proffered hand. 'Don't I need to know?'

'Nope.' He held her hand for a long moment, blue eyes twinkling, erect in his perfect English gentleman's tailored pre-war suit, a mystery to her. 'Some people call us the Firm. You'll learn a little, all you need as time goes by, but you're one of us from now on.'

Three days later, on her way to yet another meeting at the same address, kitted out in uniform khaki and blessed silk stockings obtained with a special voucher from Lillywhite's, Claudine's first realization of her new position occurred on the corner of Baker Street. Two raw soldier recruits offered her a salute, slapping up their hands with a glimmer of tortured amusement.

Claudine felt herself blush up to her red hair piled under her cap. She did not know what to do. She had become an English officer, a junior subaltern. Ensign Forestier. She felt herself give a laugh as the extraordinary nature of the change in her life struck her. She offered the recruits a grin and some kind of imitation salute. One of them winked back. The incident was over in a few seconds but it was enough to give a glimpse of the strange new adventure she had stepped into.

Being an officer gave Claudine some privileges at the place in Surrey where she was sent. She was woken in the morning by a personal servant. Peering sleepily from the bedclothes, she remembered with a little surge of pleasure that she was staying at a country house with some of Liscombe's charm about it. And here was the chambermaid, or her equivalent. She sat up and looked at a girl who was offering her a cup of tea, in her own hand without tray or napkin. She had no time to dredge up her old housekeeper phrases for the girl said, pleasantly enough, 'It's Kimble, ma'am. You have to assemble on the tennis court at 0800 hours.'

'Whatever for, Kimble?' Claudine forgot the matter of the tray for Kimble spoke again and this time, there was no mistaking it; her tone *was* pleasant. In fact, she could hardly keep the smile out of it.

'I guessed you might not have kit, ma'am, being French, so I took the liberty of having you issued with a set and I've laid it out for you in your bathroom, ma'am.' Was she sniggering? Claudine could not be sure, but looked the girl up and down, taking in the solid legs in Army-issue stockings, the thighs as thick as tree trunks. 'Servant' was written all over her though she wore a different uniform. There would, Claudine decided, have to be a reckoning, but there would be time for that.

She threw her legs from the bed. No pain now, or hardly any, but if by kit Kimble meant physical training kit, then she was going to the commanding officer to be excused. 'Thank you, Kimble,' she said. And in the bathroom there it was, a white short-sleeved blouse and something she knew were called plimsolls. It was the shorts, black shorts lying across the bathroom stool, that in one swift and painful moment brought back that time on the dreadful gaudy promenade at Bournemouth. Johnny and the glittery sea and Jane leaping. Liscombe and Johnny, all gone forever.

And everything else too. She was glad of that. Grabbing the things, she pulled them on and ran from the room, down the corridor and out into the grim, very early morning air, she whose skin had never been revealed in a state of near undress. But this was the first day of her new life.

She knew where the rest of the group she had met the night before were from the shrieking sounds that came from beyond the ornamental lawns serving as a frontage to the house. Unpractised in the loose canvas shoes, her feet feeling every stone in the path, she ran to join them. She knew only their code names.

There was Isabelle, a tall thin ex-boarding school English girl used to physical jerks. She was swinging her arms with fluid energy and giving out a series of those English shouts: '*One*, two, three, four.' Charlotte, being French, was not so practised, her short body was no less than clumsy, Claudine thought, joining her where she would be less noticeable. On the other side of Charlotte, puffed a little plump half-Russian girl who had chosen Geneviève as her code name, and in charge, slightly apart, was another English girl, a very quiet blonde who had natural authority and whom they had to call Constance which might or might not have been her real name. 'Follow me round the lake,' she now ordered, 'fast brisk pace, keep well in, one behind the other.'

Claudine kept well in last, panting slightly even as they began to run. If this was the beginning of it, if it was necessary, then so be it.

She did not much mind.

By the time she and the rest of her group had been sent up to Scotland for training in the use of firearms, they could scale a fifty-foot ladder, cross a river under-hand by rope, tackle a series of obstacles which involved wall-scaling. Her hands were calloused, she forgot that she had ever lain sick in a hospital bed, and her body became as supple as those of the girls who had spent their school years in a very similar atmosphere to the present one. At night she slept heavy and dreamless sleeps. She made no particular friendships with the rest of the group. Friendships were not encouraged amongst them, for one day, when they were ready, they would have to live without friends. They were certainly not allowed to make friends amongst the others training in different parts of the houses where they were lodged. Some of these were men, but all the women had the same training.

Claudine was excused only part of it because of her hospital months. She did not have to learn to jump with a parachute and would have to make her landing – when it came, if it came, by boat on the south coast of France. She had first to complete all her other tasks to the satisfaction of the mysterious men who came and went amongst them.

She would have liked to boast of her exploits to Jane by letter, but that was not permitted either. She could not even tell her that her new code name was Suzanne and how hard it was to get used to answering to it, nor that she had a new identity for her first trip into enemy territory. She was to be Jeanne-Marie Cernau, of 19 bis Grand'Rue, Montpellier, daughter of a seamstress and a fisherman now deceased.

She could not even tell her that she too held a gun, a light pistol, that she was quite a good shot, or how she had screamed when they had pushed a stuffed German soldier dummy out at her one dark night when she had been told to make her way alone from the house to a farm building. She had remembered to shoot twice, to be sure of the kill though, and had passed that little test.

Her only weakness, she thought later, was in the matter of the personal code to be used for her own wireless messages which would be passed from headquarters to wherever she was in France. They asked her to choose a favourite poem and she did not have one. Sitting quietly with a copy of the *Golden Treasury* one rainy afternoon, she found herself tracing words that were her own; it *was* a weakness, for they were of Liscombe but no one but she would know it.

> The rook flies high
> And the gull
> And the swallow
> Theirs the sweet sky
> And the oak
> And the hollow
> In sleep, I take wing
> With the gull
> And the swallow
> In sleep, my heart sings
> With the gull
> And the swallow
> In sleep, that distant dream
> Is mine again

Until the words came so easily out on to the page, she thought she had shut Liscombe away forever.

And then, suddenly, weeks and months had passed and only a few tests remained: field survival, clandestine life and the management of the agents they would recruit within France. This was to include a vital skill, the cut-out system, where each of them and their recruited agents would only ever know one or two other people, so that the linked groups could never betray each other. These new matters were to be learned somewhere on the south coast.

On the train going down when they had passed another station with its name boards covered up, though the threat of invasion was past, Constance suggested: 'That's Southampton.' It had become a part of their travels, to guess where they were. 'There's the water, look, the barrage balloons are reflected in it. And a damn great battleship. Oh, lovely. Didn't you once say, Suzanne, that you lived down here?'

Opposite her in the compartment, beside a sleeping Geneviève whose head had slipped on to her shoulder, Claudine was non-committal. 'It wasn't Southampton,' she said, and closed her eyes as if in need of sleep too.

Charlotte and Isabelle, yawning over a game of cards, bickered about an ace, and the sun, southern sun, streamed through Claudine's half-closed lids.

With fear and hope, she thought: could it be Liscombe, the next place, that Mrs Tranter thought was for MI5? *Nothing so much like MI5 as the Firm.* Her heart began to beat with the rhythm of the wheels. She was going to Liscombe, going to Liscombe. Liscombe in her life, all over again, and she would climb the steps as if . . .

'Wake up, Suzanne, we've stopped.' Geneviève's friendly voice.

'We can't have.' She had been going to add 'We're not there yet,' but they were, everyone was getting their bags together. Had she been asleep? She hoped she had been.

But she had not. She dismounted with the others and it was a small country stop, hardly a village.

'I think we're in the New Forest,' Constance said with her jolliest voice.

'As if you didn't know,' Claudine said sourly, picking up her two cases from the platform. Everyone knew Constance was a headquarters spy. Suddenly she was filled with her old irritability. 'And I suppose the truck coming to fetch us will be covered in so we can't learn our way and then send a message to the German High Command about where the future French resistance workers are training? As if we'd . . .'

'Come, come, Suzanne. When we get there, you can take an aspirin and go and lie down. It must be your time of the month.' Constance moved briskly towards the exit.

'Oh, shut up!' Claudine kicked a foot into a tub of flowers on the platform. She hated girl talk and here she was, amongst a collection of over-grown girls! Geneviève offered her a wink of sympathy, but she had so wanted it to be Liscombe, to go back to Liscombe once more, and for a few minutes on the train had let herself dream that she would.

At the new house, a small one amongst a group of others, each hidden from the rest by trees, there was a week of adjustment to the new venue, some pistol practice, physical training daily of course, and the appearance of a town map to be learned by heart. Claudine held her copy of the map of Bournemouth where all their clandestine practice was to take place, found the promenade and the clifftop where Johnny's Bentley had stopped by the hotel that held Jane, and pretended it was somewhere else.

Then the schedule for the following week was posted up.

Field Survival Course
Starting time: 9 pm sharp on Monday evening
Instructor: Captain Johnny Tranter

Jane puffed up the drive of the nursing home, breathless from summer heat. A little cloud of bees burst out as she threw the bicycle against the wisteria on the wall by the front door. She had no distance to go then, Joe's room was not far along the corridor, but she did not hurry. Visits to Joe had to be faced with care.

There was his door, third on the left, reached too soon. 'Lord Liscombe' was written on the nameplate. Lady Liscombe had finally managed to have his right to the title accepted by the House of Lords but it had not seemed to make much difference to Joe. She took in a deep breath to calm herself for him, knocked and waited. He did not like to be taken unawares.

'Come in.' His voice was very changed. There was no longer any boyishness in it, and anyway his injuries had reached his throat.

'It's only me, Joe. It's all right.'

He was sitting with his back to the door as he always did and today was occupied at the desk.

'Jane?' He manoeuvred his wheelchair round and there was a smile on the left part of his face that had muscle in it, and his left eye smiled too. She avoided, as always, glancing to the right side of his face and body because he hated anyone to do that. Her impulse was to put out a hand to touch the withered parts, to share his pain, but he would not let her, not yet.

'I'm late, Joe dear, another puncture! And, of course, no more of those orange rubber bits for repairs, let alone new tyres.' She sat in her usual place near the door so that the light was behind him. 'What's that you're reading?'

'It's from Claudine. Her last letter for a time, it seems.' He held up the envelope in his good left hand.

'I've just had one.' Jane felt inside the pocket of her too-short wartime summer dress. 'I've bought it for you to see. What does yours say?'

'That she'll be going away and won't be able to

write.' Joe fiddled with the paper, bringing his injured hand up and carefully easing out the letter with it. Jane gazed with pity upon his struggle with painful shrunken fingers and forbore to get up to help.

'Yes.' Joe fixed his good eye on her, as silvery-clear as it had always been and as like his grandfather Lord David's as it was possible to be. 'Has she told you where?'

Jane decided to keep up a light tone and laughed. 'Not she! *Secret* war work, no less. Can you imagine? She's in the FANYS which are far superior to us poor lowly ATS. They get silk stockings with their uniform and they're generally much posher. But wait till I see our Claudine! Mocking me for being all eager to help the war effort, then joining up herself without a word about it!'

Joe did not smile, the old side of his face as earnest as it had always been. Jane's heart turned over. She had just noticed the tuft of dark hair at the crown of his head. It was stubbornly sticking up, as it always had, just like his Uncle Johnny's. She felt suddenly about to weep. There was dark stubble too on the good part of his chin. She wondered who shaved that, longing suddenly that it should be herself, working gently with razor to make Joe look a little as he once had.

'Where are the FANY units posted? Can't you find out? I can mark it on my war map.' He pulled impatiently at the wheels of his chair. 'I must draw the curtains. The sun . . .'

'Let me,' Jane began and stopped. He wanted to do everything for himself. 'I did telephone FANY headquarters actually, Joe, because it's her birthday soon as you know, and I wanted to send her a smart blouse I've managed to find, but they said they could not divulge her whereabouts. If we write to the office, they will hold correspondence until her return, they said.'

Joe managed to pull at the curtains whilst keeping his face averted from the sunlight. He grunted. 'Auntie's coming up the drive with Gran.'

'It's a pity,' Jane said, with some daring, 'that you refused to see Claudine when she came down here just for you.' There was no answer and he kept his back towards her. Jane went on talking of Claudine because the impossible dream of her was all that kept his interest now. She knew it to be unhealthy and pointless but wanted him to have just a taste of her. And only she could or would give it. 'I'm wondering if she's working with the Free French. You know, with that General who's starting up some kind of army in exile. He and Churchill don't get on and there's a rumour he'll be setting up a headquarters somewhere in North Africa. She might well be there . . .'

The door behind her opened and there was Lady Liscombe, as calm and beautiful as she had always been, smiling now for her nephew. Mrs Tranter struggled in behind her. Cross banter between Joe and his grandmother ensued, fuelled by her love and his misery.

Jane posed her tentative question, 'Will Mr Johnny be home soon on his next leave, your ladyship?' She got up to offer her seat.

Lady Liscombe took the seat because it was easier to do so than refuse, and answered, 'Still a few weeks to go yet, I think, dear, and none of us knows exactly what he's up to. What with Liscombe being entirely shut off by some mysterious government thing and Johnny keeping absolutely mum about his war activities, then Claudine too I hear . . . What dull ordinary lives the rest of us are living, even you with that Ack-Ack battery, Jane dear. At least it's not totally mysterious!'

'No.' She smiled, half listening to Mrs Tranter, wanting to go on, about Johnny, wanting to touch a part of his life because his dark blue eyes, in those past distant days at Liscombe, had seemed to look upon her with love. It had been the first time, since her father had died and she had been eight years old then, that anyone had seemed to love her.

She stayed on in the hot room until the luncheon gong sounded and nurses began to wheel along a trolley with trays on it for those inmates who could not bear to be seen eating like toddlers. She departed then to take her own lunch with Mary at the cottage where the girl lived with Sarah and Lady Liscombe. She left behind something of herself that would like to help Joe, for they had been such close friends once. She would have been happy enough, cutting up potato into tiny squares and talking of Claudine who had helped her become this stronger self, manning search-lights to guide guns that would blow enemy aircraft from the sky.

There might also be talk of Johnny who had been father, brother, uncle all in one to Joe, who had broken Claudine's heart, and whom she herself dreamed about still.

In her dreams he was no more than a presence, a pair of strong hands, a low voice saying things she could not bear, and some rough tobacco-and-horse-scented cloth where she leaned her head and was filled with weakness, and joy.

CHAPTER 18

'The human eye,' Johnny was saying, 'takes at least half an hour to get accustomed to darkness after light. What's more, darkness is liable to play tricks. You might be lying there on the ground staring at a thistle a few yards ahead of you and you think it's a bush or even a small tree. You think it'll be able to give you cover perhaps and you make a run for it and . . .' He made a cutting movement across his throat with his hand, the hand she knew so well, that had rough skin around the finger tips, and callouses. She had kissed it.

Claudine stared at the vision of Johnny standing in the dusky light near a stream. He had on jodhpurs and an old sports shirt. The skin on his arms and neck and face, that she had hardly dared look at yet, was handsomely browned. And then, yes, his face was the same. Perhaps a little more drawn. There might have been a deepening of the lines towards his mouth that . . .

'Cor!' Isabelle, standing near her behind the others, whispered. '*He's* not bad.'

There was the same frown that he had had that night, but it was perhaps habitual now, and anyway he was scanning this new band that he had to train into something, she could not now remember what, and he had seen her. His hard blue squint moved quickly away, and back. He had seen that it was she.

Claudine held his gaze in a silent plea. Do not let it matter. She would bear it, somehow. His mouth seemed to give a kind of grimace of distaste. Oh, Johnny. She could not bear it.

His voice began again, for it had stopped, on seeing her. 'I'm going to offer you a little experiment. Each of you will go off on a separate path, I'll show you which. It'll shortly be dark. It's your first expedition in night conditions. You might as well get used to that. The landings in France naturally take place at night and all your movements that have to be concealed will be taking place at night as well. All got notebooks and torches as ordered?' There were nods. If her name was down as Suzanne, perhaps he would behave as if she were a stranger? 'Right, now as you go, I want you to write down exactly what you hear. You'll none of you be used to listening. You're going to start getting used to it now. And in that way, you're going to start learning what's listening to you . . .'

He had to approach her because he had to speak to each person individually. She kept herself to last and after an interminable time when she could hear his low, gruff voice, that had been so dear to her, and then his steps coming towards her . . . I am learning to start listening, she thought, and looked up. It was night now but there was a moon. It was enough to see his boots all dusty in the grass and then the pulse throbbing at his neck. He said, 'I suppose you're Suzanne?' His old, impatient voice, wanting always to be rid of the present, for something just as urgent, more urgent, awaited him.

'Yes.' She lowered her gaze back to his boots.

'Right, you're to go this way. See the shadows of the next house? Go round it and . . .'

He was going to pretend she was not who she was. Claudine turned away. It would be better like that. She would do the same, for after all she was not who she had been; she had a different name, two different

319

names. She listened on, trying not to hear the other words that he had said so long ago to the other woman she had been. It had been dark then too.

'Yes, yes, I see, thank you,' she said, and set off towards the shadows of the next house. The heath was behind it. She would be afraid there of the dark.

There were to be weeks of Johnny's course in survival. Claudine, lying the next day amongst damp reeds upstream and in the clarity of the sunlight, faced the prospect of a period of pretence, regret, and, she knew, longing. There could be no hiding from it. The paths of fate had led to this extraordinary renewal of contact, however distant and painful.

Over the water on the opposite bank there he lay, beside Isabelle who was simpering, eager fingers in the water. 'Like this, you mean, Captain Johnny. I hold the hazel rod like this and let the net . . .'

'Not quite.' She could hear the grin in his voice, but he was being patient, friendly. 'You've got it too far in. The fish will never float in by themselves if you hold it like that. The net's got to be open, you see . . .' He had a hand over the dreadful Isabelle's.

Claudine held her own rod and net and lowered her face towards the coolness of the water. She could see the pebbles. 'What if there are no fish the day we happen to be starving, or what if there happen to be no streams around?' She called across, loudly, sourly, because Johnny's hand was on that other girl's and he was being patient and nice, as for one brief night he had been to her, Claudine.

Johnny got up, brushing his hands on his jodhpurs. 'Then you must hope for a rabbit, and if not a rabbit, worse. Or you starve. Don't expect there to be anything else left by the Germans, Mademoiselle . . .'

All along the stream the others raised their head to listen, happily, earnestly, floating hazel rods and silly little nets like children playing. Claudine dropped hers and got up too. He had been going to say 'Mademoiselle Forestier' and had just stopped himself in time. 'Well, I'll never kill a fish.' She too brushed her hands on her trousers, because she had been going to cry and must now stop herself.

'Really?' He gazed at her from beside Isabelle whose boots were lodged against his. 'You won't be able to go shopping, not where you're going, and I understand the Germans haven't left much for the shops anyway. They didn't last time either.'

'You won't be able to waltz down the Faubourg Saint-Honoré, old love.' Isabelle was smiling sweetly up at her from the water. 'Will she, Johnny?' Claudine noticed for the first time how pretty she was with her blonde hair and English porcelain skin.

She turned away, rage and shame in her heart. *She had let herself down.* She must not do that again, but could not now lie quietly on the river bank, pretending to fish. Isabelle let out a twinkling laugh which was, Claudine conceded, unworthy of her. She was a tough girl, plucky in fact. She had English nerve, could ride and shoot already. It was how she had been brought up. She also spoke perfect French and would make a cool agent. Everyone thought that, her reports said so, but there she was, simpering at Johnny.

Claudine went straight to the sick-bay, reporting a headache. This must be the last time she would let herself be affected by Johnny or all her months of training and the new purpose which propelled her on would disappear and leave the old void. She did not want that. She would make a better agent herself. She had two advantages over Isabelle. She was French and looked it, being of average height, and most important, *taking small strides*. Isabelle took long ones and they had told her to change her walk. She had laughed and could not.

Finally and shamefully, lying down with the headache she now had, Claudine realized she must rid herself of spite and somehow learn to live near Johnny. Good resistance agents could not allow themselves personal weaknesses. And she wanted to be a good agent. Since she could not have Johnny, or Liscombe, or even the café, then she *must* be a good agent.

Captain Johnny Tranter joined the other instructors for the weekly reports. There was a comfortable sitting-room in the big house, a fire burning though the windows were open to the sweet summer night, and a glass of whisky beside each man.

'Right then,' the man down from headquarters in London, began to summarize. 'All the girls shaping up pretty well, only one or two bits of silliness, and all perfectly understandable. Isabelle does realize she will not be able to smoke once she gets to France, does she, Ted? The day French women start to smoke in public, I'll know nasty American ways have really got to Europe. Any fuss about the blood and gore, Tranter?'

Johnny grinned round the group from the depths of his armchair near the window. 'Few screams,' he admitted, 'for the dear little bunnies. It'll be in my written reports. And one or two seriously afraid of the dark, but they have to get used to it and better here than in France where it's real. I'm having an all-night trip out before the new moon. I want it pitch black if I can. They'll be taken to different spots by truck and will have to find their way back with just a compass.'

'Do we have to allow them a compass?' The PT man

grunted from his armchair. 'They won't have one out there. Nothing would be so incriminating for the ordinary French women they are supposed to be as to be arrested in possession of a compass!'

'They'll be using other signs as well, that I've taught them, and anyway the compass fuddles most of 'em, in fact, so I'm not insisting on it.'

'And somehow Constance has got to insist on Isabelle learning to walk like a French woman. Can't we get one of those mannequin women to try and change her manner of walking?'

The man from headquarters made a note on his pad. 'There'll be plenty of French women of that sort in London, I'll see if I can get one found that's suitable.

'Now, next on the agenda, the shock interrogations. Each of you has been assigned their own agent.' He looked around and then read out: 'Fellowes, you take Isabelle, Ted, you go to Geneviève, Browning, you're assigned to Charlotte, Constance we leave out, of course, and Tranter, you're to go to Suzanne's room. It'll be 0200 hours to make sure they're asleep. Any questions on this one? I know some of you don't want to burst into the bedrooms of ladies, but we've agreed to treat them the same as the men.'

Johnny, gulping whisky, choked. He had to say that he should not be assigned to . . . But he could not. He sat on, half-listening, and cursed his folly in agreeing to stand as instructor on this work. He should have known, guessed, she would be chosen. How many French women or perfect French speakers were there in England? He would not be able to do it, break into her room dressed in some grubby German uniform, make her stand on a chair in her nightgown . . . He could not do it.

*

'Claudine?' Johnny burst into the room, because the others were bursting into theirs, and whispered her name.

'What? What is it?' Claudine whispered back, sitting up in the bed. He heard the springs and the sounds of linen being thrown off. He thought he could smell a drift of the scent she used to wear. 'Turn the light on.'

And there she was, her beautiful olive skin flushed from sleep, her eyes dark green with sleep and fear. The straps of her gown had fallen away. In the flood of the light, the skin of her shoulders was like satin. 'I had to come,' he said.

'Johnny?' Her face was transformed with joy. He saw it on her face and she held out silky arms. 'You have come to me again?'

He opened his mouth to say, 'Certainly not', because of course he had not, but with horror and lust swelling his body, saw her slip from the sheets and come padding towards him. Her face was lifted up to his and he tried to say, 'I'm supposed to interrogate you and cannot, we'll have to pretend I did . . .'

She had leaned her face gently, tentatively, against him. She was saying, 'I did not dare hope you would come, Johnny. I thought you hated me, and yet I could not believe it was so.'

''Course I don't hate you.' He was glad to find a little of his old irritation. He tried to push her away so that he could explain but she thought the movement was intended to enable him to put his arms around her.

Johnny struggled with his need for a cigarette. He stood half-dressed by the window of Claudine's room and, with caution, opened it, peering out into the dark summer night where other instructors might have been briefed to spy on him, to test his interrogation techniques! There was nowhere safe from prying eyes in this place, as he knew only too well.

'How did we both get ourselves involved in this bloody game?' he muttered in anguish, to Claudine and himself. 'Can't even smoke.' He fumbled none the less for a Navy Cut and lit it behind the shield of wall, dispersing the smoke with a frantic hand. 'Why did I put this fool of a rig on?'

'Johnny darling, you do exaggerate. No one is watching us, you are supposed to be here.'

Her feet padded across to him. She had replaced her nightgown, he noticed with relief. 'They might well be, and what a fool I'd look.' He puffed smoke up towards the ceiling. 'You do realize I was meant to ... I came here for other things. Now I'll have to pretend.'

'Pretend then, my darling.' He felt her scented skin against his and held grimly on to his dignity.

'I wish to hell I hadn't got involved in this.'

'We are meant for each other, Johnny, I've always known it. I've been waiting for you to know it too, I suppose, for I've only been half living since ... since Liscombe.'

'In the course, I meant. I might have known you'd be on one. I should never have agreed to be an instructor.' He peered at his cigarette stub. 'If anyone smells smoke in your room ... And what about that poor devil, Pierre?'

'It was fate, Johnny, that you did agree.' Claudine took a deep breath. 'I have so missed the smell of your Navy Cut. Light another, please.' She leaned against him. 'Pierre knows he was not the love of my life.'

'Poor devil!' He took his arm away from her shoulders. 'Look, we've got to sort things out, you and me, somehow. We're no longer living private lives. Let's leave things as they've been for the time you're here, shall we? Then when you come back . . .'

'I'm not listening, Johnny, just not listening to you.' Somehow, she had found his cigarette pack and lighter and had set up a blatant flame.

'Careful!' He snatched the cigarette away and held it behind his back.

'I'm not listening, Johnny,' she said. 'And you cannot let me go again. I shall not let you. We shall have these six weeks, being discreet, darling, terribly English-ly discreet, I promise. Haven't I learned clandestine meeting techniques and how to live a secret life without being followed or noticed? We shall not be noticed and you need not be ashamed of me . . .'

She was keeping matters deliberately light. Johnny acknowledged this and weakened, because she was so near to him, because he had missed her, because her body matched his. ''Course I'm not ashamed.' He groaned. 'God, what on earth to do?' He took a violent puff of smoke and coughed.

'Ssshh!' Claudine giggled. 'I have learned not to cough,' she said. 'And many other things besides, for where I am going . . . Johnny, can you let me leave for France without another word when I may be going to my death?'

He groaned again and put his arms around her.

Some weeks later Claudine, bathed in Johnny, had passed the rest of her tests in a dream but with a fulsome report which recommended that she be sent out as a courier, a vital member of any resistance network and one who was most at risk apart from the wireless operators.

At the airport in Bedfordshire where she was to depart for the flight to Gibraltar and the waiting boat,

Claudine carried nothing with her of her own but the memory of those weeks of meetings, and then his final words.

'Goodbye, old girl,' he had said, whispering in her room on her last morning. 'Be seeing you one day, maybe at Liscombe, eh, when this little lot's over.' That would have been enough, for she did not want him to change, but he had added: 'You'll make the best little agent ever.'

She stood in the aircraft shed with all of the rest of her past wiped away. She was dressed in Continental clothing, each item authentically French from the very thread used in the sewing of it, to the label of a Montpellier dress shop inside the jacket which would match her new persona. She was Jeanne-Marie Cernau. She would have pretend work as representative for a firm supplying ladies' pharmaceutical goods, so that she would have legitimate excuse for her constant travelling around the country as messenger, banker and advisor to her first network, and perhaps others after that.

Constance, helping check that no English bus or cinema ticket, not even a shaving of one which could condemn her to death as an English agent, remained on her, fired a few last minute questions to ease her nervousness.

'And what's your code poem again?' she said, running her fingers into the folds of Claudine's French-issue shoulder-bag.

The rook flies high
And the gull
And the swallow,' Claudine repeated obediently, glad to do that, although she did not need to, for Liscombe lay whole in her heart again.

There were only the two of them in a ghostly dim

light. Outside on the tarmac the little bug-like Lysander throbbed, ready for flight.

'You don't smoke, do you, love?' Constance asked, knowing full well that she did not. Claudine smiled sweetly and shook her head. 'Only we mustn't leave even the merest flake of English tobacco. The Germans and the Vichy police would leap on that and you'd be finished.'

'You know I know,' Claudine said sweetly, as if there had never been Johnny or his Navy Cut. 'All my personal stuff is in the bag I left at headquarters. You will write a note to Pierre every month with his parcel?'

'I'll never miss.' Constance gave a final brush to the rust-coloured suit and handed her an aviation jacket to put on for the flight. 'I hope you're not cold going over. Hope the boat's all arranged at Gib.'

Then it was time. Claudine walked out of the aircraft departure room and into the night. She paused at the foot of the Lysander steps and turned for a final wave to Constance who yelled: '*Merde*, Claudine!', the French version of 'Good Luck'.

Claudine grinned and began to climb, awkward in her bundle of clothing. She was not afraid, not yet, and she was going to be a good agent: for Johnny, for England, and for a lost little boy with red hair.

It was dark and chill inside the machine. There was a clattering, throbbing sound. The dark shape of the pilot turned and flashed a grin at her. She sat carefully down, her back eased into some equipment, the way she had learned. Noise around her increased. The throbbing filled her and she felt herself lifted up.

Behind her head there was some rattling glass. She twisted herself about, for her final wave at England. Peering out into the moonlight, disorientated by the movement, she located the departure hut and there he was, Johnny. She could see that it was he by the tall rangy shape outlined against light. Johnny. He had come for a final goodbye. She struggled with the desire to ask the pilot to stop. It did not matter. Johnny had come. Now she would go, light-hearted and serene, to the tasks that she had been trained for. When they were done, Johnny and Liscombe would be waiting for her, and she would not let them go again. And if she could, one day she would be taking a small newcomer back across the Channel. Johnny would teach him to ride.

Back out in the night, in the lane running past the airport, Johnny got into his Bentley beside Kate.

'No luck,' he said, 'I was too late.'

'I thought so,' she sighed. 'Well, never mind, we'll have to do our best with the boy. I don't want that headquarters place of hers interfering but I did feel Claudine ought to be told. What if she doesn't come back?'

'She'll come back.' Johnny started the engine with his usual skill. 'I told you, she's got guts and she's clever. She won't let herself be caught, but if she is, she'll stick to her cover story of being an ordinary French girl. The most she'll get is a prison sentence in France. The Germans won't be able to execute her as a spy, don't worry.'

'I'm glad we didn't bring him up here with us just in case they could see each other before she left. It would only have upset him.'

'And her,' Johnny said, roaring off as if he had more than the wartime chink in his headlight beam to see by. 'If there's one thing an agent doesn't need, it's personal worries. They choose 'em for that and I'd be in trouble, believe me, if anyone knew I'd let you get involved, let alone us both flying up here to present her with the fact of her son turning up out of the blue.'

'Those Jesuits! Imagine sending a small boy across the Channel like that, even in those chaotic days when no one really knew what to expect.' Kate passed him his packet of Navy Cut.

Johnny grunted, lighting up. 'He did have the address of the café on him, though, and Liscombe's.'

'But he must have kept it a secret. He just let himself be mixed up with the Jewish boys and be moved from orphanage to orphanage. It's unbelievable.'

'In all that confusion . . . and I wonder what English, or French for that matter, he chose to speak then. If it's the same put-on dumbness as now . . .'

'It's psychological, Johnny. You just don't understand children. Who knows what his childhood was like? And then the trauma of wherever he was, with the priests I suppose, having to be left behind because the German army was advancing . . .'

'Well, the Liscombe address – he'd had that a long time. The paper was just about worn to nothing.' Johnny sighed over the sound of his Bentley running as smooth as ever; if his precious wartime petrol were to be used on this pointless trip, he was going to enjoy it. He moved up a gear, the familiar feel of the stick in his palm very sweet.

'It was written in a French handwriting,' Kate said, 'and not Claudine's, an old person's . . . Do you think they'll let us have some kind of guardianship over him? And will he ever speak enough English, or even French, to go to school?'

Kate's voice ran on, with her woman's questing for

truth at the discovery of a mystery with endless emotional problems promised by it.

Johnny grunted again, puffing smoke, letting his sister chatter. He did not want to have to settle his mind to the appearance of Claudine's son. He did not want to think of Claudine either, for both caused him trouble. They disturbed him and he did not care to be disturbed.

CHAPTER 19

Her night excursions always made her think of Johnny, though it was more than a year since she had left England. Claudine lay half-sheltered by bushes at the edge of the wood and listened, as he had taught her. Raoul, prone nearby, would not be listening; he was as restless as a trained agent could never be. He had given out one or two sighs and was now clearing his throat. Claudine fought the desire to send over a command on the need for silence but did not. She had emphasized it enough times at their first meeting about arrangements over this air-drop and she might as well have saved her breath. Beyond him, the rest of the reception committee, whose real names she must never know either, were whispering to each other.

She scanned the clearing where the Hudson aeroplane from England was to land. Were there the sixteen hundred yards by eight hundred that it needed? Raoul swore his helpers had measured it, but the measuring of such a motley crew of villagers was not likely to be as precise as her own would have been. But then, she needed people like Raoul and his group for they knew the local countryside well enough to find such places where neither German nor French police were likely to pass by chance. Any pre-arranged raid by police or soldiery, however, was another matter and the sooner they could move off, the easier she would be. She dreaded these essential drops for she had to involve other people in them and she trusted only herself.

And there it was. A faint, very faint, humming. She raised her head. Yes! '*Allez-y*' she whispered. Raoul ran out into the clearing and placed his lamp the way she had ordered. Other dark forms joined him, flashing their lamps around. A simple L-shape, Claudine groaned to herself, that is all I need. She willed them to go stealthily about the task of placing the lights into the ground for the Hudson pilot to see.

She got to her feet, as silent and quick as a fox, the way Johnny had taught her. She had lain as still as he had taught her too and that was why she could rise without effort or stiffness, for the secret lay in constant slight flexing of the muscles so they would be warm and ready to act.

She moved across to the apex of the L where she had seen Raoul's shape. All at once, the moonlight seemed too bright. Anyone would be able to see that dark shadow coming over. The hum had become a throb now and here was another bad moment for once the aircraft was overhead and its engine noise changed for landing, there would be others in the countryside to recognize that too, and if they were not hasty . . . She kept her breathing quiet and did not let herself panic. This was all she could do; her preparations had been as careful as she could make them. It was hard enough, even when the machine came into their sight, every throbbing angle of it as clear in the moonlight as an enemy watcher needed. She could not help the prickle in her back, and there could be no more listening, expecting the enemy to come upon them, for the sound of the engine filled her. But clumsily, heaving and wobbling, the thing was down. The villagers and Raoul prepared to run towards it. Claudine restrained Raoul's arm. 'I did ask . . .' She had to shout.

He shrugged. She could see his grin. 'They are too

excited, Suzanne. You must understand, we waited so long for this, it is a big event.' He too was gone, towards the aeroplane.

Claudine kept her eyes on the movement around the open hold. She would not help with the unloading of the canisters. That was men's work and there were too many of them, dragging at the heavy cylinders, for each would hold little personal rewards sent by London: a carton of cigarettes, some chocolate, coffee, from the American supplies England now had. Those probably meant more to them than the machine guns and explosives being sent for the eventual release and freedom of France from German control. Claudine knew that and accepted it. She had had little but acorn coffee since her arrival in France but perhaps tomorrow, for breakfast, her hostess would prepare her some. She allowed herself a tiny moment of weakness, longing for real coffee, and then saw that Raoul had detached himself from the group of men rolling the canisters and was bringing the expected English agent towards her.

'Suzanne?' an Englishman's voice said.

'Georges?' She took a cold hand and shook it. 'Wait here, I've got one or two things for London.' She ran across to the light of the hold where their prizes had been rolled out and handed up her package to the pilot, feeling momentary relief to be rid of the evidence that would incriminate her absolutely if she was caught with it. It contained maps of fortifications on the north-west coast of France that had passed through to her network via someone escaping to Spain. Without such evidence and the moments like this, she was confident of maintaining an innocent identity even if arrested. Back through the contact line, however, had gone her personal request, for news of a certain Jesuit seminary near a village in the exclusion zone.

A shape appeared in the dark space of the cockpit. 'London says, you all right?'

Claudine could just see the pilot. 'I'm all right.'

'Bit frisky, your lot here.'

'I shan't see them again.'

'Cheerio then.'

Claudine's heart gave a twist. Johnny used to say that. 'Cheerio,' she replied. 'Good luck for the return.'

'And *merde* to you!' His face turned away and she stepped back, her body shaking, from the rattling contraption that would soon be in England again. Where one day, she would be. She had to believe that.

The canisters had been rolled into the wood. Georges and Raoul stood together at the edge of it. They all three turned to watch as the Hudson set off with a roar that could waken the neighbourhood and any intruders too, but Claudine knew she could not afford to dwell on fear. 'Get your men to collect the lamps, Raoul,' she said. 'They're sure they can get rid of the canisters?'

'A farmer's promised they can hide them behind his sewage. And the guns go to a cowman's shed farther up in the hills. Don't worry about us, you're moving on tomorrow, we'll manage. And what's more, we'll be ready when London gives the signal for action.'

'Once I get my leader out, he'll almost certainly be calling on you to set up some lessons in sabotage. I think London wants him to plan something for the tyre-making factory over the river. But do try and make your helpers understand. One word out of place to the wrong person . . .'

Raoul sighed. 'It's difficult. You know your own countrymen.'

'Excitable!' Georges forbore to try out his French on his first local inhabitant. 'But we can't do without you all, old chap.'

'English gallantry.' Raoul sighed again. 'Now come on, you and Suzanne are to sleep down in the village tonight in my house at the back of the school. It's as safe as any. And I have coffee and I have cigarettes!' He took Claudine's arm. 'Real tobacco, you cannot know! And I managed an extra bicycle for you, Georges. They're beyond those beeches.'

'Have you my cash, Georges?' Claudine felt comforted by the presence of two men. She was so often alone, because it was safer to be a woman in the streets of occupied France where men were likely to be questioned. The wireless operator of her group had himself to move around too often to be much help to her, for his signalling was at constant risk of detection by patrolling enemy detection vans. And her leader was incarcerated in a damp prison, submitting to probable torture. It was up to her to get him freed.

'I've got about six million francs,' Georges said, 'with a few other things you asked for.'

'I need the money to get Olivier out of prison tomorrow. I can't bear to think what he's going through. And if he finally cracks . . .' She stopped. She had already said too much and must not give in to her need for real conversation.

She let Georges follow Raoul who had stuffed his precious cargo into his jacket, and took the rear on a squeaky bicycle that was too big for her. The rest of the helpers were already on their way in the other direction beyond the wood in an ancient gas-run vehicle which made nearly as much noise as the Hudson had. It had seemed to be a particularly noisy drop. Claudine knew she would be glad to be free of it and off on her next assignment so that any careless words spoken in the village area could implicate neither Georges nor herself. Each would be too far away and quite separate from the event, as they must remain. She would never see these people again.

In the room behind the school, Raoul's wife and mother had a little feast prepared for their guests. Claudine breathed in the scent of their homely soup and sat down obediently beside their fire, feeling its warmth spread into her. Raoul's fingers trembled over the lighting of his first real cigarette in more than a year. His glasses misted as he gave his wife the two packets of real coffee and the brave woman, putting her own life at risk by the mere offering of refuge for one night to British agents, opened the packet with slow care, to take in its aroma.

'I hope you have not had to spend too much on the black market, *mesdames*,' Claudine murmured, for there was cheese on the table and a whole loaf of bread. A glass of wine in her hand, she considered the figure of Georges in the opposite chair. The women had laughingly placed a beret on his head to make him look French. He had brown eyes and could, she supposed, pass for a Frenchman. She had not said much to him and would not; her sole task for this agent was to give him the railway ticket she had bought and to direct him to his own network.

At the table, conversation was difficult at first for none of the people present must know much of their visitors and the guests must know nothing of them. That way, if any arrests were to follow, there would be no information to reveal. But there was animation as Georges passed on the latest British war news and the hosts became angry over the local atrocities of the enemy occupiers and the new threat, the formation of a French Milice who were proving themselves in cruelty in the south. It was French police that Claudine herself had learned to fear for they were more likely to break her cover-story if she were caught. The Germans were easier to fool. She had felt secure enough in her identity as traveller in ladies' needs. The many times she had been stopped and her identity papers inspected, there had been embarrassment, and she had been waved on. It was, she brooded, a brilliant cover and she had thought of it herself. Tomorrow, she had to divide the money into the wrappings of cotton wool in her representative sample case and it would be easy then to take it on to the person who had promised to get Olivier free. The wireless operator had learned that so far he had stuck to his story of being an out-of-work nightclub manager looking for employment in a new area, and if the interrogation did not crack it, she and the wireless operator would be as safe as they were ever likely to be. If not . . .

'Suzanne! You are thinking too much. Finish that soup and have another glass of wine.' Raoul's clever dark eyes looked straight into hers over the table. 'Can any of us help with your worries?'

'I'm just wondering about my group leader.' Claudine gave in to a moment of sharing her troubles. 'If we lose him, more of us will be at risk too.' She raised her glass. 'But never mind. For the moment, we've had a successful drop. There's been no knock on your door, so . . . here's health to us all.'

Georges said, 'Do London know you'll be doing this prison job on your own?'

'No need for them to know.' Claudine laughed, but all at once felt too tired to go on with the soup that she had felt so hungry for. She was too tired to eat. Heat and the release of tension made her yearn to close her eyes. 'Honestly.' She struggled with her fatigue. 'And I've got it all organized. I've just the one contact to make, pass over the cash ... I'm not worried. I've done more complicated things than that.'

And in the warmth of this home she let herself give in to the need to go over her plans out loud. She could never write anything down; everything had to be held in her head. 'I shall go to the station with Georges tomorrow,' she confided, 'and from there on to the town just north of here to make my contact. He's to be the one who passes the money to the prison guard ...'

She thought they were hardly listening, heads bent over their next course, a generous piece of chicken they had probably raised and killed themselves. But she felt better, her planning all the clearer, and tackled her own portion with sudden energy.

Claudine stared with pity at the suitcase underneath the train seat of the woman opposite her. There was a kind of string around it for the catch was broken, but the string had been made with strips of newspaper and had not held in the rain. It was raining now; heavy drops ran down the windows. She and the woman opposite had remarked upon it only minutes before and had exclaimed together over war shortages with not a mere piece of string to be had, let alone a new suitcase. Now there was resentment on the woman's face and a flicker of fear as she avoided the German guard's eyes and passed him her papers which could only, Claudine thought, be innocently genuine, as her own were not. She tried to still her own pinch of fear as she counted back the weeks to the time she had had her new ration card. The enemy authorities liked to make frequent changes in vital identification papers to catch just such as she.

The woman was getting up, ordered to by the guard. She and the other passengers watched with familiar horror as the woman without the suitcase was marched off. The guard made a gesture towards it. Not mine, the woman mimed, and shrugged, glancing back at Claudine as she was taken.

Claudine closed her eyes to avoid the glance. The woman was asking her to look after the case and she dared not. There might be anything at all in it, any kind of contraband goods, and she could not risk being implicated. As it was, with one suspect taken and her own the next stop, she might escape the guard's attentions altogether. No one else in the carriage wished to do so much as glance at the case either. She held on to her own, which weighed perhaps a little more than a consignment of ladies' toiletries might have, and leaned back into her seat. She was on legitimate business, with an appointment to keep at chemists' shops where she might increase her sales. She had nothing to fear.

At the café in the town which housed a prison and which she would never visit again, she had not long to wait. It was busy with the service of lunch, meagre fare no doubt as everywhere else now. Steam from the customers' dripping clothes filled the room and obscured her view of the street outside but she was careful in any case not to have the air of watching or waiting for someone.

She did not take much note of the menu, ordering the *plat du jour* and glad to receive the surprise of a proper omelette. She was cutting into a hard apple, her dessert, when a voice said: '*Vous permettez, Madame?*' And it was her contact, for he added: '*Il y a une jolie église ici, n'est-ce pas?*' This was their agreed code.

There was not much else to do after she had risen from the table, her acorn coffee drunk and some polite conversation with the stranger later. Under the table, she left a brown paper package which the contact would, in a moment, without haste, after waiting for her to disappear, pick up and offer to the prison warder who had the keys that would release her fellow agent.

Claudine herself took a tour around the town that held not much interest. It was as everywhere else in wartime France. A few pairs of German patrol boots marched its streets, many of the shops were shuttered or half-empty of goods to sell. Some of its people were reduced to wearing wooden-soled shoes and there was an air about them of underfed weariness which the flurries of rain did not improve. They kept their eyes firmly down to manoeuvre past puddles and sullenly away from the green uniforms of the intruders.

There was another hour to be passed in gazing blankly round the pretty little church and taking a stroll in the square with its Great War monument. Claudine wondered how many war-dead would be listed when finally the present torment was over.

She did not forget to call in at both chemists' shops there in case she should be being followed, though she had no sense that she was. She carried the despatch case that was part of her false identity, for it had in it samples of the goods she was supposed to sell. Inside the shops, she paused long enough to ask if they should have such a thing as toothpaste, for which she had an empty tube for the obligatory exchange. Such small items of knowledge as the need for this exchange tube before toothpaste could be bought made up part of the messages she sent back to London so that new agents would make fewer mistakes. Once, a new man had asked for a *café-crème* in a restaurant and had been arrested. Such everyday French items had long since disappeared.

Finally, Claudine felt she might be able to book into the only hotel in the square without arousing suspicion. She hoped for a suggestion of warmth within it to dry her damp clothes and shoes and for no one to question her persona as Jeanne-Marie Cernau, Sales Representative. On her travels with cash and messages between resistance networks over the previous eighteen months, she had sometimes used another alias, for which she had a double set of papers, but today felt secure enough. With a prison escape to take place at any moment, the warder would decide when, there was a risk of the whole town being blockaded and Mademoiselle Cernau with her sales samples could have had nothing to do with it.

In her bedroom on the first floor, as disappointingly damp and cold as it had been outside, but she was used to that, she settled herself to wait. There was some comfort. She took off her shoes and wrapped her spare pullover about her feet as she set to her next task: watching from the window until her lunch-time contact should pass by and go into the café opposite for his aperitif. The cold and her training would prevent her from dozing, and her fear, because if the prison warder were not as safe as he had to be, if the escape were foiled, if the warder were caught, if he were only a false one put there to trap them, then the contact would not go into the café opposite.

Claudine set her mind to her next journey which would lead to the rendezvous with her organizer once he was free. She had another set of identity papers for him, obtained with some difficulty and which lacked the new ration cards. Somehow she would have to get food for two . . . Her mind ticked on.

But the contact had not passed by. Claudine, at last recognizing that the time for his appearance had gone, sat stubbornly on, willing him to appear, casually crossing the street to let her know that all was well.

All was not well. She admitted that to herself when night had fallen and it was already too late to venture out for her own dinner. She could not even leave the hotel and the place for soon it would be curfew. Rubbing cold hands and feet, permitting herself only the eiderdown from the bed as additional warmth, Claudine resolved to sit fully-dressed by the window all night so as to be ready to leave the moment she saw the arrival of any patrol or police activity down by the hotel entrance. If there was to be none, she had hope of a safe departure early in the morning. She, at least, would still be free and she must not think of what had gone wrong just yet.

She did doze, inevitably, but none the less heard a shuffling around her door as the church clock was striking 3 a.m. Instantly awake, she felt her heart thud with fear. They always came at three, bringing terror with them. The shuffling stopped. Claudine waited. Nothing. No boots, no shouts at the door. But there was a gleam of something pale under it. She forced herself to sit still, waiting, until her eyes had accustomed themselves to the dimness, the way Johnny had taught her. And it was something pale, a piece of paper. Moving cautiously, she picked it up. It was a mere inch from the edge of a newspaper with one word scribbled on it. *Fuyez*, it said. Flee.

And so she must.

At Beaulieu, Johnny grimly finished the last day of the last course before his week's leave. There had been another trio of females on it and he preferred to train men. It was so much more natural for men to be learning what he had to teach.

'Right, that's it, you lot. Don't forget a single one of the things I've taught you, your lives will depend on them.' He avoided looking at the girls, as he always did, for he wanted no more complications. Each would remind him of Claudine if he let her, if only because of their French accents. He preferred men.

'Shall you be at the party tonight, Captain Johnny?' the one with the code name Hélène called out.

''Fraid I'm off on leave. Cheerio to you all, and *merde*!' He had learned that much. He took in a deep breath of relief, striding away through the evening sunlight to his quarters. He was not pleased to see Constance running along the path towards him but was obliged to stop.

'Johnny!' She had a man of her own now, he had been relieved to learn the year before, but none the less still had a fancy for him, so he answered warily: 'What is it?' He had not noticed the serious expression on her face but noticed it now as she said, 'There's news of Claudine. I thought you should know but HQ will kill me if they find out I've told you.' She was panting a little, from running. Johnny hesitated between the desire to pretend he knew nothing of any Claudine and the sinking feeling in his heart. 'What is it?' he said again, steeling himself for the truth.

Constance lowered her head. 'Arrested,' she said. 'They think so anyway. Nothing from her after the radio man managed to send word she was going to try and free the leader. There's been nothing more from him either since.'

'All taken then. How long?'

'About three months.'

'Ah.' Johnny looked blindly past her and added, 'Thanks. Let me know if there's anything else.'

'Yes, Johnny. And I'm so sorry. She was plucky, Claudine. She'd done some good work.'

344

Johnny walked on. It was, after all, to be expected. One or two other women agents had disappeared They should never have been sent out.

He kept his news until the next morning, unable to bear the speculation it would cause in the three ter-raced cottages in Long Trenthide where the old Lis-combe group now lived. He spent half the evening at his stables at the Ramsays', bad-temperedly inspecting the stableman's work and cursing the war which had shut Liscombe away from him and his horses. There was then an hour or so at his club so that he would have to think of nothing in particular and the night's sleep would come the easier.

It was unfortunate that the first member of the Liscombe party he saw in the morning was the silent little lad, Claudine's boy, so that he had to start think-ing again. Paul walked quietly into the kitchen just as Johnny was fumbling about for matches with the idea of putting on a kettle himself. The boy had a tray laden with Mrs Tranter's version of a proper breakfast: thick wedges of bacon from their own pig they had to sign forms for, fat yellow eggs from the chickens she contrived to keep down by the stream. And this little creature was so like his mother, with an air of grace and self-containment she had once had, that he had to start remembering too, and to stop remembering, had to speak. '*Bonjour, mon garçon,*' he said jovially.

The boy placed the tray on the table and glanced up at him. He opened his mouth. There was a clear struggle, with fear, with habit, for he seldom spoke, then he said clearly, '*Bonjour, Monsieur.*' They both grinned in astonishment and pleasure, and he was gone.

Johnny sighed, sitting only long enough to stuff the

food into his mouth, for otherwise there would be trouble with his mother, and set off for his round quickly, the sooner to get to the Ramsays' where he had work to do.

He slipped round the back way, past his mother and Joe's cottage, directly to his sister's. She at least would be sensible about the matter and discuss the boy's future without emotional drama.

They were all there, the collection of occupants of this larger cottage, crammed round the kitchen table at their own breakfast. ''Morning,' he said glumly in the greeting he hoped would suffice, his sister at the stove, his pretty niece Sarah, the awful Mary, the boy, and Jane – home, he supposed, on leave. Everyone chorused back, but only Sarah slipped from her chair to kiss him with the enthusiasm of her spirited twelve years. 'Take us over to the horses today, Uncle,' she begged, snuggling into his shoulder.

'I haven't time.'

'Paul likes them, Uncle Johnny. He drew one yesterday and when he draws something . . .' She aimed another kiss at his chin and gave a mock grimace at his stubble.

'Oh, I'll see. Now get off. I want to talk to your mother.'

Satisfied she had won, Sarah's eyes sparkled as she chewed at a final crust. 'Come on, everyone. Boots on quick, he won't wait.'

The two other young ones left the room with her, pushing and giggling.

Johnny threw himself into a chair. 'The boy seems to understand something,' he said.

'He understands almost everything.' Jane spoke for the first time. Johnny noticed vaguely that she had a new hairstyle which made her look older and more composed; it was swept up behind. 'How's the Ack-Ack?'

'Jane's got a nasty injury.' Kate Liscombe put a fresh pot of tea on the table and cleared away plates. Jane poured Johnny tea and held up a bandaged wrist. 'Pulled tendon,' she said, 'I did it on the searchlights. Sometimes you have to drag at them.'

'I've asked her to get herself discharged,' Kate broke in, sitting down between them at the table. 'It's her second injury and I honestly need her here now Joe's home, and she and Sarah are the only ones Paul seems to like or feel easy with, apart from Joe himself, and I don't want them together too much. They don't speak, just seem to be looking at old photographs and damn war maps. It's hardly enlightening for the boy. I just don't know what to do with him, really, and until we have news of Claudine's return . . .'

'Ah.' Johnny took a superfluous gulp of tea. 'That's what I've come about, actually.'

'Claudine?' Jane put her cup down with a clatter. 'Not . . .?'

''Course not,' Johnny muttered. 'Just no news of her for the present.'

'You mean that HQ place has admitted something at last?' Kate rubbed a weary hand over her face.

'Nope. I heard on the grapevine and you're both to keep absolutely mum, do you hear?'

'Well,' Kate sighed, 'if we're to keep mum, we might as well know the truth. We already know she's on resistance work in France and we've kept quiet so far. We haven't been sent to the Tower of London.'

Johnny kept his eyes down but he could somehow still see that Jane had gone pale with fear. 'All right,' he said, 'she's disappeared, believed to be arrested, that's all I know, but we can't count . . . it may be the end of the war before she gets out.'

'If she survives,' Jane said.

'All right,' Johnny said, again. 'Don't get silly.'

'Jane's not getting silly, Johnny, she and Claudine were very close, so just let us know what you know.' Kate spoke with the authority of an elder sister.

'I've told you all I know.' Johnny pushed away his cup and dared to glance again at Jane. A dark vein had appeared at her forehead and her mouth was drawn down in an effort not to cry. He hoped she was not going to cry.

Silence fell between them. They could hear muffled chatter from the bedrooms above and the thudding of feet.

'The poor boy.' Jane did not let herself weep. 'We've got to help him now. *I* shall help him if I can.'

'You'll stay then, Jane dear? You seem to have a way with him and you're certainly the only one who can please Joe. We can pay you a salary, a proper one from his Trust. He's supposed to have a nurse and just won't.' Kate got to her feet, all the weariness of the war and her new problems written in the deep shadows around her eyes. 'If you can get Paul talking, just a little French, say, that you learned from Claudine, never mind English, then if we break into his pain and silence, we can start up some kind of future for him. For Claudine's sake.'

'Yes, I'll do it.' Jane stood up. 'For Claudine's sake, because she had been a true friend to me, my only one apart from Joe, and Joe has often asked me to stay . . .'

'I'll leave it to you two then.' Johnny got up but did not feel the relief he'd expected. Release of his news after all changed nothing.

'Of course.' Kate managed a brief smile. 'Remember

to go and see Joe and Mother before you start off for the day.'

'Right.' Johnny pushed in the chair and stood helplessly looking at the tired face of his sister who had always managed problems. 'There's plenty of hope – for her coming back, I mean,' he said. He wanted there to be hope.

He was glad to be able to show a little temper with the kids waiting for him by the gateway. 'No good you hanging there making a noise. Do something useful for half an hour at least,' he grumbled as he passed them.

Joe was sitting with his grandmother at their kitchen table in the middle cottage. She had cut up his bacon and egg into tiny pieces and was watching him spoon it into his mouth. Johnny got the greetings over with quickly and sat down for another cup of tea he did not want, frowning over Joe's struggle with the egg and his cup, an invalid's one with a little spout. He could never get used to any of that. He almost shouted, 'No improvement then?' from the depths of his anger at the boy's stupidity in trying to do good in a morass of evil. If he had not been so like his father! If the wretched episode in the Spanish War had not been enough! He refrained from saying anything until he remembered what he had come to say and felt ready to explode. 'Can't stay, you two,' he muttered. 'See you both after, for supper, eh? Got to get to the stables. That bloke's been overfeeding – there's bellies on 'em you should see!'

He felt himself slouch off, shame and misery mingled with the anger in his heart. Kate would have to pass the bad news about Claudine to Joe and it would not serve to diminish his obsession in any way, would probably in fact increase it. It was based on a dream and whether Claudine were alive or dead would not much matter. Or Jane could do it, he thought. She was fond of him and endlessly patient, like a mother. She was more of a mother to him and to the boy than she had ever been to her own child.

'Why aren't you kids ready?' he shouted, and tried to feel lightened by the load of duty he had unburdened.

In the Cherche-Midi Prison in Paris, Claudine sat obediently on her bunk opposite her companion in misery, an American girl called Mary. On a third bunk under the chink of light that represented a window sat a woman of uncertain nationality who might or might not be placed there to listen to a conversation which could finally convict them.

They had to sit this way to receive the portion of food that would just keep them alive. First in the day was this cup of something black that had no taste but the saccharine in it. This disposed of, each sat back again, waiting, for there was nothing else to do. Claudine tried to make her breathing as shallow as possible. The months of her incarceration had not yet accustomed her to the fetid air of prisons and the presence of the communal canister of sewage which stood in the corner. Another task was to try and retard the small needs of her bowels and bladder until she should be called for interrogation for then one was allowed relief at one of the more private buckets in the corridor recess.

'Examination, number 1732!' The peephole in the door was shoved back and a guard shouted.

The mysterious Polish or Ukrainian woman got up and went to the door. 'It is my turn,' she said in English, and it was the English that had made Claudine and Mary suspect her so that they had hardly spoken to each other yet. Each had been in other prisons since their arrest and knew this first and most vital act: trust no one.

'They haven't called you for two days,' Mary said, beginning upon the little toilette she preferred to offer herself away from the suspect woman's eyes. She had two inches of comb which she kept somewhere in the folds of her very dirty cardigan and two ribbons, each without colour, which she liked to change.

'Nor you since yesterday,' Claudine whispered, getting up from the bunk and taking off the jacket which HQ had had made for her and which was no longer rust-coloured. She began to scrape at the cloth of it with long fingernails she could not bring herself yet to bite off, as some women did, because every part of her was covered with unmentionable grime. 'Tell me again about New York,' she said, 'and why you did not run back there as soon as war was declared.' She lay the jacket on her bunk and took off her skirt to begin brushing that; she did not mind if Mary saw the holed grubbiness of her petticoat for hers was in a worse state.

Mary had finished scraping back her hair into the second ribbon and had begun to rub on her shoes with the back of the comb; she could sometimes get a shine if she spent long enough upon it. 'I thought I'd do a bit of noble ambulance driving first,' she said. 'They'd got up a group of us Americans in Paris. We had that woman, the one who caused all the scandal by marrying the Prince of Wales.'

'The Duchess of Windsor?' Claudine laughed. 'Bit of a come-down from almost being Queen.'

'My, was she smart though, glossy all over, you know. If she could see these shoes of mine . . . and she didn't get caught interfering in doing anything else like trying to save a few airmen who'd got shot down over Paris . . . English airmen, gorgeously handsome they were . . . stuck out like a sore thumb in Paris.' Mary considered the poor shine on her left shoe and moved to her right. 'So some of us got a few safe houses fixed up and before you know it, an escape route . . .'

Claudine laughed again, whispering, 'You must have been the first resistants. Sshh!' She stumbled back into her skirt where a strip of hem six inches long had come unstitched and the waistband was almost entirely unworked. 'I think 1732's coming back.'

Mary secreted her fraction of comb and each sank back into her gloom. The door slammed shut behind prisoner number 1732 but soon flew open again. 'Number 1879!'

Claudine rose, putting her dirty jacket over her pullover. She was conscious of the odour of her body; being deprived of facilities to bathe or change one's clothes was part of the humiliation process.

That day, they called her five times. They often did this and then left her for weeks without interrogation as if she no longer existed. It was sometimes hard to remember that she did but had somehow held on to her false identity as Mademoiselle Jeanne-Marie Cernau, Sales Representative and wholly innocent of the charges they laid against her: working for an English spy network. So far she had not broken. Though each of her fingers had cracked bones, for it was a favourite game of theirs, to crack fingers, and though many parts of her body had been bruised or burned, she had not broken.

Released finally by supper-time which brought a cup of liquid called tea and half a slice of hard dark bread, Claudine began the process that would help her

go on living and resisting. First, there was a complicated recipe to formulate in her mind, from the buying
of the ingredients in the Chelsea street where she
lived, to the serving of it by Pierre in their kitchen at
the back of the café, all steaming and aromatic. Pierre's
face and manner she sometimes had to search hard to
find again, but each of his dishes was as clear and
scented in her imagination as if she had just come upon
them. The process would bring a mouthful of saliva
but she would not permit herself to swallow the morsel
of supper bread yet, for there was time to concoct
another dish, at Liscombe perhaps, with the old cook
there re-imagined in all her temper and her plumpness,
and then old Mrs Villiers, Lady Liscombe's aunt,
peering at it with her usual disparagement, claiming
that the fowl's flesh was a little dry or the fish past its
best.

This all might end in true hallucination that the
dish was before her, and Aunt Bessie too, with her
old-fashioned fringe of dyed hair. Sometimes Claudine
made her mind run along the full Liscombe pantries as
they had been, before she stuffed the disgusting matter
into her mouth and tried to make it satisfy her hunger.

By then, the cell would be darker. They knew it
was night outside as well as in and she could lie
down in the blessed darkness to dwell again in her
imagined world that was keeping her alive. She
would start with the day she had stood at the bottom
of Liscombe Hill and climbed up until she had
reached the avenue, and it had all lain there,
waiting.

'The rook flies high
And the gull
And the swallow . . .' she would recite over and over
again, and see Liscombe lying there waiting for her,

until the very last moment when she would allow herself the final joy and let the image of Johnny come striding across the gravel.

CHAPTER 20
Summer 1945

Mordecai asked the taxi to stop at the top of the hill. There was an old faded sign saying 'Liscombe and Pugs Burrow', just as Claudine had described, and a great expanse of blue sky. The air, she had said, was special, clear and sweet with birds swirling about in it, and that was true too, he saw, lifting up his face to it. He passed the driver a pound note and waved him off.

He stood breathing in the air and noting all about him, the little patches of fields and the roll of Downs beyond and then, to his left, the avenue and the place itself that he would study in a moment. He had time. It was all as she had described it to him from her hospital bed, the long seven months she had spent recovering from the bombing when he had not missed a single evening. He had had nothing else to do. He had less now.

He wiped the band of his Panama hat and replaced it, hesitating before the task that lay ahead. He could see the way from the first two oak trees swishing and swaying in the wind. He was not expected, but Lady Liscombe would welcome him none the less. She had the true manners of a lady, always contacting him with worries about the welfare of Claudine's boy because he himself had been named her next-of-kin. He had never told the lady he would have liked to take charge of the child himself, hesitating only because of the solitary life he led. He stood brooding, wondering whether he should have asked for him.

But it had been done so quickly, the offer of a home in this place, who was he to think a humbler life might better have suited?

He set off along the avenue Claudine had dreamed of treading again. There was another old sign saying 'Entry Forbidden' with a board nailed across it, for the war was over. There was a sweet coolness there, under the leaves, and a swishing, rustling sound as she had said. And there the place was. Mordecai looked up. He saw a long golden building bathed in sunlight, many windows, two towers, each with a Union Jack fluttering over it, for the victory. Claudine had taken the walk perhaps many times and now he was taking it.

He had not thought he ever would, but when an extra daughter enters one's life, one should welcome all the new experiences she is likely to bring. He kept his eyes on the image of her dream place, and refused to let himself tire.

Kate Liscombe, working with Jane in an old bedroom in the East Tower that had been an office for the duration of the war, kneeled by the open window, scraping at the edge with a palette knife. 'There's someone coming,' she said, peering out into the sunlight. 'Looks familiar, I wonder who it is?' She got up, wiping paint dust from her face. 'I hope someone else answers the door, we've only just begun.'

Jane, also in overall and headscarf, and at work with a screwdriver taking out telephone fittings, said, 'I think Gladys is still opening up the windows on the west wing. It takes her hours.'

'What with pausing to tut-tut at the state of her precious rooms.' Kate laughed. 'I daren't tell her how many years it will take us to get straight again with everything back as it was, if we ever do.' She reached the doorway as the bell chimed. 'Ah,' she said, 'I can hear the children giggling down there. Isn't it strange how the place echoes now it's nearly empty?' She stood in the corridor and called out, 'Who is it, children?'

Sarah's happy voice came back. 'A nice man, Mummy, Mr Mordecai. I've shown him into the drawing-room that was because there are some chairs in it.'

Kate felt her heart constrict. Claudine's faithful friend, the man she had named as next-of-kin before leaving England. She turned towards Jane who had joined her. 'News of Claudine?' They looked at each other, seeing their own hope and fear reflected back. 'I'm coming down. Run and put the kettle on in the kitchen, darling,' Kate called back to her daughter and set off along the bare boards of the corridor. The War Office had been kind enough to roll up the Persian carpeting and that too lay in store in the basement and would be a huge task to put down again.

Jane, following on behind, said, 'I'll go and make coffee.'

'Bring it straight in and stay.' Kate hurried down the staircase where the oak needed thorough cleaning and repolishing. It would be their final task and lay far in the future.

'Oh, Mr Mordecai, how nice to see you again.' She put a bright tone into her voice but when he turned round towards her, she knew hope was gone. He was standing by the drawing-room window and the light from it showed his plump tired body sagging, all the lines of his face set in sadness.

'What news?' she asked, because she could not wait to go through the formalities of his visit. She indicated a chair but he did not move towards it. His manner told her what he had come to say, but she asked again, 'They have told you at last what has happened to her, Mr Mordecai?'

'They have, my lady.' She could hear the sound of his breathing, wheezing a little, laboured. She wanted him to sit down and walked across the room to move a chair so that she could ease him into it. She wanted not to know just yet, because Claudine's boy was at that very moment carrying a tray towards them. She heard the rattle of it and Jane's voice saying, 'Careful, Paul dear, you should not have put so much on. And, Mary, if you drop that cake stand . . . You know one does not serve biscuits on a cake stand anyway. Whatever has got into you all this morning?' There were muffled giggles.

Mordecai, putting out a hand towards the chairback to lean upon it, turned his head towards the door. 'The boy?'

'Yes.' Kate called out to the children, 'Let Jane take the tray and bring it in, please, and the rest of you go back down into the kitchen at once for your own milk and biscuits.' There must have been something in her tone to make them listen for it was only Jane who came in with the tray. A young hand pushed the cake stand with Mrs Tranter's home-made biscuits on it round the doorway and the giggling faded away.

Jane put the things on the office table that the War Office had left in the room and stood beside Lady Liscombe, looking as she did like a woman on teabreak from wartime factory work, dust- and paint-covered. They could see Mordecai struggling with his innate good manners and the burden of the news he carried. Jane made the effort to help him, but the words came out as harsh as they had lain in her mind since the moment she had known it was Mr Mordecai walking up to the door. 'Is she dead?' she said. 'Have they told you?' The words echoed in the bare sunlit room.

Mordecai nodded.

For the rest of the victory summer, those left at Liscombe went on with the repair work as far as they were able. There was little to be had in the way of wood or paint or the materials that would bring the Hall back to life. They worked at it, none the less, because the relief of the war's end and the first joy of it had left lethargy in its wake and a strange unsettling lack of purpose that they were not alone in feeling. The entire country seemed to lack the force to begin ordinary work again, though so much had to be done. The tasks of rebuilding a country seemed unsurmountable but because remaking Liscombe was within the bounds of possibility, Kate, her family and its adopted members set to making themselves comfortable in the East Tower and part of the east wing. There was Kate's old bedroom she had shared with her husband, next to it Sarah's in what had been Aunt Bessie's room. Mary and Paul had the nursery rooms, and the only two servants, Gladys and a cook, were above them. Mrs Tranter and her grandson Joe were in the ground-floor rooms, because of Joe's wheelchair. Johnny had re-established himself in his old stables and only called across at the Hall for his meals which Mrs Tranter and the cook contrived together with what there was available, for wartime rationing still had its grip on supplies.

Everyone had been surprised by Johnny's interest in the child Paul, who was now able to attend school in Dorchester. This slim, pale, red-haired boy who resembled his mother was amongst other refugee and war-orphaned children and was not made to feel an outcast. His polite nature, the precise and careful English that Jane had taught him, did not allow anyone but her to know much of his thoughts. He was self-contained, as his mother had been, and stood his ground between the two girls who argued as much as they always had and who were still rivals in school work and achievement at the grammar school they both attended.

He stood his ground too in the face of Johnny's attempts to persuade him on to the back of a horse or to hold a gun in his hands. He did not care for physical activity, as his mother had not.

The early September day of that year, when Kate had finally called a family conference to discuss his future, Johnny went across to the Hall early. In the refurbished drawing-room, he found Kate already waiting. 'Got these,' he said, throwing on to the coffee table a number of leaflets about schools. He was, he knew, as astonished at his action in actually sending for them as his sister was, and spoke before she could form her irritating woman's questions. 'I think he should be at proper boy's school. Yes, Sis, a public school, so don't start.'

Kate peered over her glasses at him as he strode about the messy room which was full of chairs and surfaces with bits and pieces to be knocked over on them. He had preferred wartime simplicity. 'I don't want him turning out like Joe.'

Kate said, 'What do you mean, Johnny? Joe was a lovely boy before his . . . before the war.'

'He was too soft, he had too many women about him, he never learned to be a man, for Chrissake!'

'He had you.' Kate's voice rose. 'You taught him to ride and box and hunt and shoot, what more could you want of him?'

'He should have had companions, that's what he should have had, to knock the softness out of him. I did my best, or thought I did, but it wasn't enough. D'you think he'd have gone off doing brave and noble things if he'd had more sense? Just like his father, and he might as well be dead, I say.'

'Johnny! Sshh, he might hear . . .'

'Yes, and he's always stuck here with nothing else to do but listen to you lot of women and be fussed over. He'd have done better to stay in one of those places where they rehabilitate men properly. If he had no money and no title, he would be doing a job of work by now perhaps.'

'It'll be years,' Kate reminded him, 'before his invest-ments are freed, so how are we going to send Clau-dine's son to public school?' Kate did not want to get into another argument about Joe; there had been enough of those.

'I'll pay for it.' Johnny stopped pacing and looked out into a rainy day. The grass was churned to mud and none of his horses would be able to run. He ignored Kate's intake of breath and said, 'Why not? Someone's got to take charge of the boy and you let us in for it, remember, never stopping to think about the future.'

'You know I thought Claudine would come back,' his sister said wearily. 'Let's not argue over it. You say you want to pay for Paul to go to public school . . .'

'Boarding school?' Jane came into the room with the coffee and there was a pause while she poured it out. 'I'm not sure that would suit him.' She did not realize there had been an argument and went cheerfully on with the authority of Paul's closest helper, the one who had coaxed out his first English words, 'He's so very un-English, isn't he. I mean, he has a sort of

Continental manner, so un-awkward somehow for a fourteen-year-old boy.'

'He needs to be with other lads,' Johnny said, accepting his cup and allowing himself to glance down at her bent head where the line of her unswept hair was so touching. 'Claudine wouldn't want him to be a sissy.'

'No,' Jane agreed, 'we must do what Claudine would want.' They could say her name now without hesitation. It had become easier to do so once they had learned that she had died. But they regarded each other blankly as she added: 'How can we know what Claudine would have wanted, really, for her son?'

Johnny moved away to the window. 'Did she even know he was likely to be sent to England for the war? Was she supporting him at that seminary he came from?'

Jane answered, pausing over the betrayal of a confidence. 'She had not seen him ... since the birth, I think.' She fell silent as the other two absorbed this new information.

'What else do you know?' Johnny strode back for more coffee.

'Nothing,' Jane said. It was almost true.

'Then *we* must decide, for Chrissake.' He held out his cup.

'He has no real guardian,' Kate broke in, 'and must have one if decisions are to be made about him.'

'Jane ... what about you? You know more about Claudine than any of us.' Johnny thought this was true; he only knew about her sweet body that he would never touch again and that god-damned spirit of hers that seemed now to be egging him on to interfere. What he felt was that something of her still lingered in this place.

'Me?' Jane looked up from her chair beside Kate's, her blue eyes wide with surprise. The war had, Johnny thought, brought her a kind of confidence that she had not had before. There was a calm dignity about her and no silly fluttering about being incapable. She had taken charge of the boy as if he had been her own. Jane suddenly answered, and there was no fluttering now, not even the desire for reassurance. 'I should not mind, we are ... attached to each other, and for Claudine's sake ...'

'Johnny thinks he needs a man's eye on him.' Kate finished her coffee and got up. 'I think I'll let you go on discussing it. Leave me out. I'll fit in with whatever you decide to do. I've got to get hold of enough meat for the week's meals somehow and I want to see that some potatoes are dug. Or we'll all starve, Paul included.' She went out with an unaccustomed slam of the door.

'What's the matter with her?' Johnny grumbled.

Jane smiled. 'She's tired, as you very well know. She's got the huge job of getting Liscombe into shape, let alone deciding what to do with it.'

Johnny grinned at her. 'Okay, okay. You women stick together, you always have.'

'Well, if we don't, you men tread all over us. You always have.' Jane got up too, her face alight with laughter.

Johnny thought: she is almost beautiful. He said, 'That damned Ack-Ack stuff made you a bit cocky, if you ask me, and now you've learned French, and worse, for that boy's sake ...'

'I didn't ask you, Johnny.' Jane picked up the leaflets from the boarding schools and moved to the door with a graceful turn of her body. She fiddled with a tendril of hair that had escaped from its roll. 'Are we going to talk sensibly about Paul, because I do want to. I owe a lot to Claudine, as I keep telling everyone. She was my first and only true friend apart from Joe, and I shall never let her down, ever, by letting Paul down.'

'I want to do the best for the boy too,' Johnny said. She had her hand on the door and he wanted to restrain her so added, 'What is the best for him, in your opinion?'

'A good school somewhere soon, that is sure, because he's clever. He might even be an academic given the chance.'

'An academic!' Johnny snorted.

'Or a doctor or a scientist . . . an engineer.'

'Pah!'

Jane persisted. 'Something that could do some good in rebuilding the country. And there is money. Mr Mordecai says the will is to go through Probate soon, if . . . death can be presumed.' Her face saddened but she went on, 'Claudine told me she'd left her share of the café takings to him, and if Pierre never comes back either, he'll have it all. Just because *you* think the boy should be like you, with horses and so on! It might not be right for him, and I say I know better what is right for him . . .'

At last she looked up into his face. Johnny saw a flush on her cheeks. Her eyes had changed, become darker with her anger, or almost anger, for surely she could not be angry with him? She had had a pash on him once. He moved towards her, taking in the dark, changed colour of her eyes. Before the war, she would never have gone so far towards frankness. 'Then I suppose he'd better have what you say. But I'll pay for the school and the money Cl . . . the money left for him can go into a trust until he's older.'

'Do you care that much, Johnny?' She was looking up at him, the old shy look.

'Well, I . . .'

'Is it because you once loved his mother?'

Johnny stood back, startled. 'How did you . . . women's talk, I suppose?'

'Claudine was not one for women's talk and I never had any women friends but her. Whatever sort of talk it was, we had it when we were half-buried by the bombing and did not expect to get out, so you cannot accuse her of being disloyal.'

He saw the new, sharp look was back, that women now seemed to have. Johnny tried to be conciliatory. 'And you saved her. Damn plucky!'

'And afterwards, when she lay for months recuperating . . .'

'All right, I don't mind your knowing.'

'I am glad she had some love before she died. The rest was all work, Johnny. She always had the guts to go on doing something.'

'I always thought she had guts, admired her for it, in fact.' He turned away from the blue gaze which suddenly seemed as straight as Claudine's sometimes was.

'Please admit you loved her, Johnny, don't deny her memory of that.'

'Love!' Johnny strode to the window and back again. He did not look at her. '*That's* women's talk. Most people, men and women, rub along together well enough, once they get involved. It's something else that starts it. Attraction!' He was relieved to find the right word. 'And, yes, we had that. I respected her and I was attracted to her. Yes. That was it.'

'You cared enough to want to do something for her boy, Johnny.' Jane moved to put herself in front of

365

him. 'Let's decide now, this very minute, what to do, otherwise you'll go on chipping in and interfering when Lady Liscombe and I actually get on with the matter by enrolling him somewhere this term, in a week or so. Then you'll start complaining and nagging at your sister and I won't be here to help her argue back.'

Johnny stopped the laugh that had begun in his throat and was travelling up to lighten his face. 'What d'you mean, you won't be here?'

'I'm thinking about my own future,' Jane said lightly, absorbing the sight of his dear familiar cross face that had seldom been so close.

'Whatever for?' There was a deepening of the frown between his eyes. His right hand had gripped her arm.

'Because I can't stay here for ever. Paul will be moving on, Joe really needs a nurse and I am not sure I want to go on nursing. I want to be a teacher actually. I've had such a taste for learning since I battled with French, for Paul, and then on with Latin and Greek so that he could catch up at the grammar . . .'

'Stuff and nonsense, you'll stay here!'

'I can't, Johnny. I have no real place, I am not employed officially, it was just a temporary scheme to help Lady Liscombe and Paul. I must work properly.'

'A woman like you shouldn't be working, you should be making a home. You've got a child, two now you say you'll be Paul's guardian. Listen.'

'It's a bit late for me to make a home for either of them, they're nearly grown, but I plan to rent a cottage somewhere so they'll have a place to come in their holidays.' She tried to take her arm from his hand.

'I see.' Johnny released her and stepped back. 'So you take the two of them away from the only home they've ever known, to live in penury with you in a dreary job?' He shrugged. 'All right. I thought Liscombe meant a lot to you.' He turned away.

'It does. Oh Johnny, it does. I didn't mean . . . I can hardly bear to leave Liscombe but I must.'

'Stay then.' He stepped forward, his hand on the door knob.

Jane took in a deep breath. She moved away and stopped. 'Don't you see? I have no real place here. Your sister has just had me as yet another burden all these years.'

'I've been thinking, maybe you and me could rub along together.'

Jane gasped, for he had turned around now and his hands were held out towards her. 'Better get married,' he said, 'and give those kids a father and a proper home at the same time. We'll rub along all right, you'll see.'

Jane gasped again, for without knowing it she had walked into his arms and had rested her head against the blessed comfort that was waiting for it.

The day the British troops reached Ravensbruck concentration camp in Germany, 70,000 prisoners died from disease and weakness. Claudine lay in her hut there listening to new sounds: soldiers and English voices and swearing and shovels.

Greta, from the overhead bunk, brought in a tin of condensed milk on the old plate that had sometimes held half an inch of bread. Claudine could smell sweetness before Greta reached her. The woman, who seemed to have no particular age or nationality, speaking as she did several languages, sat down on the earth floor. Claudine heard her breathing in sweetness, too. Then a bony hand reached out to take hers and guide it towards the plate. 'The tin is open,' Greta whispered, 'a soldier gave it to me. He had opened it and said it was all mine but I must be very careful with it. Here. I am being very careful.'

Claudine raised her head and opened her mouth towards the touch of white sweetness lying on her finger which would mean that she was not going to die after all.

Later that joyful day, another person came into their hut. A great thud of boots seemed to make the floor tremble and the women who had not died cried out for noise was painful too, and they were not used to it. There had been less shouting at Ravensbruck since the guards had known the British were advancing towards it.

Claudine managed to sit up in her bunk and struggle with the piece of rag around her hair, her last vanity before she had fallen prey to the fever which had finally taken most of her strength.

'And this lady, what's her name and nationality?' The soldier gave out a burst of sound which was his voice and the shape of him loomed before her as if in a dream.

'Her name's Jeanne-Marie Cernau,' Greta said, for Greta had taken charge of Claudine since she had fallen ill.

Claudine struggled. She wanted to say that her real name was Claudine, Claudine Forestier, but the fever had very nearly closed her throat.

'And where does she come from?' He was writing out a list.

'Liscombe,' Greta said helpfully; she had remembered that much from Claudine's stories.

'L'Isscomme? Well, she sounds French to me. I'll put her down as query French for the moment and someone will see to that later.'

Claudine heard the name Liscombe and tried to find the words that might take her home.

CHAPTER 21

1946

One cold morning, Mordecai rose early to answer the knock at his door. His heart was thumping at the sound of it for who could it be so early? He had had enough bad news already this year, and enough good too, that anyone at his time of life could expect. Monsieur Pierre had come, having walked half across Poland. He could hope for no more.

A delivery boy stood there, the kind with a uniform and a bicycle. He fumbled for a penny from his overcoat pocket on the hatstand, put on the kettle for his coffee, searched for his glasses, for there could be nothing important . . .

It was fortunate that he was already seated at the table and the coffee was giving its sweet drip-drip, for the contents of the envelope were so shocking. He had to read twice, three times.

Pleased to inform you Mlle Claudine Forestier alive and well.
Telephone Hotel Victoria for full information . . .

Mordecai did not telephone; he rushed through sad and icy London that the war's end had allowed no comfort, to the Hotel Victoria itself.

And she was *there*. A woman at the reception desk told him she was still weak from a long journey but he forgot his inbred good manners and demanded to be allowed to see her. 'I am her adoptive father,' he said solemnly, grimly, all his old body trembling, 'and her only family. I demand that you tell me where you are hiding her.'

The woman was officious but knew that she had no reason to keep a father from his daughter, a father who had to see if it were true, who had a duty to inform others who loved her.

And it was true. Claudine was on an upstairs floor of this hotel which was not open to the public, sitting in an armchair by a window. There was breakfast spread out on a table before her and she tipped over a cup because she rose to her feet so quickly, and held out her arms.

'Mordecai, Mordecai!' She had plenty of words to cry out, but he could find none and had to sit in the other chair to wipe his eyes until they were clear enough to see her.

She was thinner, he could see that, but slimness became her. They had given her a beautiful rust-coloured dress that was the right shade for her hair. That was thinner too but with some gloss in it, as it had always had. The change, if any, was in her face, for it had not its healthy glow, from the energy and life she had had once, but being home would bring that back. She was saying something to him, about her being listed with the wrong name, and he tried to listen, gazing at this person, his near-daughter, come back from the dead.

'I hadn't even been in Ravensbruck camp long, you see, but they emptied some of the French prisons when they learned that the Allies were fighting their way up from the south of France. They knew they'd lost but they didn't want any evidence left behind so they shunted us off in trains. Mordecai . . .' She kept stopping for breath, and he, wordless, filled with joyous certainty that this girl was there before him, let his tears run down into his collar and listened.

'The treatment I had wasn't so bad as some, they didn't dare any more, but I got some awful fever and couldn't speak and my name was all muddled up. I hadn't broken, Mordecai, I stayed plucky the way Johnny knew I would, until the end. But afterwards there was such chaos. They even made me stateless, can you imagine? I've had such trouble to get back, but HQ have been so good. If it wasn't for them wangling me a flight from Paris last night, we'd have been one more day without each other. I was afraid *you'd* died whilst I was away, Mordecai!'

They sat back and regarded each other with love and disbelief. Mordecai began to offer *his* news: that Pierre was safely back in England, having walked with his fellow prisoners who had also survived all across Poland and finally into France where he found his mother had died. 'So he came across to us, me, my dear, and I had to tell our dear Monsieur that you were also . . .' Fresh tears began as he added, 'And I had to tell him that the café was gone but his home would be with me until he found himself work again.'

'I am so glad Pierre has come through too, Mordecai!' Claudine accepted the loan of his handkerchief to wipe away her own tears. 'HQ did tell me that you and he were well. But of course, Pierre – you know there was someone else for me, in the war? Before the war, really. Pierre knew a little. I said nothing in my letters, of course, in case he did not come back. I shan't pretend now though, Mordecai. I must not. It would not be fair, would it?'

'He has been desolate to think you gone from him, my dear, but war brings so many losses. Just to see you now . . . He has been invited down to Liscombe, your grand place!'

'Liscombe! I might have telephoned there this morning, but I feel I do not dare, now the time has come ... Have you heard, Mordecai, how everything is there? Jane and Lady Liscombe and ... all the family?'

'Everyone was well when I went down last summer to tell them about you.'

'That I'd disappeared?' Claudine managed a weak laugh. 'They will have a surprise! I can't wait to see their faces. What will they say ... and Pierre?'

Mordecai hesitated with the further news that he knew he should give her, but decided that it could lie for a few hours more; it would be enough for her to see her dream place, and perhaps, if they were fortunate, the boy would not be there so she would have time to accustom herself to the shock of his presence in England before she saw him.

'We've decided to try out some aperitifs before the party!' Sarah Liscombe, at the door of Jane's bedroom in Liscombe Hall, held a tray with a number of glasses on it, each filled with a mysteriously-coloured liquid. 'Mary and I have had such fun down in the cellars.' She placed the tray with a rattle on the chest of drawers and whirled about the room in an imaginary dance step. 'And what do you think of *our* dresses for the party tonight? Gladys has been working so hard on them.' She looked dreamily romantic in a dress cut down from one of her mother's pre-war outfits, its creamy lace a perfect foil for her skin and dark glowing hair.

Behind her, also in cream, silk cut from parachute material, stood Mary holding a corsage for Jane sent up by Jed. She looked less romantic than Sarah, for there was a heaviness about her features and her body and an undeniable sulkiness about her mouth, particularly this early afternoon.

'Come in, girls,' Kate Liscombe said mildly. 'Don't wait to be asked!'

'They both look sweet anyway.' Jane sat at her dressing-table wearing a deep rose crêpe gown that had also been Kate Liscombe's in the days of pre-war prosperity. 'Both perfect for tonight's party. But let me see that hem, Mary. Doesn't it fall a little at the back?'

'Oh, you would find something wrong, Mummy, to spoil the party for me. It's practically my first ever. It's all right for you, you were young before the war. All I've ever known . . .'

'You'll have plenty of time for parties, Mary,' Kate suggested, 'and there *is* a dip in that hem. Go and ask Gladys to have a look at it.'

'It's my day as well. Everyone will be looking at me, *knowing* what I am. My mother, *Miss* Jane Beale, getting engaged. I don't know why we have to make such a fuss about it anyway.' She sank heavily on to her mother's bed, back arched ungracefully over her full body.

Sarah stopped taking imaginary steps around the room with an imaginary wedding train. 'Because the war's over, silly. Because it's our first excuse for a party. Because someone gave us two fat turkeys . . . Oh, who cares? It's a *party*.' Her dark blue eyes glowed with happiness.

Mary, whose own eyes were not of a kind to glow, being pale and small, squinted across at her. 'It's all right for you. No one ever thinks about *my* feelings.'

'Mary dear,' Jane began, 'I can no longer go on saying how sorry I am. I know I have not been a good mother to you, but am I not going to make us both

374

respectable soon?' She turned back to the glass and regarded herself. She could see herself trembling about the mouth. How familiar the sight, and how foolish!

Kate was saying, 'You know, Mary, I hope you realize that your suffering as a child was hardly as great as your mother's. You have been raised in some comfort, with far more care than she had. You won't be lifting carrots . . .'

'With a baby on my back. I've heard it all before, Auntie, and it wasn't my fault.' Mary slouched to the door. 'I'm going. I didn't ask to be born.'

'Off you both go,' Kate said. 'For Gladys to check those dresses. We'll try these concoctions of yours.' She passed a glass containing an orange liquid to Jane. 'I'm so glad Pierre came home in time for our first party, in how long? Since before the war, surely?' She chose a green liquid for herself that seemed to be some old dregs of *crème de menthe*.

'Yes, a long time before the war. With Pierre here, things seem a little more like old times, don't they?' Jane made an effort, her mouth hovering over her glass. She turned her face away from her own reflected image and thought: if Claudine were here . . .

'Only he makes me think of Claudine and that is painful.' Kate winced at her liqueur. 'I don't think we can offer any of this stuff at your party, my dear.'

'No,' Jane said obediently. If Claudine were here she would not be marrying Johnny, she would not be sitting here trembling again as she had in the old days, and Johnny would not have been at liberty to touch her.

'And,' Kate was saying, 'we can't start getting maudlin again. Go straight across to the stables – I know Johnny's there with his horse forms – go and ask him what he thinks of your new-old dress. I hope he's grateful to have such an effort made for his engagement. I'll come with you actually, I want to measure the height of the windowsill in his sitting-room. Yours soon, my dear. I think that pair of satin chairs from the old morning-room might fit nicely there. You can sit and mend Johnny's socks . . .'

Kate bustled ahead of her and Jane was glad of it for she did not have to see his face drop a little at her arrival, as it had this morning when she had taken his coffee across.

Kate and her tape measure and chatter filled the quiet there would have been between them. They, she, found so few things to say because of the first day his hand had reached out towards her . . .

'Well, I'll leave you two alone and you can tell Jane how lovely she looks in her pretty dress, Johnny,' said Kate, mock commanding. '*And* you can decide what day the wedding is to be or I shall be able to arrange nothing at all. Jed won't even be able to produce a few flowers, and we can't have a wedding without flowers.'

She was gone. Jane listened to the thumping of her heart in the silence, to the fire hissing in the grate, to Johnny's sudden and loud 'Hrrump!' as he shovelled papers on his desk.

'I fear Kate is doing more for our wedding than we are,' she said.

'She likes to keep busy.' He did not look up at her standing near the window where she had helped Kate measuring.

'Yes, of course, once we are married, I shall be in charge.' Jane struggled to find the self that had taken her with such aplomb through the war and on through to learning Latin and Greek and applying for a place at teacher-training college.

'I don't expect you'll have to do a lot.' He raised his

head and looked towards the region of her waist. 'After all, we're only getting married for the boy's sake, it won't affect either of us much. You can get on with your own plans. Teaching, wasn't it?'

Jane took a deep breath. 'I thought you didn't want me to work? You said you'd like a proper wife.'

Johnny's eyes travelled the length of the deep rose crêpe and up again. 'Yes, well, that was before.' He looked back at his papers.

'Johnny! Oh, Johnny, I'm sorry. I couldn't help it. I am so silly, I know. I'll try, I will try!'

'I don't force women, not even my wife-to-be. What sort of chap do you think I am?'

Like all the others, Jane screamed silently in her head, where the memories were. And now, most recent, most shocking, Johnny with his strong hands reaching up to unbutton her clothes, to strip away her shield, to run his fingers around her nipples until they leapt with horror and desire for more. His male skin, his male strength, forcing itself upon her. It was the same, the same! 'I am so sorry,' she said again. 'Shall I have your tea sent across or shall I make it for you?'

'Send Gladys,' he said.

Her weak legs took her down the stairs and out into the courtyard where she found Joe struggling to man-oeuvre his wheelchair along the stable doors to see the horses he could no longer ride.

'Let me help, Joe,' she cried, her breath misting out into the wintry air. How easy it was to devote oneself to helping others!

'Damn hay in the wheels,' Joe grunted. His good left arm dragged at muddy strands. He turned his head to look at her, the right side of his face still scarred and sunken, like the right side of his body, but he never tried to shield himself from Jane.

She gazed with fresh pity upon the wounded part of his face and down at his withered arm; his scars were external, hers did not show. She had thought they were gone.

'I say, what's up?' Joe threw away crushed hay.

'What do you mean?' Jane took hold of the chair handles.

'You're crying. Don't think you can hide from me by standing where I can't see you.' He tried to turn his head.

'Am I crying?' she asked. 'I suppose I am. But tears won't help me, they never have. Do you want to go for a walk, Joe?'

'Take me for a drive,' he said, 'out to Bulbarrow or somewhere. Away from the ears in this place. But I shan't go back into the car until you've told me what's up.'

Jane tried to wrench the wheelchair round towards the Hall terrace. 'It'll be a bit hard underfoot at Bulbarrow,' she said. 'What about a trip out to Paul's school? It's not far. The three of us can have a nice walk around on their smooth paths. Paul's always glad to see us.'

'Leave me here then and go and get out of that party dress. Send someone to help me into the car. And put a fur on.'

Jane flew off, thinking tuck box and fresh clothes, the suit Paul wanted cleaned, his repaired rugby boots. Of course, they must not be late back for the party, but how glad she was to fill the afternoon.

The day was as ice-cold as all the wartime winter days had seemed to be. But the driver was able to get up Liscombe Hill for there was no ice on the roads. Hoar frost remained, however, all along the hedges and across the fields, a sharp white against dark earth. The driver, no doubt following instructions, said that he would wait down in the village inn until called for. So she and Mordecai were alone under the sign which still faintly bore the words 'Liscombe and Pugs Burrow'.

Claudine let out a breath of misty air. 'I am here again, Mordecai, at the dream place. The memory of this and all that happened to me here helped me bear the prisons.'

'Yes, my dear.' He held on to her arm, feeling it so slender beneath the fur coat he had kept in mothballs for her in his spare-room wardrobe. They and the car had called back for it before starting off for Liscombe and he had been glad to delay this moment another half-hour; he did not trust what lay ahead.

All the oaks were touched with white along the bare branches where a solitary rook sat rocking. 'It has always been sunny at Liscombe, in my dreams,' she said. 'Always the sky has been clear and blue with birds gliding in it.' Her walk was straight and steady, as if she had had an ordinary war. Mordecai held on to her arm but she did not need his support. She said, 'And the oaks were always rustling and swaying, not still like today, and . . . Oh!' She stopped. 'There it is, Mordecai. Can you see? The lovely stone . . .'

'It is beautiful,' he agreed.

'And, oh, flags on the towers. I never saw flags here, is it for the victory? How still they hang, how still the place seems. Are you sure, Mordecai that everyone is here again?' She increased her pace; he had to release her arm.

'They were in the summer,' he puffed, 'and look, here are cars.'

'Several cars, yes.' Claudine stopped and laughed,

for Johnny's Bentley was there, as *he* would be; she had made herself wait to see him, so that she would be well enough to walk towards where he was. 'That is Johnny's Bentley, the green one. Look, I expect he has kept it carefully polished all these years waiting for there to be petrol again.' Here it was, all lying before her, as she had dreamed of it. Claudine's heart thumped, but it was not from prison weakness. She was as well and strong now, or almost, as she had ever been. Her body needed care, but she had never wavered. All the years of her misery and now Johnny and Liscombe were still there. Her reward lay waiting and she need not hurry.

Their steps sounded so loud, ringing out in the cold air, that she laughed again. 'I wonder Gladys does not hear us and peer out from some attic window. I suppose Gladys *is* here, and Jane in the cottage perhaps or up with Sarah and Mary and Lady Liscombe? Oh, I do not know, Mordecai, *who* is here, do I? I have been away too long. I must not expect everything to be the same.'

'Hardly anything will be the same, my dear, not after years of absence.' Mordecai had struggled with the news of her son that he had wanted to give up to her all through their car journey and had failed to do. The burden of it grew heavier with each step he took but he had left it too late.

'Too many years of absence,' Claudine said, and began to run, as light as a girl, up the steps to the oak door where she pressed the brass plate. A distant ring sounded and her heart thumped again because today was very much like the first and other time she had caused that sound. She had been unexpected then. Years of endurance had led her here for the second time. How soon before she would hear Johnny's voice saying, 'Hello, old girl' and everything began again?

There was some rattling and the door opened. A beautiful young girl appeared, all dark blue eyes and sweetness, who must be Sarah Liscombe for she was so like her mother. She was smiling and had on a surprising dress, a party dress, but of course she had the manners of her upbringing for she said at once, 'Good afternoon,' though her smile became a round O of surprise and shock. 'Claudine!' she screamed. 'Oh, can it, can it be you?'

'Of course it is me.' Claudine laughed because Sarah was so shocked. 'We last saw each other when you were how old? And you thought me dead. Well, I am not, as you can see!'

'Oh, Claudine, yes, we *did* think you were dead!' She recovered herself and held out her arms, hot young tears readily falling. 'We thought you were dead. Aunt Jane has been so upset. Wait till she comes back!'

Claudine let herself be wrapped about and kissed. 'You at least, Sarah dear, have not changed, only grown. And I am so glad.' Claudine refused to let herself cry; there would be time enough for that later and once she began she would not stop. 'Is there to be a party? You're dressed up.'

'We're trying on our dresses. They're made over, of course, because of the war, but Gladys . . . Oh, Claudine, we were having a party tonight and for some reason it's cancelled, I don't know why. But we must have it for you. You're reason enough!'

Claudine did not stay at the door any longer. Her legs, that had found new strength because she was at Liscombe and near to Johnny, took her across the floor her maids had once polished, past the hearth where the fire glowed and a real pair of homely boots stood to dry, on to the bronze pillars where all the warm splendour was reflected, the way it had used to be. The door of the small drawing-room was open. There were voices coming from it. Sarah held her arm and she saw they were all there, having tea: Lady Liscombe, Joe in his wheelchair, an overgrown Mary, old Mrs Tranter. Gladys was standing with a plate of something, about to offer it. She screamed out because she had seen Claudine come back from the dead. Lady Liscombe stood up, her hand to her mouth.

Claudine stayed still in the doorway and fought with tears and laughter. She knew she should have telephoned first; they thought she was a ghost. Another person detached himself from the mists of her vision at the back of the room and a familiar voice shouted, '*Claudine, ma petite!*' Pierre ran towards her. She had been about to fall.

There was some confusion, Claudine realized. But she sipped tea, somehow, sitting beside Pierre, and tried to understand what it was that had happened just before her arrival. There was to have been a party. Everything was ready for it. They had been given two fat turkeys which now lay glistening in the kitchens, just out of the stoves, both Gladys and Pierre had informed her with delight. How many years since any of them had seen a turkey? 'How many years since I saw *any* meat?' Claudine had laughed at them both, accepting wartime cake and bread and butter and Mrs Tranter's plum jam. She would eat anything they offered, she said, but stumbled over it none the less, for Lady Liscombe was trying to tell her that the party had been cancelled without saying why that was. She wanted to ask why Jane should have been the central figure in this party, and why she had gone off that afternoon and refused to return. Dear Joe was involved in the story somehow, he had seemed to be recounting it over again, but there was too much chatter. Mrs Tranter had gone so far as to waddle across the hearth to offer Claudine a slice of precious fruit cake. Lady Liscombe came and went. Gladys scurried about with fresh teapots, giggling, succumbing to Mordecai's charm. Joe finally stationed himself near Mordecai's chair so that he could gaze on her.

Claudine began to wilt and was glad to accept Lady Liscombe's offer of accommodation. They gave her a room in the East Wing and soon she was sitting up in bed in the Rose Suite that she had been careful once to keep in its full glory. There was a little of it still; the walnut cabinet was in place and the fire surround only needed a thorough cleaning. The rose-coloured drapes at the window looked almost as good too. She had begged Gladys to leave them open so that she could see the Liscombe sky. It was black now with a clear moon showing a roll of Downs in the distance and a few glittery stars.

She had, she knew, been weeping, but that was over now. Who would not have wept to hear that the son she had thought was lost to her had been safe at Liscombe, sent to school, cared for! And he knew about her, Joe had told her; he knew about his mother's bravery, about her solitary struggle to earn her own living. And he looked so like her, Joe said.

Claudine, sunk with exhaustion into the pillows of the bed, reviewed this conversation with Joe and wept afresh. Tomorrow she was to see her son. He had very red hair and was not to be a priest.

'Darling!' Pierre's voice. He had crept into the room with the familiarity of their past together and she had not heard him. In the dim lamplight, she saw his brown eyes were dark with sympathy and affection. 'It has all been too much excitement for you. For all of us. What an incredible day we have had, and then you coming back to us to lift us from the gloom.'

Claudine accepted his proffered handkerchief and wiped her face. She struggled to find the strength to speak. 'Is it to do with Jane, or something about Johnny? What has been happening today?'

'Don't trouble yourself yet, *ma chérie*, you will soon know everything. With all the women in this building, there'll be a day of gossip tomorrow.' He reached across her to stroke her damp cheek. 'Should you like me to heat up a little consommé, with a slice or two of Melba toast? Then you can sleep.'

'Yes, please.' She gazed upon the strange thinness of his face, the cheekbones finely shaped, his moustache a poor straggle of what it had been. 'You have had such a time of it too!'

'Yes,' he said, leaning his face towards hers for a light kiss on her forehead. 'And now each of us has to begin again, as if we have been given a new life.'

'Yes. A new life,' she repeated.

'Together, my dear, only if *you* want it.' He straightened up and was gone, quick-footed and eager, though too thin, in a suit he had said was offered him by Lady Liscombe, from her husband's unused wardrobe.

Claudine fought back more tears. 'But where is *Jane*?' she cried to his departing back. He did not turn around to answer her. The door closed behind him and she cried again, 'Where is Johnny?'

No one had wanted to answer her, either at tea or later when Lady Liscombe and Gladys and Sarah had fussed around her, bringing her clothes for the morrow, and toilet articles, and a glass of brandy.

Claudine struggled against sleep then so that she could insist upon an answer to her question, to both questions. The thought that each of them was dead, that there had been an accident, startled her heart to a frantic beat though the rest of her body seemed to sink into a stupor.

She dreamed that there was indeed an accident down on the Dorchester Road, just where the lane to Liscombe began, at the very spot where Lord Liscombe and Mrs Villiers had met their deaths. She herself was leaning over the bodies of these two who were also Johnny and Jane.

When she woke, she was screaming. She was aware of waking from a nightmare and stilled the scream at once. Making a violent effort she sat up, for if you screamed the guards came.

'There,' a voice said, 'there.' It was a low gruff voice that had come to soothe her after other dreams. But of course it was only her imagination that wanted it to be his, as it always had been.

She tried to lie back, breathing cautiously, and found herself meeting strength, and warmth. And a familiar scent came to her, but she had often imagined that too. 'All right, old girl.' His voice, in her head.

She said, 'There has been an accident? Johnny and Jane?'

'No, old thing, I'm here as large as life and Jane's gone away. She needed to for a bit. That's all.'

'Johnny?' Claudine saw that the darkness around her was Johnny's navy blue pullover with the leather patches at the elbows.

'The same.' And his arms reached forward to draw her more firmly to him.

SIGNET

Published or forthcoming

Sherry Ashworth

While her husband Richard is away, Stella embarks on a dazzling new career...

Having ostensibly conquered her own personal problems, Stella Martin – once the high priestess of Slim-Plicity – is now preparing to liberate other people from theirs.

Undergoing therapy with the slip-hipped Roland Temple after the departure of her previous therapist Gill, Stella decides that an absentee husband is no bad thing, and in a positive frame of mind she starts up her own therapy group.

Stella visualized the group; now it has formed with the terminally indecisive Sandra and her 'victim' friend Zoë, with Carol the professional patient and Jim the compulsive liar. Stella is their guru. But who, if not commonsense Sandra, will guide Stella through the storm when she finds out the bitter truth about the people she trusts most in the world: Richard and the delicately vulnerable Roland?

SIGNET

Published or forthcoming

Distant Echoes

Laura Gilmour Bennett

Rachel runs a celebrated French restaurant in California with her glamorous husband, chef Alain Ribard, and is mother to their son Oliver. She seems to have it all – so why does she feel there is some threat to her happiness?

When Alain unexpectedly takes Oliver to France on a sentimental trip to his birth-place, Rachel decides to join them. But upon arrival in Roquelaire, she discovers that they are nowhere to be found – and that rumours abound about her husband's involvement with a mysterious Frenchwoman.

Drawn into village life as she attempts to unravel the mystery of Alain's and Oliver's disappearance, she is befriended by attractive Englishman Michael Lowry, who is writing a chronicle of events in the village in the summer of 1348.

As Rachel's involvement with Michael deepens, she learns of the centuries-old tale of Margaret Prior, who became a pilgrim in order to search for her son and the husband who deserted her in their plague-stricken village – a tale which begins strangely to mirror her own …

SIGNET

Published or forthcoming

SCENES FROM THE SEX WAR

Maeve Haran

'Maeve Haran is the new star chronicler of the contemporary scene ... you feel real regret when her novel ends' – *Annabel*

Allegra Boyd, warm and beautiful, has always been there for chat-show host Matt and their two daughters. Rather like an old sofa. And with the girls growing up and Matt deep in his dazzling career, Ally begins to feel just about as noticeable.

So Ally decides it's *her* turn now. To her amazement she lands a daytime TV slot as an agony aunt and her star begins to soar, bringing with it fame and glamour – not to mention the temptation of up-and-coming Danny Wilde – just as Matt's is starting to wane. But can Matt cope with his wife's success or is Ally's bid for a little independence about to go horribly wrong?

'An entertaining writer with a delicious lightness of touch' – *Sunday Times*

SIGNET

Published or forthcoming

HONEST ILLUSIONS

Nora Roberts

Young Luke Callahan was wild, spirited, a thief – and a runaway scarred by years of abuse. Drawn to the magician's tent at a carnival fairground, destiny and hope fuse when he crosses the path of master conjurer Max Nouvelle. Taking Luke into his home Max reveals to him a new world of wondrous enchantment: magic.

As Luke's artistry and ambition grow over the years, so does his smouldering passion for Roxanne, Maximillian's beautiful, talented daughter. Revelling in their adventures on and off-stage, the trio use their magicians' skills to relieve the rich of their jewels and works of art – a lure as exquisite as that of the honest illusion . . .

'Move over Sidney Sheldon, the world has a new master of romantic suspense, and her name is Nora Roberts. *Honest Illusions* is an explosive novel of obsession, passion and intrigue that pulses with excitement from beginning to end' – Rex Reed

SIGNET

Published or forthcoming

The RUNNING VIXEN

Elizabeth Chadwick

It is 1126 and young nobleman Adam de Lacey has returned to his troubled homeland in the Welsh marches to discover that his beautiful stepsister Heulwen, for whom he has long held a secret, burning passion, is recently widowed.

She is already promised in marriage to Warrin de Mortimer, hated enemy of Adam. However, when de Mortimer's name is linked with treachery, Heulwen is unexpectedly drawn towards Adam. Their tempestuous relationship unfolds agains a background of conflicting loyalties as they become embroiled in the intrigues of King Henry's court and the conspiracies of a rival claimant to the royal throne. And then there is the greatest danger of all, the bitter enmity of Warrin de Mortimer ...

Ⓢ SIGNET

Published or forthcoming

BEACHES

Iris Rainer Dart

Once in a lifetime you make a friendship that lasts forever ...

From the moment Cee Cee Bloom and Bertie Barron collide on the beach at Atlantic City aged ten and seven, they are friends ... for life. In time Cee Cee, a talented singer and comedienne, successfully pursues Hollywood stardom, while Bertie chooses the conventional life of marriage and motherhood. But despite the striking differences between them, the two women sustain each other through thirty years of careers and children, jealousy and drugs, lovers and divorce. And when they are torn apart by a shattering tragedy, against all odds Cee Cee and Bertie find strength in their extraordinary friendship.

'Well-written, well-constructed and thoroughly enjoyable' – *Daily Telegraph*

Published or forthcoming

SUCH DEVOTED SISTERS

Eileen Goudge

Eve and Dolly are aspiring Hollywood starlets, hungry for fame and success. When one of them betrays the other a tragic chain of events is set in motion that irrevocably changes their lives and the futures of Eve's children, Annie and Laurel.

Forced to leave their home, Annie and her sister run away to New York. There Annie, drawn into the delicious, fragrant world of the chocolate business, determines to become a top chocolatier, while Laurel becomes an artist. Full of unspoken secrets they live for each other – until they fall in love with the same man and the past returns to haunt the future . . .

SIGNET

By the same author

Liscombe Hall

When an illicit liaison with Lord Liscombe ends in heartbreak, Kate Tranter sets out in search of a new life. Driven to protect a secret borne of passion, she rises beyond her humble beginnings to become a wealthy restaurateur; indomitable, proud, admired – and haunted by the searing memory of a love that could never be.

Set amidst the rolling hills of the Dorset countryside, from the turn of the century to the post-war era, *Liscombe Hall* follows the tangled destinies of two families and the powerful passions that bind them.